Advance Praise

"Form Lu Hsun, Ngugi wa Thiong'o, Wole Soyinka, Pramoedya Ananta Toer, Ghassan Kanafani, Mulk Raj Anand, to Munshi Prem Chand, national liberation struggles have always been a wellspring of stories and a source of inspiration for storytellers. *Rojava* is no exception. Gathered from the font of the Kurdish liberation struggles, Sharam Qawami weaves stories of real people engaged in real struggles into a story of the indefatigable human spirit. Far from refusing to succumb and let their humanity unravel in the face of fascism, militarism, patriarchy, ecological destruction, as well as the breakdown of comradeship and social relationships, the humanity of these characters resurface precisely in moments between despair and determination. Qawami lets the characters tell the story of a century-old struggle with all its contradictions, tensions, and dissensions in the past and present, and through the burning human desire for freedom and justice that holds them together. Whatever the twists and turns in the Kurdish liberation struggle, Rojava will continue to educate and inspire."

—**Radha D'Souza**, author of *What's Wrong with Rights? Social Movements, Law and Liberal Imaginations* and professor of law at the University of Westminster, London

"Sharam Qawami has packed much of the history of the Kurdish movement as a whole and of Rojava in particular into this highly readable and inspiring novel. In turns suspenseful, introspective, and even humorous, Quawami leaves plenty of room for nuance and the manifold stories of characters in their multiple dimension and complexity, while avoiding the pitfalls of romanticizing or heroising the history and ongoing struggle of guerilla fighters who dare to imagine and win freedom—all of which makes *Rojava* immensely gripping and worth reading."

—**Thomas Schmidinger**, author of *Rojava: Revolution, War and the Future of Syria's Kurds* and associate professor of Political Science and International Relations at the University of Kurdistan Hewlêr

Rojava: A Novel of Kurdish Freedom
By Sharam Qawami
Translated by Kiyoumars Zamani
Edited by Patrick Germain

ISBN: 978-1-945335-10-5 | eBook ISBN: 978-1-945335-23-5
Library of Congress Number: 9781945335105
10 9 8 7 6 5 4 3 2 1

Common Notions   Common Notions
c/o Interference Archive   c/o Making Worlds Bookstore
314 7th St.   210 S. 45th St.
Brooklyn, NY 11215   Philadelphia, PA 19104

www.commonnotions.org
info@commonnotions.org

Discounted bulk quantities of our books are available for organizing, educational, or fundraising purposes. Please contact Common Notions at the address above for more information.

Cover design by Josh MacPhee
Layout design and typesetting by Suba Murugan
Printed by union labor in Canada on acid-free paper

Rojava

Rojava

A Novel of Kurdish Freedom

Sharam Qawami
Translated by Kiyoumars Zamani
Edited by Patrick Germain

Brooklyn, NY
Philadelphia, PA
commonnotions.org

To everyone who has struggled against oppression to acquire freedom and equality.

CONTENTS

Foreword   i

Chapter 1: The Era of the Drone   1

Chapter 2: From Paradise to a Hellscape   34

Chapter 3: Bikinis and Military Fatigues   49

Chapter 4: The Fruit Doesn't Fall Far from the Hawthorn   68

Chapter 5: I Promise as a Woman   98

Chapter 6: The Congo River Streams in All of Us   123

Chapter 7: Doxwa and Jokes   138

Chapter 8: The Second Sex and the First Sacrifice   161

Chapter 9: Kollberî: The Ethnic Impoverishment Project /
            We Thought You Were a Man   186

Chapter 10: Heme Seyar / The Şiwan Battalion   219

Chapter 11: Arjîn and Befrîn: A Human-Animal
             Friendship   254

Chapter 12: Nighttime River Trek /
             Cave-to-Cave Relocation   262

Chapter 13: Baking Bread and Butchering Humans /
             Libertarians and Fascists   273

Chapter 14: Cobras vs. Mountains   286

Chapter 15: Jînçin's One Desire   304

Chapter 16: Heval, You Are a Kurd   325

Chapter 17: Phobia vs. Love   346

About the Author   377

About Common Notions   379

TRANSLATOR'S FOREWORD

WHEN MOHAMED BOUAZIZI set himself on fire, nobody thought the flames would engulf the dictators of North Africa and the Middle East. Decades of dictatorial rule in these areas have created huge social inequalities that have brought nothing but excruciating poverty and suffering, especially since, demographically, the vast majority of these societies are working class. Millions of people across the region have no access to adequate food, health care, or education. In such a complex environment, the lack of freedom of expression allows the ruling class to suppress the lower classes. Dictatorships, by using divisive tricks relying on religious, ethnic, and gender differences, have created gaps between the various strata of the working class. In this way, it diverts its attention away from its common enemy. This is where dictatorial soldiers, who do not share the same religion or ethnicity as the protesters, but belong to the same social class as them, are simply deceived by the dictatorial system as much as possible and respond to the protesters—who are their own peers—with bullets to the head. The unification of their resistance is of vital importance for those who fight against these authoritarian systems, which have marginalized the common people for so long and have treated them as mere objects for the production of wealth and the preservation of state power in an invisible, misleading labyrinth. *Rojava* exposes this labyrinth, a labyrinth so invisible and intangible that the reader may not feel the need to search for string to get out. By considering each of the characters, however, it can be more easily recognized, and by putting them together, a macroscopic view of the novel can be drawn.

Xemo, an Êzdî* man who has been harmed by the unique tenets of his religion and does not gain customary permission to marry his girlfriend, who is of a lower social class, decides to expose the truth and inform the lower-class Êzdîs, but his plans are foiled by the Êzdî upper class. Xemo's defeat comes after the defeat of the Kurdish people's struggle led by Mela Mistefa Barzani, who also fought in the frontlines as a Pêşmerge.† Xemo could not bear the heavy burden of these defeats, so he left his homeland and settled in Germany. There he met a German woman and they decided to get married. After many correspondences with the religious leader of the Êzdîs, he was excommunicated and expelled from the Êzdî community forever. But with the onset of war with Daesh‡ and the massacres of Êzdîs, Xemo, now a sixty-three-year-old man, returns to his homeland to save the Êzdî society from which he was expelled. He is killed in battle in Rojava and this motivates his daughter, Jînçin, to get acquainted with her Eastern roots on a trip to Rojava. Jînçin embarks on a clandestine journey through various autonomous territories of Kurdistan, from Başûr in northern Iraq (southern Kurdistan), to the remote mountains of Bakûr in southeast Turkey (northern Kurdistan), and to Rojava in northeastern Syria.

As a university professor, she decides to use her knowledge and experience to open a new chapter in the guerrillas' liberation struggle; but, seeing their existing facilities and general condition, realizes that the provision of new, Western facilities or equipment would not be aligned with the libertarians' methods. At first, Jînçin becomes frustrated because she sees that the current situation is markedly different from what she already had in mind and prepares to leave Rojava, but as the days go by and she gets to know her comrades, she realizes the reality of the situation and prefers to stay in those difficult conditions. In an environment

---

* Êzdî comes from Êzed, who is the equal of God in Mithraism. Islamicists changed it to "Yazidi" to ridicule Êzdîs. Yazid I was the second Ummayad caliph under whose rule Hussain, the grandson of Prophet Mohammad, was killed.

† *Peshmerga*, which means "those who face death," is the military of the Kurdistan region—both in Rojhilat and Başûr. Their existence dates back to the mid-twentieth century, when Mela Mistefa [Mustafa] Barzani took up arms to fight for Kurdistan autonomy.

‡ Daesh is the Arabic acronym of the Islamic State, used in a pejorative sense to refer to IS across the region.

removed from media domination, concepts such as freedom of speech and democracy are gradually transformed in her mind and she reaches a different understanding of social life.

The author's allegorical use of a "trip to the Orient" theme has been masterfully employed for the narrator. During her trip to Rojava, Jîncîn initially sought to understand her father's ideas, but now she knows her roots as well as the various layers of her personality and finds herself in a situation where she seems to have been reborn. During her trip, Jîncîn is introduced to the modern concepts of social life and the struggle for that form of freedom that is distinct from the neoliberal standards and mainstream media domination of public opinion that govern industrial societies.

The image that people of the world have of the libertarian fighters in Rojava and other parts of Kurdistan is that of warriors dressed in Kurdish costume. Jîncîn, who joins the group of guerrillas with this mindset, finds an opportunity to get acquainted with the human and social aspects of the guerrillas and realizes that they are ordinary human beings who, just like her, have their own concerns, in spite of their status as fighters. Each of these fighters, we learn, has entered the field with a different life story and different emotional tendencies, carrying these characteristics on their shoulders throughout the story to the extent that these traits affect their relationships. Jîncîn realizes that what the fighters are seeking is to build a free society for all, in which they can live away from any individual domination and censorship, beyond any individual differences, in a situation that is rarely seen in modern societies.

In this novel, the author uses an unusually flexible perspective in which the real and expressionist atmospheres intertwine within the work as much as possible. All parts of the novel can be considered objectively realistic, but due to the fluid nature of the events, the change of narrative perspective, and the philosophical mentality built on coincidence, all of these realistic narrative spaces are equally propositional and expressionist. The subjective bases of the narratives leave no room for the presence of consolidated knowledge, and no truth-teller narrates what lies within the characters' minds behind their social masks. Not only the narrators, but also the author, has been relegated from a dominant observer position and, like any other character, passes through the events of the novel. With this technique, the author explores not only the characters, but also

Kurdish sociopolitical events and touches on the characters' personalities as the they themselves are amazed, awed, or dismayed by their experiences.

Women in the novel come from different backgrounds, but they all have one thing in common: the reality of living in a patriarchal society. The paradox of feminine gentleness, coupled with the necessity for warfare and a sense of responsibility on a mountain that lacks even the most basic facilities, has made the commander of the group, Rûken, a character who reacts strongly to any gender discrimination. Sometimes she considers the contradiction between female fertility and the taking of life as a bitter necessity in the struggle for freedom and gender equality, and sometimes as a dialectical requisite to conquer the last bastions of fascism and patriarchy.

The personal complexity of the characters in the novel creates intertwined and unique relationships that emerge in different and sometimes contradictory ways at different times and places. Whether it is Tewar, a combative girl who is consistently antagonistic with all characters except Serhelldan, the tallest male guerilla in the world; or the three humorist characters of the group, Zinar, Satyar and Nadîr, who engage in a boundless struggle with other comrades like Rojano, Arjîn, Ferhad, Akam, Dêrsîm and Gulbehar, where all become victims of the decisions of superpowers dominating the land from thousands of kilometers away. Each of them carries a part of social history, and, by telling the story of their lives, they try to introduce Kurdish matters to the audience of the novel, to each other, and even to the author himself. The narrators' constant displacement in the course of the story goes so far that the author seems to have entered into a game and it is the narrators who have made a character of the author.

The author creates a unique atmosphere by gathering various characters from different parts of Kurdistan, as well as other parts of the world. He involves internationalists and civilians in this struggle throughout the work to reveal their historical commitments, which are never broadcasted by the mainstream media. *Rojava* is the story of people from the same social stratum who have decided, regardless of the present world order, to build a society free from any discrimination based on individual religious, ethnic, ideological, and gender differences. Self-made human beings, by sacrificing their lives and property, have set foot on a path based on the freedom and equality of all human beings towards each other, within a society that is all their own.

Kiyoumars Zamani

The peak of tragedy is when the writer must mitigate the tragedies.

CHAPTER 1

I HAVE BEEN curled up on the ground for a long time. My whole existence feels cramped. The pain is wrapping around my body. This is my first time being in such a situation, but the entire group is stupefied by its sudden appearance in the sky. This time, we were not informed in advance and our fast-moving life has been paralyzed by an invisible bird buzzing in the distance. A sound that has signaled danger and a need for patience since my first days here. "Patience? Until when?" I pose this question to a person whom I feel has been petrified behind me, without turning my head to him.

"No one knows. They stay up there for a few hours. Sometimes all day. These unmanned drones have unlimited stamina and also enough fuel for eighteen working hours," the man replied.

"Can I turn my head or is that dangerous too?"

"It depends on whether its camera is focused on us at this moment or not. But you can turn your head slowly. It seems very far away from us, probably about ten thousand meters high."

I slowly turned my head to the right towards his face. He had brown hair and was lying face down on the ground.

"Ten thousand meters! How do you know that?"

"You see only a black dot from here and also from its buzzing."

"Can I stretch my legs?"

"That is too risky. Such drones are equipped with a high-resolution camera, a GPS antenna, devices for satellite communications, and also laser-guided rockets."

He talked about it like an expert.

"What's your name, comrade?"

"Saro."

"What part of Kurdistan are you from?"

"Rojhilat.* What is your name?"

"I have not chosen a nickname yet."

"And what have the comrades called you so far? You're supposed to have been here for a few days."

"They call me hevala† German. I am here temporarily."

"Interesting, no one comes to visit here in the beginning of autumn. The snow will begin to fall soon."

"I will leave here in the next few days." I was surprised by my resolute and spontaneous answer. Am I really here as a guest, or should I stay for the next eight months? Although returning has remained an option for me, I had thrown it out of my life calendar for the upcoming year before I voluntarily came to this dangerous place in Bakûr.‡ I turn my eyes from Saro to the little black dot in the sky. If the drone continues to fly to the left, after a few hours it will disappear behind the top of that mountain. But what will happen if it flies to the right side and ambushes us after waiting above our heads for us to make a mistake over the next fourteen hours? Again, I felt another annoying pain in my back and my head started burning beneath the early-autumn sun.

"Hevalê§ Saro, how do you spend your summertime here? Does this *scheißflug* appear incessantly?"

"It depends on the weather. The worse the weather, the better our chances. We always have these uninvited guests in good weather. We'd prefer the storms of a mythic deluge to clear skies and shining sun. What did you call that drone in German? A scheiße-something?"

"Have you ever been to Germany?"

"Yes, I've been there a few times in my civilian life. And where did you learn Kurdish?"

"My father was Êzdî."

"Amazing! And did he get married to a German?"

"Strange, isn't it?"

"Very much so. Say more German profanities. Make a storm of profanities until the drone disappears."

---

* The east of Kurdistan, mostly in present-day Iran.
† "Female comrade," in Kurdish.
‡ The north of Kurdistan, mostly in present-day Turkey.
§ "Male comrade," in Kurdish.

I burst out laughing. "Can this tin shit hear my words?"

"Don't worry, you can even sing."

"That sounds very romantic, to sing and dance with it. My body is cramped like I'm in a telephone booth. How can you go about your everyday life if these drones appear so often?"

"Something must have gone wrong today. We are usually informed by wireless seven minutes before the drone arrives. Maybe the Turkish secret service found our informant. Tomorrow another one will keep us in the loop."

I carefully turned my head to the left and looked at the other comrades higher up. Four hours ago, all twelve of them were busy digging into the ground like ants, until someone shouted loudly "Fifty!," three times. Instinctively, everyone plunged down to the ground when they heard the code number. I did not expect everyone to camouflage themselves so perfectly. Not only did all the comrades disappear, but also the grave that had required a week's hard work to convert into an underground winter bunker. The entire group and any trace of the last eleven days' worth of hard work were swallowed up by the ground. Over the past few days, I did not have a chance to talk to anyone. We were in constant motion, digging like ants amidst the early onset of cold weather. Where did this guy, "Saro," suddenly come from today? I turned my head to him carelessly. I was shocked and petrified by my own action. I waited a few seconds but nothing happened. The drone was not aware of my carelessness. I opened my eyes and took a few quick breaths. Only then did I noticed Saro again.

"What happens if the drone gets one of us?"

"That means certain death for him and great peril for others."

"Why didn't you say a single word to me in the last four hours? I almost let myself roll down to the valley in helplessness."

"I did not know you could understand Kurdish. Your hair color suggests otherwise."

"But you could have talked to me in English."

"Why do you think I can speak English?"

"Do I not have something like brains in my big head?"

"Pardon, heval. I was afraid that it might shock you and make the drone aware of us. Besides, I was thinking of my project the whole time."

"Can I ask what plan you are dealing with? Or is it also confidential information from your party?

"But you have not yet introduced yourself to me. Do you believe that pseudonyms are not enough for anonymity?"

"I did not find a proper nickname yet. What do you think of 'Jînçin'?"

"Viva! A woman who picks up and weaves life. Where did you get this name from?"

"I have a friend who calls me that. He was teaching me Kurdish profanities online. I can turn my head and hurl some Kurdish profanities at them."

"Or shut one of your eyes and fire some bullets."

"Oh! Can I learn to shoot here?" I asked enthusiastically.

"How can you learn it when you want to return home in the next few days?"

"How long does it take to learn to shoot? Is shooting more difficult than shitting?"

"I haven't fired any rounds yet myself."

"What? You're really a weird guerrilla. So, what are you doing in this guerrilla's uniform?"

"I came from Rojava to put a project into action."

"Your confidential plan?" A sarcastic smile appears on my lips when I ask this question. He could see it clearly from ten meters away.

"Before I leave here I will explain it to you. I am your guest tonight."

"Guest? You've arrived rather early, sir. Our seven-star hotel is still under construction. We've been digging like moles for eleven days. I almost see you now like a pile of soil."

"I will help you when I get back."

"And when will you return?"

"In the next ten days."

"We will have finished all floors and even the air conditioning system in the next ten days. Nobody has smart ideas like you about running away. You should have been called hevalê Fox. What does your name mean?"

"Saro means 'bright day.'"

"Right! Very fitting. Something perfectly useless to us here. The only things of use to us are cloudy days and people who dig with the efficiency of a burrowing rodent."

Saro starts to laugh. I look at him in bewilderment, failing to grasp the cause for his amusement, as if he did not understand what I meant by my taunts. He might see me as just a female clown brought in from faraway for his entertainment. Everything in this abandoned place is ridiculous; this unarmed guy even more so. I traveled over three thousand kilometers from my hometown to offer my skills as a professional to this so-called emancipatory movement, but what have I done in the meantime? In the last three months they have taken me through different cities, villages, peaks and valleys, and we have finally settled on an abandoned mountain. Could be worse. There are no modern laboratories here for scientific experiments, but at least I was lucky enough to find a longterm location. And what should you do now, Jînçin? Bury your degrees beneath all this dirt, I guess. With a hoe or a shovel? Which one is your new specialization? What am I actually looking for in this place?

I look at my cracked hands. In all my life up until now, the most difficult job I ever did was watering my flowers. What would my mother and my colleagues say if they could see me in this situation, with a shovel in my hands and a sack full of soil on my shoulder? The image makes me laugh. Eh, I don't care about their opinions anyway. I look over Saro's head at the spring in which I washed my face this morning and realize I did not drink enough of its cool, pure water. I listen to the murmur of the rivulet flowing down the valley in front of me and the roaring of the invisible river further away. The nape of my neck is aching. I turn my head and look at the white cliffs reflecting the bright sunlight. The sky is perfectly clear. If only I could undress and lay down on this cool yellow meadow, taking deep breaths of the crisp air and marveling at the great blue sky as I drifted into sleep. But sleep means death here. I ignore my neck pain and turn my head to Saro. It seems he's gazing at the drone.

"Do you have water with you, heval?"

"Yeah, I have a little water from yesterday. But how can I hand it over to you?"

"Does this devil's toy even notice a bottle of water?"

"I am not sure. But a plastic bottle reflects light."

"Then this damn thing doesn't need to shoot us. It can stay up there and surveil us until we all die of thirst."

"Do not worry, heval. No guerrilla has died of thirst yet. Fresh water is everywhere in these mountains.

"What relation is there between thirst and abundance of water? You can't even pull a bottle of water out of your backpack."

"I can drink myself. I said I could not hand it over to you."

"Fine, drink. Let me see what it looks like for an unarmed guerrilla to get blown into the air by a drone missile."

Saro bursts out with laughter and says, "You remind me of Meursault in one of Camus' stories. The guy who's driven mad by the hot weather."

"Why don't you just call me Antoshka? I'm already a clown!"

My harsh words silenced Saro for a few minutes. Then he said, "Can I tell you my prediction, hevala Jînçin?"

"I do not believe in predictions."

"I'm not talking about fortune telling. There is a possibility that we could get rid of the drone soon."

"How?"

"It will go behind a cloud for a little while."

"And why would this drone hide behind that little cloud?"

"It will not stay there. The cloud will just stand between us. If we don't see it, then it doesn't see us, either."

"Seriously? Were you out looking for the loo while God was distributing reason?"

"What's the issue?"

"It would be feasible if you could mix up the laws of physics as you wished. If you see someone standing near a mirror then he will see you, too. What happens if you hold your palms in front of your eyes? You will not see me, but I can still see your long ears."

"But the situation up there is different. There must be a distance of over a thousand meters between us and the cloud."

"And over six thousand meters between the drone and clouds. Did you forget that or are you trying to trick me?"

"Why would I do that?"

"Have you tried to spread this stupid idea to others before?"

"No. Why did you pretend not to understand in the beginning?"

"I wanted to teach you . . forget it. I overestimated that stupid tin can. It's a toy, really. You can hit it with the simplest air missiles."

"That's our problem; they don't permit us to have even very simple defense missiles. That's why these drones have turned into fearsome monsters for us."

I asked Saro, "What kinds of search capabilities are the drones equipped with?"

"Optic and thermal."

"Are they not equipped with high-frequency or sound-searching capabilities?"

"Not yet, our situation isn't that miserable right now. We can even move with an umbrella at night."

"But you have to find a definitive solution to this problem. These drones will be optimized with HD-quality recording systems and equipped with other capabilities. Then even our means of camouflage won't work anymore."

"What do you propose we do?"

"You must have either air defense systems or anti-drone hackers."

"You have seen our existing equipment and resources. Which one of your solutions is feasible?"

"You can only dig the ground with a hoe and shovel."

"Did you ever think so much about these garden tools in your entire life?"

"Garden tools or burial tools? I hate both of them more than the 'Little Boy' they dropped on Hiroshima."

A sudden pain rises from the back of my neck. I can no longer hold my head in a rotated position. I turn my face and watch the drone. It seems to be nailed onto that point. The pain, the cramping, and the desperation are unbearable to me. Nothing upsets me more than being held captive. When I was a child, my mother locked me up in a room whenever she wanted to punish me. It did not matter for me how big the room was: broom closet, my bedroom, or the whole house. Now I'm being held captive by my own voluntary actions. I almost made the stupid decision to stay here. I'd have to live with the moles in a catacomb for the next eight months. "When the molehills in the garden are high, a long, bitter winter is nigh." The best-case scenario is that the next eight months are the same bullshit the past eleven days have been. I will have to get up at five o'clock in the morning and gaze at the same plastic walls and people until dusk. We have no electricity, internet, phones, or even bathrooms. Everything is the same as it was in the Stone Age. It'll be annoying to have the same two types of simple food every day for eight months, too. We eat lentil soup for breakfast, rice and a meatless bean stew for lunch, and again lentil soup for dinner. And it's not for a few days. So much monotony is just shitty. The *Gebietsführer* will be back in the next few days, then I can get back to civilization. Back to Germany or maybe over to Rojava. But the difficult days that I spent here won't have been pointless. How else could I know for sure that Turkey uses drones for warfare? It's not just the US, UK, and Israel that use artificial intelligence to hunt people down and kill them. I call out to Saro in the opposite position, "Heval, since when has the Turkish government been using these drones against you?"

"For the past eleven years. In the beginning, the American drones watched us; then, the Turkish army purchased a lot of them."

"Do you know how many people have been murdered by these drones?"

"No idea, heval."

"Estimated?"

"I cannot say that either. The human victims were numerous in the beginning. But now they kill animals and destroy nature."

For eleven years! And it has not been reported in the European media. All this tormenting thirst, bothersome cramping, and screaming pain have brought me to my wits' end. I would gladly let myself drop and roll down deep into the valley. Saro called me for the first time, "Look up, hevala Jînçin. What do you think?"

The black dot had moved closer to us and some distant clouds had mixed together, turning into a big dark cloud.

"Theoretically, there is a better chance. The problem is we're not just being watched by the drone. What can we do about the operators in the air control centers who are now looking at this shot directly? Do you think they won't notice fourteen people suddenly disappearing? Even if they see us as stones, won't they ask how the stones ran away after a few seconds? What would happen if they knew that we had escaped?"

"They'll send fighter jets here and throw bombs down for a few hours. Is there a safe place nearby where we can protect ourselves in case of bombardment?"

"There's a small and solid cave near our camp. I already thought about that, but what do we do after that? Can we return to our place after the bombers have gone?"

"No, we have to leave this area."

"And then we'll have to clench our teeth and dig another 165 cubic meters of stony ground. Didn't you say that you were leaving tomorrow? Only to return when the work is done, right?"

"If we encounter the worst possible luck and have to leave this place, then I promise I will stay and dig with you."

"And what about your important plan?"

"This experiment can also be a part of my project. How about that?"

"And how should we do that?"

"I'll run toward our comrades when the drone disappears behind the cloud. If nothing happens then you can run to the cave."

"I don't let anyone pull chestnuts out of the fire for me. We will try it together."

"No way. A guerrilla mustn't play games with her life."

"But I'm not a guerrilla."

"Well, you wear a guerilla's uniform."

"Would you like me to strip naked before we continue?"

He laughs. "One single person would be enough for the experiment. Is hevala Rûken* your commander?"

"Yes, she is."

"I haven't seen or talked to her in five years. Call her and explain our plan."

While I am a stubborn adventurer of a woman, I would have rejected his suggestion if I weren't completely screwed. Our little experiment would have no connection at all with real science. I did not know the height of the drone or the clouds, nor even the distance between us and both of them. We don't know other necessary parameters such as wind speed, the light's radius of curvature, the existing angles, and even the distance between us and the other comrades. Our decision was merely based on an ignorant and unscientific gut feeling. I looked at the black cloud near the drone and calculated something in my head. Saro asked me, "Why aren't you calling hevala Rûken?"

"I remembered a simple technique. Rule of thumb. This allows us to estimate the distance between the drone and the clouds, as well as determine their size. It doesn't hurt to be more reasonable with our adventure. Do you know what the dimensions of these drones are?"

---

* A woman with a laughing face.

"Eleven meters long and twenty meters wide."

"Alright. I should do some calculations. Look in the direction of that cloud. Let me know if you see a bird near it."

By rule of thumb I found out the drone was only six thousand meters away from us and was flying at nine thousand meters above sea level. After calculating the drone's distance from the clouds and their size, I made the call.

"Hevala Rûken! Hevalê Saro is with me."

"Saro?"

"You've disappointed me, heval. You shouldn't forget your comrades so easily," Saro declared out loud.

"Pardon heval, the dragon up there has disturbed me," Rûken replied with great enthusiasm.

"Never mind, heval. We want to do a revolutionary experiment. Listen carefully to what hevala Jîncin says."

"Who is hevala Jîncin?"

"That German lady."

"A nice name. Congratulations."

I thanked Rûken and asked how far they are from the hawthorn trees.

"Very close. One of us is even sleeping under the trees," Rûken replied.

"Where is hevala Rojano?"* I asked.

"Oh, that lucky devil? Out of everyone, it's Rojano. She's been spoiled enough today. She snores even when she's in a deep sleep."

"Heval is lying. I cannot sleep peacefully when my comrades are under the scorching sun. I am highly tenderhearted," Rojano responded to Rûken. Rojano was a comrade from Serdeşt. She was as tall as me and had studied civil engineering. I tried to explain to her how she could find the angles between herself, the right side of the cloud, and the drone. But I couldn't find the right technical terms in Kurdish that she could also understand. I explained it all to Saro in English and he translated it into Kurdish for Rojano.

That was the most difficult and riskiest calculation of my whole life. I had gathered a few possibilities and wrote my calculation with a stick on the ground. We needed at least twenty-five seconds to reach the cave

* The new day.

safely. Right at that time, I saw an eagle next to the cloud. Saro also noticed it, but we did not have enough time to redo the calculation. The group was ready to run away. I was the closest person to the destination. The cave's location was fifty meters up on my left side. I'd have to run fifty meters in twenty-five seconds uphill. It didn't appear too difficult. Saro had to run over sixty meters uphill at the same time. Other comrades had to overcome seventy meters of distance, but they were further up, on nearly flat ground. Saro became the advance guard and I took command, even though I was not a member of the party. They had entrusted their lives to me without hesitation. I waited until the drone reached a certain point behind the cloud, then I gave my stupid command and it worked.

I was running as fast as I could, but when I reached the cave there were already some comrades there. Gulbehar,[*] an ever-smiling twenty-one-year-old girl from a village near Kobanî, grabbed my arm and pulled me down close to Rûnahî,[†] to enable the other comrades to immediately find a safe place. Rûnahî was a Êzdî girl from Şingal, who grew up in Baghdad. Besides her duties, she was responsible for the group's health care. At the same moment, a couple of comrades leisurely approached the mouth of the cave as if they were strolling on a city sidewalk. One of them had a big sack on his shoulder and the other, with a thick black beard and mustache on his face, had a big black pot in his hands. They were our group jokesters, Zinar[‡] from Colemêrg and Satyar[§] from Xaneqîn. Then Saro arrived and sat down in front of me. The last one who came in was our commander. She sat down in front of Satyar and everyone cheered. From the jubilation of these experienced guerrillas, I could glean what devastating effect these drones have had on their lives.

The cave was small but deep enough to protect us from the drone and bombers. Zinar pulled out a bottle of water from his sack and handed it over to Rûken. She gave it to Gulbehar then went to sit by Saro, hugged him and said, "Hevalê Saro, you just got here, yet you've already taken over my command. We were already close friends."

Saro squeezed her left arm with his hand and replied.

---

[*] Spring flower.
[†] Brightness.
[‡] Rock wall.
[§] A friend in difficult times.

"If I were the commander, we would all be dead now, and without Erdoğan personally handing me a thank-you prize for it. Any mistake that I could have made was prevented by hevala Jîncin."

Arjîn* gave me a handshake and said, "Thanks, hevala Jîncin. Lovely name you have; I wish I had it myself."

"I would gladly exchange my name for your beauty," I replied.

"Thanks for the compliment, but every heval here thinks we look as similar as two sisters, just in slightly different colors."

I thought they had been deliberately ignoring me these past few days. I could not understand the extraordinary circumstances they lived in until today, even though this drone was always flying over us somewhere. Prior to today we would dig under a truck tarp in the daytime and would not notice the presence of the drone. Then at sundown we would slip into our individual sleeping tents. But tonight they were thinking about me and pointed out something that I had never noticed: my Middle Eastern eyes! Arjîn really resembled me. Everyone would think she was my own daughter if I took a sun bath, used amber-colored contact lenses, and colored my hair brown and tightly curled it. The daughter of a woman who was a young mother.

Two bottles of water passed hand to hand, but nobody drank until a bottle reached Tewar from Amed. She bore no resemblance to a female eagle; she was more like a black raven. She gulped down half of a bottle then gave it to me. I handed it to Zinar without drinking and waited for another bottle to reach me from the other side. A very long arm twirled over our heads like a crane. It belonged to Serhelldan† from Cîzrê, the one whom the comrades call the tallest guerilla in the world. He is about two meters tall, which is too much to be a partisan. The water was warm but I relished it anyway. I wanted to drink the whole bottle but I handed it over to the crane.

I asked for water again once I had seen that all my comrades had drunk enough. I drank quietly. Once I put the bottle down, Saro asked me, "Ten minutes have passed, heval. Do you think they will dispatch jets to bombard us?"

* Fire of life.
† Revolution.

"I'm not an air traffic expert. I don't know the capabilities of Turkish controllers and observers in their air traffic controls. Are they even comparing the photos taken ten minutes ago with the current ones? It's too easy to recognize the differences between various photos with today's improved technology. Fourteen objects suddenly disappeared from the screen within a few seconds. Unless the observers were snoozing, but. . ."

"Or underestimated us," Saro said. This statement brought about a jestful mood in the room.

"Do not worry, heval. They thought we were abandoned sheep that ran away suddenly," Arjîn said.

"Your theory works for thirteen of us, but they thought hevalê Serhelldan was a fallen plantain tree. How can a plantain tree run away without legs?" Rojano playfully retorted.

"You make the facts too complicated. A naughty buck kicked the plantain tree and it began to roll down deep into the valley. All the sheep panicked and ran away." Satyar declared, solving the problem.

The atmosphere of the group became unexpectedly silly, but it was even funnier when Nadîr asked seriously, "When's dinner, heval?"

Even I couldn't stop laughing. Nadîr was a strong, handsome young man with big black eyes and a suntanned face. He was from Xaneqîn, just like Satyar. His question was appropriate: we had eaten nothing since last night. Gulbehar got up, brought the pot, and put it down in the middle of the group. Once she picked up the lid of the pot and Nadîr saw the lentil soup, he asked even more seriously than before, "Should we call this breakfast or lunch right now?"

Laughter poured out of the cave. Nadîr was looking at us calmly, unaware that in that moment he had been renamed. Everyone in the PKK* has the right to pick whatever nickname they would like for themselves, but because of his questions Nadîr's close friend, Satyar, gave him a different one. Nadîr had no complaints about it. Zinar opened his bag and pulled out two pans, laid them in front of the pot, and then gave everyone a spoon. Satyar gave his spoon to Nadîr and said, "Take it, Natêr.† Eat your breakfast with this one and lunch with another."

---

* Partiya Karkerên Kurdistanê or Kurdistan Workers' Party
† Hunger, the comrades' nickname for Nadîr.".

We all liked these two guys. Satyar always had new jokes and Zinar had all the necessities a heval could want. Every so often his hands would burrow into his bag and emerge with some new variety of items.

"Here it is, heval. Bread . . . salt and . . . oh, cover your ears, hevala Gulbehar . . . lemon essence!"

Gulbehar abhors anything sour or citrus-flavored. She gets nauseous just hearing the word "lemon." Zinar then took some tobacco out from his magic bag. Rojano was still dissatisfied. "Well! How can we smoke without cigarette paper, heval?"

Zinar's right hand went into his vest pocket and pulled out a few packets of cigarette paper.

"This heval is unique. A magic box! He's got everything you need. If you tell him you want five kilos of tomatoes, he'll put his hand in his pocket and produce what you desire in various types and different colors. Tell him it's hot and you wish you had a fan; he'll disappear behind a stone and reappear after twenty minutes with a couple of fans, a stand, and a ceiling fan. I'm not kidding, I swear to Erdoğan," Arjîn announced.

"Yeah, look in your pockets, heval. Maybe you'll find an anti-aircraft missile to take care of these buzzing drones," Saro told Zinar.

"No, heval. That's illegal contraband. I don't like to get myself into trouble."

"But we're already illegal," Rojano replied.

"Yes, heval. But why should I thicken my criminal file even more?"

"As a terrorist, you'll already get a minimum sentence of a hundred years in prison."

"Yes heval, maybe you are right. But a hundred years of punishment is much better than two hundred years."

"You mean that you want to live for the next hundred years?"

"Why not, heval. Noah lived for a thousand years."

"But you are not a prophet."

"You mustn't underestimate your comrades. What prophetic features is he missing?" Satyar spoke in his defense.

"I want to drink tea now. I will recognize you as a prophet if you make some tea in this bear den." Arjîn looked at him with her big, amber eyes and said, "Yes heval, tea is not a problem."

Zinar half rose and went to the left corner of the cave, where the oldest comrade, hevalê Ferhad, was sitting. He was from Erzirom. We all respected him in a special way. When he was a young man, he had been imprisoned in Amed's dreadful prison for ten years. You could feel the unbearable torture in his eyes, in his limping, and much more in his profound silence twenty-eight years after his release. Zinar sat down opposite hevalê Ferhad and started talking to him politely, as if he had not been there all along.

"Pardon, heval, unfortunately I hid the kettle behind you. Could you please move to let me get it out?"

"Yeah, sure, heval."

Hevalê Ferhad came over and sat beside me. That made me happy. At that moment the chit-chat ended. From his hidden place Zinar took out a kettle, two bottles of water, and some tea and sugar. He made a small smokeless fire at a corner of the cave and poured water into the kettle. Meanwhile, we were eating lentils in two huddled groups, each group with their own pan. Tea was drunk and cigarettes were masterfully rolled and smoked one after another. Apart from me and Arjîn, everyone else had a smoke and nobody cared about the drone up in the sky. Although no one was making jokes anymore, the atmosphere of the group was quite pleasant compared to the previous days. Saro had the group's attention. Everyone was asking him questions about Rojava. For the first time, I had the opportunity to really notice how handsome this man was. He had straight dark hair and light brown eyes. I was attracted to his warm gaze. I asked him about hevala Jiyan,* a comrade whom I met two years ago and whose personality impressed me greatly. Saro did not know her and there was no reason for me to ask another question. Our wireless contacted us after the second round of tea drinking and smoking; the drone was gone.

Nobody was happier than me to hear this news. When I was a little girl, I always promised myself that one day I would get revenge on my mother for putting me under house arrest. She must have suffered terribly when I decided to live with my father two years ago and when I set off for Rojava against her will. I returned to Germany, but after a year I left her. Left without a trace. I do not know what reasons there are for my behavior or what names I should use to describe it. Masochism, sadism, or a revolutionary self-removal from the problematic structuring of the modern nuclear family.

* Life.

I left the cave. The sky was bright and blue and I could hear the murmur of the stream again. I went downhill towards the spring. By noon I had run this path within twenty seconds. A trace of my crumpled body was visible on the dried grass. I laid down in the same place, sat up and stretched my legs, wriggled around, and gazed at the sky. It is pure blue with no trace or trail of aircrafts, something that cannot be seen in Frankfurt for even an hour of the year. I get up and go to the spring. Clearer than a crab's eyes, as my father always said. I put my palms in front of the spring and let cold water flow into them. I am not thirsty but I drink and also wash my face. Then I sit on a rock and look at the valley opposite me. I did not have the opportunity to see this virgin nature these past few days. Virgin or abandoned? The trickle that comes from our well flows about thirty meters down into a stream that continues to the left, up to a river that is invisible from here. But it separates the mountain from the high black rocks opposite us. No trace of animals can be seen. I would like to lie down naked on this rock in front of the setting sun, but freedom is limited here, of course.

I'm struggling to make a final decision. If I return to Germany, I will forever lose the opportunity to experience this strange lifestyle, yet if I stay here I will have to throw away my identity as a free woman and submit myself to a life full of clichés and rules that fell out of some fool's mind one day. Today was a different day, just because an unordinary commander had been replaced with an ordinary one. The party claims to act through collective decision-making, so why has a fundamental change occurred just by replacing one of the four administrative members for a day? The fighters went from programmed automata to humorous and emotional humans in the blink of an eye. I turn around; nobody to be seen. They have certainly gone back to the bunker and will try to compensate for today's lost time through even stricter work.

I get up and go to them. They have stopped digging and have already started construction. They reply warmly to my greeting. Hevalê Ferhad now works as a master mason and everyone works under his command. They have already made room walls with hemp sacks full of soil and are busy constructing the room's ceiling. Serhelldan's height is quite useful for the task. Saro gives him the wooden beams, then he lays them over the sack wall and tightens the structure with ropes and stones. I look around to find where I could somehow be useful. Saro looks at me with a smile and says, "It's ok, heval. The work is advancing well. We will also take a break for dinner soon anyway."

We went to the adjoining room, which was constructed as a kitchen. Rûnahî and Akam[*] were there cooking. Akam, from Merîwan, was the second oldest comrade of our group and the only one who always wrote in his diary. He was standing next to two pots standing on a two-burner gas stove. You could guess without smelling or looking into the pots that one pot contained rice and the other beans. That means our lunch shifts to dinner.

Since the women's room was lower, in consideration of their height, Arjîn and Rojano served as ladders for the others. We helped them until all four walls were constructed. After dinner, Saro told me that he wanted to talk to me. We took two umbrellas and a blanket and went toward the mouth of the cave. I thought Saro wanted to talk to me about his project, but he brought up another topic. He wanted to get to know me. I took up the conversation thread.

"I am sure that you are well informed about me. You know who I am, that I was in Rojava, and that I asked the party to dispatch me here to stay with this group for the upcoming autumn and winter."

"And why do you suddenly want to go back to Germany?"

"You don't think that I can change my decision and correct my mistake?"

"Certainly you can. You came here of your own free will and you can always leave us. We are not happy about your departure, but we respect your decision. I just want to know why you changed your mind so suddenly."

"I see a lot of structural issues in your party."

"What, for example? I would like to hear."

"What really gets on my nerves is your arts-and-crafts apotheosis. Abdullah Öcalan is worshiped here as a God. This is antimaterialist, antidialectical, and insulting to the Kurdish nation, even to Abdullah Öcalan himself. He is not a sheikh. You're repeating the same mistakes that the communists made towards Karl Marx. Your clichés also torment me. I don't understand why a party that claims to be fighting for women's equality and freedom for humanity is, in fact, still involved with trifling

---

* The result of a goal.

things. Actually no, that term is too innocuous, better to say involved with displays of vain emptiness. It's just a contradiction to talk about freedom while it's forbidden to put your legs on other party members. Why is the party interfering with people's private lives?"

"These are little problems. We have much bigger ones in the party."

"Yes I know, but these are symbols of oppression. It shows this party does not want to change and cannot develop properly beyond it."

"When I say that it's trivial, I mean that I find this behavior small, even absurd. There are much deeper problems anchored in the history of the Kurds and of humanity in general. You cannot imagine what problems the party's reactionary fundamentalists have caused for me here. Fifteen years ago, no one was allowed to even talk about such topics. I asked you to tell me your criticisms because comrades told me some points."

"And I came to know about your plan. You promised it yourself this morning."

"I'll explain it to you later, but first I want to get to know you better."

"That's exactly what I want. I want to know who you really are, hevalê Saro! And why you suddenly came here today."

"Like everyone else here I have a long history behind myself. It's too complicated to tell you my story, but you can ask me any question you want."

"Two years ago, when I wanted to go to Rojava, the party asked me to write my story. At that time it was difficult for me to write in Kurdish, but I wrote sixty pages about myself. I don't know if you read it or not . ."

"I understand. I hope I don't bore you. I am . . let me start with my father. He had a tragic fate. His brothers saw him as a bad luck charm. His father died two months before his birth and his mother died on delivery. That's why they hated him. They would always beat him and call him wretched and unlucky. They forced him to do all of the hard work. When he was twelve, they had him mow a large wheat field all alone with a broken sickle. He worked for three days, but reached the end of his rope on the fourth day and fled to Sine.* He stayed for a while in the mosques and Dervish monasteries. His village was already known for its famous mullahs. That's why he could eventually find a permanent place in a mosque. He learned Islamic theology, enrolled in university,

* Sanandaj.

and then found a good job at the registry office. In the meantime, he met my mother. My mother comes from a rich and reputed family. Her family let my dad teach her as a tutor in some subjects that she was weak in. They fell in love and decided to marry. After a few years, the Islamic Revolution began in Iran. The Kurds saw this revolution stolen by the mullahs, so they started an uprising against the Islamic Republic of Iran. This uprising was crushed after a bloody battle. The Islamic Revolutionary Guard Corps arrested my father, accusing him of abetting the uprising. My mother served as a surgeon and they also arrested her for treating anti-Islamic forces in houses that they turned into makeshift hospitals. Maybe it was an irony of fate, a continuation of his bitter destiny. My father was arrested a few days before I was born and my mother three days after. I was alone without food or water for three days, until a woman found me in that terrible situation. She was a relative of my father's. Her brother wanted her to marry an old mullah, but she fled to Sine. She found our house, opened the door by force after knocking on it a dozen times, and found me in great distress. She told me she searched the whole city to find milk for me. The city would be destroyed after twenty-four days of house-to-house combat and countless bombardments. People left the city. She couldn't find anyone to buy a cup of milk from, so in the end she fed me with tea and moldy bread. Thus, my bones are poorly formed. You have surely seen my bowed shoulders, hevala Jînçin."

"How many days were you in that condition?"

"I do not know. My parents never talked to me about these topics. They wanted to keep me away from politics and Kurdish matters."

"It's very important to me. Please give me an estimate. One year or more?"

"No, a shorter amount of time, maybe two or three weeks. But then I grew up well. When I was a kid I had a lot of enthusiasm for electronic devices. Already at thirteen I had invented an eavesdropping device and placed first with the device in a scientific competition in Kurdistan province. I sent my invention to a national contest. All of the inventors received a receipt for the shipping costs, but I didn't get one. Next year, I saw that a couple of students on television won second place for presenting my invention. My parents knew they had stolen my invention, but they didn't support me. From then on, I rarely attended school. I stayed at home and worked on electrical appliances. At the end of the year, I took the final exam and successfully completed my compulsory education. When I was fifteen, I started to work so that I wouldn't have to take any money from my parents. During the day I worked in the wastewater treatment plant and repaired computers at home in the evenings. I was the only one in the city who could fix computers, so I managed to save up a lot of money. Then, when I was eighteen, I ran the first internet cafe in Sine. I furtively installed a satellite antenna in a house near my cafe and sold fast and cheap internet. Let me tell you something funny. I advertised in the city that the internet cafe would give customers a couple of hours for free if they enrolled there. A long queue formed in front of my cafe. It was longer than the funeral procession for Michael Jackson. You could count on your fingers the months it would take until all the enrolled people could access my free internet. Briefly, I was raking in money. Other internet cafes couldn't compete with my fast and cheap service."

"Wasn't that illegal?" I asked Saro.

"Of course it was."

"But how could you do that? Why didn't they shut your cafe down?"

"It was locked and reopened several times. The officials of the Public Surveillance Authority even became my special customers. I did some smart things, but also some stupid things. I recruited two so-called fanatic Muslims and trusted them. I often left them alone with all my possessions when I was on a trip. I spent money like water, traveled like Marco Polo, and entertained myself like a king. I didn't know that the Islamists confiscated my shop legally. I was a little annoyed but immediately found an even greater source of moneymaking. I established an internet services company and made contracts with some big legal companies to sell them a mix of legal-but-slow state internet and my own ultra-high-speed illegal internet. I threw money out the window but it was piling up constantly. Then I made my second mistake. Again, radical Islamists! I founded a software company and wanted to offer ADSL throughout the province. I had already talked to a company in Tehran and made an agreement. They would send me the equipment and I would find the customers and support the technical services. Each side should get half of the profits. I don't know where those two radical Islamists learned of my project. They came to me, calling themselves my religious brothers, and asked me to cooperate with them. They took the reins. There were only two other people who could serve as witnesses to the agreement, two Muslims who ran a notary's office. We made an agreement and established that each side would get half of the profit. In the first year we earned a profit of sixty-five million tomans. That was a lot of money in those days. How much money do you think they gave me as my share? Less than one million tomans. The blood rushed to my face. I went to them with my witnesses and asked them what was going on. They wanted to convince me that my share is fair. We were all Muslims, but they were married and had children, so there were seventy people amongst them and I was alone with just the two testicles in my pants. I asked my witness: What do you think? They said that they are right according to the laws of Islam and tradition. I shouted, "I shit on your religion and your holy books." A brawl broke out. Then I returned to using my brain. I blocked the company and established a new one, so like an ox standing before the mountain, they were at a loss for what to do. My company became the largest software development company nationwide. Twelve highly skilled program writers worked for me. From then on I had a hatred for Islam. In order to get on the nerves of the Islamists, who received all kinds of support from the government in Kurdistan, I established three more factories."

"What kind of factories?"

"It will take more nights if you want me to tell you everything in detail."

"More than one thousand nights?" I said, laughing.

"Can you guarantee that I'll still be alive tomorrow night? . . No matter, I'll tell you my life story in two more rounds, if I return safely and you stay here."

"Ok, keep talking. What factories did you have?"

"Can I smoke a cigarette first?"

"Yeah, sure."

He took a small lighter from his pocket, which he also used as a flashlight. He turned it on and the cave became lit as if by moonlight. Then he brought out a copper-colored cigarette box from his vest pocket. He opened it, took a cigarette paper out, and tore it meticulously and rapidly into three small pieces. I had already noticed his tiny cigarettes this afternoon. I asked him to make me a cigarette.

"I thought you were a nonsmoker."

"I am, but now I'd like to try your little baby cigarettes. Why so small?"

"There's a story for that. I'll tell you later." He masterfully made two more cigarettes. He put one of them in a pipe and handed it over to me. I said that I wanted to smoke when he finished his cigarette. He turned off the lighter and again the cave went dark. He lit the cigarette. The glow of the cigarette light turned red in the darkness and the cave became more luminous. It was like a living creature that breathed in and out with Saro's each breath. I could understand why most guerrillas are smokers. Only cigarettes keep a flame burning for me. Saro put out his cigarette and put another one in the pipe, gave it to me, and continued his story without looking at me smoke.

"First, I launched a pickle factory. The profit was twenty times."

"Twenty times or twenty percent?"

"At least twenty times. That means two thousand percent."

"Unbelievable! Two thousand percent is just incredible."

"Yeah, I couldn't fathom it when I had the real profits in my bank account. I bought the cucumbers for fifty tomans per kilogram in cash from a poor farmer. I put three hundred grams of cucumbers into salty spiced water. The cucumbers swelled and filled the one-kilogram buckets after a few months, then I sold these three-hundred grams of cucumber for three thousand tomans. That was over two thousand percent profit. I found a customer in Başûr. For a few months I sent him some of my high-profit pickles. Then he suggested I send him pickles in twenty-kilogram cans instead of plastic buckets. It was amazing! He not only undertook the extra costs, but also sent me the required equipment for filling and packing pickles into the metal canisters. The more pickles I sent, the more he needed. I was suspicious, although he always transferred money on time. I went to Hewlêr by car and became aware of his distribution method. Some people were well occupied with my pickled cucumbers. The process wasn't too complicated: one person opened the canisters and the next one used a ladle to put the pickles into a glass over a tub. In the final stage another person pasted a sticker on the jars. They even had their own brand, which became famous in Arab countries. Their mass production and conversion industries worked through ladles and hands smoothly. That was not all. He had other employees. He had also established a factory for canisters. It was a part of his industry. Some workers were shearing empty canisters and putting them in a press machine. From one side they put old canisters into the machine and shiny tin sheets came out from the other side. These tin pallets were not allowed for export from Iran into Iraq.

Money also flowed in from my fruit-sorting factory. I had machinery smuggled in from Italy. However, the Iranian Chamber of Industry helped me, in this case. This factory was too advanced. There were only two more like it in Iran. These machines washed and dried the fruit, sorted them by color and size, polished them, determined how long the fruits would last, and in which temperature they should be stored. Not even the government officials could compete with me. I was able to supply my fruit cheaper than they did for the New Year's market and force competitors out of the market. I didn't know what to do with so much money. Then I decided to take revenge on the fanatical Muslims. I talked to their biggest investor and convinced him to join me in a profitable financial project. We traveled to Başûr and invested in the stock exchange there. The enthusiasm that arose was as unexpected as it was twelve years ago when I opened my cafe. This time there were no free offers, just pure demand. A lot of corrupt politicians and businessmen rushed to our office. I was compelled to replace the normal windows with opaque ones, so nobody could see them. Our office was a tiny subsidiary of American Forex brokers, subject to the First National Bank, which itself dances around like a little mouse under the umbrella of the Federal Reserve. It means we're little ants in this game, but money rained down on us, nevertheless, like gold from heaven. I became so rich that I couldn't audit my bank accounts."

"How much money did you make?" I asked curiously.

"Over twenty million dollars. The richer I became, the bigger my life vacuum."

"Did you have girlfriends?"

"You want to hear that story too?"

"Well now that you've pulled us in, don't leave us hanging!"

"I was never too gallant. I was always a loser when it came to women."

I noticed he was searching for something with his hands in darkness. "What are you searching for?" I asked him.

"My lighter."

I laughed. It was in my hands the whole time and I was playing with it. I switched on its light. He picked up a tiny cigarette from the ground and I asked to light it.

He said, "Don't you know that this is forbidden in the party?"

"Why?" I asked with such wide eyes that he noticed them even in the dim lighting.

"Apparently this work demeans others."

"Then let Serhelldan light some cigarettes for you. Or is he way too big and that would belittle his great stature?! Why don't you give up these damn clichés?"

I lit his cigarette. He thanked me. Another cigarette was born in front of my eyes, glowing brighter with his inhales and then fading. I could see his face when he breathed in. He looked handsome and gentlemanly. He took the cigarette out of the pipe and laid it next to others at the corner of the cave. I turned off the lighter and he continued.

"I was fifteen. I had a friend whose girlfriend had a very nice classmate. A boy who was known as a thug in the city liked her. They wanted to get rid of him and suggested that I pretend to be her boyfriend to convince him to leave her alone. The guy's name was Eira. That girl was known throughout the city for her beauty. With my figure and style, I had to present myself as her lover. Who would have believed that? Every day with my head hanging down, I walked back and forth on the sidewalk with her while I ate lots of popcorn and stuck my gaze to the mosaics of the sidewalk. I still recognize those mosaics more than my cigarette box. One day, my friends invited me to drink. I declined their invitation because I didn't drink alcohol. They said you could drink lemonade, just come on. I didn't know it was a trap and they wanted Eira to kill me."

"Why did they want to kill you?"

"No idea. Maybe they also wanted to get rid of Eira. Once I saw Eira I was scared. Before he got drunk, I told him I wanted to talk to him. We went out of the hut and I told him the story. I advised him, 'We are in over our heads with Nina. We should stick to what we know, as the people say.' Eira took a dagger from his pocket and said he was misinformed about this case and came here to kill me. Then he hugged me and became one of my best friends.

My first love adventure almost cost me my head. My first attempt at actual love was even worse. I was going from Tehran to Sine by bus.

There were many free seats on the bus but a beautiful girl sat down beside me. Maybe she thought that I was a child. I did not want to be seen as she thought, so I requested to become her friend. She did not reject my request directly and we soon became lovers. After a year and a half, she told me, 'We have to end this foolish relationship.'

'And why?' I asked, astonished.

'Because I want to get married.'

'Well, I will marry you,' I answered.

'It's not possible. You're still a child, not even sixteen, but I'm twenty-four. My family will never let you.' I looked at her seriously and said, 'They have to be grateful if I marry you. Tell them that I am a rational man.'

'You would not have made such an offer if you were a rational man.'

'I'll talk to them and convince them.'

The next day I talked to her brother but he replied, 'Kid, don't make yourself look even more ridiculous.'

'I'll make your sister happy.'

'Can you shave your armpits alone?'

'I even shave my hair by myself.'

He looked, smiling at my shaved head, and said, 'Bravo. It looks good on elementary students.'

'I'm in vocational school and work part time. I have enough money in my pocket.'

'Well, pull out your hands from your pockets then.'

'I will ask my family to submit matchmaking if you wish.'

'Don't dishonor them; we will not welcome your family. Kid, have patience and let yourself grow up first.'

She became a totally different woman after this refusal. She even rejected my dates. It seems she was leading me on to lessen her loneliness in the last nineteen months. I wanted to be sure, so I needed the help of my parents with this matter. But again, they didn't support me. I left the house and rented a small room. After two years, when I launched my internet cafe, she appeared and wanted to make up for what she had done before. I knew that she was only interested in my money, so I rejected her. She was money-hungry and at every stage of my professional career, when I climbed to a higher financial level, she reappeared. One time I got the flu. One of my employees brought me a delicious milk soup. Until that time, I had never eaten milk soup. When I expressed my appreciation to him, he said, 'A girl brought it for you.' I immediately went outside despite my illness and drove swiftly towards her house. I arrived at her home while she was getting out of her car. I called her. She came to me, opened the door, and sat. I told her, coughing, 'you left me alone during the worst part of my life. That time I was eight years younger than you and today and always this age gap will remain between us. It has not changed. I was an innocent boy who lived off his black hands and had so many butterflies in my stomach that I could not judge age differences. Now I have changed. You have taught me how to do the calculation. I am now in agreement with your original opinion: we do not belong together.'

After a month I got married, but I wasn't lucky with that life. A life with constant interruptions caused us to finally divorce. I also separated from my friends. After ten years I was alone, so I returned to my family home, and especially to my sister's side, who previously worked for me as a computer expert. There you have the history of my boring love life."

"No, it didn't bore me. And how did you join the PKK?"

He lowered his head, turned on his wristwatch light, and said, "Near to ten o'clock. It's gotten cold. I'll bring two jackets."

He stretched himself to the cave wall and picked up one of the umbrellas. He stood halfway up and went to the cave mouth. There, he turned and said, "Don't forget to come out with the umbrella when the drone arrives."

I go to the cave mouth, half-standing, half-squatting. The indigo-blue sky, decorated with bright stars, attracts my eye. A charming image that still fascinates me after twelve nights. Here there is no light pollution from the cities or villages and the sky presents its virgin color. An ancient image that drags people deep into galaxies, black holes, and the entire universe. The sky looks like a woman's indigo-blue dress at a Kurdish wedding, with countless white spangles, exactly the way my father saw it forty years ago while he was a Pêşmerge and spent the whole night in anguish on the Qendîl Mountains, amidst the failure of the biggest Kurdish uprising of the twentieth century.

This virgin sky witnessed the forced migration of hundreds of thousands of Kurds and the destruction of thousands of villages by the Turkish government in the eighties and nineties. The lights of thousands of villages have been extinguished and I sit here in this cave, dressed up in male attire that symbolizes struggle even at Kurdish weddings. Thinking of my father's death, I try to get some comfort from this indigo-blue sky. Losing him has left a void in my life. Saro comes back from the inside of darkness. I wipe away my tears. I crawl back to the cave wall and search for the lighter within the darkness. I turn its lamp on. He walks up a few steps and enters the cave half-squatting. In one hand he has a table with two glasses of tea and in the other a jacket. He was already wearing his own.

"Wow, it's like a Christmas present," I said joyfully when I saw the tea.

I sat down on the blanket to let him lean against the wall this time. He put my jacket and the tea table in front of me then sat opposite me without leaning against the wall.

"Drink heval, it won't be hot," he said.

I took the glass and drank a sip of tea. It was pleasantly warm. He drank a sip, again brought his cigarette box out of his vest pocket and rolled up three cigarettes. He drank another sip of tea. I took the lighter from my lap and lit his cigarette. He drank a sip of tea after each time he puffed his cigarette. The cigarette was dead after four sips.

"Until which part of my story did I tell you?"

"Why did you join the PKK?"

"Out of hatred for the PKK." He laughed briefly. "I had a printer in my cafe and our customers were allowed to use it for free if they brought their own paper. We didn't control who printed what. One day, some officers from the ministry of intelligence rushed into my cafe. They were armed as if they had to fight burglars and dangerous criminals. They handcuffed me, confiscated all my computers, sealed the shop, and threw me in jail. That night an interrogator came and tried to convince me to confess that I am working for the PKK. I said I hadn't ever heard that name. He repeated his assertion over and over, but I denied it every time. Finally, he put some papers in front of me and said, 'These papers were printed in your cafe.' I said confidently, 'Impossible! These papers were printed out by a dot matrix printer, but I have a laser printer. I know where these papers were printed.' He asked, 'Where?' I answered, 'In the public surveillance authority's office.' He asked me, 'How do you know?'

I replied, 'I sold it to them and I know this serial number on the bottom of the paper.'

After a few hours they took me out of jail and dumped me on the road near the Girêze River. From that day I cursed the PKK and looked for that damn name. After a few years, I accidentally found an article by Abdullah Öcalan on the internet. I really liked it and felt very proud that a Kurd had written an article about international problems. I searched his name and learned that he is the founder of the damned PKK. I looked for his books and found a small one. I read it several times. Then I decided to meet him. Where could I find him? Somebody told me he is in a prison on an island. Fine, then I will look for his party. Some people affiliated with the PKK came regularly to my cafe and printed out free leaflets but they didn't have any news from the party. A customer told me that I have to look for them in Başûr. And where is Başûr? It's located in the south of Kurdistan? And where is the south of Kurdistan? In northern Iraq. Oh, right, I know that area well.

I went legally as a businessman to the south of Kurdistan. I was introduced to someone from Qelladizê. I told him that I will give him more than enough money, so he should take me via a safe route to the PKK. He said that all the roads are safe, because Başûr is free. I cannot remember how many minutes or hours we were driving. I was distressed. It was still light when we got out of the car near a mountain. It was the beginning of a path that we would have to climb. I wasn't accustomed to hiking. Finally, we reached a place where two poles were connected to each other by a thick chain. An armed man who was speaking Farsi was standing there. Petrified by fear, I couldn't move. The armed man came closer and greeted me. I said in Kurdish that we had lost our way, but he called me by my name. Only then did I realize that they knew me from the beginning, were aware that I was looking for them, and that I had put myself in danger by going there.

Another guerrilla replaced him and he took me to a group. They were nine young girls and boys in a pit under the ground. Their dreadful situation made me cry. In the meantime, their commander appeared. His name was Manî. He saw my sadness, but he did not let me stay there. I said, 'I want to help you. Winter is coming and these people do not have warm clothes. I can help you financially.' He replied, 'What? Money, capitalism, bourgeoisie. No, we do not need money. We are fighters.' I told him, 'Yes, but the fighters need shoes, clothes, and food. All this costs money. Tell me how I can help you.' He said to go back, that he would contact me. After that I got orders from him daily. What were the orders? To distribute CDs in front of the primary schools. To write slogans on the walls of girls' schools. To blow up thousands of balloons in certain colors and hang them on a tree. I said, 'Heval, I am a manufacturer and such activities do not suit me.' He said, 'You have to fight with your deep-rooted capitalist culture.' I defended myself and replied, 'If I were a capitalist, I would not have offered you any money.' Then he said, 'Ok, bring a truck of flour to the top of this mountain in Hewraman.' I replied, 'That won't work, heval. How will I pass the surveillance post? What story should I tell them? Does my father have a bakery on the top of that mountain? And why a truck of flour? They will ask me what my father is doing with so much bread. He feeds his livestock; is that what I'm supposed to say?'"

I laugh loudly and can't stop. "Pardon me, hevalê Saro," I said and continued to laugh, "your exaggeration is very funny."

"Exaggeration? I did all these things."

"What do you mean by 'all these things?'"

"CD distribution, slogan writing, even blowing balloons. I personally blew up all the balloons, while my cheeks stretched out like a trumpeter's. But I couldn't drive a truck very easily in the mountains of Hewraman. I said I could give them money. They asked me how much. I said as much as they needed. They began a competition. I paid out like an ATM and they sucked it up like a vacuum cleaner. Then I realized that everything was planned by hevalê Manî from the beginning."

"And why did he do that?"

"He wanted to cut off my contact with the party, so that my financial help would be perceived as his doing. For some time they stuck to me like a leech to get my money and deliberately put me in danger. One day, a guerrilla in civilian costume came to my office and told me that he would have to spend some days with me. I said 'my house is under surveillance, heval! You cannot stay with me, but I'll take you to a safe house.' He said, 'No, I will only stay with you. That's an order from the party.' The more I argued, the more stubborn he became. Finally, I took him home. In the evening, some suspicious cars appeared in front of our alley. With great effort and at great risk, we managed to flee. The party's stupidity put me in danger and the intelligence services became suspicious of me. I knew an officer in the secret service authority. One morning, he came to my office and said that I had to flee the country. I asked him how many days I had to escape. His answer was only three or four hours. It was mid-autumn. I left everything: my office, my factories . . . everything that I had. I packed my life into a suitcase, took my mother and sister, and drove toward Başûr. In the evening, we arrived at a mountain where I met hevalê Mani. When I saw him, I could not control myself and shouted at him, but he branded me as a spy of the intelligence services. I said, 'I do not want to help you anymore, you lying bastard.' We hadn't eaten or drunk anything and just wanted to go to one of the cities of Başûr. But one of them said that the comrades from above wanted to see me. I asked them when I should see them. He answered, 'Right now.' Unlike in Sine, there was about a meter of snow at the foothill, and I had to climb the mountain with my autumn clothes."

I feel cold, take the jacket next to me and put it on without interrupting his words. He talks about a difficult situation, over two meters of snow, deadly frigidity, and, worse than anything, the snowstorms.

"We were climbing with great difficulty. Sometimes we were trudging through snow up to our chests. Everyone needed someone's help to get out of the snow and, once helped, the helper would then immediately need the same kind of assistance. In that condition we passed two nights and three days. We didn't have anything to eat except snowstorms. We wandered around but didn't find a camp. Even our guide hadn't expected such fearsome blizzards. Our eyelids were stuck, our hands were frozen, and I could not even scratch the ice on my watch glass. Like everyone else, I had lost sense of the time and could not distinguish the surroundings. One of us could not move anymore and dropped into the snow. Our guide dragged him through the snow for a few dozen meters, but eventually he couldn't stand either and fell down. The storm was howling in my ears and I was thinking of my sister, who was alone down there with those villains. I went snow-blind and lost my sense of direction. We did not even know if we were going up or down. Suddenly, I saw something shining. I ran in its direction without speaking to anyone. A man had made a small fire on the snow to show us the direction. I shouted as loud as I could. Three people came down toward us. I fell down on the snow and was beaten unconscious. As I was slowly regaining conscious, a guerrilla continually asked me a question without hearing my answer.

I had forgotten even my name and lost my memory. He consoled me and said that he had seen something similar and also experienced that himself. He said not to worry about it, because the situation is temporary. I do not know how many hours passed before I completely regained consciousness. Their commander came to me promptly and asked me the first question. Go ahead and guess what he asked me after all of that."

"How can I guess? I wasn't there."

"I'm sure you could never guess, even if you could take a billion guesses. He wanted to know when I could fix their generators. I said, 'What? I'm not a repairman.' But he called me 'hevalê generator-repairman.' The blood rushed to my face and I screamed, 'Through these blizzards you brought me up here to fix your generators? Are you the heval that they told me would be waiting for me up here? I have only seen a generator once in my whole life and it was during the war between Iraq and Iran in front of a bakery and I wasn't even close to it. How could I be a generator repairman?' He always called me a repairman, a plumber, a generator repairer, and I just said that I wanted to go back home. He answered every time, 'You are free and you can go anytime.'

I asked him to let someone come with me. He replied, 'Hevalê generator-repairman, I can let you go down, but I cannot send someone to accompany you. You can go alone if you want.'

Then, inevitably, I had to live all of winter and spring in that handmade cave. The cave was not finished yet and we had to move on our knees in many places. There was no toilet. They had dug a tunnel under the snow. We crawled a hundred meters through the tunnel to shit and piss there, then we had to cover it with snow and crawl back again. I did not touch anything in that cave for a few days. I looked at the molded walls and got upset. I just wanted to prevent my descent into madness. I had a small bag of tobacco and a hundred cigarette papers. They had to be enough until the way back became accessible, so I cut each paper into three pieces and waited for spring. There were even some books, but all of them were written in Turkish. I could tolerate people there only with my silence. Finally, I was bored and went to repair the generator. I asked what tools they had to fix it.

They only had a hammer and a knife and even these tools belonged to the previous group. I told him that you cannot open any bolts with a knife. 'But a comrade previously opened all the screws of another generator with it. A guerrilla must be able to open the screws with his bare hands,' he replied. 'I'm not a guerrilla, so open it then, if you've got the hang of it,' I told him. 'No, that's your job and you have to do your own work,' he replied.

I looked at the screws and bolts. They were not opened, but had been smashed. I tried to open the screws with a knife and a hammer. Every half hour, he appeared and asked in astonishment, 'You did not finish your job yet?' Finally, I lost my patience and shouted at him, 'With your ultramodern tools, you should also wonder that the work goes so slowly. With such a knife you can only cut vegetables and with your hammer you can only knock nails or strike stupid people in the head.' He said, 'I don't know what you're saying.' I replied, 'I'm sure you don't. Just shut up.'

He ran away and didn't reappear until I had removed all the screws. I also opened the cylinder head. The piston had been stuck to the cylinders. Presumably, they had used the wrong engine oil. There was a viscous layer between the piston and cylinder. I removed it with the knife, then I mixed the existing oil with cooking oil. I pulled the starter rope around the pulley and the engine ran on the first attempt. The commander came to me and said, 'I knew that you were a generator repairer from the beginning.' I said, 'Now, you can use the wireless. I have done my duty and you have to let me talk with my sister.' He said, 'Ok,' but did not call my sister. His excuse was a bad connection. I told him it was no problem, then I made an antenna with a rope and a fifteen-meter-high towline. I said, 'Alright, I think it has a connection range to Italy.' He made a joke and called me hevalê Italy instead of hevalê repairman. Once I intercepted him when he was talking with a comrade over the wireless and he said, 'Yes, you were right, he is an Iranian intelligence services officer . . a little bird told me. He wanted to make contacts with other spies. He claimed she is his sister . . yes I know he is dangerous and I have to take care of him.'

These words made me crazy, but there was nothing I could do. Then I cried. Surely he was talking with Manî. He abused me and my sister for seven years to promote himself and now he accused us of spying.

"Where is Manî now?"

"He's still in the party."

"Has he changed his personality now?

"No, he has become worse."

"Did you experience worse in your life than that time?"

"My first heartbreak was more painful. Near the place where our bunker was located, every morning an enchanting natural theater was performing which comforted me. There was a place above the left side of our cave where the winds would collide and push up the air. In the early morning some eagles would fly there and soar with the wind. The scene looked like a natural dance for me. I had a feeling that those eagles were coming there for my sake. I could not really know if they were waiting for me to start their flying dance, or if I was arriving there at the perfect time. They flew with their wings stretched-out wide and their feathers reflected the yellow sunbeams. This early morning dance and the unclear destiny of my sister helped me survive that unbearable time. I loved my sister more than anything. She became my whole life when I returned home after ten years. We loved each other so much that she had no doubts about leaving everything and coming with me."

"Where is your sister now? Is she fine?"

"Yes, she's fine. She is also in the party."

He lowered his head, turned on his wristwatch light and said, "It's half past eleven. I have to leave here in the next three hours. I should reach another group before dawn."

"Just tell me how you stayed with the PKK after so many bad experiences."

"That has its story too. I will tell you if I return safely and if you're still here."

"I'll stay here until you come back."

"Then you have to stay here until next summer. Do you have the patience?"

"I think so. You had your eagle dance and I have my indigo-blue sky."

CHAPTER 2

THEY DIDN'T WAKE me up to keep watch and I slept well in peace. When I opened my eyes the blue sky was visible between tent nets and the dried leaves of the chestnut tree. I pulled down the sleeping bag zipper to the end, then I opened the semicircular tent zipper and went outside. There was only one other gray tent. It was hevala Dêrsîm's tent, a girl from Dêrsîm who should have returned yesterday. I fastened my sleeping bag zipper and folded it horizontally, then rolled it up vertically and put it into its case without any pressure, unlike in the previous days. I also rolled up my tent and squeezed it into its case. There was no trace of the comrades but they had left a pot beside the tree that certainly contained our breakfast, lentil soup. I went toward Dêrsîm's tent and looked at her through the gray net. She was sleeping under her blanket. I missed her all of last week. She was the first person in our group to give me a souvenir, her wristwatch. I used to have a cell phone and forgot the usability of the wristwatch completely. When I asked her twice for the time, she gave me her wristwatch. I did not want to accept it, but she told me it would make her happy if I took it as a souvenir. The same evening, I learned her left leg had been cut up by a landmine. She was walking with a simple prosthetic leg that the comrades had made for her in the mountains.

I didn't wake her up and went to the women's restroom. Comrades made it under an oak tree, not far from the camp. They showed a lot of initiative in making this latrine. They had cut the side of a plastic gallon jug into two pieces and set it up as a toilet bowl. Then they made a cross-shaped cut with a knife in the middle that could open and close easily. There was always a canister full of water next to the toilet with half a plastic bottle floating inside. I opened my trouser string, put my feet on the outer sides of the toilet bowl, and squatted without opening the bothersome eight-meter-long shawl around my waist.

Three sides of the toilet had been camouflaged with tree branches, but the front side looked onto the vast valley. I look over the valley at a black rock wall, with white clouds resting on its peak. It is said that this area had a thick forest until twenty years ago. They claim that over the past ninety years various governments of Turkey have pursued a policy of extermination in Kurdistan, just like the US policy in Vietnam during the war. Rûken told me the day before yesterday, as a witness who has personally lived in these mountains for the last twenty-four years.

An eagle's cry can be heard somewhere in the sky. The only creature that can freely flaunt itself in these mountains. I pour water into the half plastic bottle and wash myself. I get up, tie my trouser string tightly without letting my dirty fingertips touch it, then clean the toilet bowl with water and a designated twig.

I wish I could go to the spring and wash my hands and face there. If a drone were to appear, I would have to lie on the ground with dirty hands till evening. I sit down beside another canister and wash my hands with our fragrance-free and multifunctional soap. In addition to its obvious duty, the soap here also serves as a shampoo, dishwashing liquid, and washing powder.

I listen carefully to the sky, then I go toward the women's camp. Dêrsîm is still asleep. I sit down under the tree and pull the pot to my side. There are two clean spoons in a glass. I take one of them and wash it again. The lentil soup is still warm. I open the tablecloth and take a loaf of guerrilla's bread. How can they bake this bread in these circumstances? Last time when they baked bread, Gulbehar and I went above the mountain summit to look around and get accustomed to this area. From above you could not see any sign of social life within the surrounding valleys and foothills, not even in the area where we had set up our camp.

I get up and wash my spoon with soap and a piece of plastic mesh. I would like to greet Dêrsîm, but she is still asleep. I go to our future underground bunker and am surprised once I ascend the three steps and put aside the hemp door. The bunker has reached its final structure and is quite different from what I was imagining earlier. A U-shaped corridor was constructed around the rooms and the men's room, on the right side of the corridor, was finished. Except for the ceiling, all of the room walls were covered with plastic greenhouse sheets. Someone was working in the kitchen to finish the ceiling. I greeted them and they greeted me back while they were working. Rûken asked if I slept well. I said "yes" and asked her how I could help them.

"You can help us with the ceiling to let Rojano and Nadîr finish the bathroom."

"What? A bathroom wasn't on the plan, was it?"

"The previous plan has changed. The men's room will be a little smaller and we will build two bathrooms instead."

"Poor men. It's opposite-land here."

"But, we will visit you more often," said Satyar.

"But you have to bring your own tea and sugar."

"Heval, the head of logistics is already a woman. You should expect a male coup if you continue so ruthlessly."

"Then we will respond to you with feminine authority. Go back to work, you mutineer," Rûken said and pushed him out of the kitchen.

They went to the bathroom, which was being built on the left side of the corridor. I sat on the ground in front of a pile of sticks and planks. I was looking at hevalê Ferhad's hands and choosing the proper pieces. He stood on a stone, got the sticks from Serhelldan that I had handed over to him, and fastened them to the roof poles. The truck tarp that we laid on the ground for camouflage on the first day could now be seen a meter higher than the roof poles and planks. We have to wait for a cloudy day, then we can lay it on the roof.

My duty was as simple as a children's game. There was no further work in the kitchen. The walls and floor must remain uncovered. I told hevalê Ferhad that I have no more work to do and that I would like to help other comrades. He let me go with a friendly smile. I went to the women's restroom. Arjîn completely went down into the pit and was throwing out soil and stones with a shovel. Gulbehar was filling various sacks with dirt and Rûken was taking and stacking them in the corridor. Suddenly we were alerted via our wireless about a code fifty-one.

Rûken loudly repeated the alarm number and ordered me to inform Dêrsîm, but she answered from the kitchen.

"I'm here, heval."

"Did you hide everything?"

"Yes heval, do not worry."

The situation became normal again. I asked Arjîn to come out from the pit. She wanted to get out alone, but I gave her a hand and helped her up. She took the shovel from Gulbehar instead of taking a rest.

"I'll do it. Smoke your cigarettes," she said.

I went down into the pit and threw up a few shovels of stones. Suddenly a big rock appeared under my feet. Arjîn noticed the situation and gave me a hoe. Hoeing was difficult in that narrow pit. I got exhausted quickly and Gulbehar changed places with me. I was scolding the stony ground, but they were in a happy state. It seems that stony ground is better for pit toilets because it will not fill up before we leave this bunker. The pit digging was finished by the evening. There were only small things left, like the setup of the toilet bowl, which I wanted to watch. Rûken was looking for weather news from the radio while she was working. The news was not announcing any bad weather. We will have to transfer our food and necessities from a hidden store to our bunker soon, but our bunker is still full of dirt-filled sacks that have to be emptied over the roof. The conflicting weather reports were making Rûken nervous. She translated the reports from Turkish into Kurdish. I gave her a sack of hope.

"Heval, these forecasts are about the cities around us, but we sit on the ass of the world. The ravens won't even poop here."

My proverbs made everyone laugh.

"Where did you learn these Kurdish proverbs, hevala German?" Arjîn asked me.

"By a friend from Sine. He likes to pull a lot of those proverbs out of his ass."

Arjîn burst into laughter, while Gulbehar laughed softly, but the commander smiled with a mysterious expression. I could not determine whether it was a sign of secret laughter or a show of disdain for my indecent behavior.

"Well, you didn't tell us if the weather will be good or bad tomorrow," Rûken finally said.

"Heval, we are at an altitude of three thousand meters. If it is farting down there, we can expect full shit up here."

"Your speech is much too inappropriate, heval."

Rûken tried to teach me polite speech, but I was too stubborn for her pedantic behavior.

"Heval, this is how a secret language develops. It's farting; it's getting foggy; it's belching; I've fucked up; it's pissing: drones are coming; it's shitting; Erdoğan's coming for an unannounced visit."

Our commander really liked my last sentence. She laughed and tried to indicate that I couldn't say such words in front of male comrades. I answered with a serious expression, "Of course, heval, in Germany I always use suitable words in front of men. It blows, it sucks, it bangs."

"Do you teach with these expressions in university, heval?"

I answered with an academic and lecturing tone.

"Dear respectful and revolutionary hevalên, this matter requires a precise description. It is my responsibility to explain it to you word by word."

"No, well put, heval. That just surprised me. Until yesterday you were completely different, very serious. What has happened to you suddenly since yesterday?"

"Not suddenly at all. Thirty hours have passed since yesterday morning. Not only the clock hands, but also my brain have been moving forward. Yesterday I decided to stay here. We can't survive this winter if we treat each other as apathetically as before. So I suppose, at least, that we will have very foggy weather tomorrow. That is enough for us to complete the roof."

I was filling sacks with stones during all the nonsense wordplay and Rûken was taking them out of the toilet and piling them up in the corridor, while the radio was announcing in Turkish throughout. Suddenly, the radio language turned into German. Right during the science and technology news. It made me happy. Over the past eight days, Gulbehar did not forget to bring me her radio at that exact time. I was listening to the radio while working when Rûken spoke to me.

"Take a rest hevala Jînçin and listen quietly. Today's work will be finished soon."

"Are you disturbed if I listen to the radio here?"

"Not me," said Rûken.

"I won't be disturbed, no way," Gulbehar said.

Arjîn smiled at me in a way that brought her tongue out on the left side of her mouth and expressed her agreement.

The radio was reporting the new particle experiments in Cern. These will lead to a deeper understanding of the world of neutrons and should permit more precise further investigations concerning the dual nature of particles. I listened to the news until the end. There was no news about the new formula presented by two well-known physicists from Hungary and Germany. It could have triggered problems for the standard models and set a milestone in the understanding of quantum physics. Certainly, it will take more time for this new formula to be proven or denied, subject to scientific experimentation. Then there were reports about the new medical methods that a well-known German company had found. Finally, there was news about the new methods for long-term weather forecasting, which could be quite useful here.

The pit construction was finished. I turned down the radio. The time of toilet bowl installation has arrived. Satyar held it on his two fingertips, playing with it like a magician's stick and the arrangement of the lights let its shadow-dance on the plastic wall. Following him, hevalê Ferhad entered the room with some short wooden poles in his hands. With a knife he pierced six holes in both sides width-wise and four holes in both sides length-wise. Meanwhile, Satyar brought a metal plate and Rûnahî brought four short wooden poles. Hevalê Ferhad inserted all four short wooden poles into holes located on the length sides. The approximate distance between two wooden poles on the outer side was twenty-five centimeters, while a forty-centimeter hole remained in the middle space. Then he inserted the six poles into holes on the width side. There remained a big hole, around thirty to forty centimeters, in the middle, the exact size for the toilet bowl.

We just watched while hevalê Ferhad squeezed stones and splinters around the wooden poles to tighten them firmly, then tied a rope around the poles. Then it was time for the metal plate. There was a big hole in the middle with dimensions of thirty by forty centimeters, with a lot of tiny holes at the edges. He placed one half of the plastic gallon over the metal plate and with a nail made some little holes along the edges. He proceeded to thread metal wires through the holes in the plastic gallon bottle and those in the metal plate and fastened them over each other. Then he turned the makeshift toilet bowl over and placed it on the intended hole, while sticking the outer edges of the metal plate into the walls of the long sides. The toilet bowl was installed but it was not ready to use yet. The last stage of the job required surgical precision with a knife. Hevalê Ferhad masterfully cut the middle of the toilet bowl in a cross shape with a box cutter; thus, it would not have to bear any heavy loads, except for a piece of shit or two, and would open and close as easily as a mercurial teenager's heart.

I have explained the process of toilet-making in such detail because I am convinced this achievement is much more useful than any short, medium, or long-range rocket in the world.

The drone was still buzzing in the sky and I could hear it behind the hemp door. We had dinner, drank tea, and waited for the darkness. Then everyone took an umbrella and went out of the bunker. The men went to the right side and we went to the left toward our tents under the chestnut tree. Like everyone else, I opened my tent, but didn't enter and waited until Arjîn set up her tent. I sat next to her and said, "Heval, would you like to chat or do you want to sleep?"

"I don't go to sleep so early, heval. I am not a chicken."

"Of course not, you're a nightingale."

"No, that doesn't suit me. Our nightingale is Gulbehar."

"Does she sing well?"

"Like Şehrîbana Kurdî."*

I turned to Gulbehar and said, "Why don't you sing for us?"

"Arjîn exaggerates, heval. Sometimes I hum to myself."

I turned my head to Arjîn and said, "If you're not exhausted, I would like to talk to you about something."

"What about, heval?"

"About your life."

"Which life do you mean, current or past?"

"Your past life."

"I am sorry. I cannot talk about that."

"Why not?"

"We are not allowed to talk with others about our private lives."

I tried to persuade her, but Rûken entered into the discussion.

"Hevala Jînçin is not a stranger. She is the daughter of one of our respected heroes. Our party trusts in her."

Arjîn apologized in a shy voice.

"It hasn't been a long time since I came here, heval. I do not want to make a mistake."

---

* Şehrîbana Kurdî is a popular contemporary Kurdish singer.

I turned my head toward Rûken and asked her if we could talk in private within my tent.

"Even better," Rûken answered.

We went towards my tent. I gave her my lighter and asked her to go inside first and turn on the lamp, so that I could check if the light was visible from outside. There was nothing visible from outside. I entered and sat down opposite her. She sat cross-legged. It appears she was still ashamed of her answer. "Thanks for coming, hevala Arjîn," I told her.

"Never mind, heval. I wanted to have a heart to heart with you, but I also didn't want to cross a line. Again, I ask for your forgiveness."

"It's ok. You did exactly the right thing. I am proud of you."

"Thanks. What can I tell you?"

"Tell me, why did you choose this difficult life of your own free will?"

"But you chose this life, too."

"I'm only staying here for a few months, but you have decided on a new lifestyle. Why?"

"You mean for what reason probably."

"Pardon, yes exactly."

"We only had a white ID card, heval. This reveals everything."

"What is the white ID card?"

"Didn't you hear about that?"

"I know what an ID card is and I understand the concept 'white,' but I don't know what you mean by a white ID card."

"In 1960, after the Syrian regime signed a nationalist agreement with Egypt, the Syrian government took away ID cards from much of the Kurdish population. The regime claimed they would replace their ID cards with new ones, but many received one of two other types of ID cards. About fifty thousand of them received a red ID card; the owners of these ID cards have no identity officially. These Kurds and their children weren't even allowed to go to school. The population of the second group was even greater. About two or three hundred thousand of them. They gave this group a white ID card. They could go to school and even study at the universities, but they were not allowed employment in state offices or agencies and couldn't sell or possess any property, such as houses, lands, or even a car. In 1962, the Syrian regime took citizenship from my grandfather and our great misery began. My father bore this tragic fate during his schooling. Then a fifteen-year-old daughter of a landlord wanted to marry him. She had compassion for him."

"Do you resemble your mother or father?"

"My father, like two peas in a pod."

"OK, go on, please."

"Then a new problem for the Kurds of Rojava arose. In 1975, the Ba'ath regime decided to change its landholding regulations, again at the expense of us miserable Kurds. The most fertile lands in Cîzrê are said to have been taken from the Kurds as part of the so-called Arab Belt project and given to the Arabs who were displaced by the creation of the Tabqa Dam and Lake Assad. This was really a project to change the demographics, as has been done under different names in Turkey and Iraq. Therefore, in 1980, my father married my mother. She had nothing in this world except the shirt on her back, as they say. They relocated to Efrîn after two years. My mother worked there as a teacher and my father as a mechanic in a stranger's workshop. My father said they worked hard for eight years straight, on the verge of hunger, to save enough money to buy property on top of a rocky hill outside Efrîn. There were not any springs or water sources and my father was forced to fetch water with a mule from a river located three hundred meters away from his land to irrigate olive seedlings. All the villagers there derided him. My parents had a boy after three years, a girl after seven years, and finally me, after nine years. They named me . . . should I also say my birth name, heval?"

"Did you choose your own nickname as Arjîn?"

"Yes, heval."

"Your nickname is enough. Please go on."

"I was born on that olive farm, in a cottage, and raised with chickens and ducks. I always liked to compete with the olive seedlings in terms of how fast we were growing up and make my dad laugh. The Kurdish question was deeply in his heart. The PKK members came regularly to our home. Monthly meetings about social issues were taking place on our farm and the Kurdish language was taught there. So, we learned to read and write the Kurdish language before the Arab Spring entered its autumn phase, as my father would say. We had to learn Arabic in school, anyway. When the state government forces had to withdraw from Rojava, for a few days my father had tears in his eyes, tears of happiness and joy. He saw the changes as an opportunity for his dreams to come true and nominated himself for a position in the Land Distribution Council's elections. He also took me and my siblings to the people's meetings so that we could see the birth of the revolution. After ten hours of discussion about the voting methodology, he sent us home before the voting started. He was elected co-chairman of the Supervisory Board of Land Distribution.

There were many large state plots of land remaining that had to be distributed between landless and rural workers who were working for others. The work was very stressful. There were always people appearing on our farm who had nothing else in mind except to bribe my dad for their personal interests. They even brought our relatives in from Qamîşlû as mediators to try to convince my father. Many even scolded us and alleged that my father had seized our farm from the Arabs.

My father did not give up on the struggle and we got through that mess. A new election took place and he was selected by a large majority. We could no longer take care of our farm alone. My father was busy all day and night with his unpaid job. All three of us were teaching the Kurdish language to people. I was thirteen, but I became a teacher and taught people. Heval, you should have seen me in class. A whole lot of people really saw me as a teacher. In the morning, I went to Arabic school by bus and then I had lunch there and in the afternoon I taught the Kurdish language in a school next door. Then I went back home and worked in our soap factory. Many factories had been relocated to Efrîn and many skilled workers and specialists had fled to Rojava from Heleb[*] and other industrial areas. One of those skilled workers was the head of an old and famous soap factory in Heleb. With him and twenty other workers, my father founded some cooperative factories. They packed fresh olives in jars and cans, extracted olive oil, and made soaps from the rest of the pomace. My sister and I became more and more revolutionary over time, while my father and my brother avoided politics.

"Why?" I asked.

Arjîn stared at me for a long time, as if she was trying to know what was in my eyes in the darkness. I didn't say anything and waited until she finally spoke.

---

[*] Aleppo.

"Heval, I have told you these things because the party trusts you, but now I tell you something else because *I* personally have trust in you. Do not disclose it. You have to promise me."

"I promise you. Please go on."

"My father and brother's enthusiasm and revolutionary dynamism gradually declined."

"For what reason?"

"For the same reasons that you mentioned on the first day. My father wouldn't like our society becoming ideological. He believed that it would lead to polarization of the community and would provide an opportunity for hypocrites to move up the ranks through deceit and grow cancerous. This situation drove away the intellectuals from the party. As you said, if the criteria for competency are not usefulness and specialty, but absolute loyalty to the party, and the measure of this loyalty is reduced to trifles, the hypocrites can easily gain power. They don't lay their legs on each other, they just repeat some quotations from the leader without having understood or read his books. . . . My father was in contact with many experts worldwide who, for whatever reason, wanted to help the Kurdish revolution, though not necessarily to support our ideology. But many of these experts have been defamed with spurious stories and driven out by uneducated and idiotic hypocrites. Hevala Jînçin, last night when you were talking with hevalê Saro in the cave, hevala Rûken told us something that my father should have said."

"Can you tell me what she said?"

"Yes, of course. Hevala Rûken said that six years ago when she saw hevalê Saro for the first time, he had a sister, a computer scientist who wanted to take part in the war as a fighter because of frustration and depression over her own uselessness. Hevalê Saro appeared suddenly and said to her commander that she should not go to war."

"Why not?"

"Because she is a skilled computer programmer."

"'Computer scientists aren't needed here,' she must have said. Hevalê Saro got angry and replied to her, 'A party that doesn't need computer scientists, but only fighters, will hurt their people more than any enemy.'"

"Hevala Jînçin, I am very glad you are here. You have brought us a fresh, new spirit. Since yesterday I haven't been afraid of the drone up there. As Rojano said, 'It is no longer a danger, but only a risk factor same as the risk that one takes when drive a car personally.'"

"I am also very happy to have met you. We will continue our struggle together. But you didn't tell me yet why you came here."

"Because of Efrîn. Efrîn was known as an island of peace, brotherhood, and tranquility throughout the country, until the rumor became audible that the Turkish government wanted to attack it. Why? Because terrorists are living there, but everyone knew that the AKP is the true main source of terrorists. You know the AKP? The "Justice and Development Party" that Erdoğan is leader of. They are terrorists, but they are the "good" terrorists; they can be freely exported wherever the Turkish government wants. Cerablus, Europe, and now to Efrîn. We couldn't believe that global public opinion was fine with giving Turkey free rein to attack Rojava on these ridiculous pretexts. Here, the brave Kurdish women fight without hijabs to destroy the ideology of political Islam through their heroism. This oil-rich Islamic region would have polarized in favor of the radical Islamists if they had not been there. The Kurdish women, without hijabs, have not only destroyed Islamic radicalism in armed conflicts, but have also defeated fanatical and reactionary Islamic ideologies with their egalitarian viewpoints. That was an important feat that the superpowers couldn't accomplish. Many people were saying stuff like that throughout their conversations in Efrîn and the surrounding area, but my father and other pessimists saw it differently. They said that global public opinion is controlled by politicians who do not represent the interests of their people, but rather that of financial industries. Optimists asked, 'but how can they convince people around the globe?' The pessimists said that was not important, that they are manipulating global public opinion arbitrarily. The optimists would shout with anger, 'but they cannot deceive cognizant people around the world!' Then they would ask how those heroic women could suddenly be dishonored as terrorists today. Then my father, as a pessimist, would tell them a dirty joke. It was the first time in my life that I've heard something like that from my dad. It convinced them all."

"Can you tell me what he told them?"

"I am ashamed to tell you, hevala Jînçin."

"Should I turn around?"

"No, heval. One day a man comes along and tells the others in his village that there is a certain villager who has slept with his aunt. The people all wave their hands and say that it's false. The man insists that it's true, but the villagers deny it again. Quite annoyed, the man persists and tells them all, 'It *is* possible! It is! We even have a son . . . whoops.' After this bitter joke, others from Nisêbîn, Cîzrê, and Amed brought examples of world communities' silence against the crimes of the Turkish government within Kurdish areas. My father was a peace-loving person who always positioned himself against the militarization of Kurdish society. He criticized any activity that could jeopardize the peace process in Bakûr. He believed that the PKK should not fall into the trap of Erdoğan's lust for power. His activities and critiques brought us terrible troubles. But he took up an adamant position on resistance in Efrîn. He even persuaded us to participate in the military training. For him, this resistance was not a question of victory or defeat, but to challenge a world based on selfishness and greed.

Before the war had begun, the Russian government tried to convince us to hand Efrîn over to the Syrian regime, to avoid an imminent war with the Turkish regime. But it would have been a vicious destruction of our human identities as the people of Rojava. We did not like to be slaves whose destinies were determined by Russia, the USA, or Germany. The more we felt betrayed by the world community, the greater our affection for self-determination. Right away, the outcome of the war was clear to our experienced commanders. They knew we had no chance, with our ineffective weapons, against the Turkish bombers, yet they gave us great hope until the last day.

Hevala Jînçin, I do not know if they miscalculated the reactions of the world community, or whether they had not predicted the boundless brutality of the Turkish government and the shameful silence of world public opinion. Maybe they knew about both of them and gave us empty hopes. But one thing is for sure: that our commanders didn't leave us and fought shoulder to shoulder with us until the last day of the war. Even now, while Efrîn is in the hands of the Islamists, they continue fighting and do not let that scum of humanity, those dogmatist Islamists and fascist mercenaries, ever get any rest. Hevala Jînçin, they were very heavily armed, but we were not. Somebody like me, who had not done anything more dangerous in my life than planting olive seedlings, somehow managed to prevent them from advancing a single meter into Rojava for a whole month.

We were resisting decisively on the battlefield while the Turkish diplomats and lobbyists were bribing the world powers behind the scenes. Heval, Turkey is known as a corrupt country when it comes to bribery. I have been there. But even there, bribes are legally forbidden. Yet when a government bribes other governments this is called 'diplomatic negotiations' and 'coming to agreements.' At that time, I was on the battlefield. The Turkish army had gotten stuck with its modern German tanks on the border and could not move a step for a month. If during the day they occupied some villages with their drones and bomber planes, we would recapture them at night. The Turkish fascists must have bribed the world powers with a very large amount that we couldn't afford. We had nothing to offer other than our lives. The president of a NATO member-state and a minion of Putin's shouldn't get stuck at the border with such a large army. Suddenly, Erdoğan was granted free rein to destroy Rojava with aerial bombardment. Sometimes seventy bombers would fly over our small area and drop countless bombs on us. Our weapons did not even reach their height, so we could not target them. On the third day, my brother was killed and I didn't have the opportunity to console my mother. We could no longer maintain ourselves in our destroyed trenches and attempted to slow down the advance of the Turkish army and its mercenaries with guerrilla combat, in the hope that the libertarians of the world would bring our miserable situation to the public eye and display the sorrowful faces of Kurdish women in at least one of the free world's newspapers.

It was unbelievable. Even my pessimistic father had not expected such a profound silence. The two sides of the war were the same as the earlier war in Kobanî. Daesh terrorists and other religious fanatics became Turkish mercenaries. But they were called ordinary ground troops and we, the Kurdish women fighters, were simply called male combatants in the international media. The filthy Turkish mercenaries were advancing on healthy olive trees and leaving behind burnt olive farms, while the fascists were proud of the heroism of their soldiers. Efrîn was besieged. We retreated to the city, but everyone was highly motivated. My dad, too. Finally, I could hug him, a month after my brother's death.

The enemy stood at the gates of Efrîn and the majority of people did not want to leave the city. They had decided on a bloody house-to-house fight. The Russians warned us of an even worse operation, but we stuck to our decision. No one had figured out what could be worse and, on the same evening, the Turkish air force dropped some bombs directly on the city hospital. Many people were killed, including my sister and my best friend. They occupied Efrîn and it was the worst thing I'd ever seen. We left the city and the bandits came and plundered everything. Heval, when I say everything, I really mean everything they could steal. I was with a group of comrades on a mountain, watching through binoculars. They plundered the whole city, even the pitchers used in the toilets. It was agreed that some very experienced guerrillas would remain there in the mountains and continue the struggle. I also wanted to stay and fight, but they did not consider me an experienced fighter and wanted to send me to a safe place. Then I made a stupid mistake."

Arjîn was silent. I took her rough hands and I knew she was crying without looking at her face. She tried to control herself again, but her tears were pouring down in torrents. Then she told me, crying, "Heval, I tried to kill myself. Do not disclose it to anyone. My commander took pity on me and let me stay there for a few weeks, but I realized that I was not an experienced fighter and only burdened them. A skilled fighter, like hevala Rûken, smells danger and makes decisions instinctively. For twenty years, she fought under the most dangerous circumstances, but she was not injured once. I want to become such a fighter and then return to Efrîn to take my revenge on those who turned our olive groves into cemeteries."

CHAPTER 3

WE WOKE UP at five o'clock, as usual. It was windy and cold, but the weather was not bad enough to let us construct the bunker roof. The fog was light and the clouds scattered in the sky. We packed our tents and sleeping bags and laid them atop each other under the chestnut tree. My sleeping bag was the only one that did not have the initials of someone's name written on it; therefore, it was easily distinguishable from the others. After breakfast, we had nothing else to do but watch the sky and wait for a suitable time. At noon the weather conditions became bad and we happily got back to work without thinking about our regular lunch. I wanted to know how they would construct the roof. Rûken let me go on the roof with hevalê Ferhad.

While we pulled out all the wooden nails from the holes in the truck tarp, other comrades brought many sacks of dirt to a place near the roof and laid them side-by-side. All of us stayed on top except Rojano and our ladder, Serhelldan. We slid the truck tarp over the wooden poles. Rûken slowly climbed down onto the sack wall, walked on it like an acrobat, and stuffed the tarp and a tear-resistant greenhouse film behind the sack walls on all four sides. Then she covered it all with thick cloth sheets and, after that, the collective work began.

Everyone dumped sacks of dirt on top of the roof, until enough soil had collected on it. Someone jumped down onto the roof, spread the dirt with a shovel, and stomped on it with their feet. The roof was piling up layer by layer until it reached the level of the surrounding structure. The comrades then poured a layer of humus, which they had collected in separate sacks, onto the roof to enable native plants to grow on top. Hevalê Ferhad was responsible for the last stage of this work. He meticulously spread out the upper layer of soil by hand.

It was twilight when the work was finished, but I could see how perfect the camouflage was. I was exhausted, though I had not done any of the more difficult work. The hard work would begin tomorrow morning. So, after dinner, we slept earlier than on previous nights.

That night, I did not have to stand guard and I was well-rested when Rûken woke me up at three o'clock. I opened the zipper of my tent. The cold air crept in. I put on my jacket. Then I turned off my lighter and crawled out of the tent. It was dark. I could barely recognize the other comrades. We packed our tents and sleeping bags quickly, ate our breakfast by groping around in the dark, and were ready to leave. As they said, the underground depot should be two hours away from our camp. I took a Kalashnikov with four magazine cartridges with me. Gulbehar was marching forty meters ahead and Akam fifty meters behind the group. Rûken was the first person in the group and gave us instructions about what distance to keep and how to maintain proper marching form. Yesterday, Dêrsîm explained to me that I should pass on the whispered instructions from the person walking in front of me, about distance and marching style, to the person walking behind me. I always have to keep an eye on them and, in the event of an incident, immediately throw myself on the ground in the opposite direction and take the right shooting position. The marching spaces have expanded and shortened several times along the way. Sometimes we were marching normally with four meters of distance, sometimes bent over and slowly and sometimes we were running fast. Finally, we arrived at our destination ten minutes early.

It seemed that we had descended one thousand meters from our camp when I looked at the tip of the mountain. The sky was cloudy and the weather was cool. There were more than fifty guerrillas busy working. At a corner of the valley, thousands of packs of necessary goods and foods were stacked close to the underground depot for next winter: countless sacks of flour, sugar, lentils and beans, cooking oil cans, hundreds of gas cartridges, gas ovens, gas stoves, and many other things in cartons with Turkish written on them.

The guerrillas were bustling around everywhere like ants. Some of them saw us and greeted us. Apparently Rûken, Dêrsîm, and Satyar were well-known and beloved there, but the comrades embraced us, too. That place must have been well under control, because no one was worried about any danger.

There were two hidden depots, but one of them was ransacked by bears. The logistics team had to compensate for the bear's demolition with an even more risky situation. At the time, a couple of guerrillas were standing guard at the new depot. A bloody fight ensued between a bear and a couple of food guards; the guerrillas were injured by the bear's paws but they got the bear in turn with their bayonets. The commotion and the guards' courageous defense of the depot sparked a lot of jokes amongst the guerrillas.

"Heval, these bears are working for the Turkish secret service," someone said.

"No heval, based on reports we got, these bears were educated at the University of Pennsylvania; otherwise, the Kurdish bears aren't too competent," another one replied.

"Don't promote xenophobic theories on this topic. They are welcome here as foreigners. But they have to stick to the rules," a female comrade declared.

"I wish I could say to aunty bear, 'Ok darling aunty, you are hungry and eat flour. Even though you do not drink tea and do not make jam, you eat up our sugar because it tastes like honey, that's right. Would you like to smoke, dear aunty? You can smoke as much as you want, but why do you break the cigarettes and piss on them?'" All the comrades laughed at Satyar's words.

"Does anyone know what they were eating before we started hiding our supplies underground?" someone asked.

"They were eating honey and catching prey. They owe their misery to us," said a forty-year-old woman guerrilla.

Everyone went silent. Someone showed us with his finger one of the comrades who had been injured by the bear. He was standing near the depot distributing food and items between groups. Saro was there too, supervising the distribution of items. I approached him. He welcomed me cheerfully and introduced me to a blonde man.

"He's your neighbor. Do you know him?"

He was a German man from Cologne. We hugged each other. I asked Saro if I could talk to him for a moment.

"Sure, until the packs are ready to be transferred."

We went to a fire with some big black kettles on it. He took two glasses from the ground and filled them with tea. I took a glass from him and sat by the fire. I asked him in German, "What is your name?"

"My name is Têkdan,* hevala Jînçin."

"How long have you been here?"

"More than eight years."

"It must have been tough for you."

"Not worse than living in Germany. These mountains are full of beautiful things."

"What for example?"

"The mountains themselves."

"But these mountains have been emptied of all animals and plants."

"We live here and as long as we struggle, these mountains stay alive."

"Struggle? Against who? We cannot even hide ourselves here. We are paralyzed in these mountains."

"But these mountains are our hands and feet. The Turkish army has not been able to move in these mountains freely. They can make our lifes more difficult with their bombers and also their expensive military operations, but the guerrillas have taken account of these difficulties before deciding to come here. While we are sitting here and drinking tea, it's a defeat for fascism."

"What? Do you see this Tom and Jerry game as a serious fight? Do you really believe that we can bring fascism to its knees through our chatting and drinking tea?"

"We cannot do that. But these mountains will survive fascism. The fascists will never be able to dance in peace at their victory celebrations while there are left libertarians who fight against them."

I did not expect such an unworldly statement from a German internationalist. I looked into his deep green eyes and said, "Is this your poetic delirium or a real point of view? Can we fight or even disturb an army that is fully armed and organized by fascists to fight in all areas without exhausting their supplies during our hide-and-seek games? They also profit from our struggle."

"But we are not the only group in the world who is fighting against this inhuman global system. Neoliberalism is on its last legs. It is even a

---

* To destroy; to make a new structure.

ceaseless struggle between those who are working for the capitalist system and whirl its wheels. This system is built on oppression and injustice, so it will not last forever. We have a Kurdish proverb that says, 'All things tear up when they get very thin, but the oppression tears up when it gets very thick.'"

"Then why are you fighting? Let the oppression grow until it tears itself up."

"Did you get passivity from this proverb? It doesn't mean that oppression tears itself apart. The nature of oppression is based on contradictory elements within itself that make opponents against itself. In the end, the pressure of these inner and outer contradictions will tear it up. Slavery and feudalism had to end just like that."

"And what do you think about the problems here?"

"What problems do you mean? We always have enormous problems here."

"I mean self-structuring problems."

"We also have a lot of those. Which do you mean exactly?"

"I mean restrictions on freedom of speech, for example compared to Germany."

He looked at me with his ruddy, suspicious expression. "And you believe that there is freedom of speech in Germany?"

"Why not? People can say whatever they would like there."

"If such is the meaning of freedom of speech, then there has been freedom of speech throughout human history. Everyone always said anything they wanted within their family or circle of friends, or at least to themselves. Ineffectual dissent never bothered any ruler," Têkdan said and took a sip of his tea. I picked up the glass from the floor. It made my fingertips pleasantly warm. I sipped the tea with pleasure. Then I drank half of it and asked Têkdan another question.

"Let me ask you a specific and very frank question. Can you state your opinions here clearly without negative consequences?"

"No, there will definitely be consequences. But someone who wants to change something mustn't be afraid of such consequences."

"How severe are these consequences?"

"No idea, I've always kept myself above water."

"Maybe because you came from Europe."

"No, I don't think so. There are many Kurds who criticize the party policies even more radically. Saro, for example."

"How long have you known him?"

"About three years. I met him in Rojava. At that time many comrades believed that he was leaning too far out the window and would lose his head in the process. But he prevailed and became even more beloved than before. Here a harsh consequence is a conceivable possibility for our freedom of speech, but in the West the restriction of freedom is the consequence itself. Journalists are free there because they don't complain."

"But there are journalists and intellectuals who keep a close eye on the rulers and fight against the media system for which they work."

"Yes, but they quickly lose their position or have to dance for both sides. And that's an even more dangerous game for today's intellectuals."

Têkdan pulled out a tobacco bag from his vest pocket, opened its string, took out a sheet of cigarette paper, and rolled a cigarette. At that moment, Saro appeared and said that our first-round packs were ready to be picked up.

There were two mules available for our group to transport a part of our packs. We had to carry all the other remaining packs by ourselves. These goods were packed in different weights and converted into backpacks with ropes. I checked some of them. A couple of them weighed about five kilograms, the next three over twenty, one of them was over forty, and the remaining packs were ten. It would not be easy for me to climb uphill for two hours with a ten-kilogram backpack and a Kalashnikov with four magazines, but I picked up one of them and carried it like a school bag. Tewar lifted the lightest backpack after me. Three of the jokester comrades took twenty-kilogram packs and our unfit ladder, the same as his friend, took a five-kilogram pack under the excuse of having back pain. All the other comrades' packs were at least as heavy as mine. But the heaviest pack remained on the ground till Rojano lifted it up. At no point in the previous days did she seem like someone who would flaunt their strength and I worried that she would repent to choose that heaviest pack.

Akam had gone early and was positioned at the foothill. The mule whose reins were in Rojanos' hand ran obediently with six gas cylinders, a gas heater, and a pack of lentils on its back. The gas cylinders were put in a couple of hanging wooden boxes on both sides of the mules and other things were placed on top of them and tightened by ropes. The other mule was restless and refused to climb. The more Tewar and Serhelldan were pushing it to run and pulling vigorously on its reins, the more stubborn the mule became. The mule threw its legs up and down and kicked in all directions until it nearly threw away its whole load.

"Heval, send someone to help us. The smart comrades have chosen the tamed mules," Tewar loudly called to Rûken.

"Ok, Gulbehar is coming now."

"No heval, send a male comrade."

Rûken was going to fulfill her request, but Rojano stopped her. She then appraoched me and put the reins of her mule in my hand and said, "Slowly keep walking this way until I come back."

Rojano went down with the heavy pack on her shoulders. She grabbed the mule's reins near its mouth, pushed the mule's ears and head down with her other hand, and then pulled it behind herself. The mule followed her like a lamb. She brought the mule near me. It was difficult for me to hold up my pack and my gun simultaneously with only one hand. Rojano noticed. She tied the reins of her mule to the saddle of my mule and took the reins out of my hand. I smiled at her and she smiled back with a kind expression. She has been in my mind since then. I've thought of her nomadic face, nice feminine bass voice, and her unique personality. She was a proud but modest woman. This combination may sound weird, but I liked her mix of pride, modesty, and inconspicuousness. That day I found her beauty for the first time; it's not like Arjîn's beauty, defined by its feminine elegance, but rather rooted in her strength and the sorrowful life she has endured.

Rojano was our shining star on that day, when we transported the goods, and all the female comrades were proud of her. She was walking leisurely, with confident steps and without any signs of the huge burden on her shoulders, and the mules were following her without any resistance. Suddenly, I saw Dêrsîm and my thoughts ruptured from Rojano. She was walking with her prosthetic plastic leg under the weight of her pack and gun without complaining. I ran to Rûken quickly and asked her to put Dêrsîm's pack on a mule. She answered me quickly, as she had already rejected that proposal a hundred times. "Dêrsîm is not someone who puts a burden on others' shoulders."

I lower my head and look at her watch on my wrist. We have been on our way for over an hour. I think about the packs that we are carrying on our shoulders. I see Saro with his curved shoulders, a permanent feature since the first day of his life. His waist bowed under a sack of rice, of which he certainly will not eat any portion. I think of Têkdan, with whom I might one day sit in front of a café near the Cologne Cathedral and chat about the heavy loads that we carried on a cloudy October day. We have thrown ourselves headlong into this type of work and I am not a bit ashamed of it. My thoughts fly out to Frankfurt, to a couple of vendors opposite a big shop on the famous Zeil Street. They are playing a childish game that makes me want to puke. You can play the role of a tenderhearted executioner, a benevolent usurer, or a boss, but it becomes disgusting and hostile to children when people shout while playing to make passersby imagine that something serious is playing out in front of the shop window. Maybe what we are doing here now is a type of game too, but we can't take it lightly. The cold season is coming and we will die from starvation if our work is not done. Then these mountains would be submitted to the fascists. I hear the murmur of the stream, raise my head, and see the chestnut tree uphill. Some comrades have sat down in front of the spring. Rojano separates from the march and takes the mules to the rivulet for drinking. We are also thirsty, but hevalê Ferhad calls to us from uphill and says that hot tea is ready on the fire.

The bunker hemp door is hung upwards. We enter through the narrow and semidark corridor and go toward the kitchen. I put my packs down on the ground and lean on the wall to take a rest, but other comrades go out to discharge packs from the mules and bring them into the bunker. The foodstuffs are brought to the kitchen and the other goods are stacked on each other in the corridor. After setting down all the packs, we go outside and sit by the fire. The smokers smoke their cigarettes after drinking tea. Then Rojano takes the mules near the rivulet to graze them. After having lunch and drinking another round of tea and smoking, we go back to work on a steep downhill. Again, Rojano took the heaviest pack and nobody could break her record. We came back to our original location after four hours. I was dead tired and wished I could sleep there right next to the packs, but I got up after a snack to get to work when Rûken said, "Hevalên Jînçin and Dêrsîm, please stay here and sort out all of the stuff."

That was the best order I could have heard. They went away and in less than two hours we had sorted the various goods based on their importance and frequency of use in the corridor. The packs that will be brought here later can simply be placed in predetermined locations. After we finished our tasks, Dêrsîm opened some yellow packs that belonged to the female comrades. They were full of sanitary napkins and underwear. I looked in amazement at the panties and bras in different colors and styles until Dêrsîm told me, "Every woman can take two sets of clothes and three sets of underwear. You can choose your own right now."

I looked at the pile again and chose three sets in black, green and red. I imagined Arjîn in blue briefs with little orange flowers. Then Dêrsîm gave me a transparent bag containing two sets of guerrilla uniforms. On the bag in capital letters were the initials H.G. I got up and tried them on. It was as if they were tailor-made. Dêrsîm probably left here last week to get these uniforms. I neatly folded them into a big, unused blue bag and put it on a corner, then asked her, "what should we do now?"

"First, we have to prepare the bathroom. Then put some canisters of water on the fire."

"Wow, does that mean that we're finally allowed to take a bath?"

"Heval, taking a bath is not forbidden, if we find an opportunity."

I felt relieved; I would otherwise be disgusted to wear the new clothes over my filthy, sweaty body. We took one of the gas heaters into the women's bathroom and put it directly under the PVC pipe of the vent. These pipes were installed in all rooms, as they could be pushed up about one meter toward the roof. Thus, we could breathe fresh air even if some meters of snow piled up on the roof. Dêrsîm turned on the heater. Then she brought a large tub, some bowls, three wooden planks for sitting, and our magic soaps. After the bathroom preparation, we took six empty large canisters and went down to the spring. The canister edges were rounded off well and there was no danger of injuring our hands, so I tried to carry two canisters full of water simultaneously. But I was compelled to put one of them down on the ground and, like Dêrsîm, brought only one canister in my arms. We filled the other canisters full of water and took them near the fire. Hevalê Ferhad set all of the canisters around the fire. Breathless, I sat by the fire and guzzled a glass of tea. Suddenly, I heard a joyful laugh from Arjîn. Comrades came up beside the stream. When they came closer I saw a white cat in Arjîn's arms. Arjîn screamed again with excitement when she saw my surprise.

"This little guy is our food guard. I introduce you to venerable hevalê Befrîn.* But this name is not certain yet. We should call him Befrîn in a democratic process. What's your idea, heval?"

"That would be undemocratic, heval, if there is no alternative name."

"Of course heval, there are three other names and you can choose one of them.

"And what would they be?"

"Crocodile, bear, and drone."

I laughed and said, "You're right heval, Befrîn suits him well."

Then she asked Dêrsîm and hevalê Ferhad, "Heval, would you like to call him Befrîn?"

"Yes heval, it's the color of white, like snow."

"And what is your idea, hevala Dêrsîm?"

"A nice name."

Dêrsîm turned her face. Tewar was coming towards us. Arjîn pulled Befrîn up to her face and showed it to Tewar.

"We named him Befrîn. What do you think?"

"I hate cats."

"But Befrîn is a special cat."

"Six of one, half a dozen of the other."

Arjîn was indifferent to her reaction and declared the voting results.

"Only one abstention vote. Then his name has been chosen democratically."

"*Very* democratically even," I said, and everyone laughed.

"Heval, democracy works everywhere like that. Doesn't it?"

"Yes, a Turkish cat with a Kurdish name."

"No, heval. These cats with different-colored eyes come from the city of Van and they are Kurdish cats."

"Why should it matter whether they are considered Kurdish or Turkish? They are neither Kurdish nor Turkish. They are just cats." My answer made her unexpectedly angry.

"What did you say? You talked about nationality first on your own. Even in a fascist way. The Turks have renamed everything that once had

---

* Snow-white.

a Kurdish name. They dance and sing to Kurdish melodies but call them Turkish dances and songs. They even claim famous Kurdish people. Who can dare to say that Yaşar Kemal and Yilmaz Güney were Kurds? They say that they wrote their books and stories in the Turkish language and that this is enough evidence to prove they were Turks. No one asked the Turks how they could have written in Kurdish when they weren't even allowed to speak Kurdish in their homes. What would you have to do if the French people 'proved' that Bertolt Brecht was French? The Turks will soon claim that Efrîn is a Turkish city and prove it to you."

She was angry and the left side of her lip was trembling. I stood still, petrified, and could not say anything. She was right to be mad at my foolishness. Why could a cat be called Turkish or Persian, but not Kurdish, especially if it came from a Kurdish city? Jarik* was right; my internationalism has become one of my clichés. He had told me this quite delicately, because he was not a nineteen-year-old girl, but a forty-four-year-old man, who knows every trick in the book.

I was ashamed, turned my face, and went toward the chestnut tree. I think about that day when Jarik caught me red handed. I was not ashamed then like I am today hearing Arjîn's words. My comments were so hurtful to Arjîn that she was not able to control her anger or avoid ruthlessly shouting at me. If Jarik had shouted at me that time, then I would not have said such ridiculous things today. Jarik had exercised his sarcasm so gently with me that it did not hurt me at all. Why, though? He should have been angry too and shouted at me. I remember once that in the middle of a Kurdish song my best friend said, "I hate the Kurds more than dogs." Jarik smiled at her and said, "Why do you hate dogs, did one ever bite you?"

"No, I don't hate dogs at all. That's just a Turkish term. But I already hate the Kurds. They are disgusting."

"Why do you feel the Kurds are disgusting? Did a Kurd ever get you sick?"

"They are the disease themselves. No microbe has killed as many innocent people as these terrorists."

"Haven't you ever wondered why these people would want to fight, often nearly unarmed?"

---

* A kind of plant that cannot be destroyed, even by uprooting and burning.

"They are terrorists and don't know anything except terror. They should appreciate the Turks for civilizing them and not letting them live in barbarism anymore."

"Maybe you are right, but for over eighty years you have been destroying their culture, language, and homeland."

"They have no culture or language. They just bleat like sheep and their homeland is called Türkiye and belongs to the Turkish nation."

"What would you do if a cultured people like the Russians occupied your homeland, not letting you speak your maternal language for seventy years, and all the so-called developed countries branded you as terrorists? Would you take up a Kalashnikov against the modern weapons of the oppressors?"

"No country can turn the Turks into an obedient nation. We ruled half of the world for six centuries. Besides Arabic and German, our language is one of the most beautiful and richest languages in the world. You cannot compare Turkish with that semi-language that lacks grammar."

"Where did you hear that Kurdish has no grammar? Can you speak the Kurdish language?"

"You're still talking about the language? Kurdish is not a language. It was made up by Britain to weaken the Ottoman empire. Kurdish was the communication method of some mountaineers who couldn't learn the language of civilized people."

My blood boiled with rage. Jarik's composure was unbearable. He made me pay for my internationalist cliché, which had led our chat in this direction. I had said it was not important whether the song belonged to the Kurds or the Turks. We could just enjoy the song. That day, Jarik let my best friend disclose her fascist features and, amazingly, some other Turkish friends were agreeing with the claims until I screamed, "Who do you actually think you are? You are the dregs of society. Your heads are full of shit. I'm not talking about any nationalities. I'm not talking about the Turks; I'm talking about you five, the scum of humanity."

I threw them out of my home screaming. The other guests fled one by one. I was enraged and even angrier with Jarik, who wickedly let this conversation reach the point that it ruined my birthday party. But he was so calm and cool that I could not show him my anger. I was steaming but I could not throw him away. I did not know why Jarik was so quiet. Maybe he just wanted to set up an atmosphere for sex, or maybe he was just a dispassionate guy, content to let my anger burn itself out? He had injected a bitter poison into my mouth, which I could neither swallow, nor spit out. Everything was under his control. His last sentence even sounded friendly.

"Everyone has their clichés and internationalism is yours."

I turned my face to my comrades. Arjîn was not there. I went to the fire and asked for her.

"She is inside," Gulbehar told me. I walked up the steps hurriedly and entered the corridor. She was sitting on a sugar sack but got up and came to me.

"Pardon me, hevala Arjîn," I said.

"No heval, I have to apologize. I wanted to come to you but did not want to disturb you until you came back. I behaved very indecently towards you. You came here from thousands of miles away to help us. I am not allowed to react so childishly. You grew up on another continent and do not have the same feelings as we do."

"No, hevala Arjîn. My attitude really was wrong. We do not have to deny our own identities to preserve our humanity. You are my darling and you must know that."

"I know heval, every heart is a mirror to the others."*

"Where is Befrîn?" I asked her, smiling.

"Rojano is feeding him. We can wash him soon. The comrades say he lets them bathe him."

We went out of the bunker. Everyone sat by the fire. You could guess how exhausted they were by their manner of sitting. It was raining lightly, but nobody wanted to miss the heat of the fire. In spite of the rain, it was decided that we would eat dinner by the fire. Maybe it would be the last dinner under the sky. After dinner, Rojano said goodbye and went to return the mules. Even the idea of that long journey was unbearable for me. Like everyone else, she must have been tired. She had carried the heaviest loads all three times and led a couple of mules, but she went on without any complaint. Suddenly, Nadîr called her, "Heval, wait, I'll come with you. It will be dark when you come back."

Rojano appreciated him. He put his half-drunk glass of tea on the ground and followed her. The water in the canisters had been boiling for

* A Kurdish proverb.

a while. I pulled my napkin out of my pocket and lifted one of them from the fire. Except Tewar, who preferred to sleep instead of taking a bath, the other female comrades followed me and everyone took a canister. Tewar said that she wanted to take a bath with Rojano later. The bathroom was hot and bright. Our new electric lamp was turned on there. I emptied the canister into the tub and went outside to bring a canister of cold water.

I was hearing the voice of Gulbehar behind me. She and Arjîn were following me. We filled the canisters at the spring and brought them back to the bunker. Under the pretext of bringing my bath towel, I put the canister in front of the bunker and went toward my clothes. When I entered the bathroom, they were all naked. They had nice bodies. Even Rûken, whose face looked fifteen years older than her real age, had a charming body and shiny skin. None of them had the slightest trace of fat at the stomach or flanks. As perfect a form as Hollywood actresses see in their dreams. I took off my clothes without being ashamed of my fat belly. No one was interested in my imperfect-looking body or in the perfection of their own. The feminine beauty of their bodies was the result of their lifestyle, with its modest diet and constant activity. Perhaps some positive effects resulted from the eight-meter-long waist shawls that they always had tied around their bellies, too. Nobody was washing themselves. They were standing, except Dêrsîm, who was sitting on one of the wooden trunks and massaging her half-leg. It was hard for me to look at this scene. The left leg of this beautiful body had to be amputated about ten centimeters below the knee with an ax three years ago. Nobody was saying a word. They were waiting for something that couldn't be soap; some bars of soaps were already on one of the wooden trunks. I filled a bowl of water from the tub and poured it on my head. Before picking up a bar of soap, Rûnahî stepped inside. She had two bowls in her hand.

"What are these?" I asked.

"Self-made hair remover."

"And how were they made?"

"There are two kinds. One is made with sugar, water, and that thing that Gulbehar doesn't like. The other is made simply with ashes and water."

She put both of them on a plastic sheet that covered the ground. I dipped my fingertips into some of the hair remover made with sugar, water, and lime. It was as sticky as natural gum. I covered my body from navel to toe. My body hair was removed when I took it off. I screamed so cheerfully that the cat jumped up. Only then did I notice Befrîn. He had fallen asleep behind the gas heater. They were so busy with hair removal that they weren't aware that the cat was sleeping there. A new question popped into my mind. I saw a paradox between two completely different aspects of their lives. Why should a woman worry about removing her unpleasant hair and wearing colorful underwear while she's living at the butt of the world under these stone-age circumstances? Perhaps this beautification is an order of the party leaders to reinforce their manly struggle by feminine means. It must be the same old story. The instrumentalization of females to fulfill male goals. I rub the natural hair remover on my body. It sticks damn well. I pull it off with a jerk and would have screamed in pain if the atmosphere here weren't even more unbearable. I would like to ask them what they are actually doing here, for whom they are making themselves so pretty. They are practically already nuns. I don't dare to ask them such questions, which torments me so much. I have never been a woman who minced words, but now I don't have enough courage. Half an hour ago, I tried to play the role of a moralizing teacher for Arjîn, then I could suddenly only stand there with my tail between my legs. I have overestimated myself, or maybe I've underestimated that nineteen-year-old girl.

I watch the fighters intently with a head full of questions that I can't ask. The answers would be predictable. "As a European woman and a teacher, do you really think about such trifles? Yes, we live in the middle of nowhere, but in the twenty-first century." Answers such as these may sound reasonable, but they cannot satisfy my doubts. I want to ask them directly, "Why are you allowing patriarchal militarism to exploit you?" But I am afraid. Afraid of unexpected answers and also shy in front of Dêrsîm, who sits beside me and removes her leg-stump hairs. I shiver from the cold. I put the bowl in the hot water and pour it on my head, then again, then once more.

I take a bar of soap and rub myself without wishing to wash myself. From head to toe. I rinse my body. Then I take out two clean bath towels from a plastic bag. One of them is for Befrîn. I give it to Arjîn. She smiles and thanks me. I wipe myself, put on my black panties and bra, then the male uniform, and go out hurriedly into the fresh air. It's not quite dark yet, but I stumble. I am doubtful about my decision to stay here. I go to the women's camp and take my sleeping bag and tent out. I lay down in my loneliness but cannot sleep.

In the following days I had the same feeling. I kept away from the other comrades and hardly spoke. Until Saro returned. Even seeing him could not change my mood, but in the evening of the same day he brought me out of my isolation. We went toward the cave again and he asked me why I was sad.

"I'm doubting something."

"What?"

"Many things here are suspicious and paradoxical."

"What, for example?"

"Why do the women here wear such striking under garments?"

"I don't know what you mean."

"You're saying that you don't know about the colorful underwear that the women wear here? Who buys them for the women?"

"The female comrades buy the undergarments themselves. They have their own procurement responsibility. I also worked as a procurer, but I never bought female stuff. Do you find it wrong for women to wear colorful underwear here? I hadn't heard about that until now, but I think it's normal. They are women after all."

"I also have other questions which I would like to ask the female comrades."

"Good idea. Why didn't you do it before?"

"I was afraid of a bad reaction and misunderstandings. I do not want my questions to be considered as prying into their personal lives. I want to ask my questions on another level."

Saro looked me straight in the eye and said, "Can I help you with this?"

"Yes, sure. It would be better if it were seen as a topic of party politics."

"With which comrades do you want to talk?"

"Rûken and Rojano. I can ask the others myself."

He left and Rojano came to me after a few minutes. She greeted me and sat down opposite me on the blanket. It was drizzling pleasantly. "Sorry to bother you. I want to ask you some questions that may sound weird," I said.

"You can ask me any questions that you'd like. I have nothing to hide."

"Thanks, heval. I see some clear paradoxes here. We lead a completely extraterrestrial, asexual life here. How is this lifestyle related to beautification?"

"What do you mean, heval?"

"I mean makeup and hair removal. Why . . . no, sorry, on what grounds are you doing this?"

"To not forget that I'm a woman. I did not come here to turn myself into a man. I've done a lot of masculine work, even in civilian life. But I've always remained cognizant of the risk of forgetting my femininity. I have feminine feelings, though I may look like a tough man in your eyes."

"No heval, please do not get me wrong. That's exactly what I expected from a smart, beautiful woman like you."

She thanked me and left. I did not want to bother the other comrades, so I went straight to our commander. She had recently gone to the spring with a tub in her hand to wash her clothes. I greeted her warmly and she answered, smiling, "I hope you are feeling better."

"Thanks heval, I am feeling better. May I sit here?"

"Yes, please; hevalê Saro said you wanted to talk to me."

"Yes, that's right."

"Why didn't you ask me in the past few days?"

"I was afraid you would misunderstand me. I still have that fear."

"Why are you afraid? Do I look so terrible?"

"No, no way. Heval, why is beautification important to you?" I said, laughing.

"Heval, I guessed that you would ask me such a question. Since that day you've changed noticeably. Heval, we fight against a patriarchal world. I say we, because I've heard it from hundreds of other female comrades. This world is characterized by hardness and masculinity. Yet, we do not want to lose our feminine beauty and tenderness. We have undertaken a masculine responsibility, if you consider it from a historical point of view. Fighting doesn't correspond with the nature of women. They bring humans into the world and do not want to kill those they have created. We have chosen these antifeminine responsibilities because we want to bring something more important to the world. The world that men have made has become unbearable. We fight against this world, but we do not want to become men."

"Thanks heval, I have another question that is even more important to me."

"Tell me."

"Heval, have you seen a woman raped or sexually harassed by men here?"

"Here? Why do we have these weapons then? Who can rape a woman if she has a gun in her hands?

"But in other armies, for example, in the German army, the women are also armed, and they are still sexually harassed and even raped."

"No, those are not weapons, but toys. There is no jurisdiction in these mountains. A rapist is simply shot in the skull. In these mountains, the sexual harassment rate of women and children drops to zero."

"Are you exaggerating, heval? This can't be a paradise."

"It's definitely not a paradise here. We have plenty of fools, opportunists, and hypocrites. The men mess up here a lot, but never in pursuit of sex or money. Two years ago, a Belgian woman, a former teacher, was here with us. One day, she came to me and said she had caught a comrade who was sexually harassing a five-year-old girl. I got mad, took my gun, and went to find that man. I wanted to shoot him in the head. We lay in wait until a little girl showed up. She ran toward him and he lifted her up a few times and kissed her forehead. I was waiting for what he would do next. He hugged her tight again and laid her on the ground. The Belgian woman was shocked and asked me, "Did you see what that dirty pig did?"

Confused, I asked her, "What did he do?"

That teacher was not acquainted with our culture. I have lived in these mountains since I was twelve. When I was a child, the comrades often kissed and hugged me, but I did not ever feel bad. Even in our village, people were embracing and kissing strangers' children, because they are just vivacious and lovely. When I was a twelve-year-old girl, I always brought warmth and cheers to the comrades, and I enjoyed it too. Now, the children of the new generation bring us this vitality. Hevala Jînçin, your Kurdish is better than other comrades' and it is amazing, but I do not know yet how well you know Middle Eastern culture. In the Middle East, if someone sexually abuses a child, he ruins his human personality. I do not mean only in front of other people, but in himself too. To someone who rapes women, this is even worse. Such men do not appear in these mountains. The men who are living in these difficult circumstances have other things in mind than sexual pleasure, though some of them are more despicable than the worst criminals and thieves outside these mountains.

CHAPTER 4

EACH DAY ON which no drones appeared, I went to the hawthorn trees. Until four days ago, the berries were still green and unripe. They should turn soft and yellow and tickle the palate. My father told me there are also yellow hawthorns in Kurdistan that are sweet and sour and melt like butter in your mouth. Nothing in the world connected me to my father as much as hawthorn. Every year in mid-November, we would go to Raimund Street. Presumably, my dad was the only one from the Middle East who found hawthorn trees in Frankfurt, but I was the first one who found this row of hawthorn trees, just a fifteen-minute walk from our house, of all places. I do not remember how old I was when I first picked up red hawthorn berries from such trees, but I remember the berries having the scent of aftershave from my father's beard stubble, when I was sitting on his shoulder, picking berries straight from the branches and eating them right there. Those red, sweet-sour berries remained on the trees for three weeks, during one period per year, but nobody picked any of tthem, neither the native Germans nor the foreigners. What the farmer doesn't know, he doesn't eat.

My mother had endless hatred for those hawthorn trees. She found it ridiculous that we had to forgo many important trips because of them. Picking hawthorn berries turned into a custom between me and my father. Every year, in mid-November, I would go to Frankfurt, even when I was studying at Munich University and during the following years when I was living with my fiancé in Berlin.

Now, there are four hawthorn trees opposite our underground bunker and even hawthorn trees with yellow berries, something my father dreamed of for forty years in Germany.

These trees could be one of the reasons why I stayed here, in a place where the monotony of life is constant. We have to get up every morning at five o'clock. After accomplishing our mundane tasks, we eat the usual breakfast and take part in countless hours of repetitive training sessions. At the beginning, these training sessions were interesting for me, because we could discuss the historical and cultural causes for the repeated failures of the last century and a half of Kurdish struggle. Akam was responsible for these training sessions and he pointed out a lot of important context.

After two weeks, I noticed that the Kurds have learned nothing from their defeats. Disunity, incompatibility, and betrayal among the Kurds are the main causes of this recurring failure, while the Kurdish forces are as divided as in the nineteenth century. Right now, two parts of Kurdistan, in the south and the west, are ruled by the Kurds. The borders have not only not disappeared, but are even more prominently marked than before. Two years ago, when I wanted to go to Rojava, I waited behind the border for more than a month. I could only pass the border by risking my life. It was impossible to cross through the section of border that was controlled by the KDP,[*] even with the help of bribes and smugglers. The newly liberated part of Kurdistan, Rojava, was besieged and the routine lives of the people disrupted.

The Kurdish forces allow themselves to be exploited by their opponents. The PKK is no different, yet they curse historical disagreements here every day. Instead of liberating Jerusalem, Selahedîn should have fought to unify the Kurdish tribes and establish a Kurdish nation.

I listen in silence and find the accusations more and more unpleasant over time. I just find it a waste of time to listen to these discussions, which I can study by myself. I could read these books in Germany while commuting on a comfortable seat in a well-lit train. I did not come here from Germany to attend historical book club sessions.

My suspicions were gradually growing, but I kept my silence. This time in protest. When the comrades asked me the reason for my silence, I shrugged my shoulders and waited to finish the worthless lessons. Until I found Akam's diary. I asked him if I could read it and he agreed. It was written in the Hewramî dialect. I read some paragraphs of his diary, but I didn't understand what he wrote. I asked him, "Can you teach me Hewramî?" "I can," he replied. Gradually he helped me to understand his text and eventually I came up with an idea.

---

[*] Kurdistan Democratic Party

Every evening, all four executive members of the group would come together after listening to their comrade's daily reports and discussing current problems and future plans. I went to the male comrades' room and waited behind the hanging hemp door for a while. Suddenly, Rûken appeared behind me and asked me to come in with her. Instead of a battery-powered lamp, a simple candle was burning. A thread was put in a little tin can that was full of cooking oil. Between a functioning radio and greasy food, it was clear they had given priority to the radio. The tin candle was burning smokeless and the small men's room was bright enough. All other three executive members were sitting cross-legged. Rûken sat next to Gulbehar, as did I. She spoke up.

"Hevala Jînçin would like to discuss something with us."

Saro laid some papers on a dark blanket and said, "Please, heval."

"Since three weeks ago this place has turned into a primary school. Apparently these training sessions have been quite useful for our comrades, but my point is that the main contents of these training sessions could be read in books that are available here. Everybody can study them if they wish. Much is said about the past here and little about the present. Wouldn't it be better if we talked about ourselves one day out of the week instead of past events? We all have something to say about our lives. Hevalê Akam has even written his life story."

"That's a good idea," Saro was the first one who agreed and turned to Rûken.

"I'm not against it, but it could reveal the anonymity of the comrades. If you tell in detail about your private life, you are no longer anonymous. Why do we actually have our aliases?"

"But we can talk about our lives without revealing our actual identity. What do you think, hevalê Ferhad?"

"I would like to hear the story of hevalê Akam. This story was written and will be published someday. Other comrades can decide for themselves if they want to tell some low-risk but intriguing parts of their lives."

"And what is your opinion, hevala Gulbehar?"

"I would like to hear two stories: the one written by Akam and the story of hevala Jînçin. When I was in Rojava, I told journalists some memories about myself. Nobody complained about it. The YPJ* even motivated me. I agree with her proposal."

"There does not seem to be anybody against it, and we can make the final decision with other comrades tomorrow," said Saro.

I appreciated them and left the room happily. I did not expect that my proposal would be accepted so quickly. The next day at dawn, or the hour of the hare, I kept the second shift of the watch. Hevalê Ferhad replaced me and hevala Gulbehar replaced our humorist, Zinar. The meeting took place like any other general meeting in the women's room. Last night, someone had turned off the gas heater in the room after the radio announced a code fifty-one, but the room was not cold. Rûken and Tewar sat in the middle and everyone else around them against the wall. We waited until Serhelldan arrived. When his footfalls were heard, Arjîn called to him.

"Heval, bend over two meters so you don't hit the doorframe."

"She's not worried about your head, heval. She's worried about the doorframe," Satyar said, interpreting her words.

Serhelldan bent over like a malnourished dinosaur and stepped through the frame. As usual, he sat next to Tewar and Rûken initiated the meeting.

"Yesterday, hevala Jîncin made a suggestion. We want to put it to a vote today."

"What's her amazing suggestion?" Tewar asked sarcastically. Rûken turned to me.

"Would you like to explain it yourself or should I do it?"

Although I wished to explain it to the comrades, I asked her to do it so I could see how she would describe my suggestion. She took a piece of paper from the floor covering, looked at it briefly, and continued, "Instead of social history, she has asked that, for one day per week, we talk about our own lives. This does not mean that everyone has to do it, but, personally, I will tell you something about my life."

The room was quiet until Rûnahî broke the silence with an excited voice, "This is a great idea."

"What is great about it?" Tewar asked bitterly, yet again.

---

* Yekîneyên Parastina Jin, Women's Protection Units

"For example, I would like to know what hevalê Nadîr's life was like in the past," Arjîn replied instead of Rûnahî.

"Hunger thought about eating from the beginning. He used to either work in candy shops or wandered around looking for treats. Now he's spoiling his own broth and stewing in his own juices as a lentil specialist," Satyar said, making the room fill with lighthearted chuckles and chatter. Rûken didn't restore order, despite her authority, until Rojano spoke up.

"I think it's very important we get to know each other better. Why did we come here and why has everyone chosen this life? Unfortunately, I can only tell you bitter memories."

"Why should we have to hear each other's life stories? Everyone has to keep their private story to themselves and only focus on our struggle and the party's goals. We are not here for ramblings." The smug expression with which Tewar said this annoyed me.

I was going to lose my temper until Akam said, "Heval, do you think of our life stories as ramblings? Each of us carries within ourselves a large part of our social history and collective troubles. It's been a long time that I've been waiting to hear these individual stories, which are better at reflecting our individual lives than any history written by fascist enemies or Kurdish nationalists. I appreciate you, hevala Jînçin, for your attention and courage. I find the suggestion timely, overdue in fact, and think it should have been added to our organization's program earlier."

I don't think that Tewar understood Akam's speech, which he gave in Hewramî dialect, but she raised her hand to indicate an objection. Rûken interrupted her and said, "This is a suggestion, but not a discussion topic. Let's put it to a vote. Who is opposed?"

Tewar raised her left hand immediately. Serhelldan looked at her and raised his hand so quickly and spontaneously that his hand would have shot through the roof if he were seated in a chair. Then Rûken asked those who agreed to raise their hands. Everyone except Tewar raised their hands, even our rickety ladder. He raised his hand slowly this time, looking at me. I thought it was just a preliminary decision and that the lessons would continue until Rûken asked, "Who would like to be the first to tell their life story today?"

"Hevala Jînçin, of course. In for a penny, in for a pound."

I looked at Rojano. She emphasized her opinion by nodding twice. I actually would like to tell them my life story. I looked around the room. Except Tewar, everyone smiled affectionately at me and I began to speak.

"I have to begin with my father. Our lives were woven together like carpet threads through countless events and memories. He was an Êzdî from Şingal. During Mullah Barzani's uprising, as a recent law graduate, he chose to join the Kurdish resistance against the Ba'ath regime in Iraq. Like millions of Kurds in those days, he saw Mela Mistefa as a demigod and loved him more than anyone else. That's why his ideas and viewpoints about Kurdish matters changed suddenly when he saw this great uprising ruined due to the recklessness of its leader. My father always told me that after the era of the Medes Kingdom and Selahedîn,* the Kurds were never as strong as in the time of the Mela Mistefa uprising. The enemy had been knocked down and they could have liberated all the Iraqi people from the Ba'ath Party. But with his egregious mistake, Mela Mistefa stalled any solution for the Kurdish problem, leaving it for the twenty-first century. His astounding capitulation drove thousands of academics, artists, Pêşmerge, and other libertarian fighters into disappointment, depression, and even suicide.

The Shah of Iran sold out the Kurds to the Ba'ath party at the price of two rivers and the Kurdish nation, whose leader was naive enough to entrust the fate of his people to a dictator, willingly laid down their arms based on a hollow promise. My father returned to Baghdad and set up a law office. There, his classmate, or better to say his girlfriend, waited for him. They had loved each other for four years, though they both knew there was a big obstacle between them. Hevala Rûnahî knows the problem better than all of us, because the problem remains a part of Êzdî culture. My father and his girlfriend came from two different social classes and they were not allowed to marry each other.

They decided to fight against this ancient custom, which had no relation with Mithraism, the ancient religion from which the later Kurdish religions arose. They talked to their families and relatives and asked for their understanding. In the end, they were compelled, as two law school graduates, to impotently submit their petition to the Êzdî's great sheikh. Their application was rejected. After a year, his girlfriend

* Salah al-Din Yusuf ibn Ayyub.

married a man from the Adani tribe and my father left Kurdistan and then settled in Germany a few months later. He worked at the post office there as an independent driver. Over time, he was able to found his own postal company. He bought some cars on credit and hired several drivers and postmen, but he always delivered parcels to a certain place himself; that was the public library where my mother worked. Over time, my mother fell in love with him.

Their love story started one New Year's Eve, when she invited him for a drink. That night, she had had a quarrel with her sister, so she felt lonely and sad. My father made her happy and could sweeten the night for her, because he was also lonely, not having any relatives in Germany.

After a few months, my mother made my father a marriage proposal, without knowing the ritual limitations of Êzdî culture. My father had explained it before their relationship became serious, but my mother thought she could convert to the Êzdî religion to get past the obstacles. My mother's suggestion of religious conversion shocked my father. He took it as a sign of deep, true love from my mother, but, really, she wasn't hit by Cupid's arrows. Her decision was just based on her indifference to religion. My mother confessed it to me after my father's death. It was a truth that she had hid from my father throughout their marriage.

After this commitment from my mother, my father made a firm resolution concerning Êzdî culture. He wrote various letters to his relatives and the great sheikh of the Êzdîs and explained to them that his fiancée would like to convert to the Êzdî religion. After a few months, he received some letters answering him. Later, I gave those letters to someone to translate them from Arabic to German. All of the letters were exactly alike, as if they were written by a single person, "An Êzdî must marry only within his family class and no one can convert his religion to that of the Êzdîs."

My father continued his fight, which was doomed from the start. He questioned the legitimacy of many Êzdî rituals. I still have the letters in Germany. He wrote those letters in Arabic and Sorani Kurdish, and criticized the wrong and irrational heresies that had entered into Êzdî culture throughout the centuries and had caused this pure and peaceful religion to deviate from its main source, Mithraism. He believed that Mithraism was against any kind of discrimination or social classification.

In contrast with Zoroastrianism, whose intellectual foundation is based on a duality of good and evil, there is no evil in Mithraism, and that is why Êzdîs do not believe in Satan. My father wrote that Êzdîs are opposed to any social classification and took as an example another Kurdish sister religion, Yarsanism, in which there is no kind of doctrinal separation or classification of people. My father's arguments proved toothless, and he received a letter with more than five hundred Êzdî signatures calling for his excommunication and expulsion from Êzdî society.

I was born a year after my parents' marriage. My father was able to organize his job from home, so he did not have to send me to a nursery. He would announce new directions and notifications to his staff by phone. If there was ever any problem at work, such as an employee falling ill or something similar, he took me to my aunt's house. So, I was basically brought up by my father and I learned the Kurdish language as the only means of communication with him.

For years, the language had only this meaning for me. There were many people throughout my studies who presented themselves as Kurdish. They were mostly from Bakûr. They spoke neither Kurdish, nor German amongst themselves, only Turkish. During my childhood, I discovered two types of languages. The type I learned from my aunt came from her reading books to me in German, and on the other side my dad recounted Kurdish stories from his heart. For my whole life, my father spoke only Kurdish with me, except for a single time in Şêxan.

We traveled to Başûr in the hot summer. I was eight. My father intended to rent a house somewhere near the Laliş holy site. He did not introduce himself as a Êzdî, but as a Kurd from Rojhilat[*] who wanted to spend two weeks there with his family. There was no hotel or house for rent, but we could stay for free as a guest in a local family's house as long as we would like.

This trip became the best memory of my childhood. My mother enjoyed it a lot too. She got to bake bread with the village women. They gifted us some colorful Kurdish dresses and invited us to two wedding celebrations. My mother often stayed with the women in the village and had fun with them, but every day at noon my father would go to the

---

[*] Eastern Kurdistan.

Lališ temple for pilgrimage. But why in the hot noon? Even the villagers wondered about that. The next day, he left the house in the hot noon and I followed him.

Far away from the temple, my father was taking off his shoes. The pavement must have been very hot, because his soles were blistered on the first day. Although he didn't talk about his burnt feet to my mother or the villagers, I could tell that he was walking in pain and I also saw him come back from the temple, sit down under the holy tree, and squeeze those blisters to let the blood-mixed pus ooze out.

Despite the daily pain of his walks, he was glad. I could see a joyful illumination in his eyes. Every day, he would take off his shoes in the same place, put them in a plastic bag, and give them to me. Then he would lift me on his shoulders and walk across the pavement.

In spite of the scorching sun, I felt cool with my big, wet straw hat on my head, as I sat on his shoulders. Over there, the hills were green and nice and the buildings on both sides of the road were ancient.

The temple entrance was a flat pavement road located between some hills and a big spring where cool water flowed. There were no pilgrims in sight because of the intense heat, even under the cool and pleasant shade of the holy tree, where he put me down on the ground. Walking barefoot, I took our shoes to a big stone and put them on it. My father had commenced his pilgrimage before I came back.

The exterior view of the temple looked like a church built by piling up rows of stones. Its height was about fifteen meters. A couple of stony pillars had been built on both sides of the entrance with an arch between them. There was another arch a few meters above the first. There was a gap between the elevated arch and the wall behind it, creating an empty space in between that stretched almost to the roof area. My father used to kiss the pillars and the statue of a black snake carved on the right side of the entrance. The whole day, there was a man sitting under the image of the black snake. He had a beautiful, big green snake, which was creeping over his body, going up and down, looping around his neck, and rising up from his straw hat. Then the snake would come down from his collar, its tongue sliding in and out, and disappear into his shirt. The man was letting me pet the snake, while my father was telling me that the snake was a sentry of the temple and wouldn't bite me. The snake was wrapping around me and my father took photos. I saw that same man again on my trip there two years ago. He had become old and had a gray snake with him. I asked him to let me hold the snake. He was wondering why a blonde European woman wasn't afraid of it. The snake wrapped around my wrist and crawled up near my armpit. Then it came down and looped around my waist. Then I sat on the ground and it unwrapped from my waist and coiled on my thighs for a brief time, then went up my body with a raised head. On my second trip, I reached the temple in the late afternoon, so it was cool and the snake was lively, but on my childhood trip it had preferred to stay in the man's shirt.

The wooden entrance door of the temple was always open, though I was not allowed to go in alone. My father liked to touch the snake's head and give some money to the man. On the first day, my father made it clear that I was not allowed to put my foot on the entrance slab. He picked me up every time and let me down on the other side. He would also pass over the stone with a big step. My father told me that hundreds of thousands of Êzdîs have been killed throughout history to protect this temple from being conquered by enemies. We were coming down some steps from the entrance to reach a great yard. The yard was paved with big, old, rectangular stones. My father was walking so slowly that I was moving past him. I enjoyed the inside of the temple. I had never seen one like it in Europe. The further in we went, the darker it became. I didn't wait for my father and stepped down the corridor steps alone. We approached a big hall with a vaulted roof after we passed some corridors. The floor, walls, and ceiling were all carved from the same old, beige stones and those stones looked greasy and gleaming in the light of the candles. The two sides of the hall were not like each other. On the left side, against the wall, there were many large clay jugs arranged beside each other, stretching the length of the hall. A short stone fence separated them from the corridor. These clay jugs were full of olive oil and were more than one thousand years old, according to my father. On the right side of the hall was a wide stone platform against the wall. Well, until two years ago I perceived it that way. But these pedestals, on which the oil candles burned, must have been hewn out of the stony hill, as well as all the rough rooms and corridors. At the end of the hall, an exit was carved into the mountain with a niche above it, on which a large candle was always burning. We passed through that door and several narrow corridors until we arrived at the holy spring that flowed out from the heart of the mountain. I forgot to count those corridors and rooms, both on my childhood trip and the last time. Hevala Rûnahî, do you know how many corridors and rooms that labyrinth consisted of?"

"I know heval, but I would like to listen to your story."

"Ok, heval. On the first day, my dad tied a violet prayer flag to one of the colorful fabrics covering the Şêx Edê tombstone. His tombstone was hexagonal in shape, within a large hall with a high ceiling. My father tied the two sides of the violet prayer flag together several times. Each day he untied one of the knots and lifted me up to untie my own prayer flag. After fifteen days, when all the knots had been untied, he took the prayer flag from the tombstone and put it in his left shirt pocket. Then we left the temple and village and after two days flew from Baghdad to Frankfurt.

Until some years ago, all I had understood from the religion of the Êzdîs was summarized in the green snake, colorful prayer flags, the half-dark greasy rooms, the cold water of the holy spring and, above all else, the Barat. The Barat was deeply engraved in my memory, because for the first and last time my father talked to me in an exclusively German-language sentence. The Barat looked like a big pearl, but it was not as smooth as my mother's pearls. The temple sentry put the Barat in my father's hand and he kissed it several times. I jumped up to grab it but my father angrily told me in German, 'You must not play with the Barat. The Barat is holy.'

My father did not seem to be a religious person. If it weren't for that trip to Başûr, I would have considered him a completely irreligious man. He did not pray or fast, nor did he talk about religion, but a few times I caught him praying while he held the Barat in his hand. The temple guards made the Barat by mixing white soil from around the temple with yogurt, kneading it enough, then making little pearl shaped balls and drying them under the sun. The Barat was converted into a holy object in this way, like Christian crucifixes or Muslim Qurans.

I never asked my father what he wished for when he tied the prayer flag, but life became easier after we returned. Before that trip my parents were living separated from each other. My mother even wanted to get a divorce. One time, I could not see my father for three weeks and I missed him so much that I fled from the house. It was midnight and raining. I couldn't sleep. After my mother had gone to bed, I left our house without warm clothing to go to my aunt's house. My father was living there. I waited for a long time at the bus station near our house, but no bus ever appeared, though a police car did. I was freezing from the cold. I burst into tears when I saw them. They asked me why I was crying, and I said I wanted to go see my dad. 'And where is your father?' they asked me.

On the map of bus stations, I put my finger on the station where I always got off. They took me there. After an hour my mother arrived there. She wanted to bring me back home, but the police told her that I wanted to stay with my father. My mother said that she had child custody. A female police officer asked me, 'Would you like to stay with your mother or your father?'

'With my father,' I answered.

Then another policeman asked me again, 'My darling, would you like to stay with your father or with your mother?'

'I want to stay here with my father.'

My mother turned pale. I was eight and did not know how to answer equivocally. It would have been better if I had said, 'I want to be with both of them.' I realized what a destructive effect my response had when I heard the female officer say, 'How much has this woman tormented this girl that she hates her so much?' My parents reconciled and after a month we traveled to Başûr. Their relationship seemed to have improved after we returned. They did not quarrel anymore, or at least not in front of me. I was an honor student and got everything I needed. It was very important to my father that I didn't grow into a picky, spoiled woman. My mother was strict in general. I learned to play the flute and swim and never smoked. I got an admission letter from the faculty of physics at the Technical University of Munich. I was also successful in university. At the age of twenty-eight, I submitted my PhD thesis, entitled 'Safe Communication and Interference-Free Transmission of Information through Entanglement Photons.' My thesis attracted great attention. I received an offer to join a project in Berlin on behalf of the Ministry of Defense and my fiancé and I commenced work on it. A modern laboratory was made available to us. We made great progress in the first eight months.

That time was the most beautiful and productive part of my life, but I unexpectedly had to give up our project. My mother had fallen ill with leukemia. The news hit me like a bolt of lightning. I felt guilty towards her. Because of me, she had to live with a man that she hadn't loved for a long time. She had lived with my father because she could not separate me from him. Suddenly, an avalanche of guilt-inducing memories assailed me. I remember a night when she had cowered beside a lamppost next to her sister's house. She did not want to knock on the door, so she waited until she saw me through the window, but I just wanted to piss her off. Maybe my mother wasn't a bad woman at all. I was just used to my father because he had raised me that way. I suddenly doubted my father's love for me. Or maybe neither of them were to blame for their unhappy life together. They were just cut from a different cloth, but because of me, they had to continue that miserable life until my mother was trapped in death's clutches. I talked to her doctor by phone for a long time. They had found a blood stem-cell donor, but the donor's HLA features did not match enough with my mother's. Therefore, it was feared that my mother's immune system would attack the injected stem cells. So, the risks of infection or internal bleeding after her surgery were too high. Thus, to prevent the immune system from rejecting the work of the procedure, it was necessary to further perform a mini-transplantation or a transfusion right after the stem cell transplantation.

In general, in order to stop the immune reactions, she would have to carefully take medicines on a rigid schedule; only then could she survive this difficult time. So, in the middle of our experiments I decided to leave Berlin and return to Frankfurt to help my mother. My fiancé worked so hard to change my mind from this abrupt decision and reminded me constantly that this unnecessary choice would ruin my scientific career, as well as our relationship. But I was so burdened by my guilt that I could not pay attention to his logical arguments. He was quite right; I was not a doctor and I could do about as much for my mother as my father could have done. He even talked with my father to persuade me to think about my decision once again. My dad did not interfere in my private life. He called me and our conversation was very short.

'Kajîn! You think it's necessary to come back to Frankfurt? Do you think that I am not capable of taking care of your mother by myself?'

'Certainly you can take care of her even better than me. But this is not a question of nursing, but of encouragement. She requires vitality more than our medical knowledge and it is my duty to support her in this difficult time. Otherwise, I will never forgive myself.'

I had myself transferred to Frankfurt. My fiancé told me that one day I would regret my decision. I did and it happened after three years, but it had nothing to do with what my fiancé foresaw. It is true that losing an opportunity to work on the cutting edge of science and technology and separating from someone that I spent the best six years of my life with is unbearable, but I felt that I had achieved a valuable goal. My mother had recovered and once again I could see her thick gray hair. She had been cured and became so cheerful that she forgot how the sickness had crippled her.

Everything happened one evening at the hour of the rooster. I was sitting on the sofa opposite the aquarium and looking over the thesis of one of my students. The TV was on. Suddenly, my mother jumped up and went toward the TV in such a hurry that her leg hit the footstool and knocked it over. A station was broadcasting news that a new minister had been nominated. With sad, exhausted eyes, my mother stared at the TV in astonishment. I asked her what was going on. She answered, 'That man was my suitor thirty-two years ago and I refused him. I was so stupid to refuse him and instead marry a man who remained as unchangeable as a turtle.'

She was terribly sad. I wanted to console her and said, 'But if you had married him, you would not have had me.'

'Do you think that your father is the only man who has a spatter of cum in his pants?'

She was so distraught and shocked by the unexpected news that she did not realize the destructive effects of her words. My mother was not an uneducated woman with no knowledge about genetics. Like all other living creatures in existence, I was the product of pure chance. If she had slept with that man, I would never have existed and would have had no chance to live in this world. Now, let me ask you a question. How many trillions of different people could have existed if all the women in the world accidentally slept with a man, regardless of age, color, religion, and nationality?"

Nobody answered me. Then I asked Rojano directly. "Heval, can you tell me an approximate number?"

"If I'm not mistaken, every man should produce over one hundred billion sperm on average."

"Higher. One man produces over a trillion sperm on average."

"And every woman approximately should produce over one million eggs. Right?"

"Yes, at least."

"Then your theory will be a huge sum of possibilities."

"What do you mean by huge, hevala Rojano?"

"An unimaginable sum, bigger than all the stars and planets in the galaxies, no, much bigger, greater than the number of creatures and drops of water on Earth."

"Even more. More than all atoms and electrons in the entire universe. It means that all fifteen people here in this underground bunker were granted priority over trillions of people who had the same chance of being born as we had. But most ladies don't let their honored ova get fertilized by any random man on the street, reducing the chance of life to billions of possibilities. All of these people, who exist in the limbo of potential life, won't get the chance to live because of their decisions, because women foolishly believe they can determine the destiny of their eggs. They choose a man or even a specific moment, making a conscious decision to give birth to a child out of passion or lust, but in doing so they eliminate trillions upon trillions of possibilities.

This also applies to my mother's eggs. Countless opportunities in life had to be cut, a terrifying sum, for me to exist. My mother had increased my chances of existence by choosing my father's sperm. One night, she threw her myriad-sided dice, and her ovum was fertilized by that sperm, among millions of sperms, which formed half of me. This happened based on the rules of pure chance. I became a real-life fetus. I, and not any one of the other possible fetuses who had an equal chance and opportunity to enter existence on that night. I was born because my mother, with her moaning lust, by her tenderness or her rudeness, brought my father to orgasm, not a millisecond too soon nor too late.

I am the result of her throwing the dice and, after thirty years, she regrets that act because she could have been the wife of a minister at age fifty-eight. I felt empty, like my life was meaningless. From then until today, I have believed my presence in this world is a sin. Countless potential humans had to vanish forever into nonexistence for me to exist. What have we done with our chance at existence, besides sully this world?

That day I asked myself a fundamental question. What would have happened if another sperm had fertilized my mother's ovum instead of the one that came to cause my birth? My answer is always the same: *nothing*. Nothing would change if I had not been brought into this world. My life was not important even for my mother. The person for whom I had ruined my life. I felt betrayed and abandoned in this world. I would have liked to call my fiancé, but he had gotten married with another woman. I was afraid that he would evaluate my regret based on his criteria and would say his prediction had come true. I even thought about suicide, but a spontaneous sensation prevented me, one of hatred for my mother. I washed my face and went downstairs. She was still watching a TV program.

'How are you, honored wife of the minister? Potentially you already are one, right?'

'The job suits me better than his current wife. Have you seen her on Twitter?'

'No, but we'll see her more than enough. You didn't tell me what his job was when he proposed to you.'

'He was an intern in our library at the time.'

'Oh, like that,' I said out loud and continued my speech silently in my head. That's why she refused his marriage proposal. *Potentially* he was a minister, but in reality only a church mouse. She preferred to get married with a man who in reality was an employer. My father's company may have been very small, but he was a twenty-nine-year-old migrant who had launched a business in a few years and even had some German employees. It was possible that my father would have grown into a big, famous company owner in the next few years. It was possible, but my dad was not such an ambitious man and he was satisfied with his financial situation. I cannot believe that my mother was in love with my father at the time. Simply put, she had overestimated him and his good financial situation as a young migrant. Her dreams had not come true, because her calculation was wrong and she had to pay the price for having me. She would always say everything was for my sake and I foolishly believed her. From that evening on, I lost my belief in a blood relationship between parent and child. I couldn't think of anything but *Mandingo*, a novel by Kyle Onstot, in which a lord sleeps with his Black slaves to breed more slaves and sell them. Only now do I understand the concept of the lord's job. I told my mother, 'I have to correct one of my student's theses. Say "hi" to dad for me whenever he gets back.'

I went to my room, threw myself on the bed and let memories of that novel and the meaning of family take me away. The relationship between parents and children is no more than a claiming of ownership. Not only today's ordinary citizens, but also the emperors of China had several wives and lovers with whom they would breed countless children without accepting them as their own offspring, though they were from their own flesh and blood. The children were accepted and loved when they were recognized as members of the family. Then their parents wished them all the best. People wish for their own children to become better than themselves, because all of the children's abilities and strengths are attributed to their parents. Children should inherit all of their good traits from their parents, but what could I have inherited from my mother except covetousness and opportunism?

Since then, I have found the family unit to be a dangerous place, where the seeds of narcissism are sown. Every child is seen as special by its owners, God's gift to mankind, and this erroneous view is passed on to the child, although it is nothing more than pure coincidence.

All of that night I was dreaming about fertilization. I was walking on a bridge and sperms were raining from the sky onto my head. The damn things were stinging my face. In my entire life I've never seen or smelled as much sperm as on that night. Yes, you can laugh now, but I couldn't sleep all night long from the disgusting stickiness of those sperm. I vomited before dawn. I was ultimately compelled to get up from my bed and go to the restroom. Suddenly, a good idea came to my mind. I decided to put my dad to the test. Despite my bad mood, I went to the university. During my last break, I called my dad's post office after he did not reply to his mobile. I told his secretary that I would pick him up in the next couple of hours. I bought two bottles of dry wine with a packet of dates and drove there. He was waiting for me outdoors and came with me without asking where we were going. I drove out of the town to a quiet place by the Main River. I parked my car and went toward the water. My father followed me. Until then, we had not exchanged a word except for our greetings. I sat down on a wooden bench and put my purse on the left side, to let him sit on my right side. It was sunny and pleasant. I said, 'Thank you for coming, dad.'

'Most welcome, what's going on?'

'I cannot forget my fiancé in any way. I always think about him and feel ashamed of myself. I'm not a teenager anymore.'

'I understand, but that's normal.'

'It's not normal for me, not at all. Tell me how you forgot Kanî.* At that moment, you were even younger than me.'

'I did not forget her. I just got used to the reality of having lost her.'

'Well, how do you console yourself when you remember Kanî?'

'I still think about her after so many years. Sometimes it happens just when I look at a glass of water in my hand. I have only good memories of her. You must not repeat my mistakes. You have to replace painful memories with sweet moments.'

'Can you eliminate these feelings? Do they fade?'

'It must be possible. Your situation is a completely different one.'

'Do you wish you had married her instead of a greedy woman like my mother?'

'I wished it a few years ago, but not anymore.'

'Why not? Your current life with your wife is no bed of roses.'

'I would not have you if I had married Kanî.'

'But you could have been the father of as many children as you wanted in your homeland.'

'Yes, many children, but not you.'

'Nonsense dad, the apple doesn't fall far from the tree. Children get features from their parents, even spiritually.'

'Kajîn, we were fourteen children all from the same parents. But everyone was different.'

'Maybe my grandmother was too naughty?'

He laughed loudly and couldn't control himself. I brought out a bottle of wine from my purse, took a sip, and then handed it to him. He drank some sips until the fit of laughter left him and said, 'There's a Kurdish proverb that says: no fingers of a hand are the same.'

'But the fingers of two hands are the same as each other.'

---

* Source of water; a spring.

'But they were formed on two different hands. I can write with the left hand and not with the other.'

'Oh, I inherited this misery from you. That's why you didn't make me give up this ridiculous habit. Unless the Kurds did not compel their left-handed children to write with their right hands?'

'No, the poor Kurds do not have enough time for such luxuries.'

'Why did you name me Kajîn?* I've never asked you, have I?'

'No, you stockpile your questions and bombard me all at once. I called you that because I wanted to find my home with you. Indeed, I have known such happiness for years. You are very different from other women. You have grown up smarter than I could have dreamed of.'

'I'm like that because you brought me up like that.'

'No Kajîn, do not call me a master of pedagogy. You are an open-minded woman. You make connections with others easily. You are eloquent and courageous. Fortunately, you resemble neither me, nor your mother.'

He took my hand and I burst into tears. He was right. He was not eloquent, but he explained his thoughts better than any lecturer. He said exactly the sentences that I needed to be able to save myself from thinking my life was futile. It was clear that he had been thinking about this question for a long time. There was another question with me for a while that I wanted to ask him, but I didn't find a convenient moment. I picked up the bottle of wine, drank another sip, and gave it to him again. He drank the rest of the wine in a breath. I asked him, 'So you think now that I am a wicked girl who bombards you with questions?'

'You are not mean, but it seems you want to bombard me with questions today.'

'You see me as a question-firing cannon, huh? Then I'll ask you one more question. This question has been relevant since the day I was born, so please tell me the truth. Promise?'

'Ok, I think that I know what you want to ask.'

'If you guess, you may drink the other bottle alone as a prize.'

'Kajîn, you know that I would rather drink with you. Did you study physics or the science of being a smartass?'

---

* Where life is to be found.

'The first one at university and the second one with you. Tell me what I want to ask you.'

'Is it about your aunt?'

'Right, did you love each other?'

'I respected her from the deepest depths of my heart.'

'Dad, that was clear, but I meant if you had sex with each other.'

'No, we did not.'

'You must not fool me. She was much prettier than your wife. You must have at least been flirting.'

'It never happened between us.'

'Why not?'

'I expected you to ask me that question someday. I did not want to break your heart or lie to you.'

'And what did my aunt say about it?'

'We never talked about it. She saw you as a child that she never had. You resemble her more.'

Ever since that day my father became the love of my life. I do not mean metaphorically, but a real love. I loved someone who loved me more than any other man could have. My feeling wasn't the same as the feelings of a daughter for her father. I was a perfect woman to my father, without needing to change myself one bit. From then on, I did not care how other men looked at me. I only needed other men to satisfy my sexual needs, but my father was a source of endless vitality and warmth for me. I had a calm and beautiful life, both privately and professionally. Until Daesh emerged. I had heard in reports that they had attacked the Kurds and the Êzdîs. But I did not know the meaning of these words, nor did I really follow them. I knew only one Kurd and Êzdî, who was safe in Frankfurt. The Kurdish language for me was also like a kind of secret language between me and my father. Apart from a short trip in my childhood, I had never spoken Kurdish with anyone else and I did not have a strong feeling of Kurdish identity. I was on a professional trip in Berlin when my mother called me. She was very worried and begged me to do something for her, but she spoke unclearly because of her anxiety. I gave her time to calm down. Then she spoke clearly.

'Your father wants to do something stupid. You have to stop him.'

'What does he want to do?'

'He wants to go to the middle of hell to fight against Daesh.'

'And why is that stupid? He will fight for his people.'

'But he won't survive that hell.'

'Don't you wish for that? I remember you wanting to get rid of him. Now he'll go do it of his own free will.

'Why are you so stubborn? Your dad is going to kill himself.'

'Yes, but he's not a kid. He's cognizant of the consequences of his actions. He has never interfered in my life or limited me. Why should I stand in the way of his desires?'

My father came to Berlin the next day. He had booked his plane ticket from Berlin to Hewlêr earlier. He was sad and his beard was in disarray. We went to a cafe. He sat with his back to a window in a corner and I sat opposite him. The determination on his face made it clear to me that I had to spare him any resistance or he'd give me a little slap. He neither drank his coffee nor spoke a word. He probably expected me to understand him, given the circumstances of the Êzdîs. But I could not understand why he should go to war for the Êzdîs when they were running away themselves. He was now sixty-three and not a fighter. What could he do for them when the well-equipped Iraqi and Syrian soldiers were escaping?

On the cafe television, he was watching the horrible images of the Êzdîs and the countless women and children who had been kidnapped by those savage Muslims. It was not necessary for me to turn toward the TV. This news was already familiar to me. He finally told me, 'I hope you understand my mood.'

'I understand your mood but not your decision. What can you do against these barbarians? What can you do to help the Êzdîs?'

'Maybe nothing for the Êzdîs, but something for myself. I'm going for my own sake and not because of them. I would like to stand beside those miserable people who have been forgotten by God and mankind. That is a matter of responsibility, like what you did for your mother back then.'

'That was the biggest mistake of my life.'

'Maybe, but you know that I should go. In the last forty years I have not been invited to any Êzdî weddings, but you do not need an invitation for a funeral. I want you to promise me something.'

'What would that be?'

'Take care of your mother if I don't come back.'

'I cannot promise you. There are no family ties left uncut between us. And as a stranger, I am not interested in her. I need someone to take care of me. You have to come back, Xemo. Otherwise, I will forget your language.'

'You must not do that, Kajîn. Otherwise, my whole life will lose its meaning. Your mother is right. Occupationally, I'm still in the same place as forty years ago. But at least I did not let you get separated from your Kurdish roots. . . . Maybe it would have been better if I had not done that work and I let you forget that part of your identity. Indeed, your life as a pure German girl would have been a lot sweeter. Maybe it was from my selfishness that I wanted to spread something like a disease to you, which only makes your life bitter. It is very difficult to be a Kurd, and only a Kurd can bear it . . . I wanted to flee from this inevitable destiny. For a time, I hoped for a better future for the Kurds, but it happened in reverse. Maybe it is better that you forget this unfortunate language, as millions of Kurds have in Bakûr, but, please, after my death. I am used to talking to you in Kurdish.'

'Xemo, please don't put yourself in danger. Don't be a hero. Help people where you can, without risking your life. You don't owe anything to the Êzdîs. You made the right decision, even though my mother was not worth it.'

'Yes, that should be the case.'

'Can you contact me from there?'

'There ought to be some weak internet. We can send emails and maybe even talk sometimes.'

He looked at his watch and got up. I took my purse and wanted to get up, but he put his hand on my shoulder and said, 'Please do not come to the airport. It is easier for me to leave you in a cafe than at the airport, where the planes are flying in front of your eyes.'

He paid the bill for the undrunk coffees, went out, and got lost in the crowd on the bridge. I followed his gray hair with my eyes over the bridge until the backside of the river. When he disappeared, I took my phone out from my purse and searched Google for someone who can teach me Kurdish. I found someone. He was a writer from the same town as hevalê Saro. I started to learn Kurdish before I registered in online classes. From that day on, the TV in my room was turned on again. I was following all of the news about the fight between the Kurds and fundamentalist Muslims. I discussed politics with my colleagues. I was proud of the courageous fight that Kurdish women were waging on the frontlines and my colleagues were surprised by that. A special mix of excitement, passion, and political motivation had come into my life, but I was worried about the unknown destiny of my father. After sixteen days, I got a message in Kurdish from my father in Iraq. He had written that he was fine and that many Êzdîs had been saved by the YPJ and YPG.* I wrote him back a long message in Kurdish. He sent me a surprised emoji. I had used some words in my message that he had never heard me use before. He asked me in the next few messages how I learned those words.

'I am learning Kurdish from somebody.'

'Is he your boyfriend,' he asked and sent me a surprised emoji.

'No, I have not seen him yet. He teaches me Kurdish reading and writing via Skype. Would you like me to correct your grammatical errors?' I added a winky face emoji with a tongue to my sentence. He replied to me with emojis of appreciation and many kisses. I sent him back hundreds of kiss emojis. Then he sent me some photos of himself in Kurdish military clothing, the same that could recently be seen on television and in newspapers. My father looked cheery in all the photos. He would send new photos and I would ask for more. Then he sent me a new series of photos with female fighters. I was so impressed that I sent nothing but kisses for a few minutes. Those photos were the face of true fighters, without any manipulation or distortion by mass media or think tanks.

'Now I understand why you feel so cheerful. You're surrounded by nymphs,' I screamed at him.

He sent me some laughter emojis in response. They were at the foothill of the Şingal Mountains and protecting the famous rescue corridor for the Êzdîs. The photos had been taken in Şerfedîn's temple, the second most important holy site of the Êzdîs. My father was typing slowly, so I simultaneously sent photos to Jarik, my Kurdish teacher. From then on, my mobile phone was the most important piece of property in my life. I never let its battery go down and it was always next to me. It quickly informed me of any changes in Kobanî. My father worked there as a

---

* Yekîneyên Parastina Gel, People's Defense Units.

guard in the hospital. The battle was finished and on victory day I saw my father in a television report. He had a Kalashnikov on his shoulder and was talking with a journalist in fluent German. I heard my mother's shouts and footsteps running from the stairs. She came into my room without knocking on the door, leaped towards me in a panic and hugged me. I did not like to spoil her good mood and let her hug me. Right at that time, I got another message from my father and she saw his photo on my mobile screen. She could not understand the message text, but had no trouble interpreting the kiss emojis. She donned a sorrowful expression and told me, 'So that's why you were so carefree. You were in contact with him the whole time. Why didn't he send me a single message? Legally, I'm still his wife.'

'He was probably compelled to reset his cell phone, so he lost all his contact numbers.'

'Why didn't he lose your number?'

'He knows my mobile number by heart. Do you really remember his number?'

She fell silent and left the room. After two days he contacted me via Skype. The connection quality was perfect, in the middle of a military area. Hevalê Saro, it ought to have been via your satellite internet product."

"Do you know where the place was?"

"No idea. My father did not tell me about the location."

"Do you remember what that area looked like?"

"I remember a two-story building surrounded by a garden."

"Were there almond trees?"

"I only know two kinds of trees in the world, hawthorn and eggplant."

"Do you count eggplants as fruits in Germany?" Tewar asked contemptuously.

"No, they consider them organic dildos."

"What's a dildo?" Arjîn asked with a questioning look.

"A kind of sports equipment. Alright, come on, I'm not an expert in pornography or horticulture. I don't know what kind of trees they had."

"Was there a big container in front of the building?"

"Yes, I remember. A gray one."

Saro laughed and confirmed that he installed the satellite antenna there.

"Thank you for your illegal act of charity," I said.

"You're welcome. Now, keep talking, maybe some more of my charitable projects will come up in your story."

I wanted to continue, but suddenly Satyar told me, "Heval, please wait, you've upset me."

"Why?"

"*Yû puşd us aût ov da layn. Yû sed det îç ov us haz têkin de plês ov bilyons ov pîpil in dis bunkr. Wî sevin slîp bisayd îçudir layk a bundil ov spûnz. Ye, aûr nutz wil bî kruşd bitwîn us.*"

I laughed like everyone else who understood the southern Kurdish dialect. It took a long time before I could go on with my memories.

"From that day on my mother was depressed. I would pass beside her but she wouldn't notice me. I was waiting for her to ask for my father's mobile number. After a few days, Xemo said that my mother had called him. It was clear that she did not nag him the same way as before and did not complain about my behavior. After six months and twelve days, my father contacted me by video. He said he wanted to surprise me and turned on his camera. I saw behind him a tree in the background. I jumped up and screamed, 'Hawthorn!' Its branches were full of the yellow berries that I had dreamed of since childhood. Although there are some hawthorn trees in Frankfurt, they only bear red berries. He picked up some yellow ones and showed me. I asked him if they tasted the same as he always told me. The sweet-sour taste that tickles the palate. He had not eaten any of those hawthorn berries yet. I was driving to Raimund Street while I was talking with him. There were lots of hawthorn trees there. All the branches had bent over under the weight of the red berries. I got out of the car and said, 'Look, which bears more fruit, the trees there or here?'

I picked up a red berry, ate one, and asked him to tell me how his yellow ones tasted. He put a few yellow ones in his vest pocket and said, 'When I get back, we'll plant them in our yard.'

'And when will you return?'

'Once Şingal is freed. I would like to spend some nights in Şingal and then I will come back.'

Şingal was freed soon. I had been waiting a long time for that moment, but, strangely, I had not heard from my father. I called his mobile phone.

He answered. I congratulated him for liberating Şingal, but he answered in disappointment.

'What liberation? Not a single bullet was shot. Everything was just like a circus. Two years ago, Barzani handed Şingal over to the Turkish mercenaries, and they gave it back to Barzani as a corpse of a city, after having burnt it down and plundered it. It was all a theater show, with a script written and performed by the world's superpowers. Now, I know what the fundamental problem of the Kurds is and why they could not establish even a gimcrack state for themselves. By nature, the Kurds are unpredictable spoilsports. They have foiled the meticulous projects of the world powers. Daesh should have come here, massacred a large part of the Êzdîs, and then the superpowers would emerge to save the Êzdîs. They didn't expect that it would be a group, whom they have called terrorists for a long time, that would arrive there and prevent this genocide. My darling Kajîn, since the first day I have known this truth, but I did not tell you about it because I didn't want to burden you with greater sorrow. I knew that several Kurdish cities and villages had been sold out under a deal to present a real-life film in which the Kurds must be sacrificed, raped, and enslaved. All of this has happened, but not exactly as the producers and directors expected. The superpowers should really be angry with the Kurds, because they have not accepted playing the role of pathetic victims. I will send you some photos of myself. In these photos you will no longer see the beautiful little town that I came to forty-two years ago. Şingal was destroyed and the photos are more painful than those of Kobanî.

'Why, Xemo?'

'War happened in Kobanî, but Şingal was burned down without any fight. The Islamists set fire to the city only out of hatred.'

Xemo kept his promise and wanted to return to Germany, but there was no way to get out of Rojava or Şingal. The roads to Mosûl, Baghdad, and Damascus had been occupied by Daesh, while all the borders to Turkey were controlled by Turkey's army and the border with Başûr was dominated by Barzani's forces. He left the frontlines of the war to Qamîşlû. He was working in a hospital while waiting for an opportunity to get out of Rojava. I thought he was safe and that his return journey would not take more than a few weeks or months. After three months, I got a voice message via Viber from my father's mobile number. I opened it, but then I heard the voice of another man. He said, 'Probably you are the daughter of hevalê Şingal. Your father was injured by a blast today.' I immediately called him on Viber, but no one answered. I called via mobile and the same voice answered again, sadly. I asked anxiously what happened to my father. He replied, 'An Islamist suicide bomber detonated a truck in the middle of Qamîşlû and over two hundred and fifty civilians were killed. Your father was also there.' I screamed, 'What do you mean, is he hurt or dead?'

'Your father has also passed away.'

My heart was broken. My cell phone fell from my hand and slipped down the stairs. I fell to the ground. Up until three months ago, I had waited for this news in the back of my mind, but not in a hospital in a quiet city where the injured people were treated.

Some students gathered around me. One of them brought my broken mobile. I wanted to redial the number, but the phone wasn't working. Although the class was not over yet, I left the university. I had written the phone number in a notebook at home. My mother was there. I was so deeply sad that I didn't notice her upset face. She said, 'Jarik called you. He couldn't reach you via your mobile.'

She walked away. After a few seconds the home phone rang. My mother brought it to me. It was Jarik. The same person had sent him a message and he took the high-speed train from Stuttgart to Frankfurt immediately. My mother laid the phone in front of the TV, which was now turned off. Once she sat on the chair, she wept uncontrollably. I knew the depth of her grief only when Jarik entered the house. She put her head on his chest and wept. She found it impossible to cry in my embrace. When Jarik came in, she got an opportunity to lament. When she calmed down, she left Jarik alone and let him come toward me. I greeted him calmly and asked some questions in Kurdish. He looked at my mother and answered my questions in German. My mother said she understood Kurdish and asked him to speak Kurdish. I did not think my mother understood Kurdish well. My father only spoke Kurdish with her if the speech was supposed to be kept secret from others.

He stayed with us until the weekend. Although my mother had never seen Jarik before, he was her rock for that time. I needed him to return my father's corpse to Germany or at least participate in his funeral. I didn't think it would be too hard. But the statements of the PKK always triggered a new fit of rage within me. I had not been told as many lies in my life as I was told by the party. That trip ruined both my summer break and my whole temperament. I forgot about my father's death because of the lies and deception of your party's members. Only after a month, with the help of some Êzdî s, whom I had never met before, could I cross the Sêmalka border to Şingal and then proceed to Rojava."

Rûken interrupted me, "Wait a moment, heval." She looked at me and said, "Hevala Gulbehar needs to be relieved of duty. She has been keeping watch longer than she should. If someone does not want to hear this story any further, they can go stand guard."

It was amazing that nobody wanted to leave and all of them preferred to listen to my story instead of serving as a sentry. Then Rûken turned to Tewar and said, "You have to go to replace hevala Gulbehar."

"Why me? It's hevala Rûnahî's turn to go."

"She will keep watch later." Tewar got up reluctantly and went out. Before I continued, she came back and said the drone was gone.

"If so, we'd better enjoy some fresh air today. I am tired too. I have never told so much about myself throughout my life. This trip took only two months, but it tortured me like ten years in prison," I said.

"Although I would like to listen to your story until the end, if you have lost your desire to continue we can postpone it until next time," Rûken said.

We went out of the bunker. It was mild and foggy and some parts of the sky were covered with white clouds. I had a good feeling and went down to the spring. Today I told my life story in my father's language and even so well that everyone wanted to continue listening. I never thought I could speak so well in a language that, until four years ago, I considered to be basically a shared fictitious language between me and my father. Jarik would be proud of me, or maybe I should give him a pat on the back. I listen to the resonance of the Kurdish words in my head, which produce different feelings and meanings than German or English words for me. I sit in front of the spring and make a bowl with my palms in front of its cool water. I drink some handfuls of water and wash my face. The mountain opposite me sits in thick fog. You cannot see its peak. From behind, two hands come up and cover my eyes before I can do anything. I touch those hands with my fingertips. They are small, so the hiding player is surely a girl.

"Are you Arjîn?" She taps her finger on my forehead, which means that my answer is wrong.

"Dêrsîm?" She keeps knocking.

"Aha, Gulbehar."

"Right, but after three guesses. Do not open your eyes until I tell you."

"OK."

"Now you can open your eyes."

I open my eyes and see a bowl of ripe yellow hawthorns.

"Where did you find these? They weren't ripe until four days ago."

"I climbed up the tree. The upper branches bear yellow berries."

"Are they ripe?"

"I think so."

"Thank you, my darling Gulbehar."

"I hope you like them."

"Definitely."

I got the bowl. The yellow berries were big and shiny. I looked at the hawthorns for a few minutes and chose ten of them. Ten of the biggest, brightest, most yellow ones. I had a habit from my childhood that I just recalled subconsciously. When I was a child, I would collect ten of the best hawthorns, currants, or strawberries. I would eat five of them at first and the last five at the end. I would collect the best ten hawthorns at the top of the bowl. Why do I always collect two sets of five pieces? I had planted two rows of five hawthorn trees in the yard. Five of the best seedlings of the red hawthorn kernels from the Raimund Street trees and five of the yellow ones that my father had kept in his vest pocket. After Jarik told me about my father's death, I suddenly remembered those hawthorn kernels in my father's vest pocket. I called my father's number. Sêdar* answered. I asked him to keep for me everything that belonged to my father.

"I did."

"The small brown kernels too?"

"What kernels do you mean? I did not find anything like that. Your father had many things with him. But not something like that."

---

* The shadow of a tree.

"It must have been in one of his pockets. I also need his clothes. Please look for the kernels first and let me know when you find them."

After two hours, he sent me a photo of the seeds. Written underneath the photo in Kurdish was "these are supposed to be the hawthorn kernels." Later I found him and took all my father's belongings. We planted all twenty-one of those kernels in our yard and just as many red hawthorn kernels from Raimund Street. Fourteen kernels from the German hawthorns and only eight kernels from the Kurdish hawthorns grew up. I selected five of the strongest seedlings of each one and planted them around our yard. I did not have to worry about these seedlings anymore, because my mother paid much more attention to them than she ever paid me.

I take one of the biggest berries and put it on my tongue. It is round and rolls into my mouth. I push it with my tongue to my molars and press it. It is pleasantly soft and delicious. Its pasty juice flows on my tongue and releases a sweet and sour taste. Just like my father had told me. Or maybe I just wanted it to taste like that. I put a couple of berries in my mouth and push them with my tongue to my molars again, bite them with my teeth, and press them under my palate with my tongue. The berries release their flavor into my mouth and tickle my palate. These hawthorns have grown up under the hot sun, pure rain, and cold snow, and were fed from the natural soil, yet have breathed from an air full of gunpowder and TNT smoke. In the past eighty years, they have survived all the bombardments of the old propeller aircrafts and modern jets. The taste of these berries will not be forgotten until my death, or perhaps even longer, when I write the story of these hawthorn trees.

CHAPTER 5

THE WEATHER HAS been cold for the past two days. Befrîn does not roam outside anymore like before. Yesterday, after a little snowfall kept him outside, he crawled into the room under the blanket that we had hung over the entrance, did not go back out, and became an ever-present, but lazy member of our class. He was the only member of our class who could go anywhere and lie down any time he liked, behind the gas heater or on one of our laps. Last night, it had snowed again before they woke me up to stand guard. Nevertheless, the sky was cold and clear before dawn. It's a bad situation for us, but good for the roaming drone. Behind the hemp door of the women's room, on a piece of sponge cloth, I keep watch and listen for any suspicious sounds of danger. I'm hungry. Maybe that's because I was thinking about Rûken's speech for all of last night. Rûken was speaking radically about the current situation of women in today's world. About the oppressive attitudes against women in developed countries, the inequality in salaries between women and men for equal hours of work, and also the greed of capitalism in relation to this. I am very happy to hear such topics in these mountains, but her exaggeration concerning the situation of women in Rojava made me uncomfortable. Deliberately, or for lack of up-to-date information, she was distorting the actual facts in Rojava.

Legally, the situation for women was more dramatic in Rojava. There were laws enacted for women that are shameful to discuss. I would have liked to point out her lies, but she raised this topic at the end of the session. Her claims about women's equal rights and her radical suggestions on liberal female activities clearly contradicted laws enacted in Rojava. It is difficult for me not to care about her distortions, just as I can't ignore the painful cramps in my legs caused by the party's prohibition on different-gender comrades putting their legs on each other, based on a ridiculous and unwritten military law.

There is no relation between military rules and our living conditions and situation here. What country's military elsewhere in the world has to suffer these kinds of conditions? I massage my legs by hand and wait until the next guard has breakfast and takes my place. Finally, Satyar arrives, pulling up the hemp door and holding it until I get up and walk in the room. Why shouldn't this act be considered humiliating, but igniting cigarettes for each other is?

As soon as I pass the last step and enter into the corridor, the air becomes pleasantly warm. Rûken is drinking tea in the kitchen. The tripod for the pan lay next to the gas stove. With her hands, Dêrsîm takes the two sides of separated greenhouse film in which to put the dough. She rolls it once to swaddle the dough. Zenar kneads it with his feet. I look at Rûken and tell her, "Heval, why didn't you let me bake the bread? Is that forbidden for me?"

"Why would that work be forbidden?"

"No idea. I've been here for thirty-seven days, but I have yet to engage in bread baking."

"I didn't think you were interested in it. Then do the bread baking today."

"Not today. Today, I would like to quarrel with you."

"Why, because of the bread baking?"

"No, because of your praise of the women's situation in Rojava yesterday. I have had other experiences there."

"Why didn't you say anything yesterday?"

"You discussed it at the end of the session and our comrades wanted to have dinner."

"Ok, then have a full breakfast to build up your strength, because I do not give up easily."

I calmly eat the lentil soup with a loaf of stale bread. Dêrsîm opens the rolled plastic sheet and sprinkles some flour on it. She cuts out a piece of dough, rolls it with both hands, turns it into a dough ball, and puts the first ball on a plastic sheet. She will make several balls and place them in a neat row on the plastic sheet. In the meantime, Zinar ignites the gas stove, places the tripod on the flame, then puts a big metal dish on it.

I would like to stay here and watch the bread-baking process, but all the comrades had gathered in the meantime and were waiting for me in the women's room, sitting cross-legged as usual. It is amazing that some comrades can sit cross-legged and upright in discussion for five hours. These long rounds of discussions are hard to bear anyway, even sitting on a chair or sofa. I had seen sessions in Rojava that lasted more than ten hours. It was alleged that they were discussing until everyone could agree on a decision. But, in my experience, it takes so long for the opponents to lose their patience, capitulate, and accept the decisions. Not everyone can withstand such marathon discussions. You have to be trained not to eat food, drink water, or even go to the toilet for the whole day. I couldn't sit cross-legged in my yoga exercises for a single hour while not concentrating on anything. In the meantime, however, I practiced and became able to run a marathon.

There is a place next to Hunger. I sit down there and Befrîn is the first thing that I notice. He lays on Arjîn's lap and looks at me with his yellow and blue eyes, which look like two glass balls in the snow. I noticed something new. One of his eyes is the same as Arjîn's amber eyes. Arjîn lets him go and he runs to me and jumps on my lap. His fur is soft and silky. I stroke his whole body with my fingertips, put my hand on his soft, pink mouth and pull my fingertips from his ears toward his wooly tail. His body is white, soft, and delicate.

Rûken looks at me and says, "Before we continue yesterday's discussion, hevala Jînçin wants to tell us an idea she has about it. She has traveled to Rojava twice before and had some experiences there that she would like to share with us. I guess some negative experiences. Please, heval."

"If I were to only speak of my experiences and observations, I would say there are more positive points than negative ones. But I have found out, or perhaps discovered, some threatening or even frightening facts that are in contradiction with the party's claims. We cannot claim to represent the liberation and equality of women on the one hand, yet enact totally anti-woman laws on the other."

"Can you give us specific examples?" asked Rûken.

"Sure. For example, in the Rojava constitution, women are not allowed to marry without their guardians' permission."

"What? That's impossible," Rûken said with dejected eyes.

"But it is so. I have read the translation of the paragraph myself."

"Heval, it is not true. Maybe the members of the ENKS* fooled you."

"Do I look like someone that gets fooled so easily? For ten days, I struggled to eliminate this paragraph. In vain, and it remained in the constitution."

Rûken bit her lip in anger, turned to Saro and asked him, "Hevalê Saro, is it true?"

"Yes, unfortunately."

"Then why are we fighting at all? So many comrades have lost their precious lives for nothing? Then we were fooled by our own comrades. Women are not allowed to marry without their guardians' permission? I spit on the face of all the guardians and party members who enacted such laws. We are living here like Stone-Age humanoids and our comrades in the cities sit on the sofas and issue these shameful laws."

She screamed out of sheer anger.

"Why did you hide it from me? Maybe you find these laws normal? Or what?"

"No, heval. Just like you and almost all the other comrades, I don't accept this shameful paragraph of the laws. But we had no choice."

"If we go whichever way the wind is blowing, then the imperialists will embarrass us by kissing our asses. What is the meaning of our struggle if we are willing to humiliate ourselves by accepting such toxic ideas? Of course, the world powers want to thwart our plans and sink our movement into the shit. We are not politicians or lobbyists, but libertarian fighters. We do not fight for profit, but for our ideas. Then you tell me straight to my face that you were forced to swallow it. You may be willing to let the fanatics bring you to your knees, but I don't give a damn about the coalition's humiliating policies and the opportunism of our party."

She was red with anger and seemed ready to pull out Saro's eyes with her claws, but Saro listened quietly until her anger subsided. Then he said, "At that time, I showed my opposition just like you are doing. But then I had to put myself in their position. What alternative would have remained for them? Something even worse was possible. Either this

* Referring to the Kurdish National Council [*Encûmena Niştimanî ya Kurdî li Sûriyê*], one of the few right-wing parties in Rojava.

proposal would be accepted, or the entire constitution would have to be put to a vote. And what could have happened then. There are many forces that the reactionaries would like to incite against us."

"That's obvious. With this strategy we will fall on our faces. It makes us look ridiculous when we fight on the front line with imperialist forces over a supposedly brighter future. A bird in the hand is worth two in the bush. Once they've used us for their purposes, they will let any well-armed army destroy us."

"But this can only be avoided if we survive, win people over to our side, and put our plans into action. The global superpowers know our ideals and want to destroy them."

Saro turned his face to me and said, "I know that when you were in Germany you certainly heard a lot about European aid for the reconstruction of Kobanî. Can you guess how much money Europe sent to Kobanî?"

"They were talking about huge sums, but I can't remember how much they sent. They always make mountains out of molehills in the media."

"You can safely say that the mountain gave birth to a mouse. For your information, less than four million dollars. For the reconstruction of a city that they destroyed with their bombs. Some of our comrades paid more out of their own pockets than all donors from abroad."

"Do you mean our sympathizers?" Rûken asked.

"No, I mean our comrades."

"And we have comrades who have four million dollars to give away?"

Before Saro could give an evasive answer, I spoke up.

"That benevolent comrade must have been hevalê Saro himself."

"Did he have four million dollars? Five years ago, he had only lice in his pocket," Rûken said to me with a vague smile.

"You've underestimated hevalê Saro. He was once a capitalist."

"Really? Comradeship cannot be like that, hevalê capitalist. Why didn't you tell me all those ten months then? Maybe you were afraid that I wanted to borrow money from you." Rûken asked with a serious tone.

"No heval, you said the reason before. That time, I only had lice in my pocket. Only when I returned to Silêmanî did I have access to some of my accounts again.

"I took pity on him and gave him my own radio," Rûken said seriously to me.

She turned back to Saro and spoke as if we were the only three people present in that room.

"Heval, you have disappointed me. Hevala Jînçin, a newcomer, knows you better than me. Even the bourgeois should not be so faithless. What else have you hidden from me? Did you go to Mecca, hevalê hajji?"

"To be honest, I traveled to Mecca too, but not as a hajji, as a tourist."

"Then you're a hajji, nevertheless. What else have you done, hevalê hajji capitalist?

"No, I am not hajji. Don't call me a hajji."

"Why not? You visited Mecca and Medina."

"That's not enough to become a hajji. I didn't throw stones at Satan. . . ."

Saro was shocked by his own words and turned to Rûnahî.

"Pardon, heval. I neglected your presence."

"No problem, heval. That is true; I am a Êzdî, but I do not expect you to erase this word from your memory for me. Hevala Jînçin has already used this word herself."

Rûnahî continued. "Your civilian life surprises me. Now I understand how right hevala Jînçin was. I would like to know your previous life story."

I immediately picked up on her comment and said, "Yes, heval. It is your time. You have to tell us your life story."

"But you did not finish your own story."

"Nevertheless, I have told a lot about myself. Who wants to hear hevalê Saro's story?"

Everyone followed me and raised up both of their hands, except Tewar and hevalê Ferhad. I said, "For seven months, hevalê Saro was forced to live like a prisoner in one of the party's caves. Tell your comrades about it."

Saro glanced at his cigarette box, grinned at me, and addressed Rûnahî, "Before one of my so-called comrades forced me to leave my civilian life, I was in a good financial situation. So, I could support the activities of the party financially. That was good for me and also for the party. It was satisfying for me that I could give away my wealth for a just cause, but one of our enemies, who has hid himself amongst us as one of our comrades until today, deliberately put me in jeopardy and ruined one of the party's largest sources of ever-flowing income. I had to flee from

Iran immediately. Many of my bank accounts were blocked and my sister had to follow me, without time to prepare. Manî and some other fools ruined my life and all my financial resources. They set fire to everything that I had packed up a short time before I left Iran. All my documents, credit cards, check books, even the personal items that I gladly hauled around the mountains with me for a hundred years. A rosary from an old woman who saved my life when I was only a six-day-old baby and almost starved to death, alone at home. At that time, my parents were arrested and the reckless bombardment campaign of the Islamic government of Iran drove civilians out of Sine. If that woman, who was only a distant relative of my father, had not looked for me and fed me with moldy bread and tea, I would not be here to tell you my life story. I only had that rosary as a souvenir from that old woman, but some fools threw it into the fire with all my personal things. I even saw them set a big fire and throw something in it, but I did not think they would do such a shameful thing. Only when they threw my briefcase into the fire did I realize that part of my life was burning before my eyes.

I ran to the fire, but they didn't even let me save those things that hadn't been burned yet. They said it was an order from the party. Who had given that order? That scoundrel who took credit for everything I did for the party as his own work.

Then they wanted to send me to military training. I screamed, 'It would be better not to arm me, otherwise my first work will be killing you three bastards.' I refused to stay with the party and wanted to return to one of the cities of Başûr. I didn't listen to their words and when I wanted to leave there with my sister, one of them told me some comrades from above wanted to see me. We would have thought they meant the hevalên in the Leadership Council, but they just wanted to send me up a frozen mountain to fix their broken generator. A route that would have taken a few hours to travel in the summer took more than three days in the heavy blizzards. Without food or warm clothes. All four travelers almost froze to death. I fainted when I arrived there. Because of the coldness, the over-three-thousand-meter altitude, and more than anything the mental frustration, my brain switched off and I lost my memory. I don't even know how long this memory loss lasted, but after I regained consciousness the situation had not improved.

I had to live for seven months in a handmade cave which was not yet finished. An early winter arrived suddenly and the comrades were surprised by the unexpected coldness and snowstorms. In the cave, there was no toilet and food was scarce, but I still had to work as a repairman. My new job caused me a lot of stress, but it had an important advantage. Because of my work as a general fixer, I got an additional undershirt, with which I could wash my body. This was my only opportunity to clean myself under those circumstances throughout the seven months. For the last two months, we did not have any food except bulgur. We would cook the bulgur with tomato paste, which had expired more than eight years prior and had turned black. Yet, that tomato paste ended up being our only luxury item.

'What do we have for lunch today, heval? Bulgur with two spoons of tomato paste?'

'No heval, bulgur with three spoons of tomato paste.'

'Hooray.'

I didn't participate in any real war, but in that cave I came close to killing somebody by myself, due to a fifteen-meter-high antenna that I had made from a steel tow rope for our radio. I had fastened the end of the tow rope to the cast iron pipe that was attached to the wall and floor of the cave. One night I was awoken by an incredibly loud bang. A light flashed so brightly in the cave that I could not see anything for a few minutes. At the same time as the bang I heard a loud scream. Once I was able to look around, I went to the source of the bang and the scream. Lightning had hit the tow rope outside and the electrical current had transferred through the cables into the cave and hit a comrade who was sleeping next to the iron pipe. Usually, I slept in that location, with some distance between me and the iron pipe. I don't know why all of us comrades liked to sleep there. I had slept next to the victim, but at the moment of the lightning strike our bodies must have been separated from each other. I switched on my lighter and looked at him. He was unconscious and his body was livid. The lightning thawed the iron pipe and this reduced the electrical current. However, it was still a mystery to me how this comrade survived and could walk again after three months. With this lightning accident all our electrical appliances, such as the radio, TV, and the generator, were broken and I, hevalê fixer, had to fix everything.

So, what tools did we have? A hammer and a kitchen knife. Two comrades went over the mountain toward the main warehouse to get the necessary spare parts for the defective equipment. There was also one modern tool in the cave that I forgot about: a turbo lighter. I was melting the tin from defective equipment and welding the parts with it. All the defective devices were fixed again and as a reward I was exempt from keeping watch. Thereafter, I took care of the equipment and waited impatiently for spring, or better to say for summer. I wanted to embrace civilization immediately. Presumably there were no obstacles ahead for me, except snow and coldness. Then I got sick. It started with the flu and got progressively worse. Comrades said that during the last phase of my illness I was unconscious for three days and nights. When I returned to consciousness, I saw a syringe in my arm, fastened with thread. The syringe was attached to a plastic tube adjoined to a bottle of fluid, a kind of serum, that hung over my head. I asked the commander what the bottle contained.

'Water, sugar, salt and citric acid.'"

Everyone laughed. Hevala Gulbehar got goosebumps and her face turned pale. Saro continued.

"I shouted, 'What? We disinfect the toilet with that and you have this shit injected in my veins?'

'You should appreciate me, we saved your life.'

'No, you've ruined my life.'

I wanted to get up, but I had no strength and lost consciousness again. When I regained consciousness, I saw three unfamiliar faces. One seemed to be a nurse. He had a blood pressure monitor. They had been sent from above. This time they really were from the party's executive committee and not from the mountaintop. They asked me what problems I had and why I wanted to leave the party. I asked for a notebook and wrote over fifty complaints and suggestions. They asked me to go with them to the party's executive committee. I said I was sick and would visit there myself as soon as I felt well enough. They asked what they could do for me. I asked only that these idiots leave me alone. They left and told the executive committee that I am a different type of character. Rarely would they have seen someone who writes his complaints or suggestions down in such detail on paper. After they had left, nobody tormented me and I could really have my peace. After ten days, I had gained enough strength and set off with a comrade toward the executive committee. He wanted to accompany me there. I could only get rid of him when I shouted at him with all my might. The comrades of the executive committee had settled in a valley. They tried to persuade me to stay in the party. They were giving me various suggestions, but I refused all of them. I did not want to work in public relations or waste my time in the party's financial or political sectors. There was no suggestion that I join the military activities. I roamed around there for a few months and stayed with my first decision. Until, that is, I met hevalê Hîwa and he convinced me to stay with them."

"Did you feel free to leave them? I assume from your words that they compelled you to stay there. Maybe not directly, but indirectly at least." I asked Saro biasedly.

"I did not have that feeling. Their attempts were more for compensation. They offered me different suggestions and gave me enough time to think about it. Until I met hevalê Hîwa. He knew my story and had told the party about the help I had given them. For example, that I had bought all the requirements for two hundred guerillas and handed it over to the comrades of Jasûsan Mountain."

"What kind of requirements do you mean?" Rûken asked.

"Military clothes, shoes, tents, sleeping bags."

"So, you turned me into the head black sheep with those yellow Adidas shoes?"

"Were you in the Jasûsan Mountains at that time?"

"No, but someone gave me a pair of those shoes as a present."

"Who?"

"My biggest enemy. They were calling me hevala Jasûsan until some months ago. There is no harmony between Adidas shoes and lentil soup. And why the yellow ones? Were there any other colors?"

Laughter burst out, making Befrîn wake up from his sleep. He started meowing anxiously and went down from my lap. He wanted to go out from the room to sleep behind the men's room heater undisturbed, but I caught him and put him on my lap again. I stroked his forehead until he shut his eyes. Everybody remained silent until I asked Saro a question.

"Why doesn't the party throw out those people?"

"These people have the ability to wear different masks. They can camouflage their faces better than us against drones. If I hadn't met Hîwa, I would have cut all my connections with the party."

"Is hevalê Hîwa from your hometown?"

"Yes."

"That's why . . . the people of Sine stick together like bees."

"No, not necessarily. Manî is also from Sine. Some believe that they will change over time. What do you think, hevala Rûken? Can we change them?"

"Yes we can change them. But that's not the main question. We have to ask ourselves how much time and energy is needed to change these opportunists, psychopaths, and rascals. And how devastating they are to our movement, how much they deviate us from our goals, and to what degree they can be exploited by our enemies. There were people like Hogir in the party. We could feel the negative effects he caused in the party after more than thirty years. Thousands of people have become our enemies because of their crimes. I do not believe that they were all seduced by the propaganda of the Turkish state. We have made many mistakes and constantly commit new ones. The people like Manî do not belong here. They have to be kept in a mental hospital. We do not have such facilities, so we have to keep them away from ourselves."

"I agree with your suggestion, but I also see other problems. First: it is not easy to prove that the harm they cause outweighs the advantages they bring. One can only realize their true intentions, which are careerism and greed for power, when it is already too late. And second: there is a lack of instruments with which to confront such people."

"No heval, the main problem I see is the pragmatism of the PKK. How could Hogir progress upward and promptly become the chief military commander of the party? Why didn't the party do anything when he was forcibly recruiting children into the guerrilla forces and executing those who opposed him as traitors and enemies of the Kurds? What the eye does not see, the heart does not grieve over. At that time, the PKK allowed everything because, according to the pragmatist policies of the party, he was performing his duty in the best way possible. And that's why someone like Manî can stay in the party and climb the party ladder quietly. I have not seen this guy yet, but I dislike him more than any of the recognized criminals in the world," I said, taking a position against Saro's words.

"And how do you know that my claims about him are true?"

"You wouldn't have dared to talk so directly if your story about this guy had not been true. Every party that fails to remove such people necessarily becomes an accomplice to their crimes. You cannot give them an opportunity and wait until they sink themselves into the shit and bring down others with their activities. I see it as putting all the blame on just a few people who are demoted overnight from a beloved hero to a hated traitor. Paradise and the Peri. . . . ,"* I said, without thinking of the consequences of my words or possible opposition from others.

"Yeah, you're right. The PKK has often made such mistakes. But in my opinion, you are making the same mistake. Neither the history of the Kurds nor of the PKK begins with the foundation of this party. Before this incident, there was a long history of oppression. The Turkish people wanted to destroy the Kurds completely and assimilate them into the Turkish nation. I purposely say the Turkish people and not the Turkish government. Unlike in Iran, Iraq, and Syria, the Kurds were assimilated through the fascist ideas of the Turkish people. The Arab and Iranian governments have enforced many policies of inhuman extermination and assimilation against the Kurds, but as a people, the Arab and Persian nations didn't oppose us. Someone was telling me why he decided to fight against the Turks. A comrade corrected him and said, 'You mean the Turkish government.' He stuck to his words and said, 'No, against the Turks.' I asked him why and he told me something that I hear over and over again. He said that one day, when he was nine, they had guests. They were talking with each other in Kurdish as quietly as possible. Suddenly there was banging on the apartment door. The door was broken open and they saw behind it a skinny fifteen-year-old boy with his mother and sister. He said that the boy attacked them and even beat his father, who

---

* *Peri* means angel in Kurdish; she, who is expelled from heaven on charges of impurity, tries to get permission to return there by donating holy gifts. The last drops of blood shed by a hero in a battle with a tyrant and then the last moans of a virgin dying in the arms of her leper lover are not enough to remove her impurity. She succeeds to return only when she gives the tears to a repentant criminal to the Gatekeeper of Heaven.

was a boxer. His father could have killed him with a single punch, but for the future of his children and their guests, he had to swallow his anger. They were all beaten and had to wait with bleeding noses until he got tired and left, but he was repeatedly provoked to continue by his family. And this was not an isolated incident, hevala Jîncin. It was a common facet of life for the Kurdish people in Turkey."

Saro turned to hevalê Ferhad.

"Heval, haven't you experienced something similar yourself?"

A trace of deep and bitter sadness came over his face. After a long silence, he spoke, dully and quietly.

"Much worse, heval."

Saro continued.

"The PKK emerged during this period of Kurdish history and the unarmed members of this party have experienced savage torture and murder in the prisons of Turkey. The extent of the torturers' savagery in the Turkish prisons, especially in Amed, stands outside of any notion of humanity. This violence has produced counterviolence. That's dialectic. Cause and effect are not separated from each other and everything produces its antithesis against itself. In the end, it took a long time for the PKK to learn the hard way that you cannot escape from a spiral of violence with more violence, nor can you escape from a deadlock of hatred through revenge.

Until recently, I hated Manî, but I don't want to judge him harshly anymore. Now I see things differently. His father was a mullah. His mother had to live with someone who was not in good financial standing yet had two other wives. Being a mullah's son is humiliating in Sine anyway. There was a joke in Sine that sums up Manî's life better than any mental analysis. The joke goes: someone asks the daughter of the Friday prayer mullah in Sine, 'What is your father's profession?' She answers, 'My father has a black belt in Quran studies.'"

All the comrades laughed, but the joke made me think deeply about something. When I started learning Kurdish, I knew some unique characteristics of Kurdish society. One of them is the use of jokes. Jokes serve different functions in Kurdistan than in other cultures. Even in vulgar and sexual jokes there is some politics in the background. I remember a joke that sounded almost the same as Saro's, but from the reverse perspective. A boy says to his father, "Dad, every day, when you go out, the Friday prayer mullah sneaks in to see mom." The father answers, surprised, "Really?" But then he thinks and says, "God will avenge us." The boy gets older and tells his father again, "Hey dad, that bastard comes every day, takes my mother to another room and locks the door."

"Really?"

Again he thinks and says, "God will avenge us."

One day, while the mullah was preaching to the people on top of a stage, the boy sneakily put a bottle of alcohol in his pocket, then pushed the mullah from the stage to the ground. The mullah died and was disgraced when the people found the bottle in his pocket. The father came home happily and said, "Did you see, son? God has mercifully avenged us!"

The boy answers, "Had I left the matter to you and God, he would have fucked my mother to death."

Listening to Saro talk about his decision to go to Rojava, I think of other Kurdish jokes that I have heard and considered to be perverse or sexist. One day a boy sees a male donkey and asks his mother, "Mommy, what is that black thing?"

"It's a donkey."

"No, the long black thing under its stomach."

"That's nothing."

A week later, the boy sees the donkey and this time asks his father and gets an answer.

"That's the donkey's dick."

"But mom said it's nothing."

"Yeah boy, it's nothing for your mother."

I laugh and everybody turns to me.

"Pardon, Befrîn tickled me with his tongue."

I stroke the cat's head while he looks at me with his bicolored eyes. While I was thinking about the jokes, Saro was retelling us how he would be sent to Rojava to help with the construction process.

He looked at Befrîn with a smile and continued, "After eighteen months away from civil life, I was pleased to be back in a city, even in Kobanî, which had been receiving wide coverage on the radio and television. The city was recently liberated and many people from different countries went there, many of them to visit the city and others to help with the reconstruction process. The latter group consisted of Kurds from other parts of Kurdistan or left internationalists. They had already done a great job in a small amount of time. Many streets had been cleared, but due to a lack of necessary construction machines they were not yet covered with asphalt. A large amount of wartime debris from buildings had been cleared away and was used to build the substructure of new streets and roads. I could not do anything there and asked them to send me to Hesekê. I had heard about the big factories in that region. Most of them were controlled by Daesh. After a while, we freed those factories from Daesh control. Syria's largest spinning mill factory, a steel factory, and a nonalcoholic beverage factory. Within a year, we managed to get these factories operational and created over eleven thousand job opportunities, but then I had to leave this job and. . . ."

"Stop, heval," I said, and everyone looked at me. I looked at Saro and asked him a question.

"Heval, you conquered these big factories, renovated them, then made over eleven thousand jobs and you want to pass over all of this in a few sentences? People don't even skip over the painting of their apartments like that. I don't know about other comrades, but I want to hear how you did it and whether the coalition or other organizations or groups helped you and, if so, to what extent?"

I turned my gaze to Rûken and asked her, "What do you think about it?"

"You're right. I also want to hear. That's our current history and it's still going on."

"Okay, but let's have a cigarette break first."

"A good proposal. Then we can listen again with better concentration," Gulbehar replied.

We left the women's room. The smokers brought glasses of tea out from the kitchen and everyone went somewhere in the corridor. Arjîn and I stayed with Dêrsîm and Zinar in the kitchen. Although Arjîn did not smoke, she preferred to drink very dark tea. I asked her, "Didn't you realize that hevalê Saro deliberately skipped over many important parts of his story?"

"That's obvious. He is modest, but with great authority."

"In my mind, I think of hevala Rojano possessing these two traits. She is also a proud, modest woman."

"Yes, but there is a big difference between these two comrades."

"What would that be?"

"Hevala Rojano resolves the problems that exist, but hevalê Saro looks for the problems that remain invisible to others."

I was compelled to lift my tea with a smile to indicate my agreement. I drank the last sip of my tea after Arjîn had finished her sugar-bombed black tea. We went back into our multifunction room. Saro had sat down in another corner and waited until all the comrades had gathered. He asked me, "What do you want to know, heval?"

"I would like to hear the story in as much detail as possible. You certainly understand what I mean, if you do not intend to skip over some events."

"Ok, I will tell the story in my own way and you can interrupt me at any time and ask me anything that you'd like. The first factory we wanted to take away from Daesh was Syria's largest spinning mill factory. It was located on the exit road of Şedadî. Daesh had entered the factory from that side. It had been occupied by Daesh for six months. I gathered two battalions and attacked them. They fled from the back wall of the factory. Behind the wall, the terrain was about six meters lower than the factory. In the part where Daesh escaped, the river had become as wide as a lake. One could notice how flooded the Xabûr river had become at certain points. Syrian army troops were positioned in the vicinity. There was less than three hundred meters between the Daesh escape corridor and their position.

Syrian troops saw Daesh forces and might have thought they could destroy or maybe arrest them. They did not expect other Daesh forces to ambush from the other side of the river. The other side of the bank was fifteen meters higher than the riverbed. The Syrian forces pursued them on this marshy terrain. Various vehicles and about three hundred soldiers drove away the militants, who fled without hesitation. The Daesh forces on the other side waited until all of the Syrian troops had fallen into the trap. Then they shot them from different sides. I never imagined something like that. It reminded me of Russian hunting, where hundreds of hunters surround some wild boar or rabbit. They look like those hunters who sit comfortably on their saddles or run without stress and shoot with full concentration. We were eavesdropping on the Daesh forces on the radio. They were betting amongst themselves. I don't mean with money. For example, one said, 'Can you shoot the left leg of that redhead?' The other replied, 'I can even shoot his right ear.' The situation of the Syrian troops was catastrophic. If we had not intervened, everyone would have been brutally murdered. We attacked the Daesh forces and they had to flee."

"How many Daesh forces were involved in this battle?" I wanted to know.

"You cannot call it a battle. Hunting would be a better term. I do not know how many there were, but when we reached the other side of the river, I had the impression from the footsteps that there were over seven hundred people. We rescued the Syrian forces, but they set fire to our cotton warehouse as a token of appreciation. We took that warehouse after a fierce fight with Daesh because the spinning mill factories would be shut down without the cotton. Only after thirteen days did we succeed in setting up the factory, but there was not enough cotton in the warehouse. There were really only two ways to get the factory working. Either close the factory and concentrate on cotton cultivation or attack Daesh and capture the large cotton warehouse under their control. We decided to perform both options simultaneously. Quickly, we provided the seeds and fertilizer to the local farmers. It was really hard to organize the cultivation process. In Syria, cotton must be irrigated between ten and twelve times. That needs diesel, electricity, and a lot of logistical and organizational work. In the end, we harvested thirty thousand tons of cotton. Meanwhile, we attacked the warehouse that was under Daesh control. It was on the outskirts of Dêrezûr. A huge warehouse. Only clean cotton from the ginning factory was stored there, which could no longer be processed in the spinning mill. The two factories were linked to the nation's central railway line by a rail line of over a hundred kilometers. In other words, over one hundred kilometers of railway line had been built specifically for transferring the products of these factories.

After we took that huge warehouse from Daesh, the government sent some saboteurs disguised as traders. They set the warehouse on fire. When cotton ignites, it is almost impossible to extinguish the resulting fire. The cotton burned and the warehouses were badly damaged. After we found out that the government was behind this sabotage, we attacked the ginning factory and took it from the state forces. After a month, Russian forces bombarded the factory. Fortunately, there was only a small group of people in the factory and they were scattered throughout, so we did not suffer huge human losses. Only a few buildings were destroyed. But after this air attack, the factory was looted by the people. They couldn't take the giant Brazilian cotton gin, but two big generators, which produced the power for the factory, had been stolen. That was a disaster for us. We could not buy new or secondhand ones anywhere. We had to pick up six defective generators from different cities, disassemble them and take apart some parts to be able to assemble the two generators."

"Did you have a technician who was familiar with such equipment?" I asked.

"No."

"And who repaired the generators? Was it you, hevalê generator-fixer?"

"Yes. After some months we were able to eliminate the damage and redevelop the destroyed elements. The machines in this ginning factory were old, so they needed more manpower than the spinning mill. In the ginning factory, the harvested cotton was separated from the cotton seeds and shells, then cleaned and fluffed by air pressure. Then the white cotton was pressed and converted into cube-shaped two-hundred-kilogram boxes. When this factory was under state control, a part of its product was delivered to the weaving factory and the remainder sent by freight train to Heleb and Damascus. First, I have to tell you something. The two factories and also the warehouses were built in three corners of the outskirts of the city. There was a good reason for that. The harvests could be sent directly to the ginning factory located on the western side, without having to be transported through the city. There were two large warehouses in the factory: one for the harvested cotton and the other for the cube boxes. These boxes were delivered by truck through roads on the outskirts to the weaving factory and maintained within large warehouses.

These well-designed institutions looked like state public services at first glance, but in reality they were just a net for stealing from farmers and workers. The cotton was bought for about twenty cents per kilogram from the farmers, while the cotton price in the US at the same time was three dollars per kilogram. The price of threads in the spinning mill was between one and one and a half dollars per kilogram, while they were exporting one kilogram of threads between ten to fifteen dollars. When we found out this information, we decided to establish a weaving factory.

There were some famous weaving factories in Heleb. The largest and most famous factory had been robbed by the Turkish government previously. The Turkish secret service had killed the weaving factory owner with their mercenaries, the Al-Nusra Front, and drove away his family, then neatly packed away all the machines and had them sent out of Heleb. They wanted to transfer the machines to Turkey, but the city of Minbic was besieged. They had tried several times to take them out of the city under the guise of humanitarian aid, claiming the presence of injured or killed people, but they failed because our comrades had already set up many checkpoints. Before we could liberate the city of Minbic, they hid all the machines under a half-made building and then completed the building. We found this hiding place, brought out the machines, and transferred them to Hesekê."

"How could you find the hiding place?" I interrupted Saro.

"An arrested Daesh member revealed it and told us the story."

"Did you publish this confession?"

"No."

"Why not?"

"What would it bring us? Everyone knew that Turkey was in cahoots with those petty thieves. Turkey has committed much worse crimes. In my experience, the Turkish government has done more acts of sabotage than all of the jihadists, at least in Hesekê and the surrounding area. Because Turkey knows how a state works and how it can be paralyzed. There are some materials that are more important for construction and renovation of substructures, such as copper, aluminum, a special type of iron, and raw materials for cement factories. At the beginning of the Syrian war, Turkey commissioned some traders to evacuate these materials out of Syria. These materials were being bought at three times the global average for transfer to Turkey. So the people, whether out of greed or hunger, destroyed everything to get some kilograms of these materials. Lads and juveniles were climbing the power poles, cracking the transformers, and dropping them on the ground. For a few kilograms of copper, they would crack open transformers. When I arrived in Hesekê, the situation was catastrophic. The high and medium voltage lines, power transformation stations, and distribution pumps for drinking water had been broken. There was nothing on the ground, even the doors and the windows of the state buildings had been looted. We wanted to buy the missing things, but no one would sell them to us. We decided to make the missing things and repair those devices which had been cracked, but there was no copper to buy. Until then, I didn't know that independent traders in the free market couldn't buy such things. The state's approach towards these materials is the same as with gold: they are traded under state preconditions. States know that if a party does not remedy these damages in a few years, the people will protest against it and say if they are unable to solve the problems, they should go away and let the Syrian government or another state come in and provide the basic requirements. It was really a difficult time that we had to pass through.

We found those machines that Turkey had stolen and brought them to Hesekê for installation. They were state-of-the-art machines for weaving and knitting, unique throughout the Middle East. These kinds of automated machines are highly sensitive and only operate under certain conditions. Therefore, we had to build an exclusive hall for these machines in the weaving factory. The weaving factory was modernized in 2013. The new machines were much smaller, so much of the factory remained empty. A wall separated this part from the rest of the factory hall. Daesh had manufactured armored vehicles in this area during their occupation. The site was very suitable for its purpose. There were several thick layers of roof over the hall and its function and structure prevented it from being discovered by the reconnaissance planes and protected it from any suspicion. I left the hall empty. We did all the necessary restructuring and set up a standard room for weaving where humidity and light could be controlled. We got the machines running, but then they relocated me."

"Why? Who moved you after so much work?" Rûken asked in amazement.

"I had two supervisors. One agreed with my projects. He did not position himself against me in the sittings, but the other was against everything I did. He was very parochial. He thought it was total nonsense to expend our time and energy on things that could be destroyed by bombardment in a few seconds or taken by force. He confused economic affairs with logistics work. The party had great faith in him because he was not a corrupt person. The party didn't understand that the harm caused by ignorance can be more than that caused by corruption. At a meeting, he claimed that I had wasted a huge sum of the party's money because of my projects, even though the party had not given me any money for these projects, and everyone knew that some comrades had financed the projects from their own pockets."

I didn't let Saro finish his words and asked angrily, "You financed these projects yourself. Maybe the other comrades here see your self-deprecation as a kind of modesty, but I see it as self-censorship and a denial of the truth. I listen to you with full concentration to better know the problems and deficiencies of the party, but you are telling us lies. Please tell us your story factually and without false modesty. Did you design and finance these projects or did the party ask you to do it?"

"Hevala Jînçin, all these projects and many others were my own initiative, but could not ever be performed without the help of other comrades. It is true that I invested some money in these projects as a donation, but other comrades paid for these projects with their lives. I'm not talking about my supervisors. One of them did support me, but the greatest help came from other comrades, especially from hevalê Rojhat.[*] He knew me and knew how important my project was, so he collected two battalions from the YPG and Asayîş and put them at my disposal to conquer the factories."

"So, you commanded those forces?"

"Not completely. As someone from the Economic Committee, I didn't participate in the battles, but I organized the actions by radio with hevalê Rojhat and the three other commanders he had given command. There were also female comrades who supported these projects.

One day, when I came out of a financial meeting, disappointed and emptyhanded, a female comrade from Bakûr followed me and asked me to describe the project in detail. I explained what I needed another battalion for. Two kilometers away from the weaving factory, there was a high hill, Kewkeb, where the telecommunication towers of the state were installed. Evidently, there must have been an underground state garrison deep in the foothill. Unfortunately, I had never managed to visit it. That hill was important to us for other reasons. An attack on the weaving factory was easily possible from there at any time, so we needed experienced military personnel to guard the hill. That comrade listened to me attentively and, in the end, she promised to send me a

* The day has come.

battalion of her comrades to help. Some groups arrived there the next day. I felt a sense of relief the moment I saw them. They were highly motivated and even helped us with the general work of the factory. Those troops were a big help in maintaining safety and order, but my opposing supervisor wanted to pull them out of the factory. One day, he called the commander and ordered her to return the troops to the military base, but hevala Rûgeş* opposed his order and said, 'The reverse is the case. We are doing something very logical here.'

'Surely you don't want to keep our troops busy with such games in a time of war, do you?'

'Nobody is playing here. Four thousand people are working here and supporting their families.'

'But what advantages does it have for the party?'

'If you do not know, the benefits are the financial independence and satisfaction of over twenty thousand people and also the removal of the burden of responsibility from the party. When these people are working for themselves, the party is not required to provide them with their necessities.'

'But you are not allowed to use the party's forces for the satisfaction of people who have not shot a bullet for the revolution.'

'What do you mean by that? When everyone becomes a soldier, who should bake your bread and weave your clothes? We will stay here until they need us.'

'You are not needed there. You stay there because you are cowardly and afraid of the war.'

'Okay, let your brave fighters come at us. We will teach you a good lesson.'

'You not only ignore the party's command, but you even threaten your own comrades.'

'I have not received any official order from the party. You are not my commander and you're asking for something improper from me. You have insulted us and for that you have received a suitable answer.'

'Then I have to contact your commander.'

'Do whatever you'd like.'

---

* The one whose face shines.

Hevala Rûgeş hung up the phone and looked at me. She said she saw the signs of fear on my face. She came toward me, holding out her right hand, and shook my hand. She squeezed my hand, looked me in the eyes and said, 'We will never leave the factory. Even if we get an order from my commander. I promise you as a woman.'

Her last sentence calmed me much more. You can no longer count on male promises. The rule of women in Rojava was clearer and more successful than you might think. Even the skeptical, reactionary communists quickly became convinced that a genuine feminist movement with great potential had emerged in Rojava. The women there were different from a particular party's means of propaganda. They had recognition and influence, which they gained through struggle. I was familiar with this particular situation of women from the last months of my life in the mountains, but I still found their self-confidence, independence, and, above all else, their radical linguistic distancing from the male world to be exotic. As if they use a different kind of language.

'I promise you as a woman . . . if I were not a woman . . . if I were not the daughter of my mother . . . long live the sisterhood of nations.' These linguistic changes were not decorations for a redefined sense of feminine attractiveness but originated from a deep conviction in the demise of the male world, which had dragged both nature and human life into a state of catastrophe. Women had real power in Rojava and it kept expanding until the time I left there. Privacy and religious freedom were guaranteed there, quite differently from how it is in these mountains, where we cannot cross our legs, like hevala Jîncin always complains about. During Ramadan you can eat in the middle of the Kurdish cities and buy liquor from the shops, drink alcohol in the pubs, and watch the passersby running on the sidewalks. I was excited about these progressive developments, but as far as my work was concerned, the situation was more than critical."

Arjîn asked, "How are hevalê Rojhat and hevala Rûgeş?"

"Unfortunately, they were both killed. Hevala Rûgeş was shot by a worker in the factory on behalf of the Turkish secret services and hevalê Rojhat died in Efrîn from an aerial bombardment."

"Was hevalê Rojhat from Ûrmiyê?"

"Yes."

Arjîn's face became terribly sad. Her lips kept trembling, this time not from anger, but from painful memories. She wanted to cry, but she struggled against it and her whole body started shaking. No one said anything until she could control herself. Then she said, "He was our commander."

She could not talk anymore, and a sorrowful atmosphere came over the room. To change the atmosphere and the subject, I asked Saro, "What other factories did you conquer?"

"A foundry and a brickyard, which were state factories. But we also took some private factories from Daesh. Actually, you cannot say they were private. They belonged to people who were in government circles and had close ties to the president, ministers, or high-ranking army personalities. Ordinary citizens do not have much money, nor can they get permits to establish such factories and can't import the necessary machines into the country. One of these factories was a beverage factory. The owner of the factory was living in the USA. He authorized some of his relatives to manage the factory. When Daesh attacked there, his relatives sold, or better to say plundered, everything they could sell. They sold all twenty of the trucks they used to transport bottles and cans, as well as more than a thousand display fridges that the manufacturer wanted to give to its regular clients. When we conquered the factory, I called the owner. He was very glad that we got his factory out of the hands of his liar relatives. Ah! The name of the beverage franchise was Sinalco. A brand from Germany. That was almost everything that I can summarize. I experienced even more important events in Rojava that cannot be shortened."

"But you have not yet answered hevala Rûken's question. Why did the party remove you?"

"'Remove' isn't the right word. I was actually promoted. The rival supervisor had complained to the party executive about my activities. They sent a few inspectors to me. They were misinformed. When they found out that my activities had created eleven thousand jobs, they were surprised. They praised me and asked me how I accomplished all of it in such a short time. I replied that I didn't make these jobs. We only brought this half-dead infrastructure back to life. One of them said that my supervisor told them that I had given the party's property to the people. I answered that, yes that was true, and that I had given the workers some of the factory's shares. They not only get a salary, but also profit from their shares. That's how I understood socialism. To my surprise, this made them even happier and they asked for my understanding about the misjudgment of my supervisor. One said he still dreams of state capitalism. They gave me carte blanche and said that I was allowed to continue my work. But, over time, the rift between me and my supervisor deepened. Then the supervisory board of the party called me. They told me that I had lost my strength there and that I was overloading the party with unnecessary disputes between me and them. I took a new job where I could make decisions without having contact with adversarial supervisors. I was there for over two years until I came here of my own free will, for a project for the party."

CHAPTER 6

WE FINALLY FOUND the right opportunity to raid the hawthorn trees. It was drizzling and the sky was free of drones. The trees were tall and our ladder, Serhelldan, was keeping watch, but we didn't need him. Except for me, all the other comrades could shimmy up the trees like a snake. I remained on the ground, but comrades above gave me all the biggest, ripest berries on all sides. I did nothing but eat, while the other comrades were continuously picking the berries. Less than an hour before, those hawthorns were like glowing Christmas trees; after they had turned to bare autumn trees and all of the berries had been deposited into our vest pockets.

Our vests not only had several pockets on the exterior and interior, but there was also a big space between the two sides that we could fill up like a backpack.

When my comrades poured the hawthorns out from their pockets, the amount of berries was more than enough to fill two empty sugar bags. For three days, I only ate yellow hawthorns. I stopped before I developed an aversion to them.

After the hawthorn-picking operation, we got new orders that put our life-recounting sessions on pause. On cloudy days we were collecting firewood. There was no more firewood around the bunker and we had to go far away to find enough. What did we need it all for anyway? "You will learn the surprise later."

For safety reasons we were not allowed to cut off or break dried branches and we had to collect the firewood that had fallen onto the ground. We were collecting firewood by the river and piling it up in a small cave. After three weeks, the cave was full and the work was done. Apart from the firewood collecting, another novelty had entered our lives and that was mortadella.

With the onset of the cold season, our diet changed. On some days of the week, instead of lentil soup for dinner we could eat mortadella. However, we still cooked lentil soup as usual because, to my amazement, half of the group was vegetarian. What should it mean for them? We were practically all vegetarians and didn't get any meat until the cylindrical cans of mortadella appeared.

Hevalê Ferhad, Saro, Rûken, Arjîn, Gulbehar, Rojano, and, strangely, Hunger, were all vegetarians. Not me, but since childhood, I've never liked mortadella, so the winner of these vegetarian diet restrictions was our cat. Eating became his main work and interest. After two weeks, he rounded out. It was clear that if he ate more and more mortadella, we would have a Van bear instead of a Van cat soon. That's why our health care specialist personally proceeded to solve the problem and announced that nobody was allowed to feed Befrîn but her. This would stop Befrîn from gaining weight in the future, but it came at our expense in the present. Thereafter, Befrîn didn't care about anyone except Rûnahî. He always followed her and slept only on her lap. Of course, no one of us wanted to accept such discrimination, so a culture of corruption took root within the group.

The bribee was easily known and getting fatter, but the bribers couldn't hide themselves, either. The one who Befrîn followed the most and whose lap he most wanted to sit on was most likely the last to have bribed him. Everyone was a suspect except Tewar, who never touched him. The main suspect was Arjîn, who couldn't stand losing any of Befrîn's affection.

I found out that our cat had a great talent for mathematics. He took bribes by the gram. For half a can he would sit on someone's lap and only for a full can would he deign to be washed. The capitalist and counterrevolutionary culture of bribery had penetrated our group all the way to our executive members. Finally, we held a particular anticorruption meeting and after five hours enacted a rule that the cat could only be fed by one of the cooks each day.

By implementing Rûnahî's proposal, the bribery problem was solved, but Befrîn completely relocated to the kitchen. So then, since for ideological and personal reasons it was mandatory for Befrîn to take part in our training sessions, we switched to Arjîn's proposal: Befrîn would be fed by the cooks of the previous day.

With this proposal, Befrîn's problems of bribery and truancy were solved and that of his obesity forgotten. We didn't expect our pudgy cat to hunt rats, but one day Befrîn proved that he must have some panther DNA.

We were in a course session. The topic of the course was class struggle in the modern capitalist era. In the middle of the capitalist struggle, Befrîn jumped up, ran out of the room, and disappeared. After a brief moment of surprise, the course resumed until Gulbehar excitedly appeared in front of the door.

"Come and look at what Befrîn did!"

He had hunted down a rat, but he was playing with it instead of eating it. From time to time he released it. The rat hesitated for a moment and then ran away, but our cat was faster and each time he would capture it again. Although I had heard of the cat and mouse game, it was not until that day that I understood the meaning of the term. So, like Gulbehar and Arjîn, I found this game very funny. To my surprise, the other comrades were looking at the scene with indifference. For a while, Rûken looked at this game sadly, then said, "Shame this cute animal is so aggressive."

"Aggressive? He's only playing with the rat."

"No, hevala Jînçin, this is not a game. If we call it a game, then it is the filthiest game of them all. Except for humans, no creature can be more aggressive against its victims than this lovely animal. In the past twenty years, I've seen this game a dozen times. It always ends with the killing of the rat."

"But this struggle comes naturally to all creatures. Even the stronger trees eliminate the weaker ones in competition for light and water."

"No, the struggle for resources is something completely different. Trees grow up in two opposite directions because their branches grow towards the sun and their roots downwards the groundwater. But these demonstrations of power found in humans and cats have no relation to scarcity."

Before I took a position against Rûken's words, Akam spoke up.

"But bloody battles happen in other parts of the animal kingdom, where the driving force is not lack of resources. For example, in swamps, the strongest male crocodile does not let other male crocodiles mate with the females, no matter how many females are in the swamp. The other males have to wait until the strongest male grows weak and a new male gets the chance to take his place. But I think you're right when it comes to humans' aggression and demonstrations of power. It should have arisen directly from the scarcity of resources.

Akam looked at me and hevalê Ferhad and said, "I would like to ask you a question."

"Under these two meters of soil, I will gladly answer any question," I said, and hevalê Ferhad showed his agreement with a combination of a smile and nod. Akam continued,

"What event in human history had the largest effect on human nature?"

"Are you looking for a real answer or our personal opinions?"

"I expect to hear a scientific answer, especially from you, hevala Jînçin."

"Your question sounds very unscientific. There have been very many ambiguous and unknown events in human history that cannot be explained by biology, anthropology, or sociology. All of these have impacted the peculiarities of today's human beings. You expect us to ignore all these scientific gaps, pull something from our pockets, and call it a scientific answer?"

"I expect you, like the others, to give answers that you consider reasonable and not necessarily the universal answer. Can one expect such an answer from others?"

"That would be our personal opinion. At the moment, I cannot come up with a convincing answer. But I gather from your questions that you mean the story of human creation and not the history made by humans."

"Exactly, that's what I mean."

"Then you are looking for an anthropological answer to explain why people have some specific peculiarities by nature. Right?"

"Exactly."

"And what human peculiarities do you mean, demonstrations of power or aggression?"

"Aggression, I mean. Where did humans get this aggressiveness?"

"That's an intellectual question. From an anthropological viewpoint, this characteristic is said to have been inherited from our common ancestors with chimpanzees. I think I now know what you meant by the most important event in human history. Do you mean the emergence of the Congo River?"

"Bingo. Do you agree with this theory?"

"Yes, this theory is based on a number of scientific experiments and a great deal of research. At this point your question is interesting, although you formulated it very poorly."

"Yes, I know. I am not a scientist. Shall we go back to the room? Befrîn will eat the rat anyway."

"And what did you mean by the Congo River?" Gulbehar asked curiously.

"We'll talk about it in the room."

"But I'm a cook today. Please speak loudly, so that I can hear too."

"Heval, go quietly into the room. I will finish it alone," Nadîr said.

"Hunger is right, he can finish it by himself. It is like setting up a fox to guard geese. A rat is safer in a cat's mouth than food is next to Hunger."

"Do not worry hevalê Satyar, I will stand in front of the door and watch hevalê Nadîr."

We left Befrîn with his prey in the kitchen and returned to the room. I wanted to know what use Akam wanted to make of the Congo River story and if he dared to talk about the different sex practices of the two great apes. Akam waited until all the smokers had finished their cigarettes and returned to the women's double-function room. Then he started from another point.

"I would often go to the Paris Zoo, but only after many years did I figure out some unbelievable differences between two types of great apes in Lisbon. One species, bonobos, are very peaceful, sharing their food among themselves. They don't solve conflicts by force, but with physical relationships. The chimpanzees are very aggressive. They solve every conflict by force, kill each other for food, and rape the weak.

When I pursued this matter I found out these behavioral differences are even more pronounced in their natural habitat. The bonobos build a matriarchal society in which the females are on top. Meanwhile, dominance in chimpanzee communities lies with the strong males. They fight within their society continuously and kill each other. They even collectively attack those chimpanzees who are far from their territory to eat them.

And where did these obvious differences between these closest species to humans come from? The blame for this is said to have been caused by a river in the Congo. About two million years ago, this river came into being and separated the habitat of those great apes' ancestors. On the northern side of the river, the chimpanzees would have to share their territory and food with gorillas. So, there was the tension of competition and aggressiveness gave them an advantage to survive. But since the gorillas cannot swim, there was no such tension of competition on the southern part of the Congo River.

Interestingly, human genetics resembles the two species of great apes more than the two species genetically resemble each other. More than ninety-eight percent of our genes and those of chimpanzees are identical. This means that two million years ago our ancestors mated with the two great apes at a time when they were geographically separated from each other.

We must have inherited our diplomatic features from the southern side of the Congo River, and our aggressive features from the northern side, and by combining both features we became the most dangerous creature in the world. Thus, diplomats can provoke our aggressive emotions and incite us against each other with their hate speech and warmongering governors can apply their diplomatic abilities to convince us to kill and die for them.

Unfortunately, we owe this shadowy, aggressive side of ourselves to the beautiful and fascinating Congo River. So I think hevala Rûken is right. Our aggressiveness arose from resource scarcity. I also find the comparison between cats and humans to be correct, but with a different formulation. Humans and cats are among the animals that torture their victims. The cats nearly kill their victims several times in their brutal game of release and re-catch and that has nothing to do with a struggle for survival."

"Maybe Befrîn would release the rat if we offered him mortadella as an alternative," Arjîn said excitedly.

"I do not believe that. In the end he will eat the rat anyway."

Arjîn quickly ran out and shouted after a few seconds.

"He's still playing with the rat."

We got up and went out so quickly that Serhelldan bumped his head on the top of the door. His head made a loud smack and he sat on the ground from the pain. Tewar stayed with him and we went to the kitchen. Arjîn opened one of the cartons that contained the mortadella and took out a can. She removed its lid and called Befrîn with the word of "mortadella" to encourage him. Then she took the fresh mortadella near to Befrîn's eyes. Befrîn turned his face away from the mortadella and held the little rat tighter with his claws. Arjîn even tried to take the rat from his claws, but Befrîn guarded it and hissed so loudly that you would have thought he was protecting his own kittens. Arjîn was upset by his unfriendly reaction and stepped back. I also put on a surprised expression until Rojano spoke up.

"I do not see this as a kind of game. Until a few years ago, I saw it as you did, but from my life experiences I have realized that this act, which we see as a game, is actually a survival tool. One of my uncles was a kollber. After the death of my father, he took care of us laboriously. When I was a child, I saw a huge piece of baggage on his back. I saw his job, kollberî,* as a game that I could not imitate. When I grew up, I realized that the baggage was not a toy, but a painful, crushing burden in life. It can also be the same case with the rats. Maybe sometime, in a forgotten part of cat history, a mother cat wanted to teach her kittens how to hunt the rats with this act. The cats know well that they shouldn't rely on humans. Befrîn, based on his instincts and perceptions, doesn't let anybody take the rat from him, because he knows this rat is his real food."

Rojano's sentences sent my mind back to Frankfurt. A night that was going to become the bitterest night of my life. That was the first Christmas Eve that I had to spend without my father. In the final two years, my father was in Şingal and Kobanî, but we would chat on the internet until we slept. The year before, I had celebrated the night of New Year's happier and more glorious than ever. For the first time, my father called me by video from Kobanî. He was sitting with comrades behind a simple table with three bottles of wine on it. One of those comrades, who was Finnish, provided these wines amidst the war in Kobanî. My father had turned one of those wines into homemade mulled wine.

They were looking cheerful and I couldn't be happier to see them in such a condition. I asked my dad to send me some photos of their New Year's celebrations. He sent them to me and I sent them to Jarik, too. I wrote under those photos, "Kobanî, right now." He also showed his happiness by sending me back some surprised emojis and informed me

---

* A job where people carry heavy loads, usually on their shoulders, between Iran and the Iraq border.

that he was in Frankfurt right now. I invited him to dinner. He accepted on the condition that I took him back to his friends later.

He came faster than I expected and brought a mulled wine with him. I was behind the table talking to my dad via Skype. They had not started drinking yet. Jarik put the mulled wine on the table and greeted my father and his comrades very warmly, but again I introduced him.

"My ugly bald-headed Kurdish teacher."

"Bald men are fortunate," my father said.

"Yes. He's definitely got dumb luck. I answer all his scientific questions for free, but he teaches me his boring bullshit for a fee."

"Then he is both bald and smart-headed."

Jarik brought his mouth to my head and whispered in my ear.

"If you are dissatisfied, we can change our means of exchange. We can both exchange our services for kisses instead of money."

I turned to look at my dad on the screen and told him gravely, "Dad, tell me how I can kill him most quickly without a weapon."

"No, you are not allowed to kill him. He is your teacher. Besides, you will be found guilty if you kill him."

"No, he is a foreigner and has sexually harassed me. Right before your eyes he offered me a sexual proposal. You have to be on my side and banging your fist on the table."

Jarik moved into the screen and told my father, "Hevalê Şingal, you know your daughter better than me. I suspect you fled from her. Can you give me a place to sleep in Kobanî for tonight? I can even sleep on the floor without a blanket."

"I will not let you out of the country. You either have to spend all of the Christmas holidays in a police prison or sing a Kurdish song for my father. Dad, which song do your comrades like?"

"'Zara Gîyan,' do you know this Kurdish song?"

"Yeah, I know it, but my voice is not nice."

"But we are not sitting in a concert hall."

"Ok, I'll sing it to you later. Let's drink some wine."

"Yes, that's overdue. We have been waiting for an hour."

Suddenly, I remembered those couple of old wine bottles that I had recently found in our cellar. I asked my father if he knew about those Spanish wines, bottled in 1980. My father was shocked and exclaimed,

"We must have bought those wines in Barcelona! One year before your birth. Open the bottles and drink with us!"

"Ok, can you endure Jarik until I get the wines from the cellar, or should I turn off my laptop?"

"We get along well if you don't break us up."

I brought up a couple of wine bottles and put them next to Jarik. He looked at them and asked me, "Do you want to drink these?"

"Are they good or spoiled?"

"Is your basement warm or cold in winter?"

"The central heating of the building is there."

"Then these are no longer drinks, but antiques."

He put the bottle in front of the lamplight and slowly moved it back and forth. Then he said, "These are not bottles of wine, but of lifeblood. We should leave wines like these rather than drink them."

"Why?"

"You have to say 'for what reason' instead of 'why.' So far, they have lived longer than you and can live for a thousand years if we do not drink them."

I looked at my father on the screen and said, "Xemo, give me your Kalashnikov. I want to shoot four bullets into his glossy head."

"Why?" My father asked, laughing.

"I thought he was just bald, but he's actually a complete idiot. He thinks it'd be a pity if we drank this grape juice, because it would remain as wine after we've decomposed into shit. Do I really look like a stupid antique dealer?"

"No, he meant you should drink that mulled wine that he brought himself."

"He really finds his wine, which he bought from the flea market, more suitable for me?"

"How did you find out that I bought it from the flea market?"

"The bottle itself says it."

I turned to the screen and added, "His mulled wine was produced in the current year, but the bottle label looks older than the ones on the wines we had forgotten in the cellar for forty years."

"My dear daughter, you don't look a gifted horse in the mouth and you shouldn't get carried away. Who sells fresh mulled wine at a flea market?"

"Actually, they do," Jarik replied, instead of me, then added, "Hevalê Şingal, I don't know when was the last time you bought something at the flea market. Nowadays you'd be able to sell anything there except your daughter. Nobody buys such a torture device for free. Even the heroes who survived Amed's prisons wouldn't be able to bear her presence for more than an hour."

My father and I burst out laughing. Jarik opened one of the bottles while speaking English with my father's comrades. Only then did I realize that I had spoken Kurdish the whole time. I could not speak with my father in any language other than Kurdish. I asked them if I should speak English, or if they could understand Kurdish. The Austrian comrade answered me in Kurdish and the others replied to me with appropriate answers in English.

"So they understood my babbling. Now they know what an impudent daughter you have."

The Austrian comrade said, "No, we know you are friends. Since when have you been friends?"

I looked at him. He seemed to be around forty.

"Tonight is the first time I've seen him in person. But the glossy shine of the light bouncing off his head has been burning my eyes via Skype for a while."

Chuckling, Jarik opened one of the old wine bottles and filled two glasses on the dining room table. We picked up our glasses. After a long wait, my father and his comrades could pick up their glasses within the screen.

"Cheers!" shouted my father's oldest comrade, an Italian of about forty-five.

Jarik repeated it.

I replied to him, "*Noş*" and everyone else repeated it. Before I brought the wineglass to my mouth, Jarik said, "You should sip the wine and move it between your palate and tongue."

"Why?"

"Don't say 'why.' You have to say 'for what reason?' Listen to me, later you will understand for yourself."

I did that and a different taste of wine spread over my tongue. The old wine was gelatinous and I could move it with my tongue under my palate. The wine tasted dry and delicious. I wanted to talk about the taste of that old wine with my dad, but I could not. Jarik was right; I would regret it later if we were to drink both bottles of wine. That Christmas Eve was wonderful for my Êzdî father and the four atheists he had gathered on the internet.

Jarik sang the requested Kurdish song, "Zara Gîyan." His voice was not bad at all. Other comrades also sang some folk songs, but the special event of the night was playing my *şimşall*. For some years, I would play this simple Kurdish wind instrument, along with a flute, for my dad. Only after becoming acquainted with Jarik did I understand that in the previous years I had been blowing into it the wrong way. Like with a flute, I was blowing into the şimşall with one steady blow, but it should be a wavy type of blowing. Only then could the enchanting, polyphonic tone come through the instrument. Jarik noticed my incorrect şimşall technique and I was able to correct it within a few months.

On Christmas Eve of 2015, when my father asked me to play şimşall, he didn't expect me to play a purely original Kurdish piece. We were all drunk on old wine. I played by ear and my dad cried. For the first time he was hearing original Êzdî music, played on the şimşall he had bought on our trip to Kurdistan twenty-six years ago.

When you blow into the şimşall with the wavy technique, an enchanting tone comes out, like the echo of screaming in a rock valley. I played such a nice piece of Kurdish music that my father cried the whole time with indescribable joy.

That night was strange in itself. Four Europeans were sitting in a hospital in the most dangerous place in the world, a city besieged by Daesh, yet they were drinking wine and singing with us directly via Skype. My father sang a German song called "Gute Nacht Freunde, Gute Nacht." After my father's death my mother listened to this song probably over a hundred times.

Last year I celebrated Christmas Eve with my father, despite the three thousand seven hundred kilometers of distance between us. But he is not alive anymore to call me on his mobile phone and share his evening with me. He was the only person that I absolutely trusted and on whom I could rely. He had raised me into a woman whom he truly loved. A woman who made life bitter for all the men she encountered except him.

Only Jarik can understand this relationship. He can analyze human relationships well, but he is the worst possible option for an emotional relationship. He negotiates with women as if they were castrated men. I would like to call Jarik and spend this sad evening with him, but it's not clear that we won't have a quarrel by the end of it. For a few minutes I hear constant shouting and can't ignore it anymore.

"Stop it. Stop it!"

I wonder who should stop what? I head in the direction of the voice. Three homeless people are lying in front of a shop. Their sleeping bags are next to them. Somebody is sitting on a stool opposite them and playing the guitar. I go toward him, stand there, and listen to him play. He masterfully plays some Eastern European music pieces. Nevertheless, after the end of each piece the three men shout together, "Stop it. Stop it!"

I sit opposite him on a cold metal bench. He has a cigarette in the corner of his lips, wears fingerless gloves, and keeps playing without paying attention to the cold or the three homeless persons shouting. I listen with full attention. He continues to play faster and thus provokes the homeless people further. One of them gets up, hurriedly approaches the guitar player and tries to take his guitar away. The guitar player spits his cigarette down next to himself and tries to explain something to the homeless man in an Eastern European language. The homeless man grabs at his guitar and he aggressively defends it, like a hen protects its chicks from danger.

The homeless man goes back. The player lights another cigarette, puts it in the corner of his lips and plays a beautiful piece of music. His fingertips dance on the guitar strings and the area fills with mellifluous music tones. The homeless people protest again as soon as he gives up playing.

"Stop it, stop it, and stop it!"

Another German homeless man gets up, goes towards him, and orders him to move twenty meters away from them. The guitar player moves up his hands to defend his place, still smoking his cigarette, and the homeless man goes back toward his mates. I feel sorry to see these poor people annoying each other. Why are these homeless men trying to keep away someone who shares their misery? Maybe they're right and their hostility arises just because they need a quiet night after a loud day. But it's only seven o'clock in the evening and the guitarist is allowed to continue his playing.

I want to prevent the struggle between them and go toward the guitar player. I see some coins in his guitar case. Almost all passersby have thrown small change into his case. His total income cannot be more than five euros. What can he do with that amount? If he smokes just as he does when playing guitar, the money won't even cover his cigarette expenses.

I stand next to him and listen to another piece he is playing. He looks at me behind his cigarette smoke, while his fingertips dance with greater motivation on the guitar strings. As soon as he finishes his piece, I go closer and speak with him.

"It seems those people probably have no sense of music. It is better to go home and spend your night differently. I'll give you fifty euros. You will not earn more than that on this quiet street."

I thought he would take my suggestion immediately, but he thanked me and spoke with a thick Bulgarian accent in broken German, "I thank. I do not go. Here I earn my food."

What did he mean "here?" The pedestrian precinct or where he was sitting on the stool? He could get rid of those homeless guys if he would move twenty meters away from there. Stubbornly, he wanted to stay in his place on this long street. If he left that place, he might not have been able to claim it the next morning and someone else would occupy that spot opposite the Christ watchmaker's shop. Maybe looking at the different colors and brands of watches helps hasten the passing of his bitter time. I go toward the shop window. Unbelievable, there are no clocks in the window, only a myriad of expensive wedding rings. All over one thousand euros. I turn and look at the guitar player again. He plays a piece of gypsy music. He is skinny, tall, and in his mid-fifties. He is too old a man to have any ambition for a wedding ring. A couple of homeless people rush toward him. I would like to support him, but what will he be able to do after I leave? I cannot change the unwritten rules of this street. I can see how they try to drive him away from his place. They look at me smiling, as if they had driven him out for my sake.

"Shitty player! Dumbass! Gypsy!" they yell at him loudly

They say the last word slowly, but it hits me like lightning. In Frankfurt you do not hear something like that. The rulers suppress the people not through their power or wisdom, but through the manufacture of social ignorance. The homeless men continue to talk and blame that "shitty player" for their misery. As if he had caused their poverty with his five euro income instead of those who make millions of euros in broad daylight just on this street. I missed Jarik. Why did we separate from each other so suddenly? Was he guilty on my birthday? Did he really trick Güzel, or just cause Güzel to show me her true face? I grew up with Güzel, but until that day I could not see any sign of racism in her. Could she ever confront me as a racist? When she was a child, she and her family were our tenants. It is true that I would talk in Kurdish with my father, but she may have thought our language was not Kurdish. How would she know Kurdish? At that time, in the parallel societies of Turks living in Germany, nobody could speak Kurdish, like in Turkey, though the government of Germany would have fought against this language discrimination, in accordance with the German constitution. Güzel was part of a loyal, hospitable family who had maintained a good relationship with us for thirty years. Maybe they did not know that my father was a Kurd, or thought he ended his shame by marrying a German girl.

We had spent countless days and nights with each other. We traveled and ate together, but never noticed their hatred for the Kurds. They were allergic to the word "Kurd" for all of those years and saw the symptoms of that disease as a form of patriotism. Did Jarik really separate me from Güzel and her brother, or did they cut themselves off from me by revealing their position?

Güzel apologized to me after my birthday party was spoiled, but I rejected her remorse. She even sent me some Kurdish songs and poems. Maybe she is no longer allergic to the Kurds and does not see them as a plague anymore. "*I hate the Kurds more than dogs. . . . They baaa like sheep. . . . They have no culture or language. . . . Their homeland is called Türkiye and belongs to the Turks. . . . The Kurdish language is the means of communication for mountaineers who can't learn human language.*" The reverberation of their words bounces around in my head and hurts me terribly. I have to call Jarik. Maybe he has changed his SIM card in the meantime. I take my phone out of my purse and turn it on. I receive a lot of texts at once. Most of them are from Güzel and her mother, through different apps. This time, their texts bring me joy, but I do not open them and instead look for Jarik's mobile number. He had also sent me a text message after thirty-four days.

"Good evening, Jînçin. I'd like to invite you to dinner. The most delicious kifteugoşt in the world is waiting for you."

I laugh. That boy cooks the Kurdish dishes that are only made in Sine, but he claims that nobody in the world can prepare those dishes better than him. He cooks this kind of rice ball very well. He uses more than fifteen aromatic herbs for it to create a scrumptiously complex flavor. I long for that dish, forget the poor guitar player, and never could have imagined that the guitar player would later be recalled in my mind, as I sit in an underground bunker, encircled by painful feelings.

CHAPTER 7

I WAS THINKING snow would make our lives more beautiful, but it turned out to be quite the opposite. We shouldn't walk on thin ice, neither on cloudy days nor at night. This ban was like house arrest for me. I was half asleep when I heard from my comrades that the snow was falling in big flakes. I would have liked to get up and see what the snow is like at this altitude, but I will have to wake up to keep watch in the next few hours. When I arrived at the guard post, which was located in front of the women's room entrance, the snowfall had stopped.

The world had turned white. I wanted to blissfully waltz through the snow, but Dêrsîm leaped towards me, roughly grabbed my collar with one hand and handed me a bucket handle with her other. At the end of my shift, I should fill it with snow and pour it into the canister above the gas heater, bring the bucket back to its place, and remove the traces in the snow where I picked some up with my hands.

The snow around the bunker would replace the water we used for drinking, cooking, washing, and even bathing. Amazingly, our diet and even our hygiene did not deteriorate. Everyone was able to take a bath and wash their clothes at least once a week with hot water from the thawed snow and our rooms were always shining because of Rûnahî's cleaning habits.

The two comrades who were selected for daily cooking normally had to take care of the cleanliness of the bunker, but that duty was gradually forgotten. Every morning, right after all the comrades got up, Rûnahî would pull open the entrance, letting in fresh, cold, and snowy air until several comrades began to sneeze. She always had a clean cloth and a small broom in her hands and didn't let even a molecule of dust remain in the bunker.

Before and after the snowfall, our lifestyle did not change, but the compulsory house arrest was unbearable to me. Every comrade showed some sign of falling victim to the gloominess and Rojano said we were all going through a temporary depression. Frustrated and disappointed, we dragged ourselves through each day. No one was willing to tell their life story to the team. Befrîn was the only happy member of the group. He would trot outside through the snow and come back to the bunker only when he was hungry or sleepy. As soon as you could take him in your arms, he would run away to the outside, and after getting a few meters out he would no longer be distinguishable from the snow.

Thus, a new rival of love arose against Arjîn: the snow. We were going to reprimand our cat by democratically changing his name to Dewîn.*Arjîn's suggestion was rejected promptly, because we were supposed to cook a delicious *doxwa* soon.

"Is there any *do* around here?" I asked, surprised

"Yes, you can get everything from hevalê Zinar," Arjîn said. Then she brought her mouth near to me and said, "Even bras, in different colors and sizes."

I laughed and all the other women present there laughed as if they had heard her words. Zinar had a bottle of very thick do, which one could dilute with water to create a large pot of do. Well, when will we cook the doxwa? When the weather gets colder. It was November and we couldn't determine a date for cooking the doxwa based on when it would be cold enough.

I forgot about the doxwa, often stared out at the forbidden snow, and was deadly bored until one morning. I had to keep watch for two hours in a row. I did not know for what reason and also I did not care. The weather outside was pleasant and through my half-opened eyes I could see the whole environment. Gulbehar got there before my watch was over. She gave me her radio and reminded me how to reach the radio, science, and technology program. I entered the bunker and saw Saro cooking. Our daily cooks were Rojano and Zinar, who were helping him. The lunch for that day seemed to be the expected doxwa. Regardless, I asked Saro what kind of soup he was cooking.

---

* White like *do*, a yogurt-based beverage.

"In Sine we consider this a main dish, although it cannot even serve as an appetizer."

"What do you mean?"

"Because it is the only meal in the world that takes more energy from the body than it ultimately gives to the body."

"Seriously?"

Saro stirred the do with a wooden ladle and continued without looking at me, "You have to keep stirring while the doxwa is being heated until it finally becomes creamy."

"And how many minutes does it take to get creamy?"

"Minutes? It takes months or even years. Doxwa will not get creamy so easily. You might be able to prevent it from flocculating, if you are a chef." I looked at Rojano. "Are hevalê Saro's words true?"

"I was a student in Sine for four years. On a foothill of Awyer Mountain, doxwa was sold everywhere. Everyone talked about creamy doxwa, but they were lying. How can you make a creamy doxwa, when it consists only of do, bulgur, and beet leaves? You can calculate for yourself: with the manual labor needed for this doxwa, you can produce three hundred megawatts of electricity."

"Then, why are you cooking such a disastrous doxwa, anyway?"

"It is absolutely delicious."

"No, heval. It serves another function. In Colemêrg it serves as a microphone changer. There are hundreds of people in turn who want to talk. Some people do not tire of talking, but they will get tired of stirring. The one who cannot stir anymore stops talking and another takes the ladle and gets to talk," Zinar said, giving Rojano a sense of encouragement.

"Heval, you figured that out very wisely. This can also be a kind of public exercise."

"Public exercise is not a priority for people in Colemêrg, but with the stirring, they could get naughty children to fall asleep. Kids always want to imitate what adults do. Before the doxwa gets warm, they let the kids stir it with a ladle. Finally, they fall asleep with a ladle in their hands or run away from the duty of stirring."

"Heval, now I know how the people heat up their homes in the winter. I was thinking the heat should come from the heater when it actually comes from the stirring." Saro said, laughing. I asked if I could try the magic doxwa.

"Nooooo, it would lead to a calorie deficit attack. Then what could we do for you here above the clouds?" Saro shouted.

"What is the meaning of a calorie deficit attack? Is that a new term?"

"No heval, it is discussed a great deal in the unwritten tradition of Kurdish medicine. Eating non-creamy doxwa leads to an upset stomach."

"You said yourself that doxwa would never become creamy."

"Why are you twisting my words? I said that I had not ever eaten creamy doxwa. In theory, however, it must be possible. You just have to kick the butts of all the electrons for long enough."

"Electrons? Damn it, now science comes back into play. So, how can you do that, then?"

"I don't want to bring owls to Athens. You are the scientist here."

"Okay, I'm asking you as one of my students. How can you tire out the electrons and make a creamy doxwa?"

"That would be very difficult. Electrons never stop in the same place, but you have to stir in different directions until those electrons lose their natural desire and fall down like hailstones. Then the doxwa would be creamy."

"And how long will that process take?"

"Not much longer. Maybe a few million years."

"So we have to wait and stir the doxwa until then?"

"Of course not. The unwritten Kurdish medical books offer a solution. We can eat a high calorie dessert. It stops you from having an upset stomach."

"Wow, the Kurds are so science-friendly."

"Heval, what can they do? If you eat a pot of doxwa, it won't compensate for the energy you expended to make it. There is only an eleven-second period between satiety and hunger again. The miserable Kurds can't afford to starve because of their doxwa-mania, so they turn to science."

I was laughing the whole time, but I saw that they really wanted to make some kind of sweets. Rojano lifted a plastic bottle from the ground, within which a lot of pretty red flower petals had been floating.

"What's this?" I asked.

"Who says its real name here? We call it rose water. I thought hevalê Zinar had been soaking these rose petals in water since some days ago, right?"

Before Zinar answered her question, Saro told us he should be replaced by Gulbehar . Rojano asked Zinar if he had some pistachios or walnuts.

"Heval, I do not trade in capitalist foods like pistachios or saffron, but I can give you some walnuts."

"Without going out into the snow?"

"Of course, heval. I am a modern guerilla. We live in the era of the drone."

He put his right hand into his military vest, fumbled around, pulled out about twenty walnuts, and dropped them into a bowl.

"Hevalê Nadîr, can you please come and crack these walnuts?"

"Let him rest. Today we are the cooks." Rojano said.

"Of course, but who else can crack these hard walnuts apart but him? He cracks walnuts more masterfully than any squirrel."

Hunger appeared, and without asking a question, squatted down next to me in front of the walnut bowl. I watched him closely. He put two walnuts on top of each other within his left palm, closed his hand, and slapped his closed hand with his right palm. When he opened his left hand, both walnuts were cracked along their natural crevices. Rojano and I tried to imitate his act. In the end, not a single walnut would crack open. Unlike Rojano, I could not hide the pain in my hands. We turned to Hunger again and within a few minutes he had calmly cracked all of the walnuts. I found his actions and his humility very attractive and asked him if he had eaten doxwa before. He answered "Yes," to which Zinar added, "Heval, what a question to ask. It's as safe as an 'amen' in church. Since he was a baby, he has grown up with doxwa. Such a huge watermill cannot be kept in operation with doxwa."

Satyar yelled from the men's room and joined our conversation. "You are mistaken, heval. No, heval, he was fed on pure human milk. His mother's milk was not enough for him and they had to beg for milk from other women. There were no women in Xaneqîn whose nipples Hunger hadn't suckled. As a result, all the girls in the city became his foster sisters and he could not marry them."

I was laughing loudly. I wasn't expecting such a fantasy and wanted to ask Satyar a question, but my laughter wouldn't let me. Finally, I had to interrupt and ask him, "And what did this poor man do in the end?"

"That's why he became a guerrilla. Because of him, I'm here too. We could have gone to Europe. But Hunger rained on my parade and now the fat is in the fire."

"How did he do that?"

"We found the best smuggler. He was squeezing people into trucks and bringing them to Europe. He put us in a truck full of dried bread. We should have gotten off right next to the Eiffel Tower. I took a nap and when I opened my eyes, four armed Daesh members were standing over our heads. There wasn't even enough dried bread to hide behind. Hunger had eaten all of it."

"No, hevalê Satyar, this story sounds illogical. Suppose he had eaten twenty tons of dried bread; then you could have hid yourself behind his twenty-ton body."

"Why, heval? Within three hours he would have used up all the energy in the dried bread. I swear. May God cut me into twenty-four thousand pieces if I lie."

"Twenty-four thousand pieces, why not say twenty thousand?"

"Heval, are you a listener or a slaughterhouse inspector? It is my body and I shall decide into how many pieces it should be cut."

"But your story contradicts the laws of physics. What happened to the energy of the twenty tons of dried bread?"

"He used up all the energy by talking. He is a chatterbox."

"Another lie. Hevalê Nadîr is not talkative."

"You are sorely mistaken there. He speaks on different levels. Bats can't even hear some of his vocal tones. God will make me mincemeat if I'm tricking you. He disturbs even the drones with his inaudible voice waves."

Satyar turned to Nadîr and said, "Has it happened that someone around you was shot down by drones?"

"No, I will not let that happen. What am I here for otherwise?"

Hunger confirmed his speech as an obvious affair. Satyar added with more confidence, "Heval, with all due respect for your scientific knowledge and calculations, without Hunger's help, you could not have saved us from that drone."

I turned to Hunger and asked him with a serious expression, "Heval, what do you think about his thesis?"

"What Satyar says is unfair. Most of this honor must be attributed to you. I was just a clumsy soldier, but you were the king . . . pardon, the queen."

Rojano laughed loudly and I laughed louder than her. Those three comrades are very funny. You just have to let them talk.

"Heval, you said that the doxwa would not have caused the insatiability of hevalê Nadîr. What should the reason be then?"

"Heval, I do not want to bring beer to Munich. You are our scientist. You must certainly know the scientific reasons for it."

"Come on, is there a scientific reason for that?"

"Of course, that's as clear as unflavored Jell-O. But it's probably not in your area of expertise. In the head of every human, there should be a nerve that informs the brain when you are full and should stop eating. This little nerve is not in Hunger's big head. Even if every type of nutrient, such as sugar, fat, vitamins, were sufficiently present in his blood, and he was also full, he would still want to eat much more because his brain remains uninformed. His stomach says I am bursting, but his brain orders him to eat even more."

"You are not a good friend. You should have taken him to a skilled surgeon."

"Why, heval? Every rose has its thorn. So he is the greatest hero in the world. He has killed more Daesh members in total than the coalition forces. Have I piqued your interest?"

"Yes, very much."

"Then take the ladle from poor hevala Rojano and stir the doxwa. She is so exhausted that her tongue is hanging out of her mouth. I didn't even see her so tired on the day we had to transfer the provisions. Am I right, hevala Rojano?"

"Definitely. Someone should take this boring ladle from me."

I went to work, sitting cross-legged on the other side of the low, gray gas stove, where our big black pot was positioned. I took the wooden ladle from Rojano and began to stir the warm white soup. I was curious what would come of this banter and addressed Satyar.

"Tell us about the heroism of our unknown hero."

Satyar smiled and looked at the ladle in my hand, as if he had found some grounds he could use to make fun of me at some later time. He said, "The Daesh troops found us in the truck and took us to Fallujah. I did not know why they took us so seriously. They didn't find a secure prison to keep us in. In the end, they imprisoned us in their central granary. It was a dream come true for Hunger and he ate all of the grain. The next day, they panicked when they lifted the tent and threw us out of the granary and also out of Fallujah. It is said that over thirty thousand Daesh members starved because of this. Unfortunately, many civilians also starved due to Hunger's heroic action, but Daesh would have starved them anyway."

"What a big lie. Daesh was cutting innocent people's heads off, why would they just release you after causing so much damage?"

"Heval, do you know what 'haram' means? They see grains as a gift from God. They won't throw away even a small piece of dried bread. Our hero had ten silos-worth of grains in his stomach. If they had killed Hunger, it would be like throwing away ten tons of bread."

"Okay, but why didn't they kill you? I suppose you had also eaten some of the holy bread?"

"No heval, my bristle saved me. If I didn't have this thick beard, they would have killed us in the truck right away. The donkey is always the first to say it, but I was also involved in the operation and I have read the Quran."

"You can read the Quran?"

He touched his thick black beard a few times like a young sheikh.

"Of course, heval, I grew up in a Muslim family. We had a Quran lying on a niche in our living room. It was very important to our family, but even more important to me. I hid money and forbidden photos between its sheets, because no one touched it. My mother picked it up once a year before Newroz, carefully cleaned the niche, blew the dust off the Quran and put it back without opening its green cover. Nobody touched it until the following year. I could read the Quran when Daesh found us; I sang its words until the morning. But it was not for nothing.

Whenever the meat pot boils, the friendship lasts well. They were saying *salawat** outside while Hunger was going through grains like a watermill."

Rojano was laughing at these stories, which Satyar was making up out of thin air, while she was frying the flour at the same time. I turned to Hunger and asked him, "Is what hevalê Satyar said true?"

"Yes, heval, I was such a heroic guy."

Hunger said this sentence with such a serious expression that I would have liked to get up and kiss his bright plump cheeks. Rûken had just come out of the bathroom and was standing behind Zinar. You could tell that her lightly combed hair was still wet.

"Comrades, come to the men's room. We want to commence the daily criticism sitting earlier today." She called from the kitchen.

Her words reinforced a suspicion that arose in my mind a few hours ago. They must have planned a birthday party for me. It is not normal that coincidentally, on my birthday, they would cook magic doxwa and sweets all at once and that the daily criticism sitting would take place in the morning instead of the evening. So many good events cannot be a coincidence. The made-up stories about upset stomachs and high-calorie desserts must have been distraction maneuvers. That wasn't necessary. If they had informed me earlier, I would have been just as surprised. Here in these mountains, at least for safety reasons, no birthdays are celebrated.

Zinar and Rojano stayed in the kitchen, Saro was keeping watch, and everyone else gathered in the men's room. Surprisingly, Befrîn was there. I hadn't heard from him in the morning. He lay on the lap of yesterday's cook, Dêrsîm. Rûken was sitting at the front and commenced the daily criticism meeting.

"Comrades, today we have commenced our daily criticism sitting earlier, because hevalê Saro wants to give us some new instructions from the party. It may bring about some long discussions. Who wants to start with the criticism?"

Satyar raises his right hand.

"I should criticize two comrades. Hevala Rûken forgot to switch off the transmitter last night after leaving her message. Though, I must add,

* An Islamic prayer recited during the five daily prayers and also when the name of the prophet is mentioned.

after about ten minutes she came back to correct her mistake. If a drone had suddenly appeared, we would have all been in danger."

"Thanks heval, you're right. I will take note and try not to repeat it. And what is your next critique?"

"The second critique is about hevalê Serhelldan. This morning he was sleeping at the guard post. I even took his gun and he did not notice. That was not the first time and I find it highly dangerous. He has to sleep earlier so he can keep watch correctly."

"I apologize to all my comrades and will try not to make this mistake again."

"Who has more criticisms?"

Tewar raised her left hand and her face turned red.

"I have a serious criticism of hevala Jînçin. Today, she was mocking hevalê Nadîr for hours. Worse than mocking, she disgraced him. She also motivated other comrades to humiliate hevalê Nadîr."

I shouted, "What?" and continued loudly, "What are you actually saying? Did we ridicule him? Hevalê Nadîr was there the whole time and laughing with us."

"He should have cried, so that you would have stopped humiliating him."

"Humiliate? Do you really believe this bullshit? I like him like everyone else does, or even more."

"I know you like him because he lets you expose yourself by humiliating him."

"Someone here is ridiculous, but it's definitely not hevalê Nadîr. We all like him and he can speak up better than you when he feels humiliated by someone."

"You must not raise your voice if I tell you the truth. You are the black sheep here. I've even caught you many times sitting with your legs on each other."

"Bugger me. You caught me with my legs on each other? I thought you caught me while I was doing my business. You don't have to lurk around me to catch me doing something so ridiculous."

I stretch my legs as long as I can and put them on each other. Rûken looks at me and asks me with her eyes to sit cross-legged. But I ignore her look. Tewar gets louder this time.

"Do you see comrades? How can you accept her behavior? She's not even willing to refer to our leader as 'serok.'* She only says Apo or even just Abdullah Öcalan."

"It would be better to call him Abdu and try to understand his words than to worship him like a prophet and repeat some of his quotations over and over again like a parrot."

Rûken stared at me again and asked me with her look to correct my sitting style. I ignored her gaze once more. She finally complained.

"Hevala Jînçin, we're at a meeting now. You cannot sit in this style."

"I know the rules, so I've been sitting cross-legged until now, but I cannot accept the irrational logic if someone is lurking around me and wants to catch me."

Rûken looks at me silently and Tewar raises her voice.

"Heval, she wants to turn our life into a circus."

"We are already in a circus and you are its black monkey."

Rûken yells at me, "Stop it and hold your tongue. You must not call your comrades monkeys."

The blood rises to my head and I scream, "But she can call me a black sheep?"

"That was different."

I get up and go toward the exit. Before I can pull up the blanket over the door and run outside, Rojano grabs my arm and doesn't let me leave. I want to yell at her, but she speaks to me in a very friendly manner.

"Dear Jînçin, I overheard everything. You were right and certainly the other comrades share this opinion."

"But why didn't anyone say anything? Neither Satyar nor Nadîr. They've ruined my whole day, on my birthday. This is the second time. Last year, my birthday was ruined as well."

"Is today your birthday? Congratulations to you, dear Jînçin. You don't want to stand in front of a drone on this beautiful day. You'll not only endanger yourself, but all of us, who love you very much. Do you know why hevala Tewar called you the black sheep?"

"Because she couldn't directly call me a black ass. Really, I am an ass. Why should I let such a psychopath cast aspersions on me? What am I even looking for here?"

* Leader.

"You are here for your beliefs and for personal reasons. Hevala Tewar called you that because she knows well that you are the flower of the flock here, without wanting to play first violin. Satyar, Nadîr, and other comrades did not say anything because they had not taken Tewar's criticism seriously. I would not have commented if I was there."

Rûken came toward us. Rojano left us alone, as if they were aware of each other's thinking through body language. Rûken stayed silent for a while. After realizing that she couldn't make me talk by staring at me, she spoke, "Do you think anyone here can seriously assume that you wanted to humiliate hevalê Nadîr?"

"I cannot hear any thoughts, only words. 'Hevala Jînçin was mocking hevalê Nadîr for hours. Worse than mocking, she disgraced him.' Are these sentences clear, or do I not understand Kurdish?"

"Yes, she said that, but she herself does not believe it. She knows that you like hevalê Nadîr, like all of us and also that he is not someone who is viewed as a buffoon by people."

"But why do you say it now? You should have said it at the time."

"Why would we want to talk about this during a daily criticism session? It's not a public discussion or an hour for reconciliation. It's a place and time where you can criticize anyone and say anything you want. It is not a place for discussion; otherwise we cannot summarize it within ten minutes."

"Discussion is not allowed there, but denunciations are permitted."

"Nobody denounced you. But you called hevala Tewar a monkey."

"Yes, but she called me a black sheep before that."

"They're not comparable. What she said was a proverb, but you directly called her a monkey. I didn't expect that from you. I must emphasize again that I do not expect that from you. You are an intelligent woman. Hevala Tewar did not want to bother you, she's just looking for your attention. We all neglected her. She is not like you four. You cannot compare Tewar with the other girls here. Arjîn has everything that one could call feminine attractiveness. She is pretty, easy to talk with, and cute. Gulbehar and Rojano are attractive and desirable in a different way. Dêrsîm and Rûnahî are well-liked for their conduct and behavior. Tewar is neither beautiful nor affable, but still a sensitive woman. Her problems were already known to us, before you arrived here. Dêrsîm even suggested that we hand over her job as a logistics specialist to Tewar, so that she would feel comfortable in our group. But it seems she is simply not capable of getting along with other comrades. It will take some time for Tewar to get comfortable with her own identity. Honestly, I did not expect her to see your humor as humiliation. We found it funny. Dêrsîm was laughing all the way into the bathroom at your chatter. I am very happy to see our life situation become more cheerful and I hope it stays like that. Such a mood is quite rare in the PKK. You cannot get upset by trivialities and let your laughter disappear. The name Rûken was suitable for me until a few years ago, when I was defeated by worries. You mustn't commit the same mistake."

"I'm not as strong as you think. I am very sensitive and also vengeful. It will be a long time before my mood levels out. If such a bad experience does not occur again."

"Unpleasant experiences are a part of our lives. Come on, our comrades are waiting for us. We have to put a new decision up for discussion."

I don't have the right temper to participate in any discussions on my birthday. Nevertheless, I go ahead and she follows me. The discussion is my birthday party and they give me an enthusiastic reception. The room is decorated in a very funny way. Instead of balloons, they inflated plastic bags and hung them on the walls in all sorts of color arrangements. The *mirtoxe*[5] that they were making with flour now plays the role of a birthday cake and my name and age are written on it in a secret code: "3X." Even the homemade candles are made from colorful pipes, transformed from the ugly tins filled with cooking oil.

Suddenly, Arjîn and our three jokesters are blowing into some very funny-sounding homemade birthday whistles. I start dying from laughter and sit on the ground. In all my life, I have never been so surprised on my birthday as I am in this underground bunker, high up in the mountains. Only when I bring my laughter under control and step aside from the door can Rûken come in. She sits down in a corner and says, "I apologize that we changed your birthday celebration date for safety reasons. We are glad that it was you who came into being from the billions of possibilities. We have learned a lot from you during this time and thank you for it. Should we start with Saro's doxwa or Rojano's mirtoxe?"

Before I say anything, Rojano says, "With the doxwa, of course. It has cost us a lot of time and energy and must not get cold. I congratulate you from deep in my heart and I am also very happy that you are celebrating your birthday with us this year. I've never been a good cook and this cake is just about the only thing I can cook. This is my birthday present."

"Thanks heval, it will be a pleasure to eat this cake with you. But I would like to ask for another gift from you."

"And what would that be?"

"A joke. I want everyone to tell me a joke. Instead of a joke, Gulbehar may, and should, sing." I turn to Gulbehar .

"Do you agree, heval?"

"That was already on our program."

All my other comrades congratulated me warmly, except Tewar, who was keeping watch outside. Zinar went to the kitchen and brought back bowls. Rojano filled them with doxwa using her magic ladle. I wanted to try it promptly, but Gulbehar took a bowl for Tewar and we waited until she came back. After so much taunting and overestimation of the doxwa, I expected a strange taste. I tried it first.

"Yummy, yummy, yummy!"

I shouted in German like a child. They all laughed simultaneously. I always find it precious to try something that tastes good on its own and doesn't require any sauce that was made in a lab. I never thought that you could cook something edible with beet leaves and do. Within ten minutes, the huge pot was emptied and just as the two doxwa cookers had predicted, we were even hungrier than before. I said, "Where's the doxwa gone? I feel like my stomach is completely empty."

My other comrades must have had the same feeling. They were hungry and wanted to eat something; even our usual lunch would taste good. Rojano and Zinar brought out two pots containing rice and bean soup. Others brought bread, salt, bowls, and spoons. Out of joy over the unexpected birthday party, or just due to hunger, the bean soup smelled very pleasant. Only with such food can you really satisfy your hunger pangs at this altitude.

We drank tea after lunch, then began a new round of smoking. Everyone but Arjîn and Dêrsîm joined in on the smoking. I took the tobacco pouch from Gulbehar and tried to roll a cigarette for myself. I could not even roll a limp cigarette and let Gulbehar roll me up a thick one. After a month, I smoked again and my head was turning. I looked at Nadîr and his gaze directed my own to the mirtoxe. I shook my index fingers at him several times and said, "You still have to wait. First, hevala Gulbehar has to sing."

I wanted to hear her highest quality singing voice. She smoked the last puff of her cigarette, drank the last sip of tea, and sang a song in the Phrygian scale. I was shocked. In this abandoned mountain, in an underground bunker, I heard for the first time a Kurdish song in this scale. For many years, I always wondered why this scale, which supposedly originated in ancient Greece, was known as a Kurdish mode in Arabic and Turkish music, although it is nowhere to be found in Kurdish music. Where would this Eastern sound have penetrated into Greek music? My music teacher explained to me that the Phrygian mode has this sound due to its semitone step to the second degree and that it is said to have been brought to Greece from Asia Minor by Pythagoras. He was able to explain why Plato hated this mode so much. But neither then nor now have I been able to find out what people lived in Asia Minor at that time or why the scale has come to be considered a Kurdish mode.

Gulbehar is not a professional singer and her voice may be immature, but she sang that scale very impressively. Her voice is full of originality, like those photos that my father proudly sent me from a Şingal foothill three years ago. At that time, such photos were advertised as a means of fighting radical Islam around the world and the huge enterprises of political economy made a profit from them. In the midst of this brutal male world, they were symbols of freedom. Now, these women are no longer reported on in the mass media when the Turkish government rains bombs upon them. They are forced to hide in underground bunkers, confronted by modern drones and the coldness of the world.

Ironically, Gulbehar, a girl from a village area of Kobanî, who escaped from death and survived her wounds, sang a lullaby instead of a birthday song. All the comrades had this song memorized by heart and sang along.

Sleep, dear mother, sleep
The patience and calmness of my life
Let us take this endless street
Deeply hurt, the heart, the feet
Our history has gone blind
There is no present for us to find

Sleep, dear mother, sleep
Grief of my life, for you I weep
You die in the strange battle hour
And it is not within my power
Sleep, dear mother, sleep
Our fields run red with blood
Our mountain forests cursed never to bud
As before us rises a new flood
Sleep, dear mother, sleep
You, flag of my life
The way so unendingly distant
My mother in deep sleep
Arise
Dear mother, climb on
The night is a silent horse

Everyone was singing along with Gulbehar. I was shocked and could not applaud at the end of the song. It must have created a state of despair in the room because Akam grabbed a pot and struck a soft beat in 7/8, which is found in a lot of dances in a large part of Rojhilat. Then he sang a love song and helped me find my composure in the group again. After singing, he asked me, "Doesn't a dance fit your celebration?"

"We have been eating, though. I think it's better if you're the first to tell a joke."

"Just because I played the pot as a drum?"

"Yes, and whoever does not have a joke to tell should keep watch," Rûken replied instead of me.

Her suggestion was democratically accepted. Akam told his joke.

"Four people are stranded in the hot desert due to a car breakdown. A bus from the UN finally arrives. The driver says to them, 'I will ask everyone a question. If you give me the right answer, you can join us.' First he asks the Arab, 'What is the name of the capital of Iraq?' He answers, 'Baghdad.' 'Ok, you can ride.' Then he asks the Persian, 'What is the name of the capital of Iran?' 'Tehran.' 'Very good, I'll take you with us.' After that he asks the Turk, 'What is the name of the capital of Turkey?' 'Istanbul.' 'Bravo.' Last, he asks the Kurd, 'What is the name of the capital of *Habesha?*' The Kurd replies, 'Ugh, just say that you don't take any Kurds.'"

We all laughed. Then Rûnahî was next in line.

"Someone brings a cock to the rural market. A Muslim wants to buy the cock for a bargain price and says, 'I won't buy it. It is from the Êzdîs. It's haram to eat.' The seller answers, 'No, brother I swear by the Quran it is not a Êzdî cock. Every morning you can hear him cry, "Cock-a-doodle-doo-Allahu-akbar."'"

While Rûnahî was telling the joke, she was moving her arms like a cock moves its wings when it cries out. The combination of the doodle-doo and the movements was very funny.

Serhelldan was automatically nominated as the next guard. He neither tells jokes nor dances in this low ceiling room. Our bearded humorist wanted to tell us something real. The main character is as usual Hunger.

"We were in the Qendîl Mountains. The Turkish government was deliberately bombing villages there in order to incite the villagers against us. One day some women came to us and said, 'Please leave this place, the drones are said to be capable of distinguishing the blood of the guerrillas.' Our commander was a woman and tried to convince them it was just the propaganda of the Turkish secret services. Then Hunger said, quite seriously, 'Yes, the drones can. We have lentils in our blood instead of hemoglobin.'"

It led to an explosion of laughter. We almost laughed for a full minute. Then Hunger himself was next in line. He said with a serious expression, "That was my joke. Satyar stole it."

"Do you really mean that?" asked Rûken.

"Yes, heval. Haven't you noticed already? When I move, I sound like a lentil rosary."

He did not laugh at all and just stared at us. Rojano started the next round.

"Goods are transferred across the internal borders of Kurdistan by kollbers and finally loaded onto Toyota pickups. They are always chased away by the IRGC, so they drive faster than any rally driver and they don't use their brakes. Ok, now let's get to the joke. A pickup driver wants to get a driver's license. The examiner asks, 'An ambulance, a fire engine, a pickup, and a motorcycle are on the road; what should be the driving order?' He replies, 'First the pickup drives, then the ambulance, then the fire truck, and finally the motorcycle.' He failed to pass the test several times. In the end, the examiner convinces him that he must give a legitimate answer. He says, 'Ok, first the ambulance, then the fire truck, and finally the motorcycle.' The examiner asks, 'And when does the pickup drive?' He replies, 'Oh, it already drove by.'"

Only the comrades from Rojhilat and Başûr laughed at this joke. Our beardless humorist was next.

"A seedling calls to another, 'Dear date tree, how are you?' The other answers, 'You do not yet know what trees we are, do you? We are . . .' Another tree quickly shouted at him, 'Shut up! Or hevala Gulbehar will uproot us!'"

It took a long time until someone was able to speak again. It was Arjîn, "Poor lemon trees."

I looked at Gulbehar. She was pale, closed her eyes, and gritted her teeth.

"Be careful buddy, or hevala Gulbehar will kill you," Satyar said.

"No, we are friends, she does not kill me for . . . put your hands on your ears, hevala Gulbehar."

She plugged her ears and Arjîn hugged her and kissed her cheeks.

"You wouldn't uproot seedlings; you're a vegetarian. Now tell your joke."

Gulbehar took her hands off her ears. After that, hevalê Ferhad was supposed to tell a joke, but no one wanted to ask anything from him. Gulbehar looked at him as if he must tell us a joke. He looked at me and said, "Darling hevala Jînçin, I want to tell you a joke. Once, there was a competition between different countries. The representatives of these countries should bring a real green leopard to New York City. US genetic engineers modified the genes of a leopard in their laboratories and, after ten months, brought in a veritable green leopard. The British sent their orientalists to where the pepper grows and after ten weeks they pulled a green leopard out of a cave and brought it to the jury. After ten days, the Chinese found a green leopard in their mass leopard-breeding factories and brought it in. After only two days, the representatives of Turkey came back to the jury with a big sack. The jury opened the sack and, puzzled, said, 'This is a turtle.' The Turks replied confidently, 'No, dear jury, this is a green leopard. We have his written confession.'"

Everyone laughed and applauded. I looked at his white hair and black eyebrows. He became silent as a stone again. Gulbehar told her joke next.

"Once, a curfew was enacted and enforced over the city of Êlih in Bakûr, starting at ten o'clock in the evening. A police officer shoots someone at eight o'clock. Some journalists ask him, 'Why did you do that?' He answers, 'the fellow was looking for an address that he couldn't possibly have found until midnight.'"

Before our laughter began, Hunger said, "I had a nonaccurate wristwatch too. Satyar stole it." All our comrades laughed. He was moving his big black eyes around the room, looking at us indifferently, but then his eyes would open wide and shine when he looked at the mirtoxe. Next Arjîn told her joke. She said, "A boy in Rojava says to a girl, 'I love you.' The girl asks, 'How much?' The boy answers, 'My love for you extends even further than a PKK meeting.'"

My eyes lock onto Arjîn's face and I burst into laughter. I am repeating the last sentence in my head and it makes me laugh again and again. She looks at me with her big amber eyes, brings her tongue out from the left side of her mouth, and says, laughing, "Is it possible to love someone more than that?"

"Certainly not," I answered, and all eyes became fixed on me.

"A man is pacing back and forth in his house. His wife asks, 'Why are you men always so restless?' The man replies, 'I have an appointment, but I've forgotten whether I have an appointment with one person at eleven o'clock, or with eleven people at one o'clock."

All the women laughed and applauded me. Hunger raises his hand and asks, "Heval, I don't know; should I laugh, cry, or laugh-cry like all the women just did?"

No one expected such a statement from Hunger. His question was serious and made everyone laugh. Saro took the floor.

"A man asks a junkie, 'What's your biggest ambition?' He replies, 'I wish that all the prominent politicians in the country, from the leader to all the ministers and administration staff, would be my relatives. Then I would play football at the World Cup finals. I am highly motivated and dribble past all of my opponents. I pass the ball to myself over the defenders' heads. Then it would only be the goalkeeper left. I dribble past him with wild maneuvers and stand alone by the goal. Then, with all my strength, I drill the ball right over the goal post. All the viewers in the world will get angry and shout, 'I shit on your whole family!'"

I raised my voice, put down the wave of laughter, and told Saro in English, "Fuck your whole family."

Rojano, Rûnahî, Satyar, and Akam laughed loudly. English is not a secret language here, I guess. I address Saro again, "You must not censor the jokes. You have to tell a new one."

"You told a man-hostile joke. I would have answered you with an opposite one if hevala Rûken was not here."

"Tit for tat. You can tell your joke. Then we can take a cigarette break. After the break, I will tell you a real story about Suleiman," Rûken said.

This name aroused a great deal of enthusiasm. The enthusiastic climate had a minimizing effect on Saro's last joke.

"God created the vast sky and said, 'Ah, the sky is beautiful.' Then he spread out the great seas and said, 'Oh, the seas are beautiful.' After that, he erected the mountains and said, 'Wow, the mountains are beautiful.' At last he created women and said, 'They are beautiful with make-up.'"

The male comrades all laughed. Rûken replied, "Maybe, but men get even uglier with make-up."

Since the comrades preferred smoking, nobody said anything about it. Dêrsîm left the room and Befrîn ran after her. Due to the lack of rats, he relied on mortadella. Moreover, Dêrsîm and Serhelldan also left the room to change guard shifts with Tewar. All others stayed in the room. Surprisingly, smoking was not prohibited in the women's room today. Saro took a crumpled piece of cigarette paper from his copper-colored cigarette box. He tore it into three pieces and made three mini-cigarettes. His work did not attract the slightest bit of attention. Nobody, except me, asked him why he made such Lilliputian cigarettes. Everything is normal here, as long as one does not overlap their feet or talk about sexual topics. The jokes would take place again after the teas were drunk and cigarettes smoked. This was the first time I heard something funny from Rûken.

"When Suleiman reached the party headquarters, he introduced himself as the son of Tahêr Karo, the great Kurdish tribal leader who had become our stubborn enemy due to mistaken party policies. Our comrades called the central committee, stating that the son of our great enemy had arrived. Hevalê Jemal ordered that a large sheep be slaughtered to make kebab. They organized a welcome reception at the ministerial level. In the middle of this reception ceremony somebody shouted, 'he is not a son of Tahêr Karo! His name is Suleiman, the shepherd of our neighboring village.'

Before that, however, he had eaten enough kabab, enjoyed a great reception, and proved his talent as a politician. Therefore, he would immediately be nominated as the party's chief shepherd. All sheep and goats at that time were under his command. However, he wanted to continue his career and build a vegetable garden, the harvest of which the party could make good use of. During the first harvest season, he radioed that his watermelons could no longer be contained. They grew towards Ankara. The representatives of the different groups had gathered there with mules and backpacks and all are said to have come too late; the earliest groups had selfishly taken all the harvest with them.

I don't know anyone who hasn't been lied to by him at least once. One morning he sent me a message saying he had shot five wild boar in his backyard. At that time, we were besieged and had nothing to eat but tree leaves. I informed the other comrades directly by radio.

'Suleiman has shot five wild boars. All the nearby groups should meet with him to get their share.'

That was probably the only time where we talked directly to each other by radio without a secret language. I took three comrades with me and hurried along the way. Many were gathered there, but there was no trace of the boars.

'Heval, where are the wild boars?'

'Heval, you have come too late. I just hurt them, so you could have fresh meat. But, they healed themselves and ran away,' Suleiman said.

'Heval, how can that be? How could all five of them have survived?'

'Heval, they healed themselves by licking each other's wounds.'

'Heval, did they have tongues in their mouths or tubes of healing ointment?"

'Heval, you are naive and unfamiliar with the wild boars; they heal themselves through their saliva.'

I went to Suleiman's famous vegetable garden to see if there was something to eat. The total area was twenty square meters. We invited ourselves to drink tea and smoke and he reluctantly accepted. In the end, he even blamed me for letting so many comrades come.

'If you hadn't invited so many comrades, I would have stayed with the injured wild boars and their mother would not have healed her kids with her saliva.'

The vegetables in his garden had bloomed and it was undiplomatic and unwise in that besieged time to burn any bridges with him. I accepted his invitation for an unspecified future time and said, 'Thanks heval, I don't eat any sacred boars, but please call me when you've shot some ordinary boars.'"

"Did he call you?" I asked.

"Yes, of course."

"And did you go?"

"Yes, heval. His stories are as believable as the fictions you get on the BBC. They are portrayed perfectly. He never uses the same stories. He often invited us to barbecues."

"And did he actually give you something to eat?"

"I ate a lot of kebab with him. He told me he grilled lambs and goats, but it was not true. He probably gave us other animals' meat to eat. Maybe cats, donkeys, bears . . . for the central committee of the party, he will slaughter his sheep, but for us, not even a mule. One time that we were there, a dog was so freshly slaughtered that its pieces of meat were still barking."

Imagining the barking pieces of meat made me shout loudly in German.

"*Du heilige Scheiße!*"

"What did you say?" Rûken asked.

"Holy shit. He really gave you dog meat?"

"I do not know, heval, but he could not have given us that much sheep meat. Thousands of guerrillas would have eaten kebab from his sheep. He does not have that many sheep. Additionally, there were many bears in these mountains. The Turkish drones can't kill all of the bears. In the past, we used to play soccer with the bears here."

Our collective laughter made Rûkan's lost smile appear on her face again for a few seconds. I was quite pleased that it happened on my birthday. Dêrsîm was the last one to tell her joke.

"The party leaders wanted the cofounder of our party, hevalê Heyder Qeresû, to learn his mother tongue. All previous attempts had failed. So, they drew their last card and sent Suleiman to him. Suleiman could not speak any language but Kurdish and hevalê Heyder Qeresû had no other means of communication with him except Kurdish. After two months, a delegation from the party visited Suleiman. They told him, 'no matter what, you should only speak Kurdish with hevalê Heyder Qeresû. Got it?' Suleiman answered calmly, 'Bilmiyorum.'"*

Everyone laughed, but the joke made me a bit sad. I asked hevalê Ferhad, "Can hevalê Heyder Qeresû really not speak Kurdish?"

"I do not know whether he can or not, but regardless, he never does speak in Kurdish."

"But how can one say that he is fighting against cultural oppression and assimilation if, after forty years as a cofounder of the PKK, he still refuses to learn the mother language? That's just pure contempt for one's own culture and a confirmation of the oppressors' policies of assimilation. His refusal to learn Kurdish is, in my eyes, no different from a confirmation of support for Kemalism. If I live in Baghdad for a year and do not learn a word of Arabic, I am either stupid or fascist."

My unexpected rage could have ruined my birthday party. Right on time, Tewar raises her hand and says something without looking at me.

"I also want to tell a joke at this birthday party. An old maid wants to commit suicide. She goes into a large flower vase in the city's big square and holds a sign in her hands, saying, 'Please stop watering me.'"

---

* "I don't know" in Turkish.

CHAPTER 8

AT NIGHT, NATURE seized everyone's attention. The breeze rustled through the meadow, the winds howled through the branches, and the storms swept through the hanging blankets on the entrance doors. We sealed the bunker doors in time and split our lives into two worlds: the indoor world of monotony and the outdoor world of diversity. Early in the autumn, for a few nights, there were heavy rainstorms. Lightning was hitting the mountain peaks while thunder roared, then echoed through the valleys and into my dreams. Everything changed with the first heavy snowfall. For three nights, a blizzard dumped snow on us. Treading on the snow was banned and we stayed locked in our bunker. The free world of nature was always a few steps away, yet inaccessible to us.

Two areas of our bunker were designated for serving guard. We had to sit on hemp crates and listen for any sound that might indicate danger. In the middle area near the kitchen, however, we could merely enjoy the sounds of nature.

Blizzards are like visible winds, like white hurricanes. They hiss into the canyons, whistle into the caves, and screech all the way to the mountaintops. Our nights are filled with a concert of natural sounds. Nevertheless, it doesn't rouse us, but, in fact, sweetens our slumber. I often think back to my previous life in Munich. After nine in the evening, I never dared to walk around my apartment. The neighbor downstairs immediately banged on the ceiling with a stick. She was not the only one who needed absolute silence when sleeping. Since I've been in these mountains, I always ask myself why we didn't complain about storms or thunderbolts, but would be up in arms about the faintest whisper from our neighbors. I was allergic to the presence of others and called it individualism. Now, on this mountain I feel like my comrades and I are a part of nature. We breathe like the breeze, flow like the stream, and leave behind little traces of our incidental existence.

Over three meters of snow lay on the ground. The hawthorn trees were all wearing dresses of snow. The blizzards covered everything that was previously cleared of snow. Every day we bring more than thirty buckets of snow into the bunker, but each time we have to clear the newly blown snow from the steps if we want to sit outside behind the kitchen blanket door.

Nowadays, two topics are the most common points of discussion: the danger of a new attack by the Turkish army on Rojava and the yellow vests movement. Quite unlike the PKK's party media, which is one-dimensional and propagandist, the facts are analyzed here realistically, with proper details, and the chances and risks are factually put up for discussion. The world powers will not remain the laughing third party forever. Turkey's military intervention in Rojava, which was authorized by the superpowers, would not restrain the potential social, political, and historical movements in the Middle East forever, and the suppression of the yellow vests revolt would not put away or even hide a heap of problems that capitalism has caused during its long historical trend, especially apropos of the financial industry in the last decade and the European Central Bank in the past twenty years.

Practically only five people participated in these discussions, but apart from us, Gulbehar, Arjîn, and Nadîr were also interested in these topics. These two girls in our group always write new topics in their notebooks. Hunger's interest can be read just by looking at his big black eyes. Dêrsîm and Rûnahî, like Zinar and Satyar, are heartily bound to the movement, but they are more interested in practical than theoretical activities. They are ready for anything that does not engage their thoughts to the point of causing a headache.

Over time, I became accustomed to these prolonged discussions. This bunker is limited, but an eternal landscape emerges when we roll up the hanging blanket over the entrance. Without this nightly meditation, the house arrest would get to me. The nights here are sources of eternal energy with their fascinating voices and the enchanting combined images of earth and sky. During the blizzards, everything constantly changes and no landscape remains the same for more than a few seconds, neither in voice, nor in image. The sound of snow breaking, avalanches roaring, winds howling, thunder screeching, and then, suddenly, silence. Even the rocks in front of us changed constantly. Sometimes it would be infinitely white, and then the hurricane would reveal its dark, bare features.

Once the wind begins to calm and the sky becomes clear, the nights turn into a quite charming landscape. One night, when I was on guard duty, I was charmed by the beauty of that magical night. A clear winter sky, twinkling stars. Indigo blue above, white below. The snowfall reflected the light of the stars. The breeze was creeping over the snow, moonlight was shining, and the little snowflakes were swirling to the rhythm of the river. That may have been my daydream, but the landscape drew Rûken in towards the end of my watch. At that time, I was sitting near the kitchen outside of the hanging blanket. She greeted me and sat next to me on the step. Soon, Arjîn also appeared, laughing, and said, "We have invited ourselves in. Can you stand us?"

"I enjoy your company," I replied.

She had two sacks stuffed with dried brushwood and a dustpan over them in her hands. Rûken went down two steps, picked up the dustpan, and shoveled the snow down the steps. Arjîn put the sacks on the lower step and both sat down. Soon Rojano appeared with a tea tray in her hands. Four tea glasses were on it.

"May I sit here?"

"Of course, hevala Rojano. I'm not the only one who loves the nighttime."

"Yes, the night is lovely. In Rojava we always made a fire in the evening and gathered around it. But without fire, the nights look even more beautiful."

I took a glass of tea, drank a sip, and asked Rojano, "Do you believe in astrology?"

"I do not believe in that."

I put my hand on Arjîn's shoulder. She turned, looked at the tea glass in my hand and said, "You just took my tea. Give it back soon. You do not drink your tea sweet and strong."

I gave her the tea and took another from the tea tray and asked another question.

"And what about you, hevala Arjîn, are you interested in horoscopes or astrology?"

She stirred her tea with a spoon, took a few sips, and gave me an answer.

"Why would someone be here if she were interested in such things? No one in my family was superstitious or religious, and I don't know anything about astrology, either."

"Then why are you always staring at the sky?"

"I enjoy looking at the sky. The nights here are nice."

"You sit here and look at the sky at every opportunity just because it's beautiful?"

"Is that not enough? Everyone likes to look at beautiful things."

"Yes, everyone likes that. The question is, however, do you think you can look at beauties just because you find them fascinating? What do you do when a man sits opposite you and stares at you for an hour?"

"That's a different question. I watch the sky without disturbing it."

"How do you know that we are not disturbing the stars when we look at them? Modern physics points out that our thoughts and attention can have an effect on different objects."

"Is that an assumption or is it proven?" Instead of Arjîn, Rojano asked the question. I answered her without addressing her directly.

"Assumption, but if a man looks at you, it would be also a matter of assumption whether he does it for your beauty or wants to disturb you."

"Or he wants something from us."

"What could he want from you, hevala Arjîn? Your beauty? But you also want to have that from the sky."

"You cannot compare these two. What can I do to the sky?"

"You can enjoy its beauty. Is a man allowed to look at your face and enjoy it?"

"I do not wear a niqab. But two people cannot stand staring at each other for long. Eventually, one of them would want to speak."

"Exactly, and what do you say to someone who just wants to look at your face."

"I don't know. Maybe I'll turn my head around, but I wouldn't have insulted anyone yet."

"Turning the head means he is not allowed to enjoy your beauty. But still, your reaction is more decent than my reaction. For some nights I had the face of a man in front of my eyes and couldn't get rid of it. His friends played on the beach with a ball, but he was watching me furtively. I caught him a few times. A silly feeling provoked me to get up and defend something in me. I went toward him and shouted at him as he turned pale and became speechless. I wanted to preserve my so-called privacy. For a long time I had forgotten this event and this man, but I asked myself for some days whether he forgot it so easily. We deem it to be from our kindness when we are looking at and smelling the flowers or hugging animals, but we don't let other people do the same with us. What is the origin of this serious alienation of people from each other? People feed the wild animals and birds, yet will put a pot full of shit in front of the emergency shelter for asylum seekers. Five years ago, I saw this scene in eastern Germany. At that time, I thought xenophobia was the main reason for this act. Now I think it's something else, but I'm not sure if these topics are forbidden to discuss here."

"You can talk openly. I see a hidden form of domination behind every forbidden subject."

"Thanks, hevala Rûken, I believe the history of power runs parallel with the sex monopoly."

"Explain more."

"Not only in human societies, but also in the animal kingdom, power is made through the control of sexual rules. Where there is some kind of power, there are also sexual monopolies. Do you remember that day when hevalê Akam talked about the differences between chimpanzees and bonobos?"

"Yes."

"He censored an important fact on this topic. The social structure of the patriarchal chimpanzee community is based on a sex monopoly. There is always a strong male who specifies the sexual rules. These rules concerning sexual practices are also determined in human societies by superior authorities. By no other means, not even religion or nationalism, can the powers that be divide society so massively and continuously as through sex. From ancient times until now, there was an intense relationship between the outlook on sex and the possession of thought systems within societies."

"What conclusions do you want me to draw from all this? What does sex monopolization have to do with beauty?" Rojano asked me.

"In nature, beauty is the driving force of sexual relations. But in subjugated societies, this relationship is manipulated and power takes over the role of beauty. In our worldwide societies, the natural relationship based on beauty deviates and money takes the position of beauty. People are no longer attracted to each other because of their beauty, but because of money and power. Sex is the bone of contention for those in power. Women used to be the most honored of the clan, now they are property of the state. It is always emphasized that women and children are raped everywhere, even by their own parents and husbands. Only the rock-solid paragraphs of the constitution could offer them safe protection. States are portrayed as saviors in the name of the law, even though they create societies where people are dragged down and raped on a much larger scale in the companies, manufacturing facilities, and sex industry."

"Even in Germany?"

"Yes, hevala Rojano, women there are more likely to be influenced by a luxury car than by spiritual or even physical beauty. Governments around the world have drawn a bubble of loneliness around the people and call it privacy. Not by beauty, but by capital, can you expand this swollen bubble and take a breath. The rulers promise people, and especially women, a guarantee of protection in their social lives, which is nothing other than a collective isolation. And, ironically, I've been a part of it my whole life. Now, in my opinion, we cannot attain a borderless world of pervasive happiness if we fail to overcome our egos and stick to our individualistic boundaries. I am not the only person in the world who has a bit of beauty. From whom should I protect my beauty? From voyeuristic men? At this point, I see such men as harmless people who are trying to attract us through natural means. They do not scare me anymore, but the gentlemen of high social standing do. They do not need to chase skirts and stare at women; rather, they easily offer women a job and suck their life up and then spit them out. Back to my first question. Hevala Arjîn, you have very nice curly hair. How do you react when a stranger asks you to let him touch your hair?"

"When I was a child, many people would touch my hair. Our neighbors even kidnapped me to play with my hair and spoil me. My father and I had a common ritual, similar to your and your father's with the hawthorns. He liked to wash my hair and straighten my curly wet hair with his hands. The hair would curl back in a few seconds. He would do it again and again and laugh the whole time. Now, if someone touches my hair, I remember my childhood. Hevala Gulbehar often does it and makes me laugh."

"And you, hevala Rojano? Do you let others stare at you?"

"I often had to. On the border we were always under observation. Mostly I was in physical contact with male kollbers. That was inevitable. We had to take care of each other, since we would overload ourselves and get injured, or get wounded by others. The kollbers were burdened with heavy loads and couldn't possibly think about sex. They were usually so tired that they would willingly let themselves be beaten. Sexism could only be found in the eyes and words of the border guards, and I always avoided them."

"It's better to refer to such perverse attitudes and views with other terms. The word 'sexism' has become divisive. It serves the same purpose today that 'adultery' did in medieval times. If one is to condemn men's attempts to attract women as sexist, one must also prohibit the songbirds' chirps and the wing-dancing of peacocks. Such generalized feminist terms have brought no benefits or freedoms, only misery. I cannot understand why an ordinary male citizen would be branded a sexist when he just wants to show us his affection, but it's perfectly decent for an entrepreneur to publish a job advertisement that clearly states that enchanting and attractive women are needed? If I were a psychoanalyst I would have defined our relationship with Befrîn as sexist. Hevala Arjîn always wants to have Befrîn in her arms. Heval, do you have sexual affection for him?"

"Yes heval, I want to marry him."

We broke out laughing.

"Really heval, he has soft white fur and I have brown curly hair. Our baby would be a hedgehog."

I would have liked to grab her and kiss her forehead several times. Rûken asked Rojano if she had a rolled-up cigarette. Rojano moved her hand toward me and took her tobacco bag from her vest pocket. The moon was gone. The dark clouds had covered the sky and it was not bright like hours ago. Nevertheless, she quickly rolled up two cigarettes. Both of them lit the cigarettes behind their palms and hid the glowing tips of the cigarettes in their fists. Right after smoking, Rûken said, "Tomorrow hevala Gulbehar will tell you a story."

"You won't be there?"

"I have something to do. I've already heard the story."

The next morning began strangely. The training course took place in the men's room and only seven people participated. So, I guessed that they must be planning a new birthday party. Only Saro, Hunger, and Akam were there. Gulbehar, Rojano, and I entered the room, waited for Arjîn to feed Befrîn, and brought him into the room. She held him with both hands and he was turning his head back and forth, his blue and yellow eyes darting around the room. It seemed that he was looking for something or was just confused why we had gathered into this small room. Arjîn's brown, curly hair had covered some parts of his white fur. Without realizing it, I pointed and shouted, "Porcupine!" Rojano laughed. After a few seconds, Arjîn said, "Aha, hedgehog." She sat beside me, laughing. Saro started the discussion.

"Today, hevala Gulbehar wants to tell us something that I've heard about in Rojava. But I would like to hear this story from a comrade who saw the event as a witness. Hevala Gulbehar would like to tell the story of a comrade who accomplished the first self-sacrifice operation in Kobanî."

"Do you mean hevala Arîn Mîrkan?" I asked.

"No, hevala Rêvan.* She did this kind of operation before hevala Arîn Mîrkan, but her operation was not publicized. I would also like to hear the reasons for this from hevala Gulbehar."

"As hevalê Saro said, hevala Rêvan was the first person to accomplish a self-sacrifice operation to stop the advance of Daesh towards Kobanî. When she accomplished this operation, hevalê Botan and I were beside her, but I don't know why hevalê Botan didn't say anything about hevala Rêvan's operation. Maybe he gave information about the operation but it was not reported. So nobody heard about it, until I was discharged from my month-long hospitalization and could tell others about hevala Rêvan's self-sacrifice. When I returned to Kobanî, I recounted it to many comrades. At the beginning, I was reiterating the story frequently, until I met someone who knew hevala Rêvan well but wasn't aware of her self-sacrifice operation.

She was turning over the pages of one of my books with a photo of hevala Rêvan in it. She laughed when she saw her photo. I asked her if she knew hevala Rêvan. She replied, 'Of course I know this cowardly, shy girl.' I was shocked. I got upset and wanted to shout at her, but I became

---

* The guard of the path.

speechless instead. After a few seconds, I noticed that she had left the room. I asked myself if it were possible that she mistook hevala Rêvan for someone else. I went out and asked her some questions. They were classmates with each other. She said hevala Rêvan was a cowardly girl at that time. Although I was with hevala Rêvan for a short time, I found her character to be totally different from what this heval told me. A brave girl with high self-confidence.

I first saw hevala Rêvan during military training. She was sitting there with a group of comrades. They were making jokes about it, but she continuously wrote information from the training in a notebook. She caught my attention. She was always busy trying to help other comrades, from preparing them tea and drinking water to teaching the uneducated comrades.

After military training was finished, we lost touch with each other. After a year, we were busy organizing a new front against Daesh. I saw her again on 'Sêv Hill.' However, that was where hevalê Xabûr had fallen, so they renamed the location 'Hevalê Xabûr Hill.' Our comrades sent me there several times. That time, hevala Rêvan was responsible for the group. Although she was older than me by about five years, she treated me like a peer and friend. The first time I got a mission to go there, she welcomed me warmly. That area was full of dust and a red haze. Because of the advance of Daesh, I was in a bad place mentally and spiritually. Hevala Rêvan personally accompanied me and on the way we talked about routine affairs. When we separated, the air was still full of dust, but my spiritual condition had improved.

Suddenly, the Daesh advance hastened. They were raiding Kurdish villages with tanks and armored vehicles and we couldn't stop them. Comrades were sending me to various fronts and I saw hevala Rêvan once more. She was tall and skinny. Her hair was neither long, nor short. Her face was neither round, nor bony. She had a harmonious face and body. I can't forget that day; the image is still fresh in my mind, especially when I see some of our comrades. Hevala Rêvan was carrying the military equipment of two guerillas. A BKC*with associated magazines, a

---

* This is called a PKM everywhere but Kurdistan. However, this reference is occurring within a quotation, so one can imagine that Gulbehar would indeed refer to it as a BKC. —Translator's note

Kalashnikov with six cartridges, and three grenades. I approached hevala Rêvan and offered her my help. But she answered, 'These are not heavy. I can carry them.'

I know well how heavy that military equipment was on her shoulders and why she had not dropped yet. She had been numbed by a plethora of mental and spiritual troubles and couldn't feel the burden of those loads. Maybe she wanted to send me the message that there is no heavier burden on her shoulders than our historical task of resistance.

Daesh was occupying villages around Kobanî and we resisted until the villagers could flee toward Kobanî or Bakûr. Hevala Rêvan went toward the front lines and led a group of comrades, though she was only serving as a BKC carrier. That is to say, she was not assigned to command them, but she nevertheless led the group through her natural authority.

After a while, the front lines began to change. Again, our forces could focus there. I saw hevala Rêvan once more when she was with hevalê Kendal, who later fell in Kobanî. Hevalê Kendal told me that some comrades had to go to a village for positioning. Hevala Rêvan, hevalê Kendal, and I accompanied three other comrades to that village. It was neither a village, nor a hamlet. Just two peasant houses next to each other. There was a hill near the houses where we positioned ourselves. A group of eleven comrades were already fighting above the hill. When the first tank had fired a shell, hevala Rêvan got up and looked around for something within the house. She found a sledgehammer and some iron pipes, then made several holes in the wall. I approached to help her and she said to me, without missing a beat of her work rhythm, 'We have to prepare ourselves for battle. Daesh will arrive in the evening.'

The other two comrades also helped us and in a few hours we made several holes in the walls through which we could see the Daesh tanks and armored vehicles. The enemy outnumbered us and attacked our comrades from different sides. Hevala Rêvan was sitting beside us, but was thinking about the comrades who were on the hill.

After five hours of fighting, two comrades from the hill came to us. They had no more water and wanted to get a drink. Hevala Rêvan drew water from the well in the yard with a hand pump and brought them a couple gallons. Before they left us, some comrades on the hill reported by radio that one of them had been injured. One of the two hevalên told us that it was not possible to go there by car and that one of us should accompany them to transfer the injured comrade to the back line. Hevala Rêvan lifted both gallons and wanted to go with them, but I told her, 'It is better for you to stay here, because you can defend this position with your BKC.'

'Ok, I'll leave my BKC for you.'

'You have more experience with the BKC than us and should stay here,' I replied.

She accepted my suggestion. We had to find a practical solution to rescue the injured comrade. There was a donkey in the yard. I said we should take the donkey with us to transfer the injured comrade downhill, so that the other comrades would not need to transfer him and, moreover, he would not lose too much blood. We took the donkey, but hevala Rêvan again implored me, 'let me go with them.'

'No, hevala Rêvan. You are the BKC operator and it's necessary for an experienced comrade to stay here.'

'All of you can fire the BKC like I can.'

'This is *your* BKC and *you* have to shoot it. If we get into trouble I will call you. Two comrades are sufficient to transfer the injured comrade right now.'

Hevala Rêvan accepted. She stayed on the farm and we went up the hill from the back side. The Daesh tanks had put the hill under heavy fire and their infantrymen were trying to climb up the hill. The comrades above the hill had no barricades and were changing their position by crawling on the ground. We arrived at the middle of the hill and I saw that Daesh forces were closing in on hevala Rêvan's position. It was dark, but from the light of the heavy fire and explosions I could see how heavy the fighting was there. The hill and the two houses downhill had been besieged on three sides and we had to quickly extricate ourselves from the situation. We reached the injured comrade and tried to lay him on the donkey, but he was too long and the donkey couldn't support him. It was dark and we were besieged by Daesh. There was only a narrow passage left for us to retreat through.

The comrades on the hill lifted up the injured comrade and carried him down on their shoulders. They had given their weapons to a young, little heval to let themselves go down freely. The burden of those weapons made that little heval walk funny. Her name was Arjîn or Arşîn.* One of the male comrades and I stayed there to cover them as they fled far away from the front lines. We reached the houses on the back side of the hill when we retreated. The comrades went towards another group that had been besieged. A male comrade and I were trying to take the injured comrade to the rear. Hevala Rêvan and two comrades resisted heavy fire to cover us from behind and not let Daesh chase after us. I wanted to help hevala Rêvan, but the injured comrade was hemorrhaging, and we had to rescue him quickly. We were carrying him on our shoulders in turns and walked in an unknown direction. We were trying to move towards the city.

After a while, we got lost. I wanted to find hevala Rêvan and the other comrades, but our cell phone and radio batteries were depleted. We didn't know the location of the central command. For six hours we traveled around, while the injured comrade was on our backs. He was bleeding intensely as my back became soaked through with his blood. I realized that was going to die soon because the temperature of his blood was going down. I told my comrade, 'Please look around carefully. Perhaps you can find other comrades.'

I didn't tell him that the injured comrade was in such a serious condition because I was afraid the injured comrade would hear me. We heard shooting and mortar explosions from all sides and we could only walk around without knowing the path, the injured comrade on our shoulders. From the other side, comrades from the central command were looking for us. Suddenly, I heard my name in the dark. Comrades were calling me on the radio. I turned my head in the dark and I saw a driver in a car. Somebody was calling me within the car radio. It seems the battery of their radio was nearly dead or its connection was weak. I quickly replied to him. I described our situation and location to him. The comrades said, 'Either stay there, or walk toward Kobanî away from the road until we can pick you up.'

When a comrade drove by and found us, we were exhausted. We had walked from six at night until three in the morning with the comrade on our shoulders. Fortunately, he was rescued, and we reached hevalê Kendal and his group. I found that hevala Rêvan and her group were not

---

* Blue fire.

there. I asked our comrades about them and said, 'We went with each other but came back alone. Their radio wasn't working and I am worried about them.'

I called hevala Rêvan by radio several times, but didn't receive any response. Hevalê Kendal called me. I went toward him and he said, 'Why are you making noises?'

'I lost my comrades. We went with each other, but I came back alone. I am worried about them,' I replied.

He said that I should not worry and that they would arrive soon. At five o'clock in the morning, I saw hevala Rêvan and her group coming toward us. We hugged each other. We were hungry, but more than food, we needed sleep. There was no place to lay our heads. Hevalê Kendal told us we could go to his car to sleep. I sat in the front seat and hevala Rêvan, the little heval, and another comrade sat in the back seats. I wanted to take a nap while sitting, but dawn approached and Daesh forces had resumed their assault. There was near constant gunfire and any time I closed my eyes a new bang would stir me. I couldn't sleep anyway, because I was worried about the Daesh attack. They were constantly bringing comrades' corpses and injured people to that area. Hevala Rêvan was sleeping soundly, though her eyes would move whenever a gunshot pop went off.

After twenty minutes we got out of the car. The battle had been intense. Daesh attacked with many tanks and armored vehicles and we could not stop their advance with our light weapons. Hevalê Kendal said that hevala Rêvan and the little heval should go to another front. They walked away. I told hevala Rêvan, 'Take care of the little heval.'"

I interrupted Gulbehar and said, "How old were you at this time?"

"I was seventeen."

"Do you mean the little heval was younger than you?"

"I don't know, hevala Jînçin. I never saw him again. They went to another front and again we were separated from each other. A few days passed before the war reached where we were stationed. We fought for a whole day and into the next morning. The terrain was unfavorable; there were no trees around. I told my comrades, 'I would like to join hevala Rêvan's group.'

'Ok, you can go. I will call you by radio if the situation has changed,' Hevalê Kendal replied to me.

I went to hevala Rêvan's position. There were comrades there who I didn't know. That front was a small hill. Our position was on the downhill and a group of comrades held the position above there. From our position, we could see several houses that Daesh forces had occupied. But we had neither a barricade, nor a suitable place for battle. They had set some stones on each other to identify the boundaries of the farmland. We sheltered behind those stones. Daesh fired occasional bullets at us, which hit the rocks and sent stony particles flying like shrapnel. In front and behind us there were a few small olive trees. Hevala Rêvan was sitting under one of them. I sat under the next tree and we looked at the other comrades. They were making jokes.

'The enemy is perched in fortified houses and here we are sitting behind a rickety stone fence. And, yet, they don't dare appear.'

'If we had time, we could make a pyramid with these stones.'

'Could we fight behind a pyramid?'

'No, we might get buried underneath it.'

'How romantic!'

The weather was continuously changing. Sometimes the sun appeared and it became warm and sometimes it was raining and became cold. The location of that front didn't help us in either case. Daesh had modern weapons which the Iraqi army had left in Mosûl and the Turkish government also provided Daesh with modern equipment, such as night and thermal binoculars. Nevertheless, we insisted on fighting against Daesh until the last breath. Hevalê Kendal came and told me, 'I will send someone to take your place. I am waiting for her so that I can send you away from the front line.'

I didn't ask to be sent back, but he was my commander and I had to obey. Hevalê Kendal told our comrades, 'Get ready, we will attack Daesh tonight.'

I saw hevala Rêvan smiling when she heard we were going to attack Daesh. After hevalê Kendal had left, she asked me, 'Am I right, hevala Gulbehar? Will we attack Daesh tonight?'

'Hevalê Kendal said that it will happen.'

The excitement covered her face and she said, 'Tonight we have to save those houses from these bandits.'

That attack was canceled. Most of the comrades who knew the region had been injured or killed. The remaining comrades were fresh and didn't know anything about the place. That night, we didn't retreat or attack Daesh. Except hevalê Botan from Bakûr, who requested to be excused to seek treatment for his illness, none of the other comrades wished to retreat or be transferred to other fronts. The commander told him to wait until he called him. He remained there reluctantly, but when the battle began he was the most effective comrade, helping others and having a great influence on the battlefield. He was with me when hevala Rêvan died, but I have not heard from him for a long time, and I haven't the faintest idea of what he is doing right now. I really miss him and would like to see him once more and talk about our memories.

That day we stayed there and hevala Rêvan took a central role amongst the comrades. We spent the whole day without food or drinking water. Once evening neared, we couldn't transfer to another front because of the darkness. She joked with us. I still remember one of her jokes. She said, 'Hevalê Botan, we are hungry. What are we supposed to do?'

'Hevala Rêvan, a new restaurant recently opened near here called Seyran. We can go there and order all the food we'd like.'

'I heard about that place, but I haven't gone there. Bring me some delicious food,' Hevala Rêvan replied, chuckling.

'What are you in the mood for?'

'I don't know. I'll adjust to your taste. Bring me whatever meal you'd like, but don't forget to bring me a salad and a yellow cola.'

'What do you want for dessert, heval?'

'I'm no glutton. Three kinds of fruit is enough.'

Then hevalê Botan asked me, 'And what do you want to order, hevala Gulbehar?'

'For me only poisonous mushrooms! Why are you being ridiculous, hevala Rêvan? We're getting attacked!'

'Right, that's why we must keep our energy up. Botan is hungry and he wants to go to a restaurant on our behalf.'

'I have enough money in my pocket. It's on me; let's go to the restaurant. We always have time for battle.'

'Is it a suitable time to go to a restaurant when we are in this hell? This is a real battle, yet you suggest we go to a restaurant? Is it a good time for such jokes? We came here to attack Daesh, but now we can only try to defend our position. How can we defend these stones? Daesh will attack us soon and we are so hungry that we don't even have the strength to stand,' I said.

'You are right, hevala Gulbehar. We need more energy for battle, so let me change my order. Hevalê Botan, bring me energy drinks instead of cola. You are paying, but it's better to save your money,' hevala Rêvan said, laughing.

Hevala Rêvan was humoring and encouraging the other comrades with her words. There were some fresh comrades who had been scared because they had not taken part in battle yet. They were gathering around hevala Rêvan and she talked to them about routine life. She was giving them moral support for the battlefield and raising their spirits. We got a message by radio: 'Your provisions have arrived. Send someone to collect them.'

Our commander asked who wanted to go to collect our provisions. Hevala Rêvan raised her hand:

'Don't go alone. Take a comrade with you to bring them all at once.'

When they brought our provisions, it was twilight. I went toward her and said, 'How did you carry so many loads? Didn't you get tired?'

'No heval, if a comrade gets injured, I have to carry them for a long time, so a petty load is not heavy to carry anymore. Moreover, the food doesn't tire me. Let's eat.'

That load was very heavy. Besides ammunition, they brought bread, mortadella, cheese, drinking water, and, as I remember, three kinds of fruits: grapes, apples, and oranges. Hevala Rêvan gave her share of mortadella to the other comrades. We were divided into two groups. The first group would eat and the other group would keep watch behind the pile of stones. After the meal, we specified the battle formation. The commander of the first group, who was a woman, said, 'Hevala Rêvan, you and two other male comrades should take a position at the bottom of the field.' That was the most dangerous part of the battlefield, because it was within range of the houses in which Daesh troops were positioned. The commander turned to me and said, 'Hevalê Botan is the BKC operator. You can help him.'

I stayed with hevalê Botan. Our commander went uphill with two other comrades. Two more comrades positioned between us and the barricade. The remaining comrades were scattered behind the hedges. Before I took my position, hevala Rêvan told me, 'Today we fought here and the enemy is familiar with our situation. We must be careful that the enemy doesn't besiege us.'

'Go to your barricade and sleep peacefully. Daesh will shout "Allahu akbar" when they attack, so we will know when they've arrived,' Hevalê Botan said.

'I don't want to depend on hearing their cries. The battle has already arrived at our door.'

She went toward her barricade and took an apple and an orange. I took some grapes to my position, put them on the stone, and nibbled on them. I lit a cigarette in my palm and started smoking. Hevalê Botan laid on the ground and took a rest. I told him, 'Hevalê Botan, don't sleep! It is very dangerous if Daesh attacks us while you're sleeping.' He said, 'Don't worry, I will wake up quickly if they attack us.'

It was dark without moonlight. The weather was cold, foggy, and full of dust, so nothing was visible. That was an advantage that let Daesh reach us stealthily. When hevala Rêvan shot the first bullet, they were less than ten meters away. Within the darkness, we could not see even our comrades behind the barricade. The Daesh troops could find us with their night binoculars and injured hevala Rêvan and many other comrades.

The first bullet they shot was too close to us. An intense battle began. The dark night turned to red from the shower of bullets. Hevalê Botan jumped to his BKC and fired. I opened fire with my Kalashnikov, too. I couldn't see anyone, but the Daesh troops' fire was very heavy and they were firing at us from everywhere. My Kalashnikov had less effect than the BKCs of hevala Rêvan and hevalê Botan. We shot back when shots were seen from somewhere. After ten minutes hevala Rêvan screamed. I wanted to reach her to know what had happened. I lowered my head and went toward her, half-crouching. The glowing red bullets were constantly tearing through the dark night. I heard bullets buzzing. I dropped to the ground and called to hevala Rêvan. Her voice was coming from somewhere near me. Evidently, she wanted to reach us after she was injured, but hevala Rêvan lost her strength across the way and had fallen on the ground.

'What happened, hevala Rêvan?' I asked.

'I've been injured. They shot me, hevala Gulbehar.'

'Don't worry. I'll save you, heval.'

She said that her flank was hit by three bullets or stone particles. I said, 'Heval, cover me until I reach you.' But she replied, 'Go and save yourself, hevala Gulbehar. I will remain here.'

'I will not leave here until I've saved you.'

But hevala Rêvan answered again, 'You have to go. You cannot save me. Go and take care of the other comrades. I have pulled out my grenade's pin.'

'Throw your grenade away! I will save you.'

While I was shooting at the enemy I yelled, 'Cover me, hevalê Botan! I will go toward hevala Rêvan.'

I wanted to go toward hevala Rêvan in the darkness. I noticed there were no other comrades who remained around me. Many of them had been injured or were transferring injured comrades. At that time, I just saw hevala Rêvan and hevalê Botan. Except us, nobody remained there. I wanted to save her anyway. I asked hevalê Botan to go on shooting until I could reach hevala Rêvan. Hevala Rêvan was shooting her BKC and I was shooting my Kalashnikov in any direction from which they were firing at us. I wanted to reach hevala Rêvan when the firing slowed down. Once I reached her, she couldn't stay up anymore and fell down to the ground, after which the Daesh fire began again. I knew she was in a critical situation. When I stood up to go toward hevalê Botan, she again stood halfway up and started shooting. I reached hevalê Botan and said, 'I couldn't reach hevala Rêvan. Take your BKC and go back to cover me better. I will shoot them and go toward hevala Rêvan to save her.'

We were surrounded. Daesh had also advanced from behind hevala Rêvan. I gave hevalê Botan's BKC and its cartridges to him, changed my Kalashnikov magazine and opened fire on the enemy. Hevala Rêvan also started shooting again with her BKC to let hevalê Botan take an appropriate position to cover us. I reached hevala Rêvan and told her, 'Let's go.' When I put my arm around her neck to pull her up, she said, 'Hevala Gulbehar, you have to go save yourself. The enemy has arrived here. You and hevalê Botan have to go away. I have pulled out my grenade's pin.'

'Throw them away, heval. I'll take you and will not leave here without you.'

Hevala Rêvan told me several times, 'No, heval, I have pulled out my grenade's pin and can't come with you.'

I didn't listen to her and picked her up and said, 'Throw them away. Hevalê Botan is covering us.'

My foot had been shot by a bullet when I was going toward hevala Rêvan, but I didn't notice. The enemy threw a grenade at us once I had picked up hevala Rêvan. Some shrapnel hit my head and I fell down onto hevala Rêvan. Over and over, I would faint for a few seconds and come back to my senses. In this situation, hevala Rêvan called for hevalê Botan. When I came to my senses, I hung onto hevalê Botan's shoulder. He had tied a cloth on my head wounds. I asked him, 'Where is hevala Rêvan?'

'She remained there. I could only save you.'

'Why did you save me, but left her alone?'

'I had no other choice. I had to save you. It was hevala Rêvan's demand.'

'We have to return to save her.'

I was becoming motionless. The weather was cold and my whole body was soaked in blood. The coldness was turning me senseless.

'Don't you hear the enemy voices? It's too late to save her,' Hevalê Botan said.

'We have to save her.'

I wanted to go back toward hevala Rêvan. The enemy voices were getting louder. They were speaking Arabic. I didn't understand what they were talking about, but it was evident they had reached hevala Rêvan. Though hevalê Botan didn't know Arabic, he said he was aware that Daesh troops had arrived near hevala Rêvan. I was trying to go toward her, while hearing their laughing voices. Suddenly, hevala Rêvan's grenade detonated. After that hevalê Botan told me, 'We can't save hevala Rêvan anymore. She has performed a sacrifice operation and I have to save you.'

At that moment I was confused and moved continuously in and out of consciousness. After some minutes, I couldn't speak and became completely unconscious. I couldn't remember how hevalê Botan saved me and got me to the other comrades nor how they transferred me to Bakûr. When I was in Bakûr for treatment, I felt indebted to hevala Rêvan. I have to do something, because she was the first one to perform a self-sacrifice operation. After a month, my wounds were healed and I was able to talk about hevala Rêvan's self-sacrifice with other comrades. They officially announced her death after hearing my words.

There is another thing that I want to tell you, hevala Jînçin. Hevala Rêvan said something on that same evening. I hadn't paid attention to it at the time. When we reached near Golmet village, the place where she performed the self-sacrifice operation, we could see that the border and Kobanî were behind us two kilometers away. She repeated a statement twice. The first time when we got down from the car and the second while she was joking about the restaurant. She said, 'We have to stop this humiliation. How far do we want to retreat? We must either submit Kobanî to Daesh, or fight 'til the last breath.'

She had no patience to see Kobanî falling. Her self-sacrifice operation not only saved our lives, but also slowed down the advance of Daesh. From then on, Daesh troops were scared of Kurdish women. They understood not only that they couldn't capture sex slaves in Kobanî, but also that they had to fear the corpses of Kurdish women. She showed the jihadists that they couldn't easily touch the bodies of women who are ready to sacrifice themselves for freedom. Her goal was to announce this message to the enemy. Apart from that, she also saved our lives.

The more I insisted on saving her, the more she demanded to help me. She didn't want the enemy passing over her corpse and reaching us and the other comrades. She showed the enemy, with all their barbarity and inhumanity, that they couldn't defeat our will for resistance. After a month, when I returned to Kobanî, Daesh had been defeated ideologically.

I was shocked when hevala Rêvan's classmate talked about her previous life. From that day until now, I have asked myself how it is possible that for three years, a cowardly girl who was scared of frogs could become a brave and gracious guerilla. Hevala Jînçin, I'm not an educated girl; I didn't even go to school. But I know with certainty that I would not be with you now if she had not sacrificed herself."

"You really didn't go to school? Where did you learn to read and write so well?" I asked Gulbehar, astonished.

"In the party, the comrades taught me."

"That's another surprise. I was already surprised by hevala Rûken teaching in the party. What great persistence you both had!"

"Thanks, hevala Jînçin. We also have another surprise for you."

"Really? Maybe you want to hold a wedding ceremony for me."

"Even better than that."

"My story is finished," Gulbehar said loudly.

"Then come outside," Rûken replied to her from within the kitchen.

We all got up and left the room. At the door, Rûken told Arjîn to stay inside until she called her. Then she told me, "We'll take you to our surprise now."

Rûken grabbed my two legs, Saro put his palms in front of my eyes and another comrade, probably Rojano, bear hugged me and picked me up from behind. For a few seconds they were spinning me around. Then in a certain direction, very slowly, they threw me up in the air. I fell down backwards on the snow. My eyes were open and I saw myself within the snow outside. Snow was falling in large flakes like popcorn. Before I could say anything, the comrades started throwing snowballs at me and I rolled around in the pure white bliss. I got up and threw snowballs at them, but they were greater in number and my comrades, especially the female ones, were not letting me defend myself. I grabbed Rûnahî's leg and threw her into the snow. A relentless rain of snowballs fell down on her, until Rojano pushed Saro and threw him into the snow. We must have thrown over a cubic meter of snow at him. He tried to get up, but the snow shelling prevented him until he got Rûken's feet and dragged her into the middle of snow. We attacked her with snowballs as if she were our enemy. Within ten minutes all of us had turned into snowmen, except Rojano, who had run away. From far away she was beaning us like a baseball pitcher and running like a hare across the snow. Finally, we stopped the futile hunt for Rojano and went back to the men's room, where Hunger hadn't let Arjîn exit. From our loud noises she understood what was happening. She did not let us cover her eyes. Then I hugged her from behind, while Rûken and Rûnahî quickly grabbed her legs and lifted her up. We took her outside. She was floundering, until she saw the heavy snowfall. She fell down of her own accord into the snow before we could throw her up and started rolling around. It was not necessary to fire snowballs at her, since she was diving and rolling deep in the snow.

Then it came to the second surprise. The comrades had set up a snow slide. It was only forty meters away but was not visible under the heavy snowfall. Rojano screamed and threw herself on the slide and slipped very fast to the creek. We also went up toward the start of the snow slide. With each step we got stuck in the snow and had to free ourselves. Before we reached the top, our heads had turned white under a collection of snow and Rojano made the second slide. First round, I slipped alone. I slid over two hundred meters under heavy snowfall, as if I were slipping inside of a snowstorm tunnel. I screamed like a kid and did not know what was waiting for me at the bottom, but the necessary precautions had already been taken and the end of the slide had been flattened and blocked by a mountain of snow.

The next few times, we were slipping together. The men were at the front and we were behind them, while we held on to each others' waists. Befrîn was always on our laps. He also enjoyed the snow slides and snowfall. He purred with pleasure the whole time. The slide sessions gave us a good chance to get Rojano, but she stayed far away and grabbed the waist of the last person, when our train had already started sliding. Before we came down completely, she would separate herself from the group and run quickly toward the top of the slide. Over an hour we slipped, laughed, and had fun. Only Rojano escaped our snowballs.

On the last round, the female comrades slipped alone. Many of them had a blue plastic bag on their laps. I asked them about the contents of the bags and Rojano exclaimed, "the biggest surprise!"

Before the last round, the two jokers appeared from downstream. They were climbing up with hevalê Ferhad in the middle of the valley. Gulbehar was our train driver now. She held Befrîn on her lap with one hand. She lifted her feet from within the snow, slipped down, and we all moved behind her. Our speed only got faster and faster. All the comrades were screaming and the snow was hitting my face in big flakes. I had to lower my head and stick my mouth to the back of Arjîn's neck. When we reached the end of the slide, Gulbehar got up and we followed her toward the creek. There were a couple of snow walls about three meters high that surrounded the stream. A narrow frozen path lay between the snow walls and stream. We went along this way toward the little cave in which we had hidden firewood in early autumn. As if we were passing through a snow tunnel whose floor was a stream. I felt a waft from a fire. I looked around but saw nothing. They had excavated the snow around two meters deep and had put a big metal barrel above the fire. I asked in amazement, "Do we take a bath here?"

"Yes," Dêrsîm replied.

She bent over within the snow hole and put firewood onto the campfire. Steam was rising from the metal barrel and the snowflakes were melting before falling in. There was a ring shape of mud around the barrel. At the end, three Kalashnikovs, their magazines and a couple of shovels lay on the snow and the snowfall was slowly covering them. Immediately, I took off my clothes and also wanted to take off my underwear. Rûken stopped me.

"Hold on, heval. First you have to wash your clothes."

I came out from the snow hole and stood half naked beside the stream. I didn't feel the cold. The snow was falling on me like cotton and it was not at all chilly. All the comrades took their clothes off and covered themselves with a jacket. I also wore my jacket and, like the others, wiped the snow off a round stone beside the creek to sit on. Arjîn asked me, "Do you need washing powder?"

"Is there washing powder here?" I asked, surprised.

"Of course, heval." She bent down and picked up a bar of soap from the ground.

"The bottom side is washing powder, the top is soap. You have to use it correctly."

"And what about the other sides? Our soap has six sides."

"I wanted to explain it to you later. The long side is dishwashing soap and the wide side is shampoo."

"But there are still two sides. Are they pumice?"

"No, they are . . . toothpaste. Right, hevala Rûnahî?"

Our hygiene expert replied, "Don't I give you enough toothpaste?"

"Why didn't you tell me earlier? I just thought it was cheese and ate it," I said.

Everyone laughed, until Arjîn said dejectedly, "We don't know yet what the application of these two sides of this unique soap are and our health minister won't tell us anything."

"You have to ask me if you don't know something. The other sides include bath cream and shower gel," added our agile hare.

"Such an exaggeration for this vapid cheese. It's just a simple, no-fragrance soap."

"No, heval, you are wrong. This soap has several scents. When soap smells one way, say like strawberries, it smells like strawberries, but when it smells like nothing, it smells like millions of things that do not have a smell. Our soap is not only multifunctional but also multifragrance," Arjîn said, smelling the soap deeply as she talked about it. "I almost faint from its various fragrances."

She handed me a bar of soap. I sat on the stone, soaked my clothes within the stream and rubbed them with enough soap. It was like butter but cleaned my clothes well. I washed them quickly. I got up, made a hole in the snow wall, and put my clothes into it. I felt cold. I ran along the creek toward the fire, poured some bowls of hot water into the canisters, mixed it with the water from the stream, then poured it on my head. I screamed with joy. I took off my shoes and went into the tepid stream water. The water was crystal clear, the landscape opposite me was white, and the snow was falling continually on my naked body. The other comrades were naked, too. Arjîn and I were more excited than the other comrades to take a bath under the snowfall. She asked me to wash her back. She put a stone within the stream and sat on it. I took her soap and wanted to wash her gleaming neck. Suddenly she yelled at me, "What are you doing? Do you take me for a fool?"

I stood in open-mouthed wonderment. Then I asked, "What have I done, heval?"

"Heval, you are washing me with the washing powder."

Everyone broke out in laughter and the mood became very funny. When I wanted to wash her hair, she screamed even louder.

"Heval, you can just take a lighter and burn my hair. That's a faster way to ruin it."

"Pardon, heval. I forgot which side the shampoo is on."

"Heval, you have to be careful. Otherwise, my father will kill you. He loves my hair."

"I also love your curly hair. If you scream again, I will pour hot water on your head." Arjîn screamed again. Gulbehar asked, "What happened again? Did she do anything?"

"I am going to freeze! Pour hot water on my head."

I brought out some bowls of hot water, mixed them with cold water in the canister and gradually poured it on her head. She brought her tongue out of the left side of her mouth and closed her eyes with joy. As she told us last night, for a few seconds her brown hair became smooth and then turned curly again. This repetitive scene made me laugh again and again. Rûken and Gulbehar got up and did the same several times, laughing a lot. Her hair resembled the spikes of a hedgehog suddenly curling up. When Rojano came to do the same, Arjîn didn't let her.

"No, no, no, I can't let you do that. First, I have to hit you with three snowballs."

Rojano made three snowballs herself and handed them over to Arjîn.

"How far away should I go?"

"Five meters is enough. I'm not a good ball thrower."

Rojano went upward beside the creek and snow wall, then turned and stood backwards. I went into the water to see her from the back. For the first time I saw her body in daylight. She had an attractive body with tanned skin.

"I won't hit you, heval. You deserve to be unbeaten," Arjîn said.

With this decision, Rûken fired snowballs at them, both the forgiven and the forgiver. We all followed our commander and threw snowballs at them. In that narrow path, all of the snowballs were hitting their target and could avenge the hour of running away, except Tewar, who had not engaged in our game from the start.

I asked Rojano to wash my back when I had no more strength left. She turned to me. A couple of nice cheeks and a long neck. She took a plastic net and rubbed some soap on it. I turned back and went into the stream. She began to wash my back. Her hands were strong and she washed so vigorously that I nearly fell into the stream. She grabbed my arm with her left hand and it felt as if I were a little girl and she were a strong man washing me. My dad washed me often, even when I was studying in Munich. He regularly went there on weekends to visit me. Whenever I knew he was coming to Munich, I didn't take a bath and waited for him. His strong hands gave me a sense of calm and confidence.

I stand stark naked at the end of the world, in a creek, listening to the crunching snow, looking at the white mountain before us and the snowflakes falling from the sky. The snowflakes melt on my body as Rojano washes my back. Without even realizing, in the midst of my euphoria, I screamed so loudly that our comrades above heard it and Saro still remembers it after three months.

"Only with that loud cheer did I first realize that you were happy to be with us."

CHAPTER 9

"I NEVER SAW my father. Before I was born, he died of an incurable lung disease caused by the 1987 Serdeşt poison gas attack, perpetrated by the Iraqi Ba'ath regime. He was a Kurdish libertarian activist. Before the chemical attack he had been imprisoned for one year at Dizel Abad prison in Kirmaşan. That is why the Iranian intelligence forces did not let him depart to Europe with those people who the UN had accepted for treatment. The primitive treatment in Iran only prolonged his painful life for a few years and cost the only source of our family income, a little shop, a great deal. My mother was working as a housemaid, but her income could not even pay our rent. I cannot imagine what would have happened to our family if one of my uncles had not taken responsibility over our lives. He had to work as a kollber at thirteen.

Every evening, when he came back exhausted, he could not move anymore. When I was five, I understood that he would like for me to walk over his body. At that time, I thought it was a kind of game, but over time, it became my duty. If I didn't massage him for an hour, he couldn't sit on the ground for dinner. In the meantime, luck was on our side for once and someone wanted to build a poultry facility next to our land. He got our land for a steal, but in that situation it was a lot of money for us. This allowed us to buy an old pickup. My uncle did not have to carry loads on his shoulders anymore and I went with him to the border.

At ten, I learned to drive and could help him if our pickup got stuck in the mud. Later I could carry loads alone, if he could not get to work. The work went well and we were happy, until he was called by the Iranian intelligence services. They wanted to force him, like many other drivers, to spy for the government. He told them that he is responsible for the lives of two of his orphaned nieces and wouldn't like to get involved with politics. They released my uncle and let him go on with his work, but from then our life was turned upside down.

There are unbelievable rules at the border that I couldn't possibly have learned in a school or university. If I had not worked there for twelve years, I couldn't have figured out those complicated and ambiguous customs. Smuggling is like a natural organism. One should only need to provide certain basic conditions and all the organs should function naturally. The roots and branches of a tree instinctively pursue water and light, thus allowing the tree to rise upward. That's how smuggling in all corrupt countries is.

Where something is forbidden, an ideology of prohibition will be devised around it. Something has to be forbidden for some reason and then the mechanism kicks in. Such forbidden things are profitable, but they cannot exist legally based on the dominant ideology in power. So, a smuggling network builds up.

When I was in university, I did an exact calculation one day with some experts and found that it is impossible that more than two percent of the illegal goods that pass through Iran's borders are transferred by kollbers. The remaining ninety-eight percent is shipped by the Revolutionary Guard in containers on safe, but illegal sea routes. Working as a kollber is pure slavery, but it's worse than other forms of servitude because a kollber in Kurdistan must invest his own capital in his slave labor. Only then can he sell his life force to continue his miserable life.

There are two sides to the Iranian smuggling system. On the one hand, there are the pure winners, including the IRGC members and traders, who bear zero percent risk for the smuggling. The kollbers are on the other side. Not only do they have to carry a load of a hundred kilograms through the cold mountain routes and minefields, but they must also take a hundred percent responsibility for their loads.

At first, kollbers pay the price of the load to the goods owner and only then can they carry out the load of a mule on their shoulders. This means, the kollber needs to bear one hundred percent of all physical, financial, social, and political risks for a small percent of profit. Zero against one hundred. The share of profit and loss in Iran's criminal laws and in the real life of the kollbers in Rojhilat is firmly established in this manner and no excuse can change this, even if a kollber loses their feet in the minefields, if they or their mule is shot by the border guards, or if they die under their load or their car is blown up by the IRGC."

"Can you call someone a kollber if they have their own car?" I interrupted Rojano.

"Certainly, even many human rights activists have not yet come to understand the meaning of kollber. A kollber is not just someone who carries a heavy load on their shoulders. They always remain as kollbers even if they have some mules or several cars, as long as they have to bear one hundred percent responsibility for their load. There are two risky routes during the process of transferring illegal goods from the border. The first is between the borders and the border towns in Rojhilat and the other is between the border towns and other major cities of Iran. In border towns, the illegal goods are considered legal goods. Dealers are allowed to sell them in their shops or via telephone and internet.

Once an agreement is made, it is again time for the kollbers to take up one hundred percent of the risk of transferring the goods. IRGC members and traders sell their goods to other traders in major cities of Iran. Once these goods arrive in the major cities of Iran, they are no longer illegal and hajjis, mullahs, and the IRGC's generals trade them as legal goods.

The whole process of goods laundering is accomplished with the kollber's body and soul and it does not matter whether they only use their bodies, or their mules, or pickup trucks. We had our own pickup, but we lost everything when my uncle refused to work as a spy for the intelligence services. I remember well that day when our pickup was shot by border guards.

It was a Thursday. At midnight, I was feeling sleepy, riding with my uncle in our pickup. Since I had to go to school that morning and had not rested enough in the evening, I fell asleep when I sat down on the seat. I would wake up at each break and hear my uncle and the other drivers' voices. At the Kurdish border, the discussion doesn't begin with greetings or talk about weather. The topic of discussion is always the same: 'What is the border situation?' That midnight, I was hearing these answers: good or very good. That should mean that the guards on duty are not the kind of soldiers who not only take bribes, but also torment the kollbers. On the borders of Kurdistan, a simple soldier is more powerful than the presidents of some countries in the world. They can simply shoot and murder those kollbers who are not completely subjugated. Anyone who refuses to pay the required bribes will get murdered in a few days as a smuggler.

While in other parts of Iran, the soldiers assigned to these positions are the most miserable, pathetic members of society, in Kurdistan they soon turn into bribers, oppressors, and sexual criminals. Their power and authority in Kurdistan is greater than god. In other parts of Iran, the soldiers are ready to give up money to serve less, just to be able to scratch their balls at home, but at the borders of Kurdistan, the guard shifts are sold. Some soldiers earn more than five million tomans a day, in a country where a shop assistant has to work for four hundred thousand tomans a month. 'The border's situation is good!' That means the guards who are there will take bribes and won't beat us. The border was good, but the drivers had to drive with the lights off.

The kollbers were constantly made to feel that they were doing something secret. I had the same feeling myself. Only after I gave up that job could I understand that that was not true. A kollber lives in a cycle of guilt and must always hide their acts, but their acts are not at all secret. I was like a heroin addict who tries to hide their addiction, though their wrinkled face and constant weight loss reveal their situation.

Only after leaving my civilian life, when I was no longer an organ of the smuggling network, could I understand why we were driving with the lights off and constantly had to change our smuggling routes, even though the picking up and unloading points were constant. I thought, like other kollbers, who timidly hid themselves under their loads, that it was to conceal our illegal job. Our transferring of goods was no secret at all. There was no one on the border who could not be bribed, except one alleged commander, from whom the soldiers and other officers had to run away in fear.

On the border routes it was not possible to install speed limit signs for the smugglers, but they could force them to drive with their lights off when they shot at the cars with lights on with a machine gun. On those winding roads, no drivers could drive fast when their car lights were off, so drivers couldn't increase their meager earnings.

We had to change our goods-transferring routes several times per year and would naively think that we had found a safer way. From my perspective today, this constant change of routes was not determined by us, but the IRGC headquarters in Kurdistan, so that all bases on the border would get their share of this profit from the smuggling, or perhaps to take advantage of the intense natural competition between border bases for profit.

On the evening of our most miserable day, I was not interested in border reports as a twelve-year-old girl. I was tired and only wanted to sleep, but I was jerked out of sleep by the brakes and border reports until we finally arrived at the depot. We had arrived early and there were only a couple of eleven-year-old boys as guards at the bottom of the enormous hoard of goods."

"Two eleven-year-old boys were protecting a mountain of goods? And what would have happened if someone had attacked them and stolen all the goods? What can two children do against adult villains?" I interrupted her.

"Most likely, they had just left them with the goods. It is not easy for poor people to attack children. In my experience, children can be more useful as guards on the border than professional boxers."

"Ok, that's reasonable, but how do you know exactly that those two children were eleven? Did you see their birth certificates?"

"Hevala Jînçin, I know that an eleven-year-old boy is one year younger than a twelve-year-old. If you would let me talk, I will go on about these topics. They belong to my story."

"Thank you for your explanation. I will listen well."

"I remember these two boys well, because we almost died in an accident from hidden bullets. One week before, we had to stay with them besides the loads for four hours. They did not know us and my uncle had left the prepayment voucher from the merchant at home. A few weeks before, he had deposited five million tomans of credit with the merchant, and that was enough for fifty boxes of tea in thirty-kilogram packs, but those boys didn't know and we had to wait for the agent's representative to come and hand us over the fifty boxes of tea.

It was early spring and that night was cold. They had made a campfire next to the pile of goods. Over time, the pickup drivers appeared and loaded goods onto their pickups. My uncle asked me to go home with one of the drivers. I said I would go to school tomorrow afternoon and I wanted to stay with these boys. They sat by the fire and only when a new driver came would one of them get up, get a prepayment voucher from the driver, and let him charge the goods on the receipt. It was getting colder. I had sat next to them by the fire. It was a scant fire, but it gradually warmed the ground. After an hour, an explosion arose from the soil.

'It must have been a cartridge left over from the Iran-Iraq war,' one of the pickup drivers said when he was packing some heavy loads onto the pickup. Before his warning, we had run away from the fire, but we came back because of the painful sting of the cold. We kept our distance from the fire as much as possible, but the next bullet exploded right near Xebat's[*] head. We moved away from the fire again. One of the drivers warned us of the danger of these leftover cartridges and gave me his jacket and said, 'You should alternate wearing it.' My uncle asked him for the time. It was half past one and the agent's merchant shouldn't return until around four.

We walked around the goods depot for half an hour and no bullet exploded. Our noses were running and my body was shivering all over. Xebat's cousin even started coughing. None of the coming drivers had warm clothes with them and we returned to the low burning fire. Xebat put some sticks and dried brushwood on the fire and we sat down again. It wasn't ten minutes before a bang rose up from the fire again. This time, the bullet flew close to my face and singed my hair. This time my uncle took us away from the fire and stifled it with his feet. He told me to go to sleep in our truck, which was parked about fifty meters away from the depot. It let the coming trucks turn around easily. The drivers had told us to stay in their trucks during the goods loading, but Xebat and his cousin rejected their suggestions. In this time of chilly trembling, a plane flew through the sky.

'The passengers of that aircraft are now seated with underpants on,' Xebat said to himself.

Maybe because of this sentence, I still remember Xebat. I've completely forgotten the other boy. Surely Xebat was not in a situation or of an age to express any sexual fantasies. He was merely thinking about the pleasant warmth within the airplane. That sentence shaped a fantasy in my mind that did not leave me for years. I wanted to know what the people traveling in planes looked like. Only after many years, when I

---

[*] Activity for moral, spiritual, and social purposes.

was a student, did my dream come true. My boyfriend wanted to give me a birthday present and I had refused to ask for any gift, but he had previously heard about this desire from my conversations. He booked me a trip to Armenia for three days, all alone. The fulfillment of this simple wish took me ten years."

"How did you feel when you saw the airplane passengers?"

"Not great. Often people are too old to enjoy the realization of their dreams."

"Can I ask you something about your boyfriend? I would like to know what kind of person he was who financed a solitary journey for you."

"He was from Bane. I do not want to say more. That's a forgotten story."

"And do you know what happened to Xebat?"

"No. I have seen thousands of such children on the borders, hevala Jînçin. Before they talk, nobody can figure out if they are girls or boys. All of them have the same short hair, wear male Kurdish pants, and carry heavy loads on their shoulders. On the day of our misfortune, I should say the day on which the IRGC was ordered to shoot at us, we had easily loaded goods onto our pickup. Our load was two times higher than the pickup itself. At the first guard point, my uncle paid the bribe and drove on. At a place where the slimy soil had turned into a swamp as a result of heavy rain from the previous three days, a soldier stood like on any other day. My uncle gave him the usual bribe, but he demanded a tremendously higher sum in a furious and hateful voice. My uncle found it to be a dangerous situation and quickly paid him the requested money. The front pickup truck pulled out of the slime with the help of the other drivers. Then we drove on and got stuck there. With the full power of the engine we could not get the car out. My uncle got out of the car, I slid behind the wheel, and the soldier pointed his weapon directly at us and then started shooting at the car. My uncle ran around the car and took me out of it. Agitated, we ran to the first car that had been released from the swamp. The soldier was blindly shooting at us in the dark.

We could save our lives, but we never saw our pickup and the five million toman deposit. Everyone advised us to be silent about the event, otherwise we would be charged as smugglers and would have to pay a much higher fine for smuggling.

The next day we went back to the border, but in someone else's car and as kollbers who carried the loads of others on our shoulders. My uncle did not want to let me accompany him, but I knew about his back pain and wanted to ease some of his burden. A small load that was increasing over time. During my school time and all summer breaks when I was student, I worked at the border. My older sister was shorter than me and I wanted her to focus on her education, but she could not obtain her high school diploma and got married with someone from our social class. I can't tell you anything interesting about my studies in Sine. Everybody already knows what's going on in Kurdish cities in Iran.

Every summer break, I returned to Serdeşt to work at the border again. The end of my studies became the beginning of my greater misery. My uncle, the great hero of my life, was shot by border guards for no reason. My mother had four more brothers and I had another three uncles on my paternal side, but no one was responsible for our lives. When my father was alive, he lived with us because there was no high school in their village. My dad must have been kind to him and he had not forgotten my father's compassion until his last breath. At the borders, I have seen blind or disabled people carrying seventy kilogram loads rather than begging, but they are doing it because of their family needs. Their work is instinctive, even egoistic. There was no father-child relationship between us. He was helping us out of pure responsibility, or perhaps a promise that he gave to my father as a thirteen-year-old child. We do not live in a world where someone does something like that. He was a symbol of devotion. I have not seen any mother in my life who has surpassed his generosity. He didn't get married because of us and even he left his high school, which was the reason for him coming to our house in the first place.

He always wore a pair of plastic boots, while my sister bought expensive shoes and handbags. His death left a void in my life that could not be filled. Only after his death did I notice how little I had talked to him. We were always together, but never had the opportunity to talk with each other. Either we had a heavy load on our shoulders or were fatigued from the load. Who was he really? What dreams did he have? What did he imagine his future would be like? Had he ever loved a woman?

I never asked him such questions and every time he called me he wanted to know if I could handle my life and how he could help me.

When he was murdered, I felt guilty. We had taken advantage of his generosity and ruined his life through our silence. I could imagine any destiny for him but murder. He was no adventurer and was not interested in political affairs, but he was finally murdered for political reasons that had nothing to do with him.

At a certain point, the Iranian regime had executed four Kurdish political activists. This caused great social antipathy in all the cities of Rojhilat. After a call from the Kurdish parties for a general strike, the citizens of the cities demonstrated in a great parade of empathy and social solidarity. In Sine, over ninety-five percent of all the city's shops closed on the appointed day. The widespread civil protests must have enraged the IRGC enormously. They decided to destroy the unity of the civilian resistance and struck at the weakest link in the chain by murdering a lot of kollbers and their mules in Serdeşt.

Most of the Kurdish people may have thought that the publication of horrific images of the murdered kollbers with their mules would cause a wave of social sympathy in other cities of Iran, but the result was quite the contrary. In fact, it actually led to lots of government saber rattling and influenced many naive people in the other parts of Iran. They were shown how widespread smuggling in Kurdistan was. I had never read such disappointing comments before. Many commenters saw the work of the kollbers as a major economic threat to the country and as a risk factor for the territorial integrity of Iran.

The Iranian people were led to believe that the murdered kollbers were not ordinary, miserable people who carried goods for others, but a few separatists who were smuggling drugs, weapons, and ammunition on their mules to accomplish subversive activities. I took the bus to Bane. There I immediately switched to Serdeşt. My uncle's body was said to have been in a mortuary cell in the coroner's office. My mother, my sister, and all my uncles and aunts stood in front of that place and begged a guard outside to let them in. Without talking to anyone, I yelled at him to go away. He stood there like a tower of jelly. I grabbed his collar and bashed him against the wall with a supernatural force before he could reply to me. I opened the door and went inside. My family and the relatives of other victims followed me. One of the doctors, a Kurd from Îlam, had compassion for us and supported us when the police raided the location and tried to kick us out. I was the first one to go inside the mortuary cell. I looked at my uncle's corpse. He had two big bloodstains on his gray shirt and wore a wristwatch that I had bought him in Yerevan. It was the only real property that he owned and he had worn it for just three weeks. He was only thirty-four, but looked like a skinny fifty-year-old man."

The whole time, Rojano was subconsciously pressing on her male wristwatch.

I asked her, "Were the killers of these victims punished or found?"

"No, these so-called poor, young border guards commit all kinds of crimes and have never been punished or put on trial. As if murder and rape were part of their job."

"Rape? Something like that should be a red line for the Kurds. How is this allowed?"

"What can they do? The loads, which are heavier than they can bear, don't allow them to shoulder any further social or political burdens and they bend over under twofold pressure. They are dependent on daily work and the soldiers of the Iranian regime know this well. Not only the children and women, but also strong men have been sexually harassed by frail soldiers at the border. They call to kollbers and say things like, 'come here bunny baby' or 'fucking fag,' and shout at them, 'you are my delicious salami!' The kollbers are more impotent against soldiers than us versus the drones.

It was very difficult for me to stay in Iran for the few more months I needed to finish my studies. After graduation, I left Iran and went to Başûr. But I soon realized that this so-called liberated part of Kurdistan was actually the backyard of the IRGC. One month ago, hevalê Saro was talking about the sabotage plans of the Turkish government in Rojava. Turkey must have learned a lot from the sabotage work of the Iranian regime. There must have been a time when hundreds of thousands of Kurds fled from Başûr to Rojhilat. Many people in Merîwan still dream of that time when their city was booming economically. They forget that that glamorous time was the result of the plundering of Başûr. Within a few years, all the economic sources of Başûr were destroyed, robbed, and transported to Iran. I am sure that Rojhilat's share of the profit from this plundering was lower than one percent.

Twenty years after the liberation of Başûr, the living conditions of the Kurds there were more catastrophic that you can imagine. Ordinary citizens had access to electricity for only four hours a day and they were supplied with tap water for a few hours per week. Through corruption, the social gap grew unbearable. Başûr was practically divided between two main enemies of the Kurds. In the green zone, Iran ruled and in the yellow zone, Turkey.

The liberation of Başûr not only failed to help the other parts of Kurdistan, but it also became the biggest obstacle for the Kurdish liberation movements. Under the pretext of preserving the achievements of Başûr and not giving the enemies an excuse, all the political activities of the opposition parties of Rojhilat were banned and until today they are passively wasting time in their unprotected bases.

I did not want to wait there for an uncertain future and joined the PJAK.* I soon understood that they did not want to do anything for the rights of the Kurds in Rojhilat, or at least could not do anything. In my opinion, the PKK in the past and today is dependent on the help of the Iranian regime and, in view of this, its sister party cannot oppose the repression of the Iranian regime in Rojhilat. I said to myself, never mind, I can at least fight for the rights of the Kurds in Bakûr. But, at that time, the PKK was in the so-called peacetime, despite everyone in the party knowing that the AKP was taking advantage of this peace process to strengthen its power bases in Bakûr and also to stabilize itself in Turkey.

For some months I got bored with different departments of the PKK, but then I read a lot of books, improved my English skills, learned how to work with various weapons, and waited until conditions changed. It took four years. Then Daesh appeared out of nowhere. After conquering Mûsil and Tikrît in June 2014, our party's leaders were also alarmed. My commander told me that I would be sent to intensive military training within the next two days.

'To which front will I be sent?' I asked with joy.

'No idea. To Rojhilat, Rojava, or Şingal, I do not know exactly.'

The next day, they sent me to the training camp. A battalion of fifty-six experienced guerrillas was already there. They did not expect a person like me, who had no battle experience, to endure the tough training so easily, but I was doing all the battle exercises and served as a driver, as before. One day before the Daesh attack on Şingal, we received an

---

* Partiya Jiyana Azad a Kurdistanê, Kurdistan Free Life Party.

order from headquarters. There would be a battle ahead of us. We drove from Xakûrkê and Xinêrê toward the Gara Mountains. The area was very familiar to me. When we get off there, a comrade told me, we would meet hevalê Jemal* soon after. I was the only one who had not met him yet.

I knew it would be an important mission. We were escorted to a stream in the shade of dense trees. There were two very long benches opposite each other, made of stone and wooden masts that were filled over with mud and covered with clear plastic. Between the benches, there was a long table. Some in our group knew that place well and led us to the spring. The sound of the flowing spring could be heard from far away. The spring water was clear as tears and cold as ice. When I washed my face, I felt refreshed.

The spring was flowing into a stream downhill. We washed our faces with one of the multifunctional soap bars😊 and returned to the benches. The comrades stationed there came and greeted us. Many of them knew each other. They brought us our favorite thing in a black kettle.

By the time we had drunk a glass of tea and smoked some cigarettes, the other battalion arrived. Around noon, a hundred and two guerrillas gathered at the dining table. Our lunch was brought to the table. Many comrades did not consider themselves as guests and helped to set the table. Spoons for everyone, enough metal glasses, bread, and salt, which was in jars. At that time, hevalê Jemal appeared. He welcomed all of us in a very friendly manner.

'Good day, hevalno, I hope that you are all fine.'

We stood up and he shook hands with all of us warmly. It did not take more than three minutes to shake hands with everyone. Then he came and sat down right opposite me and said, 'Are you our famous rally driver?'

'No heval, I was only a pickup driver. The comrades exaggerate.'

'They are not allowed to do that. They say it is safer to ride on a scud missile than in the front seat of your car.'

'No one has been hurt in my company.'

---

* Mirad Qarayîlan, cofounder of the PKK and current commander-in-chief of the organization's military wing, the People's Defence Forces, HPG [Hêzên Parastina Gel].

'Yes, you haven't had any car accidents, but you've scared countless comrades half to death. Can you drive in reverse under one hundred kilometers per hour?'

'If someone gives me a guarantee that we will not be shot, I will even ride in fifth gear at ten per hour.'

'Nobody can give you such guarantees in Kurdistan.'

'That's right, heval. So, I have to drive quickly to save comrades from peril.'

'What peril? You create peril yourself. The comrades fear your driving more than a barrel of bombs.'

'Heval, the guerillas should not be cowardly. We have to be brave like you.'

'You cannot deceive me. I've never been a passenger in your car, but there is no smoke without fire.'

'Heval, you should not believe the rumors.'

'There is always something in rumors.'

'Maybe, but our commander should not be frightened by it. Why do the Turks keep putting a higher and higher price on your head?'

'They like my head because it's round.'

'Mine is even more round, but no one has put a price on it.'

'Then you have to send an application to the MİT.'*

'Why don't you just give me your price? When it comes to round heads, my head is rounder than yours. If you do not believe it, I can shave my hair off.'

Hevalê Jemal took my hand and said, 'Maybe a head like mine is tastier. Turks like *kelle paça*, but we have rice and bean soup here. Please eat.'

That was a nice start to the conversation. Everyone laughed along with it. In front of every six guerrillas, they placed a pan of rice and a pan of bean soup. Hevalê Jemal, four other comrades, and I ate from the same pans. During lunch, he asked me if I play volleyball as fast as I drive. I told him I did and he said that we should play on the same team in the afternoon. That afternoon we played volleyball and laughed even more. For dinner we ate lentil soup with fresh baked bread and, before it got

* *Millî İstihbarat Teşkilatı* [National Intelligence Organization], the intelligence agency of the Turkish state.

dark, everyone went to a tent. Early the next morning, after breakfast, we gathered under a huge walnut tree for tea drinking and smoking until hevalê Jemal arrived. There was no sign of a smile on his face anymore. He commenced his speech with a frown.

'Hevalno, what we had foreseen, has unfortunately come to pass. Last night Daesh attacked Şingal and the KDP disgracefully handed the city and its associated villages to those jihadists and ran away with its twelve thousand Kurdish fighters, although they knew well that radical Islamists would regard the Êzdîs as pagans and ruthlessly slaughter them. Based on reports we've got, more than a hundred thousand Êzdîs have taken refuge in the Şingal Mountains. They are besieged from all directions and there is a great danger of genocide against them. Throughout history it is said that more than seventy attacks against the Êzdîs have been perpetrated, until a large part of the Kurds inevitably converted their religion to Islam. This time we cannot allow another massacre to be carried out against the Êzdîs. This peaceful, ancient community of Kurdish people is about to be destroyed and we cannot wait any longer. We have to send you into the fire. These jihadists are not ordinary fighters. They firmly believe that, after death, virgin girls and rivers of wine are waiting for them. Many of them would like to die and see eternal happiness in martyrdom. You have to try your best for the salvation of the Êzdîs. This is a historical mission. This is not just about winning on a battlefield against the radical Islamists, but about an ideological struggle.

This is a struggle between our social model, namely democratic confederalism, and the capitalist model of the nation state. We strive to build up a society in which all people, regardless of nationality, religion, or gender, can live in peace without any classification or discrimination. Therefore, we must win this for our social model against the inhuman model of the nation state, which makes people and religions fight with each other.

In essence, Daesh is nothing more than another means of dividing society. The capitalists want to distract people in the Middle East and around the world from the real problems their greed has caused. So, we must win this fight against the warped, fictitious concept of the nation state. The upcoming battle is the first step. That's why you have to be cautious and coolheaded. No heroic deeds, no adventure. Until now, all the militants who have stood in front of Daesh have been defeated and have run away, which is why the Daesh fighters have become arrogant. You have to shock Daesh with a sudden and dramatic attack to break up the ecstasy of their victories. These radical jihadists must finally understand that there is no paradise for them in Kurdistan, only a devastating hell waiting for those enemies of humanity and their inhuman ideology. You must show them what a guerrilla war really is. But first you have to understand for yourself that a guerrilla has to lead a completely different way of life. Militants are used to having everything in their hands, but you will have to produce your own provisions from nothing and defend the Êzdîs in the Şingal Mountains.

These mountains are sacred for the Kurds. Throughout history, the Şingal Mountains have saved the Êzdîs from massacres a hundred times over. In Şingal, there will not be as many springs as in the other mountains of Kurdistan, only five to six. But there should be very tasty figs. I have not been to Şingal yet, haven't eaten any of its figs or pomegranates, but I have already heard about them in Kurdish folk songs and I can imagine how tasty they are. But it takes time for them to ripen; until then you will have to feed yourself with something like chestnuts or acorns when the situation gets tougher. For Êzdîs, the situation is already dramatic. I will repeat that famous Kurdish proverb, 'The Kurds have no friends but the mountains.' We must not hand over our faithful friends to the enemies of humanity. No one is allowed to come back until all Êzdîs are saved and the mountain is under our safe control. Once you have entered the Şingal Mountains, you must drive in stakes and organize the Êzdî people. One month ago, we sent some of our comrades there and created the basis for a Êzdî defense unit, or YBŞ. You are to train more Êzdîs, expand this unit, and transform it into an army to protect the Êzdîs. Your mission is a real challenge. Anyone who does not wish to journey through hell is allowed to stay here.'

Hevalê Jemal talked for more than two and a half hours and tried to instill a fighting spirit with his epic speech, but it was not necessary at all. I was just in a hurry to get to our upcoming battle. We had lunch there and in the afternoon collected the necessary requirements. There were only five Toyota pickups available. I sat as a driver in one of the pickups, four other comrades sat closely next to me, and more than twenty comrades sat in the back of the pickup. At six in the evening we drove to the border point between Başûr and Rojava.

Although it was still hot, the comrades above the pickup were singing revolutionary songs and smoking all the time. Not a single car was traveling in our direction, but innumerable cars passed by from the opposite direction at full speed. Suddenly, a long military convoy appeared. Many armored vehicles, trucks laden with cannons, and countless pickups laden with heavy machine guns had parked by the side of the road. They were the twelve thousand members of Barzani's Pêşmerge who had fled from Daesh. They ran away from Daesh with great haste in Şingal, but here they leaned on their cars and drank Coke comfortably. The fleeing civilians drove beside them at full speed. Hundreds of thousands were fleeing from Daesh, but we were like a group of crazy people heading for them. When we got close to Barzani's military convoy, the comrades raised their voices and sang louder. I heard our comrades, laughed with all my heart at our madness, and was proud of it. Some comrades, who had not fought for a long time, even yelped with joy.

At the checkpoint over the Dîcle River there hung countless yellow PUK flags. The Pêşmerge who were positioned there wanted to prevent us from crossing the river.

They said they were instructed not to let us pass, because we were blacklisted as terrorists worldwide. Our female commander told them that we wanted to go to Şingal to help the Êzdîs. But a PUK* commander appeared and emphasized that we must not cross the river. At that moment, our commander in chief, hevalê Serhed Efrîn jumped from the back of the truck and shouted at him, 'You fled from Daesh and left hundreds of thousands of our people to them and also want to prevent us from helping the Êzdîs. You are not fighters, but cowards and lackeys. You are not Pêşmerge of your people, but mercenaries. You are a disgrace to the Kurds. Your bullshit cannot stop us. We care neither about you, nor your boundaries. We did not fall out of the sky. We are the children of these people and do not need your permission. We will cross the river and you can try to prevent us.'

Hevalê Serhed Efrîn reloaded his weapon and all the other comrades imitated him.

'I will give you only fifteen seconds, then we'll pass by force,' hevalê Serhed told him.

---

* Patriotic Union of Kurdistan.

An armed man at the roadblock immediately lifted up the barrier. We parked our pickups at the border point and passed the last checkpoint toward the Dîcle. There were only three motorboats, but in an hour we were all on the other side of the river in Rojava. When we arrived it was already dark. A group of YPJ and YPG were waiting for us. A female comrade sat down beside me and showed us the way to the YPG headquarters near Til Koçer. We should drive over the Kuprî and Qaraço areas. At midnight we arrived there and were able to have dinner. From then on, the age of lentil soup was over.

They brought us kebab and rice from Rimêlan. Many of our troops were vegetarian and had to eat rice and yogurt, until an explorer like our hevalê Hunger opened one of the refrigerators and gave the order to attack. With this refrigerator operation, the humorists of both groups immediately showed up. The refrigerators were full of products like watermelon, melon, apples, pomegranates, thick grape juice, clarified butter, and soft drinks. Outside the fridges there were also plenty of items, even capitalist luxury ones. They served more as fodder for jokes than as meals.

'Heval, we have too many beautiful mountain summits and colored stones up there. More than enough cold, as well. We can exchange some of these things for your refrigerator's contents.'

'Ok heval, a mountain for a watermelon.'

'Heval, didn't you used to be a banker? A mountain for two watermelons and three honeydews. And definitely some quinces as a gift.'

During the tea drinking, we exchanged all the mountains of Kurdistan for watermelons and melons. Then we went to sleep, because early the next morning we would have a meeting with the administration of the YPJ and YPG. Before going to sleep, we were informed that Rojavan comrades were trying to recapture the two important towns of Rabia and Sinûnê from Daesh to enable us to go to Şingal. The next day at breakfast we were informed that the comrades of the YPJ and YPG had successfully completed their mission the night before and, after an intense battle, freed these places. At the meeting, our plans and logistic needs were discussed until ten o'clock. Then we drove to Şingal.

On the way, we saw painful scenes. Thousands of cattle and sheep ran around in the fields without shepherds, and people fled bewildered, either towards Rojava or to Dihok. Many people tried to chase cars or overload the cars they had with people and things as they fled as far as possible from their residences. No news was announced yet of the release of Rabia and Sinûnê, or if they had heard of it, they did not believe it. At that time, Daesh was deemed invincible. All the well-equipped armies had been defeated and fled from Daesh and we were going to challenge them with Kalashnikovs in hand and two grenades hanging on our waists.

Once we arrived in Sinûnê, they gave us some bad news. Daesh had conquered the entrance path to Şingal. There was a wedding hall and a small village. These two places were under their control. Our comrades who were in Sinûnê explained the situation to us. They said Daesh would certainly be spying on us and an immediate move would be very risky, but hevalê Serhed insisted on moving there soon. There were some Êzdî comrades from the newly formed Şingal Defense Units and they informed us that there was another way to Şingal. An old forgotten path, from a desolated and abandoned village called Adîka. Based on their claim, many years ago people would go on horseback from Borik to Kersê. One of the Êzdîs came with us and we set off. We drove as fast as we could, but we were shot at by Daesh from the village and the wedding hall with mortars and some DShK. Two of our cars were damaged, but we managed to penetrate the mountain and reached the village of Kersê.

Behind the last turn of the road, where Daesh couldn't shoot us, there was an alien world, even for me, although I had been familiar with frightening scenes since childhood. Tens of thousands of frightened people were huddled together in fear of being massacred. After all of the gunfire, they must have thought that Daesh had penetrated into the Şingal Mountains and Kersê Valley, but they began to cry when they saw young, smiling, and clean girls and boys in Kurdish costumes instead of the bearded Islamists who shout 'Allahu akbar.'

I have never seen that kind of crying. We are used to applying the same verb to describe everyone who sheds tears from their eyes. But at that moment all the Êzdîs were crying, even those whose eyes were dry. Their crying did not express any human emotion like sadness, joy, fear, or anything. An aversion to life itself hung within their eyes. What was screaming in that valley was only the silence. Nobody was saying anything and they were not revealing any feelings that we could notice. Gleams of hope could be seen in the eyes of the young girls and boys, but older people had fallen into pure despair.

The Êzdî men embraced our male comrades, put their heads on our comrade's chests, and wept. Their children and women hugged us tightly, but not because they thought we could save them. They had lost that hope when twelve thousand well-equipped Pêşmerge had abandoned them. They no longer believed in salvation. Their tears were a sign of indescribable gratitude. We had gone into the fire to die with them. That's how they understood our mission. Doom and gloom prevailed there. They said that the end of the Êzdîs had come and that they would never return to their villages and cities, nor to Lališ and Şerfedîn, their holy places. We were uninvited guests to the hell that their enemies had devised for them and it was a great comfort to them. We tried to give them hope, swearing by all holy things that we would save them, but they could not believe it. They saw us as some kind of Muslim Kurds who had disappointed, seduced, and betrayed the Êzdîs throughout history. I still remember the words of an old woman who was speaking to hevalê Serhed:

'My son, Barzani's Pêşmerge told us these words for a week. They did not let us out of the city. Even until the last hour, when many of them had already run away. The Muslim Kurds have sold us to the enemy. Your bosses will sell us too. I do not mean you. You came here to save us, but what can you do with one hundred and eleven boys and girls against those monsters? With what can you save us? With a Kalashnikov and two grenades. Our men have such weapons too. Many of you are even girls.'

It is always advised to abstain from absolutism. But that day the Êzdîs were absolutely hopeless. Maybe they were right. Twelve thousand of Barzani's Pêşmerge had run away from Daesh with cannons and armored military vehicles, and after that, about one hundred young boys and girls had come and wanted to stand up and confront Daesh. When we told them that we would soon attack Daesh to open a rescue corridor, no one took it seriously. Each of us tried to convince some young men and women to accompany us for the upcoming battle. After a few hours, we were able to organize many Êzdîs. Then the administration distributed our hundred and eleven fighters into six groups and the Êzdîs were integrated into these groups, making six battalions. Each battalion was taken by car to the various peaks of the mountains. We had to walk on foot and positioned ourselves at a suitable point of the Şingal Mountains. I was selected for the Battalion of the Rescue Corridor.

Hevalê Serhed wanted to begin the attack immediately, but the administration decided to postpone the attack until the next morning. At night I could not sleep because of my excitement. I was continually asking myself, 'What will be the outcome of this battle? Can we open a rescue corridor, or would Daesh launch a counteroffensive and invade the Şingal Mountains?' If such a thing happened, the radical Islamists would slaughter the entire Êzdî community. At the time, I did not think that in the twenty-first century anyone would come up with the idea of sexually enslaving women and children and selling them for about twenty dollars in their so-called Islamic caliphate. I was awake before the comrades woke me up. Everyone received a bit of bread and some cheese. I put my breakfast in my vest pocket, hung my BKC on my shoulder, and climbed the mountain with a group of four people. We positioned ourselves on the foothill that looked over the wedding hall. Our mission was to cover our comrades downhill as soon as the Daesh forces noticed them.

I took some night-vision binoculars from one of my male comrades and saw our comrades crawling like snakes across the grass to the enemy. There should have also been a member of the Daesh forces somewhere observing the environment through night-vision binoculars; otherwise, they would not have noticed the presence of our comrades so quickly. The shooting began. We saw the firing point and kept it under fire. Comrades were running towards the enemy half-squatting and in a few minutes arrived behind the walls of the wedding hall. Countless grenades were thrown over the wall at the enemy. Other comrades, who attacked the village, had an easier job chasing the enemy away. We kept the Daesh fighters under control and killed them all in the blink of an eye. They were running away and our sniper picked them off one by one.

In less than twenty minutes, the village and the hall fell under our control. Comrades chased the enemy to an important point necessary for the opening of a safe corridor. All the Êzdîs were awakened by shooting and grenades exploding. When they learned that Daesh had run away and a corridor had been opened to save them, they stood with their mouths wide open. Within three hours, over fifteen thousand Êzdîs were transferred to Rojava through the rescue corridor. However, many adult men came back after they had taken their families to a safe place.

As expected, Daesh, who could not believe such a defeat after continuous wins, began a massive counterattack. Countless Daesh fighters stormed the mountain. They were climbing like ants on all sides of the mountain and as we killed more and more of them, more and more would climb up. We were well aware that Islamist forces must not be allowed to conquer the Kersê Valley. If they were to invade the valley, it would be a bloodbath. Fortunately, enough ammunition and five DShK 26s were brought from Rojava to the mountain during the opening of the corridor.

After four hours of fierce battle, Daesh was unable to sustain any further losses to conquer the Şingal Mountains and retreated. It could also be a trap, but many people were starving and had nothing to eat. Administration took the risk and decided to attack the Daesh barricade at nightfall and open the permanent rescue corridor.

Our victory broke down the dignity of Daesh and gave the Êzdîs a feeling of greater hope. Many of them were asking to participate in the next attack, but the administration was trying to prevent this. We told them that attacking the barricade was not a task for common people. Any mistakes could ruin the entire attack plan. We talked with them for a long time, but some were not persuaded by our arguments and insisted on joining in. Under the condition of staying behind the line of attack, we let them participate.

The arrogance of Daesh, despite its recent defeat, facilitated the implementation of our attack plan. They wanted to attack us at midnight and did not expect us to attack them first. Our comrades in Sinûnê were on alert and would have attacked Daesh from their weak front side if our plan had gone wrong.

At eleven o'clock in the evening, the first group crept quietly to their barricade lines. Another team crept toward them with thirty meters of distance. The enemy did not notice us until the first group threw their grenades into the enemy barricade. Then a huge shootout began. Bullets were flying in all directions and the sky was red from the gunfire. The leading group of comrades fortified the first barricade of the Daesh forces and then started firing on the second barricade so that our second group could storm it. After ten minutes, the second barricade was conquered. Our team was in line. The comrades positioned on the second barricade gave us cover as we attacked the third barricade. They did not give up and shot at us the whole time while throwing grenades toward us.

We had to fall to the ground not to be shot by the enemy and to give our comrades a chance to fire at them. Two of our comrades had already crawled near the Daesh forces and had thrown their grenades into the barricade. Our comrades were advancing and taking over the other barricades. Daesh had no chance to defend their barricades and decided to attack us laterally, but this was foreseen in our attack plan. In the conquest of each barricade, two more teams took positions on the two sides and took care of the lateral attacks. Within three hours, we not only conquered all of the Daesh barricades deep in Rojava, but were able to extend the rescue corridor over two kilometers and strengthen our positions. We even decided to conquer another village on the left side of us, which was not part of our original plan. Some groups of comrades nearly recaptured it, but the enemy blew up a large gasoline tank and four of our comrades fell there, while three more were seriously injured. Comrades had to take care of the injured ones and retreated to our fortified positions. Such a great victory was unbelievable, even for our experienced commanders. When it was light out, we prepared to expand the corridor under our control, through which thousands of Êzdîs could safely move to Rojava. Only then did I have enough time to eat my breakfast.

In less than half an hour, the flood of people came down from the mountain. Only then could we see what a large mass of people had sheltered in the Şingal Mountains and Kersê Valley in the past three days. An incredibly long train of people, cars, and livestock passed along the way. Many of them barely had strength left. The vehicles were overloaded. Many were almost starving. Someone was carrying the corpses of their children who had died of thirst. From Rojava, several cars had been sent to transfer children, sick, and exhausted people to a safe place, but the number of miserable people was much higher than could possibly be transported. The exhausted crowd reminded me of the kollber trains in Serdeşt, where no one could take care of anyone else's burden. Everyone would have to take responsibility for their own burden. Here, in this rescue corridor, children, pregnant women, and exhausted people who had no strength to carry their own bodies, fell down and died on the ground. Suddenly, a comrade put her hand on my shoulder and gave me the radio.

'Please come to Serdeşt quickly,' a woman told me.

I thought she was talking about my city in Rojhilat. 'Serdeşt?' I screamed in surprise.

'Yes, the comrade there knows where a pregnant woman is,' she said.

There was an expanded valley above the Şingal Mountains called Serdeşt. We ran to an SUV. I got in and drove up the hill. After many years, I felt gloomy and tears poured from my eyes when I saw Serdeşt. The whole valley was full of people who had been helpless under the scorching sun. Such a dense, disorientated crowd cannot be seen anywhere, even at the concerts of the most famous singers. I took the pregnant woman to Rojava and never saw Serdeşt again, neither my hometown, nor the tragic valley of the Êzdîs in the Şingal Mountains.

"I was with you behind the SUV," hevala Rûnahî said.

"Really? What happened to the pregnant woman?"

"She gave birth to healthy children. After that day you were very famous in Serdeşt. But we thought you were a man."

"Yes, I almost turned myself into a man."

Rojano said this sentence with her sharp, bass voice, an impressive voice that has feminine tenderness and masculine strength. This voice could have been the result of her frequent need to act like a man at the border. After this sentence she got up and said, "I need some fresh air. The rest of the story can be better told by hevala Rûnahî."

Rojano went to the door, pulled up the hanging blanket, and walked out of the women's room. I turned to Rûnahî and asked her a question.

"I did not know that you were in Şingal on the day of the Êzdî tragedy. You have a lot to tell us then. I have heard many contradicting stories from those days. The members of the KDP have claimed that they fought besides the Êzdîs against the jihadists until the last bullet."

"Hevala Jînçin, their lies are the most unbearable part of the whole tragedy for me. Even many Êzdîs distort the truth, though everyone knows the facts. The pure reality should not be sullied. As sure as I am right now that the animal on hevalê Ferhad's lap is a cat and not a dog, I am just as sure that the KDP sold out not only Şingal and its associated villages, but also the Êzdîs. But that's a long story."

"Then you can tell us your story after lunch. For a whole month nobody has told us anything about themselves. Anyone opposed can lift his or her hand," Rûken said.

Nobody was against it. There was a lot of smoking in the kitchen after lunch. Rojano must have been behind the hanging blanket in front of the men's room, because Arjîn was on guard in front of the women's room. She was back with us for lunch and during the afternoon story-telling session I sat down opposite her. Rûnahî began her story.

"I was born in Baghdad, but my family was from Şingal. Every summer break, we would travel to Şingal and stay there until the end of the summer. My mother was a well-known midwife and hairdresser there. Therefore, this trip was also important to us for financial reasons. She would not only travel during the summer break, but would also make a pilgrimage to Şingal, to cut clients' hair and shape their eyebrows. Many women in Şingal and the surrounding area wouldn't go to any other hairdresser and waited for her. During the summer in which Daesh invaded the Êzdîs' land, she traveled to Koço because her younger sister was pregnant there. That's why I took her job and looked after her clients, who entrusted me with their beautification. Suddenly, Daesh appeared. It was said they were advancing toward the Êzdî territories. As a minority, the Êzdîs have always been afraid of Muslims. Not only the Arab ones, but also the Kurdish people who speak exactly the same language as us. In Baghdad, we had no problem with the Muslims Kurds. My mother had many Kurdish clients and helped many pregnant Muslim Kurds to give birth to their children and circumcise their boys. But the Kurds in Şingal and the surrounding area were hostile people. They did not buy the Êzdîs' dairy products, the meat of their cattle, or even eggs of their chickens. Therefore, the Êzdîs were very reluctant to connect with them. We felt the peril early because we were hearing horrible news about the Êzdîs in Mosûl and its surrounding areas. We wanted to escape the danger at the earliest possible time, but could not go back to Baghdad, because the roads to Baghdad were already under Daesh control. Escaping to Başûr was our only option, but the KDP soldiers did not let us leave the city under the pretext that they were protecting us from any danger. Daesh was getting closer and closer and the fears of the Êzdî population were growing. On the evening of August 3rd, when Daesh began its attack, the chairman of the state police drove around the city in his car to give the Êzdîs a sense of security.

Around two o'clock in the morning, we got news that Daesh had attacked Êzdî villages, such as Sibaşêxidir and Gilzer. Even then, Barzani's

Pêşmerge didn't let us leave the city and told us repeatedly that there was no reason for panic and that the twelve thousand well-equipped soldiers of the KDP would destroy Daesh and drive them away. But it was just a trap. Their forces suddenly retreated from the front line without shooting a single bullet or informing anyone.

The Êzdîs were compelled to prevent the advance of Daesh with their light weapons until the people could flee to the Şingal Mountains. It caused an incredible panic in the city. Barzani's Pêşmerge had fled ahead of the civilians and the miserable people stood there alone. Those who had a car took as many people as they could along with them. The others escaped with their children towards the Şingal Mountains. Apart from our armed men, who are said to have fought to the death, some Pêşmerge of the PUK are said to have fought for the rescue of the Êzdîs until the last breath. Their resistance failed to create enough time for all the Êzdîs to reach the mountain, but enough to slow Daesh down until many like us could reach the Şingal Mountains.

My dad's car was full and we were taking anyone from the road who could not run away. As we reached the Şingal Mountains, hundreds of cars drove up the mountain's curves. From our place at the foothill, we were watching the Daesh fighters in their armored cars driving at high speed toward the mountain. Some Êzdîs left their broken cars on the way to slow down the advance of Daesh. Something good and unexpected happened there. A pickup from the escaped KDP forces was left on a curve of the mountain because of a breakdown. On the car was mounted a DShK 23. That was the only real weapon they had left. With this DShK, it was possible to prevent the advance of Daesh to the mountain, but none of the Êzdîs could use this weapon. Suddenly, two guardian angels appeared. Two soldiers in male Kurdish garb. One of them was a girl who she said could use the DShK. She got into the pickup and brought the car to a suitable position, then got down off the car and climbed onto the back of the pickup truck. She swiftly pointed the DShK at the Daesh combatants and fired. The sound of the gunfire was loud and some of the Daesh cars got shot, while others had to slow down, so the rest of the cars and people on the foothill got an opportunity to reach the mountain.

We ran toward the girl. Her name was Hedar[*] and she said that she was part of a nine-member PKK force who had arrived there a month earlier and had hidden in the mountains from the KDP. We had not heard of the PKK. Hevala Hedar said there were twelve people at the beginning and three of them were arrested by the KDP in Sinûnê. Her comrade got a message by radio and she announced to the people that we could not escape because Daesh had besieged the mountains from all sides and also that the small city of Sinûnê had already been conquered. That was a terrible message. As hevala Rojano said, the absolute hopelessness grew immeasurably at that time and the only consolation was that the DShK we had was preventing the Daesh convoy from climbing up. In spite of seeing how this lone girl brought the convoy to a halt, everyone wanted to escape. Until, that is, hevala Hedar stopped shooting and yelled to the escaping people.

'We will not hand over this mountain to the enemy! They have never fought in the mountains and will not dare to come up. You just have to believe in yourselves. These savages will be smashed with your help. The PKK will help you. Soon we will get reinforcements from our party.'

Nobody knew the PKK and they could not even pronounce that name correctly. Someone asked, 'Who are these PPK?'

'PKK, not PPK. They are the children of the people.'

Hevala Hedar certainly meant the Kurds, but no Êzdîs wanted to hear the name of the Kurds. We saw them as our biggest enemy. We owe all our miseries to them. They had tied our hands and thrown us into the lap of these wild animals.

'We are nine people, but we have a lot of fighting experience. We will teach you how to defend yourselves until the reinforcements come. You are many and this mountain will help us,' she said, even louder.

In the end, a small group joined them, but not because we believed her or the PPK. We had no choice. She explained to one of them how to use the DShK and then asked some Êzdîs to go down the mountain with her to block the way with broken cars. The courage of this girl impressed us. They blocked the way and came back safely. So, the foundation of the defense forces of Şingal was set up.

---

[*] A person who shelters someone.

In the previous few years, I had gone with my family several times through that mountainous path when we wanted to go on pilgrimage to Şerfedîn or on the most important pilgrimage to Lalîş or visiting our relatives on the northern side of the Şingal Mountains. But never did I think people in these mountains could die of thirst or starve to death. On the way, the high water columns were jumping up from the water pumps of the deep wells and you could see several farms and gardens with various products such as cucumber, eggplant, watermelon, zucchini, and pepper that caressed our eyes and bellies. There were many restaurants and small food shops, where you could stop if you wanted and eat everything you wished. There were also two villages along the way. The route was well prepared for passengers, and everyone could enjoy the quiet ride and be served. Nobody had predicted such a huge crowd in the middle of summer when the max temperature reached nearly fifty degrees Celsius.

During our trip the year before, we were able to enjoy pure, cold water from the wells or springs which ran deep under the valley beside the path. But the Şingal Mountains were vast and the Êzdîs' villages were scattered around the mountains; not everyone had a car or enough time in the dangerous situation to take the main route. Tens of thousands of people had to go to a nearby location on the mountain, where no water could be found. Everyone cared about the safety of their families and did not know that in other places on the mountain many other people were dying of thirst under the blazing sun of the third, fourth, and fifth days of August.

After two days, we heard that one hundred and two other PKK fighters had come to save us, but we did not trust them. We saw them as Muslim Kurds, although almost all of them were atheists. We did not know what atheist meant and that was for the better. How could the Êzdîs rely on nonreligious people when the Muslims believing in Allah slaughtered the Êzdîs in front of our eyes? Some Êzdîs were so naive that they returned to the city when a few Arab Muslim neighbors had promised them that Daesh would not kill them. They went down to accompany their Muslims neighbors and we eventually saw that Daesh had cut off their heads or shot them in the skull.

When hevala Rojano came to take my pregnant relative to the hospital, I thought the whole time that they would kick us out of the car or shoot us. She was flying in that SUV, but I did not think she wanted to save the mother and her children. Once we arrived at the hospital I calmed down. There, I saw women and men in white uniforms and they dispelled my fear. The hospital was simple, but clean. The nurse took the pregnant woman to the treatment room and escorted her husband and me to a small kitchen. Two pots were on a four-burner stove. They told us to serve ourselves like we were in our own homes. We looked with hesitation at those pots, which smelled of rice and bean soup, and at the bread on the table, until an armed man came and brought four plates for the rice and bean soup from a cupboard, poured the food on those plates, put them on the table, and asked us to eat. I asked him if I could charge my phone and he answered, 'You should feel like this is your home. This is the People's Hospital.'

His answer was so friendly that I allowed myself to ask him if I could have the opportunity to call my mother. He gave me his cell phone. I wanted to call her, but the pregnant woman's husband also wanted to call his family. That's why I decided to call my cousin in Dihok instead of calling my mom. Her husband answered the cell phone. He knew my voice and worriedly asked me where I was. I said in Syria and added that the cell phone was not mine. He told me to hang up and he would call back. I did. In a minute the phone rang and I heard my cousin's voice. She asked what had happened to my family and the other Êzdîs. I told her that the PKK had opened a rescue corridor for us. A great cheer went up in the house upon hearing this news. They had gathered with many other Êzdî families and waited anxiously for a message from Şingal. I told her that I'm in a hospital because Şevger* would soon give birth to her children. I asked her to call my mother and Şevger's mother-in-law in Koço and tell us immediately about their situation.

The armed man left his cell phone with us and left the kitchen, after which we ate the food. After about ten minutes my cousin called me back and said they were fine and that they had not been attacked yet. Three days before, some Arab Muslim neighbors from the village are said to have guaranteed that they would be secure if they gave their weapons to them. 'They should not have done such a stupid thing,' I shouted ferociously and told her what had happened to the surrendered Êzdîs who had submitted themselves to Daesh.

---

* A woman who wanders in the night.

This news hit me like lightning. I went to the armed man, gave his cell phone back, and said that I would like to return to my father in Şingal. He said he would talk about it with his superior. He came back soon and said I could go back with the first convoy.

After an hour, the convoy was ready to go. I said goodbye to Şevger and her husband and left the hospital. In the yard, three trucks waited for me with running engines. Many tents, blankets, and a few cartons of medicine were loaded on them. An armed girl from the YPJ was sitting next to the driver. He also wore military clothes. They filled up the cab space with a revolutionary song. The girl fighter helped me get up the truck. I greeted them and they shook my hand and greeted me warmly. Then the drivers drove off. Unlike hevala Rojano, he drove very slowly, in spite of the excitement and fast tempo of the song. The other trucks passed us.

There was no sign of war in Rimêlan and the surrounding area, but right at the exit of the city, the streets were full of cars. A long, tightly packed train of cars blocked the streets. The driver took a detour and drove out of the city with difficulty. Along the way, he was driving on the edge of the road. Kurdish soldiers were stationed in some places on the path and at every crossroads. The girl fighter made me aware that my mobile phone was ringing. Once I got my phone, it had stopped ringing and instead I got several messages. Rojevîn* had sent me credits. In one message, I could choose an option to get unlimited internet access for a month. I chose the option and sent her an appreciation message. Then I called my dad. He was in Serdeşt, waiting for me. Rojevîn had sent him and my mother the same credits. I announced to my father that my cousin was well and that she and her husband were safe.

We reached the rescue corridor. It was a real hell there. Because of the dense dust you could hardly see ahead of you. The drivers were driving as fast as they could and those who didn't have a car were trying, with their remaining strength, to make it to Rojava before Daesh could attack again and the corridor would be closed. People knocked on the passing cars and asked for a sip of water. We had two big containers of mineral water, which lay at my feet. The fighter girl asked me to get down so that

* Day of love.

she could hand over the water to those in need. I got down and she got the two containers out of the truck and called out to the driver.

'I'll stay here. Call me when you come back so we don't lose each other.'

I stayed alone in the car with a strange armed man but was not scared at all. Every truck that brought food, tents, blankets, and other necessary items from Rojava also took people who had no car to Rojava. The required food and water were provided and the fear of an Daesh attack decreased, but the destiny of the Êzdîs who were besieged by Daesh was our greater concern. The situation in Koço was more frightening. The pressure on the Êzdîs there must have increased after being persuaded by their Arab fellow villagers to hand their weapons over to the Islamic jihadists. On the fifth day of the siege, the same Arab neighbors came to the Êzdîs and said they have only two choices: either convert to Islam or be killed as pagans. We all knew how dangerous the situation was. We resorted to every means possible to help the besieged Êzdîs in Koço. We called countless human rights organizations and governments around the world and informed them of the mortal danger the Êzdîs were in, but we were given only empty words in response. The Êzdîs in Koço also called around everywhere.

Those days, I was working at the People's Hospital in Rimêlan, so I could follow up on the news with the TV and radio. Every channel was talking about the daily anti-Daesh coalition airstrikes against Daesh positions in the Şingal Mountains and surrounding areas. Such brazen lies could hardly be endured. The Daesh positions were not bombed even once. Reconnaissance drones and military planes were flying over Koço the whole time, as the people from Koço told us, but not to bombard Daesh positions. They were recording the destiny of the Êzdîs.

At that time, I did not understand anything about the effects of aircrafts in war, but now I realize that the coalition, with the help of their aircrafts, could have easily saved two thousand besieged Êzdîs. Hevala Jînçin, your beloved father was perfectly right. The tragedy of the Êzdîs was just a scenario conceived of and approved by the superpowers. The directors of that tragedy needed a much higher number of Êzdî victims, but about a hundred Kurdish girls and boys arrived and ruined their film production. The world powers ought to be angry at the PKK, because it meddles in everything.

The Êzdîs in Koço did not convert to Islam and, so, the Daesh ultimatum ended on August 15th. We contacted the people from the besieged village on every matter. Daesh had separated the women and children from the men and taken them into a school yard. Over a thousand women and children are said to have been brought together there. Some Êzdîs from the villages around Koço who had fled there also became trapped in Koço. The women in the schoolyard are said to have heard several vollies. Later we learned that Daesh had shot all the men in Koço. These scenes were recorded by the flying planes. One day we will be able to watch such films, when the new governments of the superpowers want to disgrace the ex-governments and blame them for such tragedies. At the end of the phone calls, we could only hear the screams of women and children.

I was continuously following up on the news by radio and TV. All the channels were reporting on the anti-Daesh coalition and the airstrikes on Daesh positions in the Şingal Mountains, as if all the Êzdîs on the top of the mountains were blind. Not a single fighter aircraft bombed Daesh or its military convoys, which were stationed in specialized areas during this time. At that time, the Êzdîs were living through an inferno. Every day we received frightening news of the murder of Êzdîs and enslaved women and children. After two months, Şevger called me and said that seventy Êzdîs, who had earlier been enslaved, were being ransomed, or, it is better to say, exchanged for a merchant. Our comrades had arrested an Arab trader. He is said to have been very important to Daesh and they had sent a message by radio to our comrades to trade him for ten hostages. One of our comrades from Rojhilat said on his own initiative that we would release him only for seventy hostages and they should all be Êzdî women and children."

"Was the proposal accepted?" I asked with excitement and she answered yes.

"In the hospital I explained that story to my superior and asked her to send me to Şingal. Less than ten minutes later a pickup appeared at the door and I was taken to Şingal. On the way, Şevger called me back and said that my mother and my five-year-old brother were also among the released hostages. I was overcome with joy until I arrived in Şingal and saw them. They were like living corpses. Within two months, the Islamic jihadists had crushed them like pomegranates. They were thin and pale and acted shy. I ran to my mother and hugged her. She looked at me, expressionless. My brother was much worse. He could neither stand nor sit normally. Countless Muslims had allegedly raped him. I later overheard my mother saying that a religious sixty-year-old hajji had bought my brother for one hundred dollars and raped him several times. How is one to believe that someone can stand before Allah after committing such crimes and pray without any conscience? My mother had been traded over twenty times within two months and resold for ten dollars as a sex slave. That was the day I decided to join the women's defense units of Şingal. I wanted to fight against Daesh and also against the Barzani clan. My hatred for that clan was and still is greater than my hatred for the radical Islamists."

"Why?" Akam asked.

"We trusted them and not Daesh. Either they are not Kurds, or we will not let ourselves be called Kurds. That's not just my personal opinion. Many other Êzdîs think the same way as I do."

"Do you know that thirty-one years ago the same tragedy, or even worse, happened to the Barzani clan? That year, eight thousand Barzanis were abducted by the Ba'ath regime. All the males were murdered and thrown into mass graves, and all the females sold in the countries of the Gulf region. Many of the abducted Êzdî women were ransomed or saved, but almost none of the Barzanis returned. The tragedy of the Êzdîs was recognized as a genocide worldwide, but the genocide of the Barzanis was not named anywhere outside of Kurdistan, because it was the beginning of a plan of annihilation against the Kurds. In the following massacres of the Barzanis through 1988, within a period of five years, one hundred and eighty-two thousand Kurds were murdered and thrown into mass graves, but it was not judged to be genocide by a single country. The world powers have never deemed it as such for diplomatic and economic reasons and haven't recognized the Anfal Campaign as genocide.[*] Maybe they even had to hide and cover up this genocide. How could the Germans explain to the world community that they themselves had provided the chemical weapons that Saddam's regime used to perpetrate

---

[*] The UK appears to be an exception; see UK Parliment, "Debate Debate on the 25th anniversary of the Kurdish genocide," February 28, 2013, https://www.parliament.uk/external/committees/committee-news-pre-oct-2020/2013/february/25th-anniversary-of-kurdish-genocide-debate/. — Translator's note

the largest chemical weapons attack in human history, against a Kurdish city, murdering five thousand civilians within a few minutes."

"Hevala Rûnahî, with all due respect I must tell you that the recent Êzdî tragedy is not the only massacre in the past hundred years of Kurdish history. In Dêrsîm, more than seventy thousand civilians were killed by the Turkish army in 1937. We Kurds did not have anything to offer the world community. We are not at the forefront of any political, scientific, social, or literary fields, but we do lead in disasters. The biggest collective suicide in history must have taken place in 1938 near Dêrsîm, where thousands of Kurdish women, besieged by the Turkish military, threw themselves off the Munzûr Mountains into the Laç River. For the first time, chemical weapons were used against a Kurdish city: Serdeşt in Rojhilat.

We Kurds have seen many tragedies in the last hundred years, but we are also to blame. Apart from our dissension, our ignorance has also been a reason for our successive disasters. We helped our enemies to destroy other peoples. I do not believe that the Armenian genocide could have been implemented on that large of a scale without massive support from the Kurds. We helped the Kemalists to implement their genocidal plans against the Armenians."

"But aiding the Hamidiye army cannot be attributed to the Kurdish people. I have often read that many Kurds even helped the Armenians to escape from the genocide," Rojano took a position against Akam's words.

"It might be that Kurds saved several thousand of their Armenian countrymen and neighbors. But they participated on a greater scale in the destruction of hundreds of thousands of Armenians. Not only should Kurdish victims be described as Kurds, but the Kurds who killed innocent people as executioners should not be separated from their original identity either. At that time, the Hamidiye army represented a large part of the Kurds, who allowed themselves to be exploited by the ideology of Islam and by their own selfish motives. The later generations of that army are still present in Bakûr and help the Turkish fascists and Islamists. The population of Kurds in Bakûr is supposed to be over twenty-five million. Where are they? To whom do they give their votes in the elections? More than half the population gives their votes to the fascist and Islamist parties, giving them the opportunity to split their society into Turks and non-Turks, Muslims and non-Muslims."

CHAPTER 10

WE TOOK BATHS in the river again whenever it snowed. Then a thin sheet of ice formed over the water. It was hidden under three or four meters of snow after several blizzards, and was not recognizable from the surrounding area. Nevertheless, bathing under the snowfall brought a lot of energy into my life. It was a unique form of relaxation for all of us. On such days, two male comrades were responsible for cooking lunch. Two others of them would pull out the metal drum and gather enough wood from the hiding place, then boil the water for the females' bath. The women would take three Kalashnikovs and Befrîn with them. That became a firm rule without ever being discussed. One of us would keep watch continuously. She would take a bath at the end and then a couple of women would fill up the drum and heat the water for the male comrades. The women's baths usually took longer. After the bath, we would promptly dress up in our clean military clothes, run next to the snow wall until the crossroads, then go up to the bunker. A warm room, hot lunch, and cups of fresh tea awaited us there.

The male comrades had already eaten lunch and waited a while for us before we returned to the bunker. Sometimes they had to take baths at night, which I also wanted to experience. Then the women were responsible for cooking dinner and removing footprint traces in the snow when not enough snowfall had fallen to cover them.

After my first bath under the snowfall, a pleasant rhythm came into my life. I felt free and calm. I kept the necessary distance from Tewar and Serhelldan as much as I could, but I felt very close with the other comrades, as if I had known them from childhood. Thinking about leaving them after a few months made me sad, so I tried to get to know them better in the time that we had. Akam had not yet read us his written story, although his writing was the reason for commencing our storytelling. One night I followed him when he went outside to smoke a cigarette behind the hanging blanket. It was dark, foggy, and cold.

"May I sit down?" I asked.

He puffed the smoke from his cigarette into the night and said gently, "Sure, darling hevala Jîncin."

I put my sack stuffed with dried brushwood next to him on the step, sat on it, and asked, "Hevalê Akam, why don't you read your novel for us?"

"I feel like I can't finish it."

"What's the problem?"

"I have a lot of problems with it, especially with the choice of narrative perspective. I have tried with different styles, but every time something goes wrong. I have lived through some parts of the story, so these parts are very familiar to me. But some parts of the story I can only guess. I am completely convinced of what happened for some parts, but I don't have any evidence to prove it. In the past few years I've rewritten the story several times, but it's far away from a real novel."

"Maybe the conventional narrative perspective does not fit such stories. I have a friend who is a novelist and he basically does not believe in using a conventional narrative perspective. He believes that the principles on which the narrative perspective are built no longer exist in the age of social networks."

"What does that mean?"

"Narrative perspectives are classified based on three main pillars; position, outlook, and attitude, but nowadays these three elements have undergone basic changes. Today, people in Vienna can know what a Brazilian peasant woman cooks for dinner, but they probably do not know their neighbors. For this reason, spatial and temporal distance don't exist anymore. Interior views and exterior views are no longer distinguishable. They are either intertwined or distorted by think tanks. Even in a science like quantum physics, scientists are infected by antiscientific viruses. This has happened because scientists receive budgets for their projects from institutions and states that are not interested in improving the intellectual capabilities of their societies. When I wanted to write my father's story earlier, he suggested that I use a flexible narrative perspective that he called an 'unmasked narrative perspective.'"

"And what does that mean?"

"This narrative perspective is rooted in a theory that all narrative perspectives have been created based on a false thesis. A writer is one person and can only represent himself, but since the beginning of the history of the novel, he has taken responsibility for representing the whole world. The Renaissance might have become an atheist era, but today rulers can control people more strictly and more comprehensively than any gods. Therefore, we really are living in the era of Jaam-e Jam. Have you heard about it?"

Akam puffed his cigarette for the last time behind his hand, killed its glowing tip with snow lying on the step, and put the rest of it in his vest pocket. Only then did he raise his head, which appeared even grayer due to the darkness and the falling snow, and said, "Jaam-e Jam is a famous myth, hevala Jîncin."

"And what do you know about this myth?"

"It's about a king who had a magic chalice with which he could observe all his people."

"But how can hundreds of thousands of people be seen in a single chalice?"

"The myth already had an answer for that. The faces of the people who were planning something against the king would appear in the chalice."

"Maybe thousands of people wanted to do something against him. How many people's faces fit in a chalice?"

"His biggest opponents appear first in the chalice and he could also track other opponents down in it."

"I am very glad that you have already heard this story. I heard about it only last year. Nowadays, that mythical chalice has become a part of our real life. The people who own Google and use artificial intelligence technologies actually have this mythical chalice in their hands. They can know how many millions of people looked for, clicked, searched, or shared a specified subject. The Orb of Jamshid is just a myth, but the king could profit from it for as long as his people believed in its existence. Yet, modern AI and search engines are not only fearsome, but also an effective and real means of controlling the population."

"I agree with that, but what is the relation between these things and narrative perspectives? I have technical problems with writing my novel, but not with the content."

"Because literary and artistic techniques reflect the worldview of the artists. An author who puts himself in another person's shoes conceals his true face. The author is actually a unique and true character, even if he wears a dozen masks. Authors are utilized to speak on behalf of other people. I do not understand why, when using an authorial narrative perspective, I have a right to read the minds of my novel's characters, but I can't do that in my real life. I am that same person and I know that the methods of logic, deduction, and induction in literature and the spiritual sciences often lead to irritation. I'm really excited to hear your story. I mean the story of hevalê Akam and not some unknown imaginary narrator."

After a week, Akam told me that he would like to read his story the next morning. The drone was in the sky and only Serhelldan was keeping watch. Akam read the story by heart, even though he had his notebook with him.

"I would like to tell you one of the most bitter tragedies of Rojhilat. The extermination story of the most legendary battalion of the Komele Party. This party was founded by Kak* Fouad from the village of Almana, near Merîwan. During his university studies, he became acquainted with the Marxist movement and then founded 'Unity of Farmers,' which developed swiftly and from which Komele later separated.

It takes a long time to talk about this party, but I will talk about the Şiwan battalion, the party's most famous battalion. The fierceness and competency of this battalion had been a thorn in the eyes of the Islamic government of Iran for eight years. During a period when the city of Sine was one of the most militarized cities in the world, this battalion broke the authority of the Islamic republic of Iran and teased its power structure. They were always settled in Sine and its surrounding areas, and conducted military and political activities whenever they wanted.

This battalion, which had destroyed the defensive lines of the mullah's Iranian regime thousands of times throughout those eight years and mostly came out without any losses, was finally exterminated within ten minutes by a destructive decision of Komele's central committee. But those committee members, after thirty-one years, still do not accept any blame for their wrong decision, and even try more than ever to blame

---

* Salutation to a big brother.

other people in this tragedy. Surprisingly, they blame someone who was actually the only person that made the right decision and who endangered himself to save the battalion. It's a tragedy that I want to tell you.

The carnage of beloved members of this battalion was painful for me, but more agonizing are the instruments that the culprits have used to blame the innocent people in this tragedy. The first secretary of Komele managed to deceive not only the people, but also the majority of the Pêşmerge, and one of them was me. I had believed his false story for twenty-two years and knew someone as a traitor who should have been respected as a great and glorious commander and who should have been honored by us and by society for his sacrifice. All persons in this story are real and I will use their true names.

It began with a decision by the Komele central committee to dispatch a battalion to Biyare. This village is located in Başûr near the border with Iran. At first they decided to dispatch the battalion of Merîwan there, but the battalion denied their order and didn't go because of the perilous situation in Biyare. The artillery units of the Islamic republic of Iran were constantly firing on the village. Apart from the Merîwan battalion, there was another person who opposed the decision of the central committee from the beginning. He was the person who was later blamed for the whole tragedy. His name was Heme Seyar and, at the time, he publicly opposed the decision of the chairman.

Before that, a rumor had been spreading that the Iranian army was planning a major attack on these areas. There were many signs indicating an imminent and major military offensive. We received news about mobilizations of massive IRGC forces and also the construction of a new military road to transfer these forces. Some PUK members who were supposed to participate in this military attack had even informed the central committee about the exact time and place of attack. But all this evidence did not persuade the Komele officials to withdraw their battalion from Biyare. The answer of the executive committee to Heme Seyar's yelling about a prompt retreat of the Şiwan battalion was nothing but mockery, 'Why are you scared of death?'

At that time, I was too stupid to ask myself why Heme Seyar should dread the battle. He had already proven his courage as a Pêşmerge and commander in the past nine years. Apart from that, his life was not in any danger. He was just trying to save the lives of his comrades. The more perceptible and obvious the signs of the IRGC attack became, the more unconcerned and carefree the executive committee reacted to it. The only ones who worried about the destiny of the comrades in the Şiwan battalion were Heme Seyar and his commander Heybella Kêllane. He was also a military genius and foresaw the impending danger a month in advance. He was the commander of the Sine eleventh brigade and responsible for the mobilization of all troops in Biyare at that time.

Twenty days before this tragedy, Heybella and Salah Mazooji had gone to the first secretary of Komele, Sey Ibrahim Alizadeh, and had explained the dangerous situation. But Sey Ibrahim not only did not listen to him, but also decreed that he was taking back all responsibility over the troops' mobilization from the Sine central committee and handing it over to the executive committee of Komele.

Two days before the beginning of the IRGC military attack, the situation was awful. The executive of the Şiwan Battalion had a meeting with the Sine Area Committee in Çinare. Not only was withdrawal not decided on for the battalion, but some others went to Biyare with them. They knew that the situation in Biyare was terrible and wanted to be with their partners and close friends during that dangerous time.

I have not forgotten that no one was more worried than Heme Seyar that day. He stood yelling in front of the Toyota Land Cruiser and tried to prevent the other people from going to Biyare. He even came to Heybella and asked for help, but, in the end, everyone who had already made their decision went to Biyare.

At that time I was with Heybella. He was in constant wireless contact with Şokê Xêrabadî, the Şiwan battalion commander. After two days, Şokê reported by wireless that the attack had commenced. Only then did Heybella order him to leave everything there and promptly retreat with their weapons. This overdue order was issued by Heybella without informing Komele executives, but it was too late. They marched toward the Zellm Bridge, but it was already under the control of Iranian troops. The Şiwan battalion was besieged on three sides and the other side was Lake Derbendîxan. Their situation was already awful and what made it worse was that none of them knew the regions.

For eight years they had fought successfully in the region around Sine, because they knew every corner, valley, and mountain like the back of their hands. But none of them had ever known the geography of the Şarezûr and Biyare regions. That legendary battalion is said to have been running around all day in the midst of a battle between two large armies. In the evening they were exhausted and wanted to take a rest. So, they went to the town of Sîrwan and spent the night there. That night, Heybella announced that the Iraqi government had promised to provide him with some inflatable boats so that they could pass across Lake Sîrwan to the safe side of the reservoir.

The next morning, something unforeseeable happened. The Iraqi army, which had been utterly defeated and lost control of a lot of territory, carried out the largest chemical bomb attack in history over this area. The Şiwan Battalion was in the wrong place at the wrong time, near the city of Helebce, where five thousand people suffocated from the poisonous chemical gas within a few hours.

That same morning, Heme Seyar drove with several Pêşmerge to see Ba'ath Party executives in the city of Erbet, receiving just a few rubber boats, despite all sorts of help they could have provided them. Late that night, Heme Seyar announced that they had arrived near the reservoir and had been given only one or at most two usable boats. By this time, the battalion had reached the shore of the lake. Heme told Şokê to shoot some flares for him to find their position. It was done and Heme told Şokê that he found their location and that they were supposed to walk upward from the edge of shore until they reached that location. However, the boat failed to reach there and the Iranian forces fired at them with RPGs and machine guns until we did not hear from them anymore.

Our guess was that all of them had fallen. The first rescue operation for the Şiwan battalion failed and the battalion, which was exhausted, hopeless, and poisoned with chemical gas, had to seek a hiding place and wait for the next rescue attempt. But there was no real rescue plan to save them and Iranian forces discovered their hiding place and attacked them before they tried to set up a second childish plan. The troops of the Islamic government of the gallows, who were once frightened even by the name of this battalion, knew exactly what kind of a dramatic situation our comrades were in.

'Our guard says that some military cars are coming towards us and a few soldiers are running behind them,' Şokê said via wireless. The Iranian troops knew well that those tigers opposite them were unarmed and had laid down on the ground, injured. They had lost their strength to move at all. Many of them had been poisoned and had already thrown away their weapons or magazines on the way. So they became sitting ducks for the troops of the Islamic republic. The struggle did not take more than ten minutes and the whole battalion was put under fire. That was our first assumption. After a few days, it was reported that twelve members of the Şiwan battalion had been arrested and the IRGC decided to expose them in the Azadi sports complex. None of the prisoners appeared on Iranian TV and none expressed any regret, so after a few months all twelve prisoners were executed.

After the tragedy, we realized why Heme Seyar was against the dispatch of battalions to Biyare from the beginning. Everyone asked why our forces were locked out in this wide place near the Iranian border. That was contrary to every rule of guerrilla warfare.

Over time these questions were posed more loudly, more exasperatedly, and more frequently to the Komele executive committee. Some members of the Pêşmerge had even launched a protest campaign and prepared a tough petition, which several members of the party had signed. Ibrahim Alizadeh, who since the founding of the Communist Party of Iran in 1983, and to this day, has screwed up all sorts of crap as party leader and has never once admitted to a mistake, nor been held accountable for his mistakes, blocked the proposal for an investigation into the causes of that tragedy. His excuse was that it would make our enemies happy and weaken the fighting spirit of the Pêşmerge members. We would need renewed strength and absolute unity to avenge our fallen heroes. With these demagogic slogans he was able to stay afloat and remain chairman."

"And what do you think? Why did Komele, in spite of all the obvious dangers, dispatch this battalion to Biyare? There should have been a good reason for that," Rûken asked him.

"They had a reason, but a childish one. The reason was the profound enmity between them and the HDKA.* They were possessed by such an incurable animosity for the HDKA that no argument or illustration could stop them from dispatching the Şiwan battalion and throwing them into the fire. They refused to withdraw the battalion from hell in order to prevent our Kurdish rivals from gaining a foothold in that area."

---

* Democratic Party of Iranian Kurdistan.

"It sounds illogical, hevalê Akam. How could the HDKA do something in that region when it had been turned into a battlefield of two government armies? Maybe there was another reason."

"Like what?"

"Perhaps the Ba'ath regime did not let them pull their troops back from there."

"No, hevala Rûken. Neither Komele, nor the HDKA had ever been mercenaries of both governments. The culture of resistance in Rojhilat is very distinct. Unlike the other parts of Kurdistan, where the parties cooperate with and even bow to orders from the fascist governments of Iran and Turkey, none of the parties in Rojhilat have ever become servants of other governments. They may have messed up a lot, but they have followed a couple of their ethical maxims until now. They had never been servants of national governments and there had never been a terror or boycott within the party. The profound enmity between Komele and HDKA was the main reason for stationing their troops in Biyare, but neither of the two party's leaders accepted any responsibility for this destructive mistake and have not apologized to this day.

After two months, the first survivor of the Şiwan battalion, and two weeks later the last one, came back to the Komele forces. At that time I was a confidant of the Komele central committee and had the opportunity to read the reports of both of them. Through these reports, I realized how this battalion, which was exhausted and poisoned, had been destroyed within ten minutes by a small force of twenty soldiers. I went ballistic and wanted to avenge them, so I asked the party to send me to Rojhilat.

Seven months after the tragedy, a hundred and eight other Pêşmerge and I were positioned on Şanişîn Mountain, close to a very nice spring which is called Çawrreş. Suddenly, a man appeared from the green valley, came uphill, and headed straight toward us. One of our comrades who was watching him through binoculars said, 'This man is walking like Heme Seyar.' We had thought he was dead, but he climbed along the edge of the stream. He put down the binoculars and went downhill. After a few seconds he ran and they hugged each other when he reached Heme. All of us comrades ran down toward him.

I was not the only one who stumbled several times out of sheer excitement and fell onto the meadow. He was our commander for a long time, one of the most beloved members of Komele. Nothing in the world could give us as much pleasure in that moment as his appearance. I hugged him and kissed him all over his face. His lips were chapped and his face was sunburned and had become red. It was clear that he had spent a long time in the darkness.

All of us comrades spent the whole day rejoicing on Şanişîn Mountain. We cooked a broth from fresh sheep meat. Our nurse treated his sunburned face, and the battalion's commander informed the Komele central base about Heme's return by wireless. The news was broadcasted within all the bunkers and military bases of Komele via loudspeaker.

We were given an order by wireless that no one should bother him with various questions. Six other comrades and I got a mission to accompany him to Silêmanî in the evening. Heme also took a Kalashnikov and we went from Çilçeme downward to Bestam. At dawn, we arrived at the IRGC base. There we waited until the next evening, then crossed the border into Iraq. The party leaders had sent us a Toyota Land Cruiser. We got in and after three hours we arrived in Silêmanî. There, the deputy party chairman was waiting for us.

Here I want to clarify something to you. A week ago, I had a talk with hevala Jînçin about narrative perspective."

He turned to me and continued,

"You were right. Although I was not present at some places and I did not hear some conversations, I want to tell these parts with direct speech because I am convinced of their truthfulness. In the last thirty-one years, I have talked with countless people and researched the cases well. I'm sure my recountings are true, so I will tell it as if I were present there.

"When we arrived in Silêmanî, the assistant of Sey Ibrahim talked with Heme. He informed the deputy party leader that he had been imprisoned in an Iranian jail eighteen days after the tragedy. He told Heme not to talk about it with anyone.

Some Pêşmerge accompanied us in a convoy from Silêmanî to the Sine camp of Komele in Çinare. There were many comrades there waiting for us. It was a more enthusiastic welcome than anyone had ever received before in Komele history. For three days there were celebrations, dancing, and singing. Only then was Heme called to the political office. There he explained what had happened to him and how he had spent the previous seven months. When he told how the Islamic intelligence officials had shot our comrade in the head right in front of his eyes within a dark shooting tunnel, he broke down and cried. The executioners are said to have pretended that they had photographed him with a pistol in his hand while shooting his comrades. They were there to scare him and persuade him to return to Komele as a spy for the Ayatollah's regime.

When Heme finished his story, Ibrahim Alizadeh embraced him and said, 'I absolutely believe you and know that the Islamic intelligence services wanted to perform a character assassination on you.'

Within a week Heme had comprehensively written his story about the previous seven months in a sixty-page report. I have personally read his report. He wrote:

Ednan Hewramî was opposed to a rescue operation using the motorboats. He said several times to the party's PR chairman that he knew some places in the reservoir that were not deep even in the springtime. We could cross the lake from these spots and lead our comrades back to the safe side of the reservoir. Unfortunately, Heme Nebewî repeatedly rejected his proposal. Ednan was local, knew the terrain well, and was willing to go to hell with us, so we had to follow his recommendation.

It took over twenty hours before we were approved for the three inflatable boats. We carried the boats on our shoulders to the shore. We had only two to three hours to blow up the rubber boats by air pump, reach our comrades, and bring them back. One of them had a leak after we had inflated it. We threw it away and inflated another one by air pump, then put it on the lake. Those two boat lovers stayed on the safe shore and Ednan, two Iraqi soldiers, three other Pêşmerge, and I boarded the boat and crossed the lake on that pitch black night toward the other side. The darkness was so complete that even the other side of the lake could not be seen. I turned my head to the comrades who sat behind me, but they were not visible and I heard only their whispering. The Iraqi soldiers drove the boat, while Ednan sat next to them and translated my instructions into Arabic. I had nothing to say on that pitch-black night, so I kept silent while they drove the boat. Tahêr Bêsaran was sitting beside

Ednan and I was on their left side. Reza sat opposite us and Qubad at the head of the boat.

The side of the reservoir that we wanted to cross was eight hundred meters wide, but a troop of Iranians had noticed us because of the motorboat buzzing. On the other side, when we arrived near the shore, I asked Ednan to tell the soldiers we should no longer go forward, but head to the edge of the shore. Ednan told them my instructions and I contacted Heybella by radio again. At that moment, an RPG rocket was shot at us and the IRGC troops put us under fire. Qubad and I fired in the direction of where the shots came from. We both emptied our magazines. Our immediate and quick response left their weapons silent for a while. I used this time to find out what was happening. Then I noticed my head was injured. The RPG rocket exploded above us and some shrapnel hit my head. I pulled my handkerchief out of my pocket and tied my wound.

Ednan and those two soldiers had fallen. So, the boat was continuously whirling around itself and my vertigo was increasing. I was hearing some voices from the radio. Muzefer and Mohammad ordered us to withdraw. My vertigo was getting worse. I could hardly contact Heybella by radio and announced to him our dramatic situation. Shooting began from the other side again. The engine of the boat was on fire and its flames revealed our position to the soldiers opposite us. Tahêr Bêsaran ran toward the engine and threw it into the lake but, simultaneously, a bullet hit his head and he shouted loudly, 'Tahêr has become a martyr!' He died at that moment. I ducked under the constant shots and looked around to see the other comrades' situations. Qubad's head was hit by a bullet. He leaned onto the boat next to me and died. Reza was opposite me and was also hit by several bullets to his chest and stomach. He was in a critical situation. Hopeless, I laid down on the bottom of the boat and thought about a possible solution.

Except Reza, who was badly injured, all of my comrades died on the boat. Those comrades who were behind us did not even shoot a bullet and IRGC troops put us under fire with glee.

Heme Seyar also wrote in his report that he spoke with the radio operator in the group and asked why didn't the comrades on the other side of the reservoir didn't shoot at the IRGC troops to give them a chance of retreating? 'Once the shooting began,' she replied, 'Heme Nebewî and his buddy escaped toward the Iraqi army base and ordered us to follow them.'

Poor Heme was suffocating under the rain of bullets and the rush of adrenaline. He was trying to find a sudden solution and unstrapped the handkerchief around his head, washed it in the water that had come into the boat, and again wrapped it tightly around his head. Heme Seyar's report continued:

> The radio was in the water and didn't work anymore. I took off my clothes while lying down. I shivered in the cold weather. My head was spinning with the boat whirling in the darkness. Reza raised his head while he was moaning in pain and asked me, "Could you help me?" But at that moment a bullet struck his head and he fell.

> There was no point in staying in that boat anymore. I crawled over the boat and threw myself into the lake. I wanted to swim back to the place that we came from, but because of my head injury, the cold weather, and the darkness, I accidentally swam toward the enemy. After fifteen minutes I reached the wrong side of the reservoir. I walked for about ten minutes looking for a hill where there was an Iraqi army military base. I did not find the hill, so I went back in the opposite direction and walked for twenty minutes until I heard the voice of the Iranian military forces. I realized that I had reached the wrong side of the reservoir. The Iranian troops were talking loudly. They might have been the troops who shot us. They carried with them two killed and three injured soldiers. I threw myself on the ground and tried to crawl to the reeds near the reservoir, but by now it was dawn and they noticed me. I got up and talked to them in

a broken Persian accent. "I not soldier. I PUK. I hurt. Saddam chemical bomb."

The soldiers took Heme Seyar to their commander to identify if he was a member of the PUK. The Iranian commander asked him, 'Where is the PUK headquarters?' Everyone in Komele knew the answer, but he was confused because of his injury and exhaustion and did not remember the place name, so he told them another quarter's place name. The commander says, 'He used to be a PUK member.' They considered him to be an Iraqi Kurd and took him to join the other Iraqi Kurds they had gathered from that area. Heme Seyar was sent to Iran with many other Kurds, and then sent to Hersîn near Kirmaşan and settled in a school.

Eighteen days after the tragedy, Heme Seyar stole shoes from one of the refugees and fled at night. Heme Seyar wrote about the event like this:

> In the previous days, when they sent me to Hersîn for interrogation and changed my head bandage, I remembered the path and direction to escape to Kirmaşan. On that night when I escaped, I did not dare to take my dinner with me. After I had my dinner I wore some shoes that I had tried on in the previous days and went to the yard, under the excuse of using the bathroom. There were no walls around the school. Besides the two or three meters of the school yard that were illuminated by the light of the room lamps, the whole vicinity of that area was in darkness. The water tank was located under the light of the school. I filled up the ewer but left it there, and then I crawled toward darkness. I got up after a while and ran quickly. When I was far away from the school I started running parallel to the road, with fifty meters of distance in between, so that I wouldn't lose my sense of direction. I walked for a long time. The shoes that I thought fit me were small and hurt my feet. I could not endure my foot pain and finally laid down behind a rock.
>
> Everywhere was dark and quiet. Sometimes cars crossed with a roar, then the scene returned again to pitch black night. I took off my overcoat which, seventeen days ago, an Iranian soldier had taken from an arrested Iraqi soldier and gave to me near the Derbendîxan reservoir. It had a tough lining inside. I tried

to tear it up by hand, but I couldn't and had to put it on a stone and slowly split it up with another stone. I removed the lining of the sleeves and wrapped it around my feet. Then I tied my shoelaces and walked until morning. It was twilight when I arrived at Ferraş village near the Qeresû rivulet.

Heme Seyar misspelled the river's name, perhaps because the real name 'Gamasîyaw' seems to have the word 'black' in it as well. Heme Seyar didn't expect the river to hinder his escape. Heme was saying:

> For a while I was looking for a bridge. I couldn't find one. I briefly considered crossing the rivulet, but the weather was cold and the water even colder. I thought that even if I didn't freeze in the rivulet I would be exhausted and lose the last of my strength. Also, I was too hungry. I went to the left side and entered an underground concrete tube that led to the other side of the road. I really don't know if I slept or fainted. I woke up to the voice of a shepherd lad who was cursing in the Lekî Kurdish dialect and throwing pebbles at his sheep and goats, who refused to stop loudly bleating. I crawled within the tube towards the other side of the road before he noticed me. There I leaned on a rock. It was sunny and the weather was warming up. I fainted but again woke to the sound of people's voices. There were many people gathering there. In the previous few days, at the school, the radio was constantly broadcasting that the Iraqi army was attacking western Iran with bombs and rockets. I thought they were refugees who came there to flee the bombing. Later I found out it was Sêzde Beder, a holiday where people go out into nature. There were so many people that my presence was no longer noticed. When the night came, I hid myself near the road until a bus that was transporting refugees to the city came back. When the people got off the bus, I went to a man who was going toward Ferraş village. I said in Farsi, "Brother, I am a soldier. Where can I find some bread?"

> "We are refugees ourselves, but I can get you some bread."

I went to a house with him and stayed at the door. He went inside and after a few minutes came back with some bread. I was putting the bread in my pocket, but at that time a boy came to me with a couple dishes of rice and stew. I was afraid to draw attention if I ate there, so I asked the man, "Can I go into the yard to eat my food?" He accepted. It was a wide yard of nearly two hundred square meters. A pool was located in the center. It appeared that they were a rich family. When I wanted to leave, his wife followed me. I listened to her earlier; she was speaking in the Lekî dialect. She said in Farsi, "Take it," and put sixty tomans in my hand. She went back to her room, before I could express my gratitude. I asked the man, "How can I get to Bakhtaran?"

"There is no straight road to Kermanshah. You have to go to the Bistoon crossroads first. There you will find a lot of cars going to Kermanshah."

I left the yard and went toward the road. After a while a car arrived. I asked him in Farsi if he was going to Kermanshah. "No, but at the junction there are a lot of cars for Kermanshah."

The car's radio was broadcasting news about the bombardment of Iran's cities by Iraq. When I woke up, the car was stopped in front of a police checkpoint. An armed soldier looked inside and then let us go. We arrived at the junction. I paid six tomans to the driver, like the others, and got down. I knew already that there was another police checkpoint nearby, so I turned to walk to the other side and waited for a car. After a while, a car came and I went to Kirmaşan. I asked him to let me off in front of a telephone booth. He dropped me off near a building that used to be a cinema before the so-called Iranian Revolution. I paid him twenty tomans and he gave me back two tomans. The telephone booth was crowded. I picked up an empty cigarette packet from the ground and tore a piece of it. In front of the telephone booth, I asked a man who was selling cigarettes to give me a pen to write down a phone number. A lot of people were standing in the queue. I asked a man, "Brother, do you have a coin?" He gave me one. I wanted to give him money, but he did not accept. I called 118, the phone number for information, and asked them for the number of my friend Perwîz Mohammadi and his brother. He replied that there was no phone number registered in that name. I asked again for his father's phone number. He gave me his phone number. I let it ring a lot but they did not answer.

Twenty-six years after the Şiwan battalion tragedy, I met Heme Seyar in his home. His wife, Mahrox, brought us tea and a Norwegian song was playing on the TV. Both of his daughters were sitting on the canapé opposite me. Neither Heme nor Mahrox complained and they hosted me like an old friend. Heme Seyar took my hand and stared at me. 'Let me tell you something amazing,' he said. I thanked Mahrox for the tea, picked up a glass and said, 'Anything even weirder, Heme?'

'Yes, when I was on my way to visit you in Şanişîn, I waited for dark for a few hours in the teahouse next to the village of Kewlle with one of my friends who drove me there. Meanwhile, a car arrived and stopped in front of the tea house. People were returning from a trip to Turkey. I saw my friend Perwîz among those getting out. Although we had not seen each other for eight years and I had lost a lot of weight in captivity, he recognized me immediately. He ran up to me, hugged me tightly, and burst into tears.

We were close friends. After vocational school we lived together in a room at the university for two years. Later we remained close friends. When the Islamic army took possession of Sine, he moved to Kirmaşan with his family. Nobody knew them there and they could continue to live like normal citizens. I told him I called him in Kirmaşan seven months ago. He said they lived in their garden outside of town at that time. When I arrived in Norway, I heard that he had died in a car accident.'

Heme Seyar started to laugh, which surprised me. Well, what was he laughing at? I stared at his laughing face and saw that tears were running down his cheeks. I stared at him wide-eyed and couldn't say anything until his elder daughter, Sara, said, 'Only a few months ago I realized Heme laughs when he is crying. This is something completely different from the simultaneous smiling and crying of the women. He reacts to all strong expressions of emotion with inappropriate facial expressions.'

Sara was talking calmly, as if Heme were not there.

'Three months ago, Heme talked to me about his prison time. The experiences were horrific, but he laughed about them. After Heme finished his words, I couldn't stay at home. I took a train to Oslo. There, I cried in my boyfriend's arms for hours. I asked myself why my father would tell me those things and think they were funny. My mother called me and told me that on the first day that we came to Norway, one of our friends called Heme and told him that his father had passed away. Heme laughed loudly and told the host that his father had died. The host was astonished by his reaction. Heme was deeply upset and talked about his old and patient father's sorrowful face and then cried. Your father always had this habit. He laughs when he is crying.'

I sat up and said, 'No, Mahrox is wrong. Back then, Heme laughed when he was happy or found something funny. I haven't seen him in twenty-four years, but we often laughed and cried together.'

Heme Seyar stopped laughing.

'Heme, I still don't know how you spent your prison time,' I said to him.

He told me with a bitter smile, 'I was at war with the lice. In the intelligence prison of Sine, they threw me into a room full of lice. I have never even seen as many ants in one place until then. A hundred thousand lice were crawling up and down the room, on the walls and between the two dirty blankets. During the first three weeks, I was tortured so violently that returning to my cell was a comfort for me. I knew they would break my will if the torture didn't stop soon. One day, my torturer told me that an imprisoned Pêşmerge would come talk to me. They covered my eyes and I couldn't see his face. I'm sure that he couldn't see me either, otherwise he would recognize me. He said, "I don't know who you are. A sympathizer, an ordinary Pêşmerge, or one of Komele's commanders. The torture here knows no bounds. They will break you. The sooner you confess, the less you will be tormented."

His words broke me down. He was a member of my forces in the Arêz and Kawe battalions. One of the best humans that I have seen in my whole life. A handsome revolutionary with a brave heart who was arrested based on the foolish decision of the central committee of Komele. I liked him very much. They took him out of the room. A dreadful silence engulfed the torture chamber. I told myself that I should try to deceive them instead of taking any heroic action. Under my blindfold, I saw my torturer's hands. He put a sheet of paper on the table next to me, then sat behind me and said, "Remove your blindfold." On the paper was written: "1. Spy and counterspy names, 2. Secret forces names, 3. Location of hidden ammunition." I wrote some information and they brought me back to my cell. After a week, my body had recovered and I could feel the presence of the louse colony in my cell. Suddenly my whole body itched. Then my armpit and lower abdomen started to hurt and it became unbearable over time.

I was alone in that small cell and those hundred thousand lice had only me to feed on. They bit me and sucked my blood. They laid eggs, which scattered with every movement that I made, and when they hatched a new colony of lice emerged. I hit the wall in pain and scratched my skin with my long nails, until one night, a nightmare woke me up. It was dark and I was stark naked. Mahrox sat near me by a great fire on Mount Şanişîn. I wanted to get physically close to her, but suddenly I saw some lice on my arm. They were huge like cockroaches. They climbed up and became locusts. Mahrox moved closer to me. I got up and ran away. Mahrox called after me desperately. When I woke up, I was sweating profusely and fearful that I had typhus.

During my operations when I was a Pêşmerge, I kept nightly watch over the IRGC's bases and stared at them so much that my eyesight weakened. I couldn't see the lice until the sun came into my cell from a little window on the ceiling. I waited until noon. Once the sunlight was shining into my cell, I sat next to the toilet bowl and began to comb my head with my nails and scratch my body. The dimensions of my cell were two cubic meters and on a given day sunlight came in for only two or three hours. I poured some water onto a broken dustpan and hunted lice. Before the sunlight disappeared, I had caught thousands of lice. The water in the plastic scoop seemed black. I shook it into the toilet bowl.

From then on, catching lice was my only mental and physical occupation. After the sun left my cell, I waited impatiently for the next rays of sunshine. I thought my action had to be kept secret, otherwise the prison guards would have stopped me. The huge amount of lice within this cell was not accidental and it must have been a part of my physical and mental torture. I pricked up my ears and immediately emptied the plastic scoop down the toilet as soon as I heard the sound of a footstep.

Gradually, this act turned into a rescue action for me. I had to stay sane and try to gain the trust of my interrogators.

Once I filled out the new papers with harmless information, I went back to cleaning the lice. After three months I was able to eradicate them. For three days I woke up at dawn and looked for the lice until dusk and found none. I thought my eyes had gotten worse by now, but that wasn't the case. There were no more lice in the cell. I had waited for this moment for ninety-four days, but I wasn't happy. How could I have spent the long summer days without something to do?

I waited for the Iranian secret services to take me back to the Çilçeme Mountains by military helicopter to show them our hidden ammunition dumps that never existed. You know that we didn't have an ammunition store there and we hid our weapons and ammunition with the villagers.'

Heme Seyar stared at me again. He could have raised his voice and even kicked me out of the house. Like many other members of the party, I had spread the rumors behind his back that Heme had betrayed our ammunition depots to the Iranian secret services. His younger daughter turned off the television. Heme was still scratching his face with his nails. Then he touched the cup with his fingertips. The tea must have been cold. Mahrox leaned toward the teapot standing over a glass warmer, under which two candles were burning. She lifted the pot and poured him half a glass of hot tea. Heme Seyar mixed the cold tea with the new one, drank it down and spoke.

'The first time, the intelligence officers must have known that the Pêşmerge had not returned to the mountains yet, but they were afraid to stay there for a long time and search under the snow for the ammunition. They took me back to my dirty cell early without showing anyone. My two interrogators were the only people whose faces I was allowed to see and whose voices I was allowed to hear. After cleaning the lice, I didn't see anyone for two weeks. One hand always opened the little door three times a day, filled my bowl with cold food and put a piece of stale bread at my feet next to the toilet bowl.

After a while, an interrogator came to my cell with a box in his hand. For the first time he sat there. Apparently, he knew there was no trace of lice.

'Do you think we have an insider in the central committee of Komele?' He asked.

'No, I don't think so.'

'Well, look, we have a copy of all the photos that you had recorded with your camera.'

He opened the box and threw some photos at me. He wanted to show me the strength of the Islamic government and bully me even more, but when I saw the first photo, my lips moved and formed into a smile. After a hundred and forty-two days, it was the first sign of human emotion. My friends were in this world. For three months I had drowned the lice without hating them or making sense of what I was doing. The food was bland and I was feeling numb. I picked up another photo from the floor. It was the Kawe battalion Pêşmerge standing in some rows. I burst out laughing and crying and couldn't stop. My interrogator looked at me in astonishment. He probably thought I'd gone insane. Can you guess who I saw in the photo?'

I looked into Heme Seyar's eyes and said, 'Hesen Mîrawa.'

He said yes and Mahrox burst into laughter. I laughed louder and Heme Seyar laughed too."

"Who is this Hesen?" I asked Akam.

Akam burst into laughter in our underground bunker, too. After a while hevalê Akam controlled his laughter and said, "Hevala Jînçin, Heme's younger daughter, Hana, asked me this question instead of her father. I told her nobody can describe Hesen better than Heme. Hana looked at her father and said, 'Heme!'

'Hesen was a strong chatterbox with a tiny head and a very long tongue,' Heme said.

'Hesen was a member of your father's forces and wouldn't go to any other battalion. Your father has told me dozens of jokes about Hesen. Heme, please tell us something about him,' Akam said.

Heme Seyar didn't notice the request. He lifted the remote control from the table and wanted to turn the TV on. Hana slammed her hand on the table slowly and begged, 'Heme!' Her voice sounded like a final warning.

'When Hesen was sent to me, he seemed so brave-hearted that they may as well have sent a lion,' Heme said. 'We were two large battalions and in the middle of a dangerous area. He claimed to know the area well. I told him to go in front and the groups to follow him twenty yards apart. He climbed up a hill about two hundred meters, and suddenly descended again. I thought he might have seen a government base. Soon he was running uphill again to the top and then downhill again to the bottom. He did that three times and around three hundred Pêşmerge were coming up and down behind him like ants. I said to myself that there couldn't be too many bases. I got off the train, ran to him, and asked him, 'Why are you going up and down, Hesen?'

'I am picking up mushrooms.'"

'You're kidding,' Hana burst out.

'No, it is true. This happened in daylight. One night, we were passing near an IRGC base. The soldiers were shooting aimlessly to demonstrate their presence.' Hesen asked me, 'Why would the soldiers do that?'

'Because they were scared,' I replied.

'Then why don't we shoot?'

Hana's older sister said as Hana giggled, 'That's why the Kurds can't free themselves. We have such warriors.'

'Hesen was not a fighter, but a diplomat. Heme, tell us about his literacy attempt,' Hana's mother said, rejecting her thesis.

'Perwîn was Hesen's teacher from the Pêşmerge battalion. In a session, she criticized Hesen for his laziness and said that Hesen didn't do his work.

He couldn't bear this criticism and replied, "Perwîn, have I ever asked you why you've remained a virgin until now?"'

Laughter stormed through the room. Heme Seyar picked up an apple from the fruit dish on the table. 'Just one more, Heme! Tell us about the day we were going to arm the villagers,' I said.

Heme put the apple back on the table and said, 'Muzefer, the leader of the village organization in Dîwandere was an eloquent rhetorician, famous for his agitational way of speaking. We took him to a big village. He explained to the people that the only way to get their rights is to take up arms and fight for them. He talked for two hours and fifty-six minutes and charmed the people. Everyone wanted to be armed. At the end of his speech, Hesen, who sat next to Muzefer said, "Bah! Kak Muzefer is an idiot. I was imprisoned for six months for a hunting gun and now he tells you to get militarized. They will certainly kill you." At the end of Hesen's words the villagers shouted. "God bless you. That is right."'

'Hesen is right. Why don't you get married, Sara? You're the elder sister and you're in my way,' Hana said.

A roar of our laughter echoed through the neighborhood, until Heme spoke again.

'When I saw the photo of Hesen posing with a bulging stomach and puffed out cheeks, the prestige of the Islamic secret service crumbled before my eyes. They had archived our photos and documents without understanding any of it. Otherwise, they wouldn't have tried to smother me with a photo of Hesen Mîrawa. Hesen was more famous in our party than Imam Hesen in Najaf. He was the epitome of satire for us.'

'Tell me Heme, how could it be that an experienced fighter like you, who managed to stay alive in hell next to the Derbendîxan reservoir, was so easily arrested in a big city?' I asked him.

'I spoke on that in my report to Komele at that time and even in my story later. I was too sloppy when I arrived in Kirmaşan. I wore a torn Iraqi army jacket with military antichemical pants and a pair of used plastic shoes. Add to that a half-shaven, injured, and infected head. I didn't look like an ordinary urbanite. I wanted to go to Sine anyway, after Perwîz and his family did not answer my phone call. I walked close to the walls but a crazy man reached me. He thought that I had stolen his stuff, as somebody had stolen from his home on Sêzde Beder. I begged him profusely but he did not give up and took me to the police. They had been informed last night about my escape by the interrogator's officer in the school and identified me as the person who fled by a photo that they had taken of me there earlier.'

Heme Seyar was obviously tormented by having to recount those memories. He had explained his situation well in the report and I had read through it several times twenty-five years earlier. It explained in detail how he was received by intelligence officials and sent to the Intelligence Central Detention Center in Sine. Heme Seyar had described the torture methods in detail. Like all the other comrades, I saw in him a true hero who tried to deceive his torturers with false and unimportant information in order to get back to the party. For a month, he was honored. But then, overnight, as a result of a new statement from the party leader, he went from a hero to a traitor who alone caused the destruction of our legendary battalion.

One day, the Komele executives called the party members to a meeting. There was discussion about routines. At the end of the meeting, Sey Ibrahim Alizadeh said, 'Comrades, please come closer. I would like to discuss something with you. Now is the time to disclose the truth to you. As a libertarian, I must not keep silent about this case. I find it to be my historical duty to tell you something, so that future generations will know the truth about the tragedy of the Şiwan battalion. When Kak Heme Seyar reached the other side of the reservoir, he was in the hands of the Iranian state security. I do not want to explain further. Please do not ask me any other questions.'

Hemey Sayar was ruined with this speech. Everyone asked themselves what happened that Sey Ibrahim could not explain? He had thrown a ball onto the field and let everyone arbitrarily play with it, so to speak.

'Heme Seyar is said to have revealed the hiding place of the Şiwan battalion to the IRGC, so they had dared to charge ruthlessly and destroy the entire force in less than ten minutes.'

'It is said he must have helped the Islamic regime a lot, otherwise they would not have released him.'

From that night on, there was only one topic for discussion and that was Heme Seyar as the greatest traitor in Komele history.

A day before Sey Ibrahim told us about Heme's betrayal, they had apparently sent him to Baghdad for treatment. Seven months of solitary confinement and torture had left him with mental and physical health problems, but in Baghdad, instead of speech therapy and psychotherapy, they ran frequent electric shock procedures on him. After two weeks, he saw the world upside down when he returned disturbed from Baghdad. Nobody wanted to talk to him. Everyone saw him as a leper. Apparently, they sent Heme to the city of Silêmanî for relaxation, but in reality he was disarmed or, rather, fired from the party. The Komele executive reached the peak of shamelessness when he ordered his wife to divorce him. Now, when I think about what we did to him and his wife, I feel ashamed. For twenty years, I continuously saw him as a traitor and mercenary. Only then did something happen that persuaded me to rethink.

The first was a speech by Sey Ibrahim on the twentieth anniversary of the Şiwan battalion tragedy. In a television program, he claimed that Biyare was a place of rest and that the Şiwan battalion was sent there to take rest. Although I had left the party eleven years earlier for a variety of reasons, I did not expect Sey Ibrahim to tell such an outrageous lie. Two months before the Şiwan battalion tragedy, I was in Biyare. The Pêşmerge forces were housed in two schools. Another thick layer of concrete covered the concrete roof of those schools, and this thick concrete roof was under constant artillery shelling by the IRGC. And now the irreplaceable first secretary of Komele claimed the place was a resort. Heme himself showed me the second point.

After twenty-two years, Heme finally wrote a book about the tragedy. Some friends told me about it, but I was not interested in reading it, until I heard from someone that Sey Ibrahim claimed that Heme Seyar had told us a very different story back then and he had just contradicted himself with his book. I asked my friend to send me a PDF file of the book. He sent it to me and I read it. Amazingly, I saw that Heme wrote exactly what he had written in his report twenty-two years ago.

Although I no longer had any contact with Sey Ibrahim, I called him and asked him to send me a copy of Heme's report. He claimed that the report was lost through the various changes in divisions in Komele. That was another lie. I worked with him for many years and knew he would not lose a single document.

I followed up the case and found out other secrets of Komele's. It became clear to me that Heme Seyar was not the only person in the Şiwan battalion tragedy who was arrested and released by the Iranian government. At that time, the Komele executives knew it but kept it quiet the whole time. One of our comrades had found an ID card from the Iranian intelligence services that displayed a picture of Jalal Kaki and on which was written, 'The owner of this card may pass all checkpoints.' At first, the comrade thought it might be a fake ID that the party's antiterrorist unit had printed so that he could pass through supposed dangers. Nevertheless, he informed the party. After a week, Salah Mazooji told him that the ID card was not issued by Komele, but by the Iranian intelligence services. Salah had told him that he must not talk to anyone about it.

I read Heme Seyar's book again, this time in more detail, and realized something about the intentions of the Iranian secret service. Something that Heme himself had not understood or maybe didn't point to. We had underestimated the Iranian intelligence ministry. They had access to the SAVAK archives, which had been founded by Mossad. They had released him consciously. What better thing could they have done with him? If they had executed him, he would have become the greatest hero in Komele history. He was one of the party's most beloved commanders, the one who loudly opposed the positioning of troops in Biyare and a dedicated commander who would volunteer to help his comrades within that hell, even though he was newly married and everyone knew how much he and his bride loved each other. I can't understand how we forgot that Heme Seyar was yelling at Heme Nebewî, in a way that didn't suit his character, because of the fate of the Şiwan battalion.

'You donkey, stop with such nonsense! Should the Şiwan battalion attack from one side and the Iraqi army from the other and recapture the Zellm Bridge? Is the Şiwan battalion in a position to take part in a battle? Do you want them to be crushed by the tanks of the two armies? Do you have a brain or shit in your head?'

Let me tell you something about Heme Nebewî. There were a lot of incompetent people in Komele and most of them were promoted because they were flatterers and Sey Ibrahim and his gang were abusing them. One day, we came back from Iran after we had not eaten anything for four days. We were informed by radio that Heme Nebewî was coming to transfer us from the border to the camp. After a while he arrived, but he did not bring us any bread. Heme Seyar was upset and said to him, 'Do you know that we've been trying to cross the border for the last four days and didn't have anything to eat? You couldn't throw a few loaves of bread in your car?'

'What are you saying? Border, border. You say it like you came through hellfire,' Heme Nebewî replied.

Hesen stood up straight and said, 'Listen, you big hero, go and just put a toe on the boundary line once. Then come and shit on my head.'"

"Again Hesen is right!" All the comrades laughed at Rojano's comment, as if there were also many show-offs and paper tigers like Heme Nebewî in the PKK. When we stopped laughing, Akam continued his story.

"The execution of Heme Seyar would be more expensive to the Iranian government than his release. He wrote in his book that his interrogators referred to him with a code name, so as not to let anyone identify him. They wanted to prevent anyone knowing that he was arrested, so that later they could send him back to Komele. They must have thought about at least three different possible scenarios after his release. First, he goes back to Komele and does not tell them about his imprisonment, as they advised him. That was exactly what Jalal Kaki had done. If Heme had kept silent about his imprisonment, the intelligence service would still hold the reins. They could publish the evidence of his imprisonment at any time and ruin him. Second, Heme would inform the Komele leaders about his imprisonment upon his return. The intelligence service must have been well informed by their spies about the serious situation that Komele's leaders were involved in. They were under pressure from the Pêşmerge and looking for someone to blame for the destruction of the Şiwan battalion. Another scenario could have been the case, but in order to make this case a reality, Komele needed some leaders who could admit their mistakes.

At that time Heme Seyar had kept the Komele executives under pressure to investigate the causes of the Şiwan battalion tragedy and announce the guilty persons to Komele's members and sympathizers. That is why Sey Ibrahim decided to eliminate Heme Seyar forever with a subtle plan. The Komele leaders pretended as if Heme had concealed his imprisonment and that they had uncovered it themselves. But Heme informed Sey Ibrahim's assistant of his imprisonment within the first minutes and then the other Komele leadership members on the following days.

The IRGC's reason for releasing Heme became clear to me, but another question remained. How did the Iranian troops know the hiding place and the condition of the Şiwan battalion at the time?

There were many civilian and military groups on the other side of the lake. It might be that they informed the Iranian army, or simply that the Iranian troops were intercepting our own radios. There was also something in his book that could prove his innocence concerning this topic. Heme claimed that the intelligence services had discovered his true identity only eighteen days after the Şiwan battalion tragedy. As he had written in his book, they should have thought of him as a mentally ill Iraqi Kurd before. He mentioned three people as witnesses in his book. One had already died of cancer. The others were still alive. I found their phone numbers and called the first one. 'It was a long time ago and I've forgotten almost everything about the case,' he said.

Then I called Yûsêf Pawe. He remembered the case very well and said, 'Heme Seyar informed Komele that he had seen a group of Iraqi refugees in Silêmanî with whom he spent over fifteen days in a Harsin school. At that time, Iraqi refugees were constantly coming back to Başûr from Rojhilat. He asked the Komele executives to investigate the case and talk to them, but they ignored his demand until Heme threatened them with setting himself on fire if they refused his demand. We talked with many of them for a long time and they told us exactly what Heme had told us before. They said that the man was injured at that time and they thought that he had gone crazy. After two weeks he stole one of our pairs of shoes and fled. They put the fences on the windows and did not allow us to go out alone. After two weeks, the head of the camp said that the crazy man was a commander of Komele and had been arrested.'

'But why did Nesan tell me he had forgotten the case?' I asked Yûsêf Pawe.

He laughed and answered me, 'Maybe he forced himself to forget it.'

That evening I found the phone number of Heme Seyar and called him. I informed him about the ID card of Jalal Kaki. Heme already knew about that ID card and all the other stories from twenty-two years ago. My whole world seemed to come to an end. He knew everything but he did not reveal them.

When we argued against him that the Islamic government does not release anyone who did not cooperate with them, he could have said to us, 'Yes, but Jalal Kaki was also released.' This generosity and gentleness impressed me. He was very pleased with my call.

I did not expect him to answer me so warmly. Although I wanted to talk to him about the time that we had spent together and to recall the memories, I was ashamed of him and my wife. She knew full well how I had abandoned him in his time of need, like many other comrades. I told him good night after a ten-minute conversation.

It was about ten o'clock in the evening. I asked my wife if our son was in the attic. She answered angrily, 'How could I know? Haven't I been here this whole time?' I went up the stairs. The door was half open. He was sleeping on the bed and the lamp was on. I went into the room, switched off the lamp and turned to the attic. There were many books scattered on the table and the room smelled of cigarettes. His thermos flask and open laptop were out on the corner of the table. I shook the flask; it was half full. I stacked his scattered books and put them in a corner of the table, then poured tea into a glass. I opened the covered window. Paris lay beneath me in radiant light. I dragged a chair close to the window, sat down, and looked at the Tuileries Park Garden. The Ferris wheel was turning with its colorful light bulbs. I drank tea and smoked a cigarette. I tried to imagine the current atmosphere of the park, but I could not. My thoughts were fluttering around the topic of Heme Seyar.

The first time I saw him was in Merîwan. At that time, the residents of Merîwan had gone out of the city in protest of the Islamic regime's military presence, following a call from Kak Fouad for a public sit-in. The entire city migrated to the banks of Lake Zirêbar. This comprehensive and unified protest got the support of other cities in Kurdistan. Thousands of people from Sine and Seqiz walked to Merîwan. This historic march of thousands of people triggered tremendous solidarity amongst the entire Kurdish population. All the needs of the marching people were intimately provided by the villagers along the route. After seven days, the protesters from Sine arrived in Merîwan. I cannot put into words the social atmosphere that was created there. The people felt able to influence not only Kurdistan but all of Iran and put the train of revolution back on the right track. Kak Fouad gave a speech there and at the end he read the petition of the participants."

"And how did the government respond to these protests and demands?" I asked Akam.

"Stop, heval. We should take a cigarette break now," Rûken interrupted hevalê Akam before he could reply to me.

We left the room. I went toward hevalê Ferhad. He was seated on a gas cylinder in the corridor behind the men's room. His tobacco pouch was on his lap and he was rolling a thick cigarette. I asked him to roll me an even thicker one. He rolled it up and gave it to me. I put it in my vest pocket and dragged another gas cylinder on the ground to the wall and sat opposite him. I looked at him for a long time. He realized that I had no lighter and handed me his. I lit my cigarette. I would have liked to light his, if it were not forbidden in the party. Then I got up and gave back his lighter with two open palms. We smoked our cigarettes without saying a word. I went to the kitchen and brought us two glasses of tea. He took a glass. "Thanks, heval."

Unlike us, he was wearing gray military clothes. His face was always clean shaven and had the same expression. His dense black eyebrows showed an invariable contrast with his white hairs; nevertheless, his long-lasting silence and his deep gray gaze never became normal to me, and I wondered again every time I saw him. When we were drinking tea, his gaze was permanently directed toward an unrecognizable place. I could not break his silence, drank my tea, and waited until he drank the last sip and got up. To my relief, Tewar relieved her mate and Ferhad and I went back to the women's room.

Everyone was gathered there and waiting for us. There was a place next to Dêrsîm. I sat down there.

Akam continued, "On that day Heme Seyar was armed but . . ."

"But you didn't reply to my question. How did the government respond to these protests and demonstrations?"

"As you wish, hevala Jîncîn! After about two weeks, Khomeini called on all the Shi'a of Iran to wage jihad against the Kurds. Heme was already armed, but I served as a messenger for a long time. On the twentieth day of the war in Sine, when the situation became very harsh, the party assigned me to deliver a letter to Kak Şiwan. The city was fully besieged, and we had to bypass the Sine Islamic government army garrison. Some sympathizers took me to the village of Kêllane from behind the Awyer Mountains. I stayed there until late at night, then we drove to Sine in a pickup with the lights switched off, which brought food for the Pêşmerge via a detour. The food should be brought to a bunker on Baxmilî Street. There I had to wait until their commander came back.

Meanwhile, I helped the comrades unload the foodstuffs until Heme Seyar appeared. He was responsible for the Baxmilî bunker. We were surprised and hugged each other. I said that I had a letter and should hand it over to Kak Şiwan. He said he was at the frontlines and that he could take me there himself if I had to hand the letter over to him personally. I was very tired and gave him the letter to deliver to Kak Şiwan. We went to the upstairs of the bunker. It was a very simple place above a café. There were only three rooms. He gave me a key to one of the rooms and said I could sleep there undisturbed.

The next morning, I was woken early by bomb blasts. I heard voices from the other rooms. I got up and followed the direction of the voices. One of my comrades was speaking into a wireless. I had breakfast there and then visited a few bunkers behind the front lines with some comrades. The city was under constant artillery and mortar fire. The helicopters and phantoms of the Islamic regime were constantly bombarding those areas that still remained under the control of the Pêşmerge. All Pêşmerge forces were under the command of Kak Şiwan, the person after whom the legendary Şiwan Battalion was later named in his honor. I was very eager to see him, but he was coming and going between fronts.

He had never attended any military training and had not participated in any war before the revolution. Also, his forces were not even heavily armed, yet they wouldn't let the Islamic regime's army or the IRGC penetrate into the main parts of Sine.

Many people had been evacuated from Sine and the city was brutally bombed by the Iranian air force. After four days of massive bombardment, on the twenty-fourth day of the war, the party decided to pull all the troops out of the city.

Even from my viewpoint today, this action was a Herculean task by Kak Şiwan. The city was besieged from all sides and two thousand Pêşmerge had to be withdrawn under his command over a low mountain range, Kuçke Reş, around Sine to a safe place. The operation that Kak Şiwan performed was a masterpiece that consisted of precision, concealment, and coordination. The withdrawal went by so unnoticed that the Islamic troops suspected that it was a deception operation and would not enter the city for three days. Hevalê Saro can well imagine what kind of military art went into withdrawing such a large number of troops over this small mountain."

"I often heard about Kak Şiwan's abilities when I was a child, but later I thought it might have been exaggerated by Komele. I also heard he killed his father. Is it true?" Saro asked hevalê Akam.

"Yes, his father is said to have raped his own daughter. That's why Kak Şiwan killed him with a knife. At that time he was nineteen. He met Kak Fouad in prison, was impressed by his personality, and later joined his newly formed party."

"Do you know how he ultimately fell? I have heard many different stories about it."

"Heme Seyar and I were there when he fell. We had attacked some Iranian troops a day before. They launched a large military offensive against us the next day and a couple of combat helicopters supported them. They besieged Hallegere village, and burnt all the houses there. People fled to the mountains. Fortunately, the herds of sheep and cattle were out of the village and had not returned from their grazing. Suddenly, one of the helicopters turned and flew to the village of Efrasyaw, where we were positioned.

Kak Şiwan ran to a military vehicle that we had confiscated the previous day and tried to shoot down the helicopter with the fifty caliber on it. But before he reached the vehicle, a rocket was fired from the helicopter. The missile hit him and severed one of his arms. His arm fell to the floor. One of the comrades immediately hid it behind his back. Kak Şiwan noticed his posture and said, 'A Pêşmerge can't have just one hand?'

Those were his last words. Shrapnel from the missile hit one of his eyes, and one of his magazines exploded at his waist, ripping through his stomach. He could not survive these deep wounds and after two hours fell in a grove. We were deeply saddened by his death. One of our Pêşmerge ran into the house and took one of the captured Revolutionary Guards outside and was about to shoot him. The other Pêşmerge prevented it and brought the situation back under their control. Heme Seyar was shocked and said he could not stay there anymore. He was assigned to a group responsible for taking prisoners to the central jail of Komele. Twelve other Pêşmerge and I were given the job of compensating for the losses of the Hallegere villagers. We helped them to reconstruct their houses and collected fodder for their livestock from other villages.

After that day, I was in charge of the battalion's logistics and did not participate in any military actions. After a year I saw Heme Seyar once more. Two battalions of Pêşmerge were ordered to attack a base of mercenaries in Sine. This base was hidden in a police station on Sirus Street and most people weren't aware. According to our plan, we would sneak into the city at night and throw a pressure cooker filled with dynamite into the yard, then raid the police station. Heme Seyar, two other Pêşmerge, and I were selected for the probable counter attacks against Islamic regime forces and we hid ourselves behind a wall in an alley close to the police station.

A few minutes before the operation began, a military patrol drove with its lights on into the dark alley. They did their usual surveillance, but one of the inexperienced Pêşmerge got frightened, ran down to the other side, and drew their attention. He could escape, but they shot him, and another military patrol turned into the alley and fired at us. I would've been killed if Heme did not react quickly. He returned fire on the patrol car.

Another comrade and I were shocked and ran away. Heme Seyar followed us and said, 'Where are you running? Come back, we should take their weapons.' I went to the car, carelessly and ashamed of my cowardice, and then Heme saved my life once more. Two members of the IRGC were still alive, pulled their weapons out of the car window and kept us under fire. Heme reacted with lightning speed and killed them, but his knee was injured. We moved back toward the Beharmes hill district. There, all the inhabitants had come out of their houses. They were extremely glad to see the Pêşmerge forces. Everyone—men, women, children, and the elderly—were embracing and kissing us. They gave us a lot of food and drink and put money in our pockets. Also, they dressed Heme's wound and gave him a stick.

Some youths ran over the roofs and showed us the safe ways to escape. Soon we arrived at Giryaşan and found other Pêşmerge troops. Our mission failed because of the clumsiness of our group, but Heme did not tell anyone about it. I felt unsuited for military missions for a long time afterwards.

I only heard good things about Heme Seyar over the following years, until the time of Komele's deterioration began. The fratricidal strife between Komele and HDKA had caused dramatic damage to the two parties and also to the Kurdish people. During this time, the party wanted to dispatch Heme to Sine to take over the secret party activities. Heme Seyar refused the order and we were shocked by his reply. The reason for his refusal was that he believed the party should draw a line between their overt and covert activities. If the party sends him or another Pêşmerge known to the Iranian intelligence service then it could endanger our covert operations.

At the time, that argument didn't convince me. Like many other party followers, I expected absolute dedication from him. After a year, however, his prediction became a reality. Almost all of the skillful members were spotted and eliminated. Many more of our hidden forces, activists, and sympathizers were hanged or sentenced to life imprisonment.

The next year, the party wanted to dispatch him to Kamyaran to solve some problems that had arisen there. But Heme Seyar also rejected this order. He said that the political situation and balance of power are now unfavorable in Kamyaran. Şaho Mountain is under the control of the HDKA and, in the city, there is no network of sympathizers. This time I even thought his decision was based on cowardice. The Komele chairman wanted to suspend him, but they could not do without his skills. They wanted to bring two battalions across the border from Merîwan. They had tried this before with different teams, but all their attempts failed.

Heme went to the reconnaissance mission with three people, found a way through the various bases and minefields, and after three days brought two battalions into Iran. Then the party ordered him to take care of the bad situation in Dîwandere. I asked the party to send me with them. Under his command, two battalions crossed the Merîwan border and then we parted. I went with Heme and sixty other Pêşmerge towards the Çilçeme mountain range.

The political situation there was catastrophic. The previous commander in charge destroyed everything that had been built up in previous years. Due to the lack of political and military activities, there was severe disappointment and hopelessness among the population. The Revolutionary Guards had forcibly recruited many men from the area. They had to stand guard at their bases one day per week or month to prevent the Pêşmerge from attacking them. Heme spread the word in the villages that we would soon storm the bases and asked the people to lay down their arms.

In the meantime, we targeted three major military bases. Heme Seyar himself went on the reconnaissance operations of all three bases. Our commanders rarely did that. A week after our arrival, we attacked the bases and in one night took control of all three without any casualties. The armed villagers took their guns to Dîwandere the next day and returned them to the Revolutionary Guards.

One day, the inhabitants of a village asked us to go there and solve a dispute between two families. Heme, six other Pêşmerge, and I went there and convinced them to agree on a solution. We wanted to return to Çilçeme, but the people didn't want to let us go back and asked us to spend a night there. The next morning, a housewife came into the room and told a female Pêşmerge, 'There are over a hundred IRGC forces and mercenaries within the village and inspecting all houses.' I wanted to inform Heme by radio, but the battery was dead. The housewife said she would go personally and tell him. Before she left the house, we heard the voice of Heme Seyar from the loudspeaker of the mosque.

'Those pigs have fallen into the trap. Hesen, you come with your troop to the house of the redheaded women. Pari and her group should go toward the house with the dark green walls. The other troops should block the escape routes.'

A female Pêşmerge and I went up the stairs to the roof. Our comrades had already opened fire on them and they ran out of there without looking behind. We also opened fire and ran over the roofs to the mosque. That day we took fourteen prisoners and confiscated many weapons without having Hesen the Lion with us.

Heme Seyar was a great man, but he also had a major flaw that all the Pêşmerge in our party had. He never positioned himself against the fratricidal war between Komele and the HDKA. Like all other Pêşmerge, he knew how damaging this war was for both parties and the Kurdish people. In reality, in Rojhilat, we were not defeated by the despotic Islamic government, but by ourselves. We left the mountains because we could no longer bear the casualties of the civil war.

In the final years of the war, the Islamic troops lost their fighting spirit and we were ahead. They launched an offensive against us with two hundred fighters and Heme sent only ten Pêşmerge against them. If he had been informed that a hundred more new soldiers had been sent, he would send no more than four or five more Pêşmerge to support them. Nothing more was needed.

But in the war against HDKA it was very different. If they increased the number of their fighters to twenty, we would have to send thirty more fighters against them. It was the same for the other side. Heme knew all these facts, but like me and all the other Pêşmerge in our party, he never opposed the stupid, devastating civil war. At HDKA it was better. There were the Pêşmerge, who demonstrated in public against the fratricidal war. One of them was Tahêr Elyar. He positioned himself against this war in the party's fourth congress and fought against an extension of the war. Unfortunately, he and like-minded people remained in the minority. In my opinion he was the greatest hero of the Civil War era.

After the fourth general meeting of the party, he resigned from the Central Committee and also from the party. There is a famous phrase he said sarcastically to the party's arsonists and warmongers as they sent seven hundred Pêşmerge on a surprise attack against Komele. He's believed to have said, 'Leave the oil wells on the Nermellas Mountains for Komele. With seven hundred Pêşmerge we can free Seqiz.'

CHAPTER 11

WE MADE ALL the preparations to celebrate Newroz. Because the bunker didn't need any further cleaning, Rûnahî could not force us to clean up our rooms. So that's why she proceeded to have us women beautify ourselves. We all had our facial hair threaded. I asked her to form my eyebrows like Arjîn's. She did it so masterfully and curled up my hair with a simple curling iron so well that even hevalê Ferhad could not hide his astonishment at our resemblance. However, we were not able to start the Newroz fire, though we had taken all the necessary measures a week beforehand; we had stored a lot of firewood in the guard cave. In order to start the fire faster, we brought alcohol there, as well as all of our shovels, so that if there was a report about the drone's departure, we could quickly extinguish the fire and its traces with snow.

Until five years ago, Newroz was only an abstract word for me. But then I saw many impressive photos and video recordings of it. The rituals of this festival were like a religious ceremony for me. A huge fire in the middle and thousands of people dancing hand in hand around the fire to a Kurdish musical rhythm. They were dancing with a harmony commanding their feet and torsos and howling with joy.

In previous years, I did not have the opportunity to attend any Newroz festivities, but I often danced with the Kurds. Kurdish dance also produced a ritualistic feeling in me. However, over time, I have noticed that both Newroz and Kurdish dance serve as political symbols, rather than rituals.

I would have liked to have set the Newroz fire and, for the first time, to have celebrated this festival in a circle of Kurds, but at noon a drone appeared and remained in the sky until late at night. We had to stay in the bunker and celebrate Newroz there; the atmosphere was very gloomy. Saro knew a Kurdish radio channel that was broadcasting only Kurdish dance music that night. We gathered in the women's room and danced for a long time. Even our ladder danced, half-squatting. I asked Gulbehar to sing us a song and she suggested that each one of us should sing. Her suggestion was accepted. That night, we sang in several languages. Saro sang a Farsi song. Other than Kurdish songs, Gulbehar also sang an Arabic song, and I sang a German tune. But the biggest surprise of the night was hevalê Ferhad. He joined us again and sang a Turkish revolutionary song in a nice bass voice. Unfortunately, nobody dared to ask him for another song.

That night I was the last to stand guard behind the hanging blanket-door. Rûken told me that the drone had flown away. I let her roll me a cigarette and put it in my waistcoat pocket. With a hemp pillow in hand, I went out through the ceiling door on the men's room side. I put it on the step, sat down on it and waited until the mountains could be seen, then lit the cigarette. The cliffs opposite the men's room were light gray again, and the frost-covered branches of the hawthorn trees were visible.

Nothing had fallen from the sky for two weeks and the snow lying on the ground had already begun to melt. This caused a minor problem and a big headache. Our cat caused this problem. He walked around outside and returned to the bunker with his mud-stained paws. Nobody cared except Tewar. She always made a fuss about it. Arjîn, Gulbehar, and Rûnahî immediately wiped away any trace left by Befrîn. Soon the others helped too. Anyone who saw Befrîn coming first immediately cleaned his paws. But one could not write up a program of his excursions. He went outside and returned as he pleased. Sometimes we didn't even notice him when we came back.

One day Tewar screamed so blood-curdlingly that we thought a snake had bit her. We were outside playing a game of catch. When I heard her scream, I suspected anything but that she was angry with our cat. We ran into the bunker. She was sobbing with a heartbroken expression, as if her father had died. Befrîn had pawed her new clothes and scratched them. She was already angry and Arjîn made her fully enraged.

"What a beautiful signature. No bank director has such a nice signature."

"Then let him sign your clothes, if you like his signature so much."

"Gladly," Arjîn said. She called out to Befrîn, but he had escaped after Tewar's screaming. She followed Befrîn and found him outside of the bunker. When Tewar saw Befrîn in Arjîn's arms, she screamed again. His fur stood up and Arjîn went outside. Gulbehar washed Tewar's clothes in the spring, but she was unwilling to wear her clothes anymore. She could not calm down, even when Dêrsîm gave her a set of new clothes. Supposedly, she would now have to wear two sets of same-colored clothes. Everyone in the group was ready to give their clothes to her to stop this show, but she made a formal complaint about the event and submitted it to court. She complained not only about Befrîn, but also Arjîn. Why are you complaining about Arjîn? "She intended to ridicule me. Arjîn is interested in having fun and playing around, when her only interest should be a total dedication to our party."

Her irritation with Arjîn was idiotic, but it gave her an excuse to blame me as well and keep my name on her blacklist. Allegedly, I grinned when Arjîn made her quip about Befrîn's masterful signature.

After a few days, Befrîn suddenly disappeared. Arjîn waited impatiently for him until the next day. When the night was over, she hastily went out from the bunker to search for him. She took a little radio with her so that we could inform her when a drone showed up. At noon she came back. Befrîn's carcass was in her arms and she was ghostly pale. When I asked her what had happened to Befrîn, her lips trembled uncontrollably before she could say anything. Beneath her big, disbelieving eyes, traces of weeping were noticeable on her pale cheeks. She was trying to show us something with her shivering fingers but she couldn't. I could not stand her suffering, got up, went to her, and took Befrîn's carcass from her arms. His body was soaked and cold. Presumably, he had been dead since yesterday. I pulled aside his neck fur and found the trace of a fastened rope. Someone had strangled Befrîn with a rope. His bicolor eyes remained open, as if stunned by the asphyxiation.

Rûken was watching the situation, came to me, and stared at the traces of strangulation, though she remained silent. She looked at Arjîn and hugged her, but she did not react at all and was shivering all over. Gulbehar ran and took Arjîn into her arms. When she released her, she fell down to the floor. We were almost in a panic. Fortunately, Rûnahî was ready with her blood pressure gauge. She measured her blood pressure and told us to give her a serum. We left the room and Rûnahî stayed alone with her.

In the afternoon, the case of our cat was investigated in the men's room. Nobody took responsibility for the incident, nor did anyone have news about it. After Rûken's speech failed to convince the guilty to confess, she raised her voice and screamed.

"What piece of garbage strangled this cat?"

Nobody answered her. She looked at me for a while, then she turned to Tewar and shouted, "Do you know something about it?"

"I, I, I know, I stand, I'm suspected, I, I, I, I cannot. I swear by Serok, Serok, Serok Apo. I did not strangle this cat."

Rûken turned her head and spoke to us in general.

"Only a coward can do something so disgusting. Whoever did this is the scum of humanity."

After two days our lessons started again. But our sessions took place in the men's room until Arjîn had recovered somewhat physically. She was able to eat and talk again, but she continued to suffer from depression and nightmares. After Befrîn's death, like many others, I had a vacuum in my life. I missed him a lot. My eyes, my hands, and my ears longed for him. We stopped hearing his meow, no longer gave him mortadella, and the white world outside thawed faster.

I knew that the twenty-third of April was Arjîn's birthday, so I wanted to surprise her with a special gift. I asked Zinar if he could get me a forty-seven-centimeter, thin plastic pipe.

"I can bring you as many meters of it as you want."

I hugged Zinar and kissed his cheeks, although I knew it was not common in the party. He laughed and asked me what exactly I needed a forty-seven-centimeter pipe for. But before I answered him, he said it himself, "Aha, you want to make a şimşall."

"Bravo, it would be a good idea to organize a birthday party for Arjîn. It will be good for her mood."

"Yes, hevala Arjîn is very sad."

"When is your birthday?"

"Mine already passed two months ago."

"Why didn't you tell us?"

"It's not important here. The birthdays of Satyar and Hunger have passed unnoticed. But yours was fun. I think it would be very good to celebrate Arjîn's birthday. I miss her loud laughs."

After two days he brought me a forty-seven-centimeter-long pipe. I told Rûken about my plan and explained to her that I hadn't practiced şimşall for a while and wanted to play in the cave at the creek on a few occasions. She said, "Ok, but Gulbehar should also accompany you."

Certainly, she sent Gulbehar to protect me from danger, but it was the best option. She was not bored at all. One day we were informed of a code fifty by radio and had to stay there until evening. That day she sang a lot of Kurdish songs and I played şimşall with her. After a few days she learned to sing with the musical instrument. Her nice, strong voice got the musical rhythm and it motivated me even more to play şimşall. Like the other comrades, Gulbehar and I had planned a nice birthday party for Arjîn, but on her birthday something unexpected happened.

After breakfast, our administration dispatched Arjîn with Dêrsîm, Tewar, and Serhelldan to a hidden depot to bring back a canister of cooking oil and a sack of flour. On their return it seemed they had seen a mama bear and three of her cubs. Serhelldan grabbed his gun and wanted to shoot the mama bear, but Arjîn tried to stop him. Nevertheless, he is said to have stuck to his decision and taken an offensive position. Arjîn claims to have stood in front of his gun and said, "The bear has three cubs; they will starve if you kill their mother."

"That's better. Then they will not be able to steal our provisions."

At that moment, the bear and her three cubs stood up as if they wanted to surrender themselves. The more Arjîn begged him, the more he insisted on his decision. In the end, Arjîn told him, "Today is my birthday. I will not let you shoot her."

"Ok, because of your birthday, I'll give you her fat cub as a present. I know that you like the fat ones."

This sentence from Serhelldan made Arjîn angry. She unlocked her gun and yelled, "Drop your weapon, you bastard!" She yelled again, "I'll count until three and then you'll be shot."

Serhelldan looked at her with torn eyes. Arjîn shot a few bullets over his head. Serhelldan immediately dropped his weapon.

"Now go to the bunker. If you turn around once, I'll leave you headless faster than a guillotine, you cat-killer."

I was with other comrades in the women's room and making the final preparations for her birthday when they reached the vicinity of the bunker. Satyar left his guard post, came to us, and told Rûken that something strange was happening outside. From far away it was like a theater performance. Dêrsîm and Tewar, the smallest people in our group, had walked ahead. Serhelldan, our tallest comrade, had lifted his hands over his head and was walking like a lamppost behind them. Our taller, younger comrade was following him with her weapon aimed at his back. If it were a comrade other than Serhelldan, I would have thought it was a game. But I knew that Arjîn hated him and didn't like to engage in play with Serhelldan. As soon as Serhelldan saw us, he dropped his hands. Rûken ordered them to hurry straight to the men's room. I also went there without asking for permission. Immediately, all four members of the administration arrived there together, but Rûken led the emergency session alone. She first asked Serhelldan.

"Tell us what happened. Why did Arjîn get mad at you?"

"Heval, you should ask her yourself. She shot several bullets over my head. She might've killed me if I had not submitted."

"And why did she put her gun on you? Did she have no reason for that?"

"Because of a bear, she wanted to kill me."

"What? Because of a bear she wanted to kill her comrade?"

"Yes, heval. We saw some bears near our hidden depot. I wanted to shoot them, but she prevented it and, in the end, even threatened me."

"And why did you want to shoot an unarmed animal, hevalê Serhelldan? Don't you know that we are not allowed to kill animals?"

"But that's just an assertion. I saw many comrades shooting the animals."

"What animals did they shoot?"

"All kinds. Roe deer, partridges, wild boar."

"Nobody is allowed to shoot at roe deer and partridges in these mountains. We shoot boars if we do not have anything else to eat. Do you eat bear meat?"

"No, but they eat our provisions. We bring our foodstuffs into the mountains with a lot of effort and they eat it up and piss on it. You can do whatever you want, but I cannot let it happen."

"Did you carry foodstuffs into the mountains with a lot of effort, hevalê Serhelldan? I don't recall seeing that."

Rûken turned her eyes to Arjîn.

"Hevala Arjîn, do you think you're allowed to point your weapons at your comrade because of that?"

"No heval, I did it for another reason. He said to me, 'Because of you, I won't kill all her cubs and will give you the fat one, because I know you like fat things.'"

"What? Hevala Tewar, did hevalê Serhelldan say that?"

"No, heval, I didn't hear anything like that."

"And you, hevala Dêrsîm? What do you say? Which comrade is telling us lies?"

"Hevala Arjîn has told the truth."

Rûken turned to Serhelldan, "And what did you mean by the 'fat things' comment?"

"I meant the bears. They are fat, right?"

"Take off your ammo belts and give them to me."

Serhelldan untied his cartridges and grenades and handed them over to Rûken.

"You are disarmed until a decision is made about you."

"What, is this upside-down world? Instead of punishing her, you disarm me, because I said 'fat' to the bears?"

"I will not let you take me for a fool. You will stay in this room all day. The whole group will make a decision about you tomorrow. You can tell your ass the story about fat things."

We left the room and Serhelldan stayed there alone. Arjîn looked at me as if seeking confirmation of her behavior from me, but I averted my gaze. Rûken took her outside and the other comrades scattered into other rooms. I had an unpleasant feeling and thought to myself *you can't shoot sparrows with cannons.* Both of them had unbearably overreacted. Gulbehar reminded me about the surprise music for Arjîn. Reluctantly I said okay, though I didn't really want to do it. I went with her into the women's room and waited until Rûken had brought Arjîn back to the bunker. Then I played her favorite song. I was kind of sad and that grief flowed out of my şimşall. Arjîn came up the corridor and stood near me. The melody was not sad, but Arjîn looked upset. The other comrades were impressed by the music. It was a long time since they had heard live music. In our plan, Gulbehar was supposed to sing along, but she did not and let me play on my own. When I took the şimşall out of my mouth, Arjîn embraced me. I reacted cautiously. She burst into violent weeping and asked me, wailing, "Do you think that I went too far with hevalê Serhelldan?"

I did not say anything, and she kept crying until Rûken answered instead of me.

"No, hevala Arjîn. You did exactly what was right."

CHAPTER 12

AROUND TEN O'CLOCK at night, Rûken woke everyone up. She said that Serhelldan had fled and we had to leave the region immediately. We could only take essential items with us. That meant almost everything, except the heater, oven, and associated gas cylinders. Each one of us took an empty sugar or flour sack, tied it on three sides with rope, filled it with stuff, and carried it like a backpack. Within half an hour, we had put the essential things on our backs and journeyed away. We went down the valley toward the creek's edge. From there, we had to walk through the water. The night was pitch black, but we couldn't turn on a flashlight and had to follow the flow of the river. At first I actually enjoyed walking through the water, but I soon realized it would be an unbearable ordeal. The rivulet was not deep, but in some places the streambed would fall out from underneath my feet, or would be deeper, and the water would suddenly reach to my chest. Soon I was soaked and the cold water was biting me like a snake. We were going downhill and the roaring of the rivulet was becoming louder. An enchanting voice to meditate on if we hadn't been on the run.

Two hours earlier, when I was on guard, I listened to Serhelldan and Tewar whispering. They were talking in Turkish, but I suspected that he wanted to persuade Tewar to do something. I even guessed that he wanted to leave the party, but I did not expect him to escape so sneakily. I thought he was disappointed with his comrade's behavior today, and he has the right to go on his own way, but I expected him to decisively speak his mind to the administration the next morning. It's clear he must have run away after his conversation with Tewar. An individual decision that caused a collective calamity.

After an hour we reached the main river. From the loud rush of the water I could guess that there was a huge waterfall further on. We walked in the opposite direction along the shore. The cold water was reaching my waist, flowing towards us, and making our march even more difficult. The sky was moonless, the water was cold, we were quiet, and I kept slipping on the stones in the river and falling further into the water. We had to leave that region as fast as possible, but what exactly was meant by "region?"

For the first time in my life I had to run against a cold spring river, in the pitch black night, with a heavy load on my back. I couldn't walk fifty steps in the river without slipping and falling face-first into the water. I was soaking wet and shivering. My legs were cramping up. It must have been bad for the others, too. Nobody said anything. I saw the spooky shape of Rûken walking at the head of the pack. Akam was the last person. Gulbehar was beside me. I wanted to ask her for help, but she also seemed to be powerless by the look of her walking rhythm. She hadn't done a proper march in five months, like everyone else, and was carrying an even heavier burden, so I couldn't allow myself to burden her anymore. Suddenly I felt nauseous, fell into the water, and could not get up. Gulbehar came over to me, took my arm, and helped me get up, but I could not move my legs. She said, "Put your arm around my neck."

"Thank you, hevala Gulbehar, I do not want to burden you."

I tried to keep running, but my legs were numb and I fell back into the water. With Gulbehar's help, I could stand up. She held my left arm around her neck and put her other hand under my right arm. We walked in this condition for about two hundred meters until she was exhausted and could not help me anymore. She left me and went back in the darkness to call Rojano. In the last two hours, Rojano was helping Tewar. She came to me, untied my load, took it, and asked me if I could walk without the load. I looked at Rojano shyly. Again she had the heaviest load on her back and I had overloaded her even more, but I was as exhausted as the cat behind the stove and wasn't in a situation to think about ethics. Surely they would not have left me there alone, even if I had asked them to, so I said, "Thanks, hevala Rojano, I will try."

She went back toward Tewar and Dêrsîm to help them, but soon came back. Saro and Hunger had taken their loads. I could not move even without a load. I not only lacked any strength, but my legs were cramping. Rojano and Gulbehar took my arms and brought me to the edge of the river. Rojano bent over and searched with her hands for a large stone, found one, and put it on the edge of the river for me to sit on. The comrades in the rear had not arrived yet. Gulbehar took off my shoes and stockings, rolled up my pant legs, and massaged my leg muscles. She bent my feet back and forth at the ankle, then put them on her knees and started to rub and slap them. She was slapping some points on my feet with one palm and massaging other points with the other palm. I slept during her work. When I woke up, it was still dark and my arm was in Rojano's hand. She had tied my load onto her own.

"Get up. I'll help you," she said.

I looked at my wristwatch. It was ten past three.

"How's Dêrsîm?" I asked Rojano.

"She is well. Tewar is also back on her feet."

Gulbehar and Rojano had dressed me again without me realizing it. I got up. I could move my legs again, but they cramped up as soon as I went back into the cold water. I fell once more into the river. Rojano grabbed me by my armpits and lifted me out of the water into a standing position, then put my arms over her shoulder and started to run. I tried to gather the rest of my strength to at least take some of my weight off of her, but soon I fell asleep and for two hours she dragged me like a ladder down the river. When I woke up, it was dusk and the comrades were out of the river, taking a rest. My head was on Rojano's shoulder, my left arm curled around her neck, and my wrist firmly in her left hand. With her right arm around my shoulder, she put her hand under my armpit and over my chest and her fingers tightly grabbed my shirt collar. Against the current, across the stony course of the river, she kept walking and didn't make me run. I kissed her neck and said, "Thanks heval, I will never forget your kindness."

"I've had this kind of problem before, too. You will get your strength back soon."

To our left, some comrades were spreading clay on their backpacks by a creek that flowed into the river. Arjîn came towards us, relieved Rojano of my burden, and put it on the riverbank. Then she untied the crock pots and pans from their backs. Only then could Rojano free herself from her own burden and sit on the river stones. Arjîn and Satyar smeared their things with mud at the stream. I would have gladly carried my burden myself, but I lacked any strength. I hobbled over the stones to a rock on which the comrades were sitting. Soon, the last of us had shown up. Tewar was on Hunger's back. She looked pale and powerless.

"A few hundred meters higher, there is a cave where we can have breakfast. Hevala Gulbehar, are the loaves of bread with you?" Rûken said, calling to us.

"Yes, hevala Rûken."

"Give the comrades bread to eat on the way. Unless the drone appears, we will reach the cave within an hour."

She looked around and continued, "Take as much water as possible. We will not find water until evening."

Gulbehar put her backpack on the ground, opened it, and brought out a big plastic bag. The bag was tightly tied; she had to open it with her teeth. Then she got up and gave bread to all the comrades. I had lost my appetite because of exhaustion, but I took a thick loaf of bread from the plastic bag, divided it into three pieces, and put them in my wet vest pocket.

For seven hours I had run continuously in the water without eating or drinking. I untied my canteen from my cartridge belt and opened the lid. It was empty and I laid there like the naked fugitive in the Garden of Gethsemane. Arjîn came up and gave her canteen to me. I drank it to the last drop. Then she took both canteens and filled them in the brook. I massaged my legs until the group was ready to go. We began to climb up the mountain. My load was light and I did not want to burden my comrades even more.

There was not even a footpath. Our train ran diagonally up the left side of the rocky mountain. There was no cave visible in the heights. The soles of my feet were burning in pain and the cold early morning breeze stuck my wet clothes to my body. My comrades were carrying my loads and I could not expect any more help. I turned my head and saw Gulbehar behind me, five meters away. "Do you need help, heval?" Gulbehar asked me out of courtesy.

"Thanks heval, but I have to do it alone."

I brought out a piece of bread from my vest pocket. It smelled like fish. I held it in front of my nose and laughed at my own imagination. Hevalê Ferhad turned his head back and smiled. He was carrying about ten kilograms on his back, in addition to his weapon and cartridge belt. I put the piece of bread in my left hand, touched my Kalashnikov with my right, and looked at the four magazines and two grenades on my belt. It was loose. I fastened it to the shawl around my waist and wondered whether I would use this weapon in the next few months.

In a fish-odored fantasy, I eat my bread and follow hevalê Ferhad with the feeling that I will never be a real guerrilla. Rûken and Satyar have stopped uphill. They must have reached the cave. The tip of the comrades' train is about forty meters below them, so I should have less than ninety meters to go. *The dog always bites the last one*, as we say back home. Not wanting to keep hevalê Ferhad waiting for me, I gather the rest of my momentum, focus on his shoes, and run faster. Bloody hell, in Germany I considered myself fit as a fiddle, a bona-fide athlete. Three times a week I would run for an hour beside the Main River and sometimes walk all day long. My weakness may be because I have not done any real exercise over the last six months. Otherwise, I was an agile girl. I was running faster and wanted to move past hevalê Ferhad, but, not long after, he stopped. I raised my head and found myself at the terminus. Satyar had a big red snake in his hand and turned its head towards us.

"Wow, are you a snake catcher too?" I asked him.

"No, I'm a dragon catcher. Hevala Rûken caught this worm."

"What do you want to do with this two-meter worm?"

"I wouldn't bend over backwards for a little thing like that. We couldn't catch a skinny twenty-kilogram fish with this worm. We always threw this kind of fish back into the Elwen."

"I'm guessing the Elwen is an ocean that I've never heard about from hevalê Satyar?"

"Heval, I don't want to make a mountain out of a hill. We call it the Elwen rivulet."

"Where did hevala Rûken catch this worm? In that cave?

"Yes."

"Eeeeeugh, and we have to sleep there?"

"Why are you breaking out into a cold sweat? The landlord is now in my hands."

I imagined a deep and dark cave. I ran up a few more steps and found myself in front of the hole in the mountain. It was a bit bigger than our previous women's room, but its height was about a meter and a half. Rûnahî was sweeping inside the cave. I laughed once I saw this scene and could not stop laughing. Even my sudden giggles could not prevent

Rûnahî from continuing to sweep. She looked at me and swept on. In a question punctuated by laughs, I asked her, "So even the snakes cannot prevent you from cleaning up?"

I heard another laugh behind me. It was Rûken. She added, "Oh, that's why you walked so well today. You knew you'd have a new place to clean at the end."

"Heval, we will eat and sleep here. It has to be clean."

Rûnahî kept on sweeping over the jokes. I asked Rûken, "Heval, didn't you say that you had ophidiophobia?"

"Yes, but that was a long time ago."

"And how did you manage to overcome this phobia?"

"Next time, smoke with me. I will reveal something to you."

I didn't notice any sarcasm in her voice, although I could have guessed it from the context. After a while the remaining comrades reached the cave. They untied their packs and wanted to sit down, but Rûnahî shouted.

"You should first take off your wet clothes!"

The men went outside and the women took their clothes off. My clothes were in Rojano's backpack. I went out of the cave. The male comrades were sitting scattered a few meters below the cave. I sat down in front of the cave slab and stretched my legs. Below, Rojano pulled Tewar and took her up. Behind them, Akam was walking. The women came out of the cave with dry clothes and the men went in. They had changed before the three comrades who were coming up reached the cave. I grabbed my load from Rojano's shoulder, then untied the remaining stuff and put it on the ground. She released her arms from the upper rope of the pack and sat. The sack slipped down and fell on the ground with a slap. I pulled the plastic bag containing my clothes out of the sack, opened its tie, and took my clothes out. "Heval, I would like to take off my wet clothes back there. Can you accompany me?" I asked Rojano.

"Okay, heval."

She opened her sack, brought out the plastic bag, and got up. Tewar went into the cave and we walked around the mountain foothill until we couldn't see anyone. The other side of the mountain was sunny. I took off my pants and underpants and sat down to pee. After I was freed from this last burden, I felt relieved. I undressed and sat stark naked under the sun. Rojano also undressed and sat down to pee. Then she went toward her plastic bag and tried to open the tie with her trembling hands. Her fingers did not bend to open the ties. I got up, went stark naked towards her and opened the bag's tie. She slipped on her underwear while seated, then got up and donned her military shirt, pulled the zipper up, put on her pants, put the shirt in them, and tied the trouser strings. She wanted to tie her long waist shawl without my help, but I bent over and took the end of her shawl in my hand and moved a couple steps away so that she could easily wrap it around her waist.

When she was turning to wrap her shawl, I looked at my waist. My belly had become flat. Maybe it also had to do with this shawl. After Rojano was fully dressed, she tied her cartridge belt over her waist shawl and put her vest on over it.

The early morning sun had warmed my body. I sat and lay down naked under the sun, but Rojano reminded me that the drone could appear at any time. I got up, dressed neatly like a real guerrilla, and said, "Heval, are you tired?"

"Yes, I'll take a brief nap."

"Then sleep, I'll awaken you when the comrades call us."

"Thanks, heval."

She threw her wet clothes into the plastic bag, laid her head on it, put her right arm around her BKC, stretched out her legs, and immediately fell asleep with half-open eyes. Only on that day did I notice that Rojano didn't close her eyes completely while she slept. My aunt had this feature, too. That's why my mother always sarcastically told her that she suffered from lagophthalmos. My aunt had keen eyes with which she could see the beauty of the world and leave it in peace. Both in German and Kurdish, there is a better term for this human feature than the terrible word lagophthalmos; it's "rabbit sleep." It certainly fits those two personalities much better. My aunt was calm and cute as a rabbit and Rojano was fast and agile as a hare.

What would have happened and how would I have reacted if my father had divorced my mother and married my aunt? Could I deal with it?

My aunt was deeply rooted in my life. Her cafe-bakery was my favorite childhood place. As far as I can remember, my dad always took me there when he had important appointments. Unlike my mother, she would let me do what I wanted there. Her house was above the cafe-bakery and from the yard I could go directly into the baking area. There I would play with the dough balls and shape them into all different shapes. I was even able to sell them to customers.

She let me work with the coffee machine and even serve coffee to some customers, too. It didn't matter if I shook half of the cup onto the floor on the way to the table. She or one of her employees would bring them another coffee. Not only my aunt, but also her four employees and all the customers were very friendly to me. I wanted to stay there all day and night. So, my father took me to her cafe-bakery more often and stayed there longer, which caused my mother quite a bit of annoyance. She always accused my aunt, "You've spoiled my daughter so much that she does not listen to me anymore."

Even from my point of view today, she had not spoiled me. I learned from her not to be fussy about eating. She would read a lot of children's books to me and I learned to read and write well before I went to school. I heard the name "Karl Marx" for the first time from her and his thoughts had a big influence on my adolescence, even at a time when it was claimed that Marxism was doomed to fail. In the 1990s, her cafe-bakery was one of the rare places in Frankfurt where anticapitalists could gather. I also often met my friends and classmates who were not interested in politics there, like Güzel and my boyfriend. I never supported my mother when she was suspicious of my aunt because of her intimacy with my father, until my first love cheated on me and had an affair with another girl. I was heartbroken.

Instinctively, I approached my mother, who would have been in a similar state of shock for years. Suddenly, I saw my aunt as a whore, especially because my boyfriend had met that girl in my aunt's cafe-bakery. After a year, I was able to cope with my heartbreak and find a new boyfriend, but my reticence towards my aunt remained unchanged even when my mother called me to say that my aunt had been in a car accident and was in the hospital. She died the next day. A cloak of grief fell on my shoulders when I heard the news of her death. It sent me back deep into my mind, where the recollection of those fond childhood memories made me cry. In that mental state, I drove to the hospital immediately. There she laid on her deathbed, eyes half-open. I look at Rojano. She is sleeping in dead silence. I get up and look at the surroundings. The gray river curves away downhill. I walk a few steps and find my heels hurt terribly. How can I walk with this pain tonight?

"Code fifty-one. The drone is on the way," called Rûken loudly.

I turned back and wanted to inform Rojano, but she was already awake. She put her BKC on her shoulder, stood up, and lifted her plastic bag from the ground. I went to her and took my stuff, and we ran toward the cave together. For breakfast we ate cheese with bread and sweet tea. I wanted to get into my sleeping bag right away, but Rûnahî brought out a kind of brown dough in a bowl and put it in the middle of the group. She said we should rub it on the soles of our feet.

"What is this?" I asked Rûnahî.

"Don't your soles hurt?"

"Yes of course, very terrible actually."

"I made it with chestnut flour. It will relieve your pain. Rub it on your soles and leave it for a few minutes, then put your stockings back on. Your pain will be gone until evening."

I did it like all the comrades, then I spread my sleeping bag between Arjîn and Rojano, and squeezed inside. The comrades slept tightly together, like two cans of sardines, with the men on the right side and women on the left. They didn't wake me up to keep watch and I was the last to wake up. All the sleeping bags had already been packed. The comrades sat cross-legged by the cave wall. A little fire burned near the cave mouth, our black kettle over it.

"Good day comrades."

All greeted me back, "Good day."

"Did you sleep well?" Saro asked me.

"Yes."

I looked at my watch. Just about five past five. I waited a few seconds. Then I pulled down the zipper of my sleeping bag and came out of it. I knelt and pulled up the zipper, folded it horizontally, rolled it up vertically, and stuffed it in its case. I looked at my watch again. It took twenty-three seconds.

"Very quick. Soon you will beat the record of hevalê Nadîr," Arjîn said.

"Come on, you better forget it. Hunger has been practicing his ambidexterity with a spoon and fork since birth. Nobody will beat his record."

"Where there's a will, there's a way."

"You're right, hevala Arjîn! But when you have a glutton for competition, you have to throw in the towel at the beginning. Were he not a Kurd, his name would be inscribed on several pages of the Guinness Book of World Records."

"For what, sleeping bag packing?" I asked Satyar.

"For all activities involving the hand or stomach. In manual work, he has no competitors anywhere in the world. He even practices while sleeping."

"You made that up! He does not move in his sleep."

"His movements are too quick to see with the naked eye."

"Then how can you see it? Perhaps your name is already in the Guinness records and we just don't know it."

"It's nothing to boast about. Honestly, I don't notice it, either. I feel it with my whole body. If I didn't have this thick beard and mustache, I would not have teeth in my mouth for chewing."

"And no jaw for chatting."

Nadîr made that last comment and everyone burst out laughing, except himself. I would have liked to provoke them into going further with their jokes, but Tewar was there and I knew that I couldn't withstand any new turbulence with her. For lunch, or better to say dinner, we had cheese with olives, as well as some mortadella for those who would like it. I felt thirsty. I took my canteen out from my sack and asked, "Hevala Rûken, when can we have water again?"

"Drink it, on the way there are a lot of springs."

I drank all of the water in my canteen. The drone was buzzing in the sky. We ate dinner and drank several teas. The comrades were rolling cigarettes and smoking, but we still had an unpredictable journey ahead of us. Either the drone would fly away and we could leave safely, or we would have to wait for night and go under umbrellas. Apart from me, everyone else had marched under umbrellas, but Rûken asked for my advice.

"Hevala Jînçin, hevalê Saro, what is your opinion? How many hours can we walk under an umbrella?"

I pointed my index finger to Saro. He said, "All night."

"Are you sure?"

"Yes heval, during this season there is no danger in walking under an umbrella in the darkness."

"And what do you think, hevala Jînçin? I have often heard that after a few hours, the body temperature becomes distinguishable under the umbrella. That's why I was always afraid to walk for a long time under an umbrella."

"Hevalê Saro has already said it. There is no danger during this season. In winter, especially early morning, you can only walk for half an hour without risk under an umbrella. But in spring, and after a sunny day like today, there is no danger. Until morning, the heat radiates from several places on the surface of the ground. The observers in the air base see countless heat spots on their screens, which they cannot distinguish from our own indirect, upward-moving radiant heat."

"Thanks, heval. Then we can reach our destination before dawn."

Everyone put a loaf of bread in their pockets and we left the cave into the darkness. With solid, dry ground under our feet now, we ran down the slope without worrying about the drone buzzing over our heads. As Rûken predicted, we reached our destination before dawn, even though we had paused at some springs and rested a bit.

CHAPTER 13

THERE WAS A spring close to our camp. Before dawn, we drank from it while carrying umbrellas, filled all our bottles, and went diagonally down a hundred meters until we reached some trees. There, we closed our umbrellas, unloaded our packs and waited for dawn. The space under six medium-sized oak trees and two big chestnut trees became our camp. That area was warm and the trees were fully covered in leaves. The other comrades were probably hungry like me, but again it was Nadîr who was the first one concerned with eating and who asked Rûken, "Heval, where should we build the hearth?"

"The female comrades should take a position under the left chestnut. You can remain under the other one. Build the hearth between them, but prepare a great space to let us cook our meals."

Nadîr went under the trees to the rock wall to look for suitable stones. Hevalê Ferhad got up to collect firewood and all the other comrades got up quickly to help him. Once we had breakfast, I lay beside a tree and slept. After four hours, Saro woke me up to take over guard duty from Gulbehar. Our guard points were uphill beside two oak trees around our camp. Akam was keeping watch below to my left. I leaned against the tree and kept watch over the downhill area. Both the women's and men's camps and the terrain behind Akam were in my sight. He was keeping the space behind me under control. There were no natural or handmade barricades, and if an enemy were to storm us from uphill we would have been easy prey. Ironically, it's precisely this weakness that should protect us from attacks. Based on Rûken's claim, the observers in the flight reconnaissance centers would be least suspicious of such locations. We should just go unnoticed, then we would notice all the movements of the enemy.

Our pot of bean stew and canister of water are on the smokeless fire. Dêrsîm is sitting on a stone by the hearth. The stew is odorless, the comrades are asleep, and we are silent. So, we cannot be traced and the dense trees hide us from the drone. Theoretically, Rûken could be right. Our watch is only an extra precaution.

Dêrsîm pours a cup of oil into the other pot on the fire, adds the rice, and turns it with a ladle. She adds a canister of boiling water and lets the rice boil until it is no longer sitting in liquid, then turns down the flame and takes the saucepan off the heat, letting the rice cook with the lid half-closed until all of the moisture has evaporated. For an hour, it smelled like a myriad of things that don't really smell like anything, until Tewar and Satyar took over guard duty from me and Akam.

After lunch we slept again, but they woke us up soon after. The drone had disappeared, and we had to get to work. I decided to go with Rûken, Zinar, and Satyar to get some things from a hiding place.

The terrain below was green. In some places we had to walk through dense bushes that were shoulder-height. The spring grasses tickled my nipples. Rûken constantly observed the surroundings with her binoculars until, after three quarters of an hour, we finally reached a rock face. She asked me, "Do you want to climb with me, or would you rather stay below?"

"Why do you think I came all this way, sister Rûken?" I replied with a laugh.

Satyar untied his waist shawl, handed it over to Rûken, and stayed below. We climbed up around twenty meters. There was a cleft on the rock wall that was not visible from below. Rûken switched on her lighter flashlight and went into the cleft. We also followed her. At the end of the cleft there was two-and-a half cubic meters of handmade space. There were six ammunition boxes leaning against the rock wall, four metal barrels, and lots of tools. She pulled down one of the tin barrels and put it in the corner. There were four gallon-sized plastic containers in the barrel. She placed the lighter flashlight on one of the ammo boxes and used both of her hands to pull another towards her. They didn't need my help and dragged the box to the entrance of the cleft.

"Give me your shawl," Rûken told me and untied her waist shawl. Zinar and I also untied our shawls. She entwined both shawls together. Then she tied the box handles with those two shawls and we dropped the box down slowly. Satyar released the shawls when the box had reached the ground. Zinar stood at the entrance and we returned into the rock cleft.

In order to be able to bring the tin barrels out through the crevice, we folded them. It took us no more than ten minutes to lower the two tin drums and plastic containers. But we still had the biggest challenge ahead of us. How could I get off now? Rûken tied the scarf around me in such a way that they could almost rappel me down like a box.

Below we undented the tin kegs and put the containers inside. The two of us took turns grabbing either side of the box handles and dragging them about a hundred yards at a time. The others carried the tin barrels and gallons on their shoulders. On the way, Rûken asked me if I would like to bake bread like before.

"Yes of course, with whom?"

"With hevalê Ferhad and hevala Gulbehar."

"I would like to bake only with hevalê Ferhad. Is that possible?"

"Okay, then you'll bake less bread tomorrow. Soon we will bake bread collectively."

"Can I ask why?"

"We need to also bake bread for another group of comrades. Tomorrow you can be alone with hevalê Ferhad."

"That's great. Thanks, darling hevala Rûken."

By the time we returned, the comrades had already flattened a two-square-meter area and had built the baking hearth on the corner. Dêrsîm had put some dough in a plastic bag for acidification early in the morning and the sourdough was ready when we arrived. The dough making recipe was basically like my aunt's bakery, but it was made in a plastic bag rather than in a dough machine and, instead of electricity, we used the power of our feet. I was looking for hevalê Ferhad. He was sitting cross-legged behind a tree reading *Çinara Min* by Musa Anter. I went toward the cooking hearth, poured two glasses of tea, and returned to hevalê Ferhad. I gave him a glass of tea and said, "Hevalê Ferhad, we will bake bread together. Can you stand baking with an amateur?"

"Heval, bread baking is not like quantum physics. And thank you for the tea."

He got up with the tea glass in his hand and went up. I followed him. He placed the tea glass next to the baking hearth, opened a sack, pulled out a rolled greenhouse film, and laid it on the floor. I left my tea glass next to his and together we spread a double layer of greenhouse film on top of the tarp and then put another layer on it. He said nothing and did not ask for my help. I had to follow him with my eyes, legs, and hands.

He went toward a flour sack. I immediately grabbed it and wanted to pick it up, but it was very heavy. It must have been the sack that Rojano had carried. Hevalê Ferhad and I took both sides of the bag, brought it over, and emptied it on the plastic sheet. He brought a smaller flour sack there and I brought a bag of salt. Then we sat down on the ground and drank our teas. He didn't say anything, even though I kept staring at him.

I finally got up, rolled up my military shirt sleeves to above my elbows, picked up a water bottle, and sat down on a rock. I put the bottle between my knees, tilted it down at an angle, and washed my hands and arms with the soap. Hevalê Ferhad also soaped his hands, although dough-making was a woman's task.

I sat cross-legged close to the plastic sheet and covered my lap with it. With my hands I dragged the flour near myself and made a heap, pushed the flour pile aside in all directions, and made a little pit in the middle. Hevalê Ferhad went to the fire, brought the canister of warm water, and poured it into the pit slowly. He also poured two bowls of salt into the water. I dipped my palms in the pit and mixed flour, salt, and water together to make dough. Then I added the sourdough to the dough. I was continuously dipping my palms into the dough, kneading and rolling it. It was like a children's game and I didn't want to give it up until hevalê Ferhad picked up the opposite side of the plastic sheet and covered the dough. I also lifted my side of the plastic sheet and pushed the dough into the middle. He thoroughly covered the dough with the plastic sheet from all sides. Then funniest part of the work began. We had to knead the dough over the plastic sheet by stomping on it. I took off my shoes and stockings, put my left foot on the plastic sheet and pressed the dough. It was moving under my foot. A pleasant feeling waved within me and I kneaded it more rigorously. Suddenly, I remembered a German nursery tune and began to sing and dance with one foot over the dough to the rhythm of the song.

A good three hundred years ago, there was a little boy
whose talents were so grand, they still bring people joy
A famous little child who mastered keys and bow
Amadeus was his name and how they loved him so!

Hevalê Ferhad was looking at me, smiling. Soon other comrades appeared. Arjîn ran to us and said, "Heval, I want to knead the dough by dancing, too."

I continued singing and nodded simultaneously to give her permission.

Mozart was the biggest star
Since his songs were wunderbar

On piano, on piano, he played the sweetest tunes
At only four, at only four, he practiced all the day
On piano, on piano, he played the sweetest tunes
And still today, across the globe, you hear his music play

Within a few seconds, our dough station had transformed into a dance stage. The other comrades either whistled the song or laughed like little children. Until Rûken screamed, "Stop! What are you doing?" Grimly, I looked at her and said, "What's wrong? What's the problem with our joy?"

"It's sinful. Kicking the dough and dancing on it! God will blind you!"

All the comrades burst out laughing and only then did I realize this had a funny story behind it. As if, twenty-four years ago, when she was twelve and saw her comrades kneading dough with their feet, she shouted at them, "What are you doing, heval? God will blind you."

"Do not worry. Let us go blind."

Rûken also came on stage and danced with the dough. We were dancing and kneading the dough uninterrupted until hevalê Ferhad told us, "That's enough, heval, otherwise the dough will spoil."

The dough stayed under the plastic sheet and a blanket until five in the morning when Rûken woke me up. Hevalê Ferhad was seated by the fireplace in the far-right corner. It was cold. I put on my jacket, put the sleeping bag in its container, and went to him.

"Good morning, hevalê Ferhad."

"Good morning, hevala Jînçin."

He took some handfuls of ash from the hearth and poured it into the concave side of the pan. He added a lot of salt, poured some water on it, mixed them with his hand, and made a kind of black mud. Then he rubbed this mud all over the side of the pan that sits directly on the fire. I washed my hands and wiped them with my handkerchief. I went to the dough, pulled away the blanket, quickly made some balls, and laid them on the flour-covered plastic sheet in rows. I caught a whiff of the fire. Hevalê Ferhad brought the pan, put it on the fire, and sat opposite me.

My eyes were on the flames through the hearth stones. I heard the crackling of the burning brush wood. Its sparks were flying toward the outside as I made dough balls efficiently and consistently like an experienced baker. He pulled a cloth out of the salt bag, soaked it, and rubbed the top side of the pan. Bubbles and steam rose up from the surface of the pan. I threw some dough balls on the sack in front of hevalê Ferhad. He picked them up calmly, quickly patted the balls into a circular shape, and put them over the pan. Soon the five dough balls were baked and the scent of bread filled the air.

Calmly and lightly, he would change the locations of the bread in the pan, as if he were picking up sheets of paper, and was also aware that the fire remained smokeless. He turned my dough balls into circular shapes with only three slaps of his palm. Once one side of the bread was baked, he picked it up and put it beside the hearth to let the other side of bread bake directly in front of the flame. The first batch of bread seemed to be baked. I went toward the hearth, lifted the bread, and threw it on the spread sack. Three more loaves were ready by the time the first ones had cooled.

I cut the bread in two pieces and gave a piece to hevalê Ferhad. He put it on a stone near the hearth and went on without thanking me or showing any reaction. To rid myself of the disappointment his response, or lack thereof, caused, I put a piece of bread in my mouth and yelped with joy.

"Wow, heval, this dance-kneaded bread is delicious."

Hevalê Ferhad picked up the bread, bit off a piece, and smiled at me. I threw some dough balls on the sack in front of him and instead of complaining I asked him directly.

"Heval, I want to ask you a question."

"Go ahead, heval."

"Have you read the book *Prison No. 5* by Mehdi Zana?"

"Yes, heval."

"And what do you think about it? Is it true how he described the prison of Amed?"

"It was even worse."

"Is there anything worse than that? I am not a tender heart, but a tough woman. Yet, it was unbearable for me to read his diary. I felt like I had died several times before I finished the book. After two years, I still have these terrifying images in front of my eyes. I said to myself that savagery must also have a boundary and wondered how the torturers of this prison could have treated prisoners like that, going beyond all the boundaries of brutality. But now you tell me the situation was even worse than he described. How can it be? Were they not humans, did they have no feelings? Were they monsters or humans?"

"They were people like us and had human feelings. They loved each other and we could clearly feel it. I believe that everyone can commit such crimes, they just need legal authority, legitimacy."

He formed a new ball of dough into a circle and slammed it on the pan. I made some balls and added, "heval, I do not expect you to talk about what happened in Amed prison. Just tell me your opinion."

"Do you wonder when you see a butcher slaughtering?"

"Unfortunately, no. I also eat meat."

"A butcher kills a sheep and chops it up. How does he do it?"

"Because he considers it his job."

"I will explain it in another way. They believe that their work is legitimate. Muslims call this legitimacy 'halal.' They believe that God created edible animals to be eaten by humans. If someone considers his deed legal, halal, and legitimate, he will do something with his victim similar to what we are doing with the dough right now. If a torturer considers his works halal, legitimate, or legal, then he can ruthlessly tear people to pieces. It is even worse when the torturer is not only convinced of the legitimacy of his crime, but also hates his victims.

The Turks in the prison of Amed hated us. We were the hated barbarians who hurt their fascist feelings. They could not even bear to hear the word 'Kurd.' Atatürk called their country Turkey and all the people who live in the country had to automatically become Turks and be proud of that. But, in my opinion, both legitimacy and hatred were not enough alone to create Prison No. 5. Our torturers had to be sadists. The Turkish intelligence services had filled the minds of a group of sadists with aversion and hatred for Kurds and let them torment us savagely. They were not only indifferent to our screaming and crying during the torment, they enjoyed it. Hevala Jîncin, the camp at Auschwitz couldn't have been worse than the Turkish prison in Amed between the years 1984–1990."

"If that's the case, why don't you write your experiences, or let someone else write about them? Those crimes will be forgotten soon."

"That'd be better, heval. Those things must be forgotten. Such crimes should not happen anywhere, even within books. People should not know or believe that such a level of brutality exists or is conceivable. As Hannah Arendt once said about Auschwitz, such brutality should never have happened."

"But these crimes happened again and you are a witness to the brutality. You have to tell and record them."

Hevalê Ferhad didn't give up his work and was working like a programmed robot the whole time, turning balls into circles and slamming them on the pan, continuously shifting the locations of the bread, taking them from the pan, placing them in front of the hearth, throwing them on the spread sack once they were baked, being sure the fire remained smokeless, and simultaneously talking with me. I just had the simple job of making dough balls, but I lost my concentration while talking. As if he were the woman and I the man.

"Hevalê Ferhad, I know that recalling bitter memories is unpleasant for you, but as a libertarian you have to recount your stories."

"Heval, it's true that I don't like talking about my imprisonment, but not because it bothers me. That is one side of the story, but the main reason is that the recounting of these savageries harms us even more. That level of brutality in Prison No. 5 radicalized our liberationist movement. It led us to perform many acts of sabotage and it was exactly what the fascists wanted and still want. At that time we were able to obliterate that hell, not by struggle or violence, but by six years of uninterrupted resistance and hunger strikes. In the meantime, several Kurdish libertarian fighters died in hunger strikes, until people outside heard our voices. We were like pieces of meat in the hands of the sadistic torturers, but for six years we yelled incessantly until Prison No. 5 became an ordinary prison again. Some of us were freed and explained to people what had happened. I was one of them. We talked about the savagery and tyranny of the Turks, but it caused hatred to fester and our society to split even more deeply.

The PKK has responded to the brutality of the Turkish government with violence, polarizing society. Today the situation is different. We have Turks in the mountains and in prisons who are fighting for the rights of the Kurds. At that time, it was out of the question for the Turks to hear a word of Kurdish; today, we have Turkish comrades who speak Kurdish. 'Prison No. 5,' the burning of thousands of villages, and the evacuation of millions of Kurds must be forgotten. These have nothing to do with the new generations of Turks. We must not hold them accountable, either militarily or morally."

Hevalê Ferhad became silent. I knew that I could not ask him any more questions. I look at his skillful hands moving and think about his masterful rhetoric. I did not expect that from someone who is more silent than a tree. He is completely silent, perhaps to talk with himself, undisturbed, in his mind. I turn all the remaining dough into balls and go toward the fire to see how you can have a smokeless flame under a large pan. Rûken did not ask anyone to cook lentils and the comrades ate the cheese and bread instead. Right now, nothing is more delicious than freshly baked bread.

After breakfast, Saro carried his backpack to leave. Rûken called him, "Do not go alone, take hevala Jînçin with you." Rûken fixed her gaze on me and asked, "Are you exhausted? Would you go with him?"

"Why exhausted?! Hevalê Ferhad did all the work himself. I will go with him."

"Then take water and some bread."

I quickly turned a sack into a backpack, put three loaves of bread and two bottles of water in it, and put it on my back. Then I swung the Kalashnikov over my shoulder and went downhill. For about twenty minutes, we descended from the right side of the foothill, jumped across a stream, and climbed up a slope until we reached the plateau. There we were surprised by a wonderful sea of blossoms. With every step, petals fell closer and closer to us. Besides the apricot trees, which caught the eye with their stunning red and white blossoms, there were also many apple, walnut, and almond trees. Saro and Rûken planted them five years ago with some other comrades. On the edge of the plateau, on the other side of the mountain, one had a beautiful view over the Çemê Miradê,* the long source of the Firat.†

The river flowed through a green valley at the foot of the mountain, a place that had endured a hundred years of war between Turks and Kurds. Beyond the river, the mountain peaks were much higher. From the plateau upwards, the ridges, passes, and all the peaks were white. The excellent harmony between the crystal-clear mountain water, the green shore, the picturesque meadow, and the contrast between the steep, black slope and the snow standing on it represented a natural aesthetic spectacle. Behind us stood a plantation in a sea of flowers. I would have happily stayed there for hours, looking at these pristine, technology-disconnected areas devoid of humans. But we had to leave the spot immediately after drinking some cold water from the well that flowed around the planted fruit trees for five years before flowing into the Çemê Miradê. The area was known for Turkish air force bases and it was highly risky to stay there.

We ran to the left on the plateau and went toward our hidden depot. It had already been discovered by bears. A heap of soil was visible on the spot, but we were not discouraged and went on anyway. Our food was untouched. The comrades had covered it with a steel net on all sides. The bears had dug until the steel net, but they could not tear through the steel and, with an empty stomach, left our food intact.

Saro wanted to notify Rûken by radio, but he suddenly saw a shepherd. His herd was grazing on the meadow across the river and he was following them. Saro sat down immediately and I imitated him. He took the binoculars from his magazine belt and looked at the shepherd. Then he pulled out the radio from his vest pocket and called Rûken.

"Do you hear me, heval? Saro is here."

"Yes, heval I hear you."

"We're at the cooking pot. The aunty was here too, but she couldn't lift the pot. The lid is said to have been very hot."

"Ok, should we come there and take the lid?"

"No, heval. The fox seems to be naughty and to have red eyes."

"Okay, then stay there and let me know when you see his toys."

"OK."

* Murat River.
† Euphrates River.

We go to a huge stone and hide ourselves behind it. He looks at the shepherd several times and finally gives me the binoculars. I look at him. He sits hidden behind the goats and sheep, holding his stick in front of his eyes and watching the surroundings.

"Holy shit! Does he work as an agent for the Turkish secret services?" I asked Saro.

"No, I don't think so. He works as a very poorly paid shepherd. If he doesn't cooperate with the MİT, they won't let him work as a shepherd peacefully. That is very unfortunate, but most of these poor shepherds cooperate with the MİT. The few of them who do not work with the MİT get in trouble every day. The Turkish secret services shoot shepherds and their herds with rockets. If they don't kill the shepherd, but eliminate his cows and sheeps, then these miserable people have to work for free. You can guess what a dirty and dangerous game it is."

"So, how do you fight against such problems?"

"There are two kinds of shepherds. Some of them are familiar with Kurdish matters and sympathize with us. We connect with them and help each other, but we hide ourselves from others. In the grazing seasons, we move with such caution that they don't look at us. If they see us anyway, we will immediately evacuate that area."

"And what do you do when they appear outside their pasture areas to look for you?"

"What can we do, hevala Jîncin? Shall we kill them like in the time of Hogir? They are poor people who live from hand to mouth. Such people can be easily hired and deceived. You can ask them to do anything if you give them some sheep and read some verses of the Qur'an. The AKP is building mosques in their villages and they are consenting to their misery. We not only have to hide from the drones and hidden cameras, but also from them."

Saro picked up the binoculars again and looked at the shepherd. Once he put them on the ground, I lifted them and looked at him. He sat next to a campfire with a black kettle on it. Rûken called by radio.
"Heval, do you hear me?"
"Yes, heval."
"Code fifty-one, drone is on the way."
"Got it."

We walked half-crouched for about two minutes, until the shepherd was no longer visible. Then we got up and ran toward a big mulberry tree. Once we arrived there, we freed ourselves from our backpacks and sat down under the tree. He sat stiffly cross-legged and I leaned against the tree trunk, stretched out my legs and placed my weapon on the ground beside me. After a while, the buzzing drone reached over our heads. I opened my bag and took out a water bottle, drank some water, and handed it over to Saro. After he took a few sips, I asked him.

"You talked about hidden cameras. Are there really any around here?"

"Yes, there are a lot of them."

"Why haven't we seen them yet?"

"We already know the locations of many of the hidden cameras and move away from them. Others are still invisible to us and they transmit recorded images to the MİT daily. They are hidden in the shapes of natural elements like stones or trunks and it is not easy to find them. The MİT is constantly installing new cameras in the mountains."

"Who installs these cameras? The Turkish armed forces don't move very secretly."

"The shepherds do it. They are convinced by the MİT that these cameras are used to protect them from possible air raids."

"Can uneducated shepherds install such complicated things?"

"Hevala Jînçin, do you want to lecture me again? Shepherds stick or screw them where they can. You yourself know better than me how to run these cameras after installation."

"What is the effect of these cameras on your movements?"

"They make our movements more difficult. The Turkish regime can combine the drones' recorded videos with these close-up images, then analyze the information with GIS and other data analysis software, and discover our bunkers and passage directions. But none of this is our biggest problem yet. Our unsafe communication methods, these radios, hurt us even more."

"And you think that I can help you?"

"I think so. You once talked about an absolutely safe and fast way of communication through entangled photons. Is it possible to run such a system in these mountains?"

"If you have the necessary hardware and a secure energy source, you can even build it on Mars."

"I can provide you with secure energy."

"Do you mean hydro or solar energy?"

"Both."

"The second does not work. The first one also has a lot of problems."

"Doesn't water provide enough energy?"

"The question is not about sufficiency. But, if you weren't always on the run and had unnoticed stations stationed next to the photon transmitters and receivers, you could also use the energy from water sources to produce electricity and charge the batteries of the devices in time. There might be other ways to solve this problem, but how can you buy the devices and smuggle them into these mountains?"

"Are these devices big?"

"No, many parts can even be bought in Bakûr or Başûr. The other parts can be mounted in two sets of laptops."

"Then we can easily transfer them from Turkey or Iraq."

"And where can you find this equipment?"

"Can't we buy them in the black markets?"

"No, the devil is in the details. Such equipment is very difficult to obtain, even among allied countries with common interests."

"Can't you help us with it?"

"I think you've got a screw loose. Do you want me to steal it from the university lab, too?"

CHAPTER 14

ONLY AFTER THREE days could we transfer our things from the hidden depot to the camp. The night before, the sky was covered with black clouds. We got up at five o'clock, as usual, but it was still dark out. Before we left, it was already raining. Except for hevalên Ferhad and Dêrsîm, everyone else went to carry out the goods, and before lunch we had transferred all the contents of the hidden depot, even the steel nets and plastic sheets used as covers. After the first round of transportation, Rûnahî, Tewar, and Akam stayed in the camp to prepare a huge pile of dough and collect enough firewood for baking.

In the afternoon we all engaged in bread-baking and, before our guests arrived, we had baked over a thousand loaves of bread on two convex pans. The group of guests consisted of nine female comrades and twelve male comrades. Two of the men had musical instruments with them, but they were tired and, like other comrades, crawled into their tents just after supper and slept. They had breakfast with us, stuffed their backpacks with bread, put them on their shoulders, and went downhill.

After about an hour we were informed by radio that some attack helicopters had taken off. Since they were flying in our direction, the Turkish air force had probably tracked down our comrades. We left everything there but our weapons and ammunition and evacuated the area within a minute. Rûken ran up the mountain under a drizzle of rain and we followed her. It only took seven minutes until we arrived at another hidden depot that had been dug up and plundered by bears.

"Hide yourselves under the bushes. No one is allowed to move or talk, no matter how many days it takes." Then she called Arjîn, "Heval, can you find the hidden depot again?"

"Yes, heval."

"Then go and keep an eye on the situation. You are not allowed to step on the snow, just run over the stones."

"Ok, heval."

Everyone hid somewhere under a bush. I looked at Arjîn, who was running to the big rock under the rain. Along the way I lost sight of her and soon many combat helicopters appeared above us in the sky. We didn't have any weapons more effective than RPG-7s, but they were trying to descend on the top of the mountain. The last helicopter wavered over the summit for a long time and finally the special units rappelled down via cables. We were below them and our situation seemed almost hopeless. Through Gulbehar's binoculars, I could see the special forces from under the bushes. They stayed up, while the other soldiers descended the mountain and searched under every stone. Some turned in our direction. They must have been well informed of our position. They moved cautiously and slowly descended the mountain.

It took two hours for the first group to approach us. Rûken had determined our position correctly; they didn't suspect that we would be there. In other places, they pulled the bushes aside and looked under them. It was raining and I was wet and shivering with cold and fear. They didn't want to leave. Suddenly a group came right up to us. They wore bullet-proof vests and hats. There was less than five meters between us. During this time, their dogs started barking. A group of them downstream must have kept their dogs on a leash. They must have smelled us and kept barking. If there wasn't another group of them standing next to us, they would have unleashed their dogs. The dogs went silent and the group continued downhill.

Later, another group came to us. I don't doubt an officer saw me. There were only two meters between us and he looked straight into my eyes. I could only look into his black eyes. He went downhill without saying anything. My heart was pounding like a snare drum out of fear. My whole body was shivering and it was raining harder and harder.

All the helicopters had flown back to their stations and the last groups also left the mountaintop and ran down. A major is said to have guessed that we were hiding near the excavated landfill. He approached us with three soldiers, saw me, and quickly drew his gun on me. However, Gulbehar shot him in the head. His hat flew into the air and the battle began.

The other three were also shot. A group standing above us opened fire and the enemy also fired on us from other sides. The groups below wanted to climb up. So, our comrades had to shoot in different directions under the bushes and rain. The situation was dramatic. But soon the tide turned. Arjîn fired several volleys at the enemy from above. Some of the forces above us were shot and killed. The others had to throw themselves on the ground and stop shooting. Arjîn was firing without interruption as if she were in an ammunition warehouse. All the comrades pointed their weapons down and fired accurately. I found my peace again, but Rûken saw the situation differently and said, "Heval, the danger has not passed yet. They will get air support soon. Until then, we have to get out of here. Hevalên Akam and Nadîr, some of them must have been hiding behind the ridge. Arjîn doesn't see them. You have to go up and hunt them down with a sniper rifle, otherwise they will soon be able to shoot Arjîn. Once you've neutralized them, give us a shot signal of one-three-one."

They both climbed up half-crouching while Arjîn shot at every moving object. She was shooting from different places.

"Hevalên Satyar and Zinar, you have to run as fast as possible downhill and drop yourself on the ground in four seconds. Not a second longer. Then continue crawling as you reach behind that big stone. Take care that the enemy does not climb up until you hear the shooting signal of Akam and Nadîr. Then you have to run back up to the top. We will meet each other there. Are you ready?" Rûken said, issuing another order.

"Yes, heval."

"Get up and run when I say 'now.' Ok?"

"Ok, heval."

Rûken and the other comrades leveled their rifle barrels at the remaining group above, and Satyar and Zinar awaited the command to go. Not wanting to see them fall, I looked up to where the enemy group was hiding. Satyar and Zinar ran. The group above raised their heads to shoot at them, but all four were hit. Satyar and Zinar reached their positions. They started shooting and Rûken gave the next order.

"Hevalên Ferhad and Rojano, you must climb over the valley on the left and prevent the enemy from rising up the back valley until hevalên Tewar and Dêrsîm go over the escarpment. Hevala Dêrsîm, you have to position hevala Tewar in a proper place to enable her to surprise and shoot enemy troops moving up with the RPG. And you yourself should give us some covering fire until we can reach the ravine."

All four comrades went, half-crouching, toward the top of the mountain and Rûken continued.

"Rûnahî stays with me and everyone else goes up until you hear the signal shots, then you have to run to the top. Their air support will appear soon." Rûken turned to me and said, "Hevala Jînçin, you stay near hevala Gulbehar. You mustn't shoot. With every bullet you shoot you put yourself in danger. Our situation is not bad and you just have to walk near hevala Gulbehar and cross the ravine as fast as possible. Ok, heval?"

"Ok."

Rûken took her binoculars and looked at the position of the unit that had remained above. We ducked under the bushes until we heard the gunshots, then we got up and ran to the top of the mountain. In the meantime, Rûken had shot the two other special units who had stayed above. We turned. Rûken and Rûnahî ran to us and Satyar and Zinar followed them. Nobody shot at them and they were able to reach us unscathed.

A new battle soon began. One of the enemy groups tried to climb up the valley behind us on the left. However, Rojano was already positioned behind a huge rock and shot at them. Hevalê Ferhad leveled his gun at the valley we were climbing. The enemy groups below must have suspected that the comrades had left their positions on the plateau and climbed up. Arjîn didn't react and they may have assumed that she had fallen. Rûken said that we had to keep climbing and not shoot at them. I was out of breath and felt that we were in grave danger again. Hevalê Ferhad went down, gave one of his cartridge chains to Rojano, and climbed back up with us.

Arjîn began to fire again. I turned back and saw the soldiers fall to the ground, either from the shots or to duck in defense.

Arjîn observed the situation from above and was ready on the wall below the peak when Rûken and Rûnahî joined us. Arjîn had her BKC on her right shoulder. Her entire torso was wrapped in a long chain of cartridges and, additionally, she had a sack of cartridges on the other shoulder. I ran to her and took the sack from her. It was full of BKC rounds and very heavy. I put it on the ground and hugged her.

"Hevala Arjîn, this many cartridges were hidden up there?"

"Yes, heval. What I could not shoot, I brought with me."

Arjîn laughed and, for the first time after Befrîn's death, her tongue protruded out from the left side of her mouth as she did it. Gulbehar came up to us, hugged her, and said, "I was worried about you. A group of enemies was landing on your nose."

"Luckily I have a little nose."

"And when did you come out from your hiding place?"

"When the group that had dogs reached you. Two groups of enemies were already positioned up there. I brought down three sacks full of cartridges from the rock, then moved away from their range and stationed myself in a safe place. But I was in doubt whether to shoot when they spotted you or to wait until the last group had climbed down and was under me. Hevala Rûken, what should I have done in such a case?"

"I'll explain it to you later. We have to evacuate this area right now."

Rojano brought out a bandolier of cartridges from the bag and tied it around her waist and chest. We walked three minutes on top of the mountain to the left until they announced via the radio that a large squadron of fighter planes had taken off from Amed. Rûken said in response, "Got it," and turned to the comrades.

"Hevalno, together we cannot save ourselves. Arjîn, Gulbehar, Jînçin, Nadîr, and Satyar come with me. The others go with hevalê Saro."

She grabbed the small radio from Gulbehar's hand, turned in the opposite direction, and shouted, "Run as fast as you can. We have only six minutes left."

Under the rain, Rûken ran like a sprinter up the mountain. For two minutes we ran after her. She was fifty meters ahead. During this race, I saw that she hid the small radio under a big stone. Before we reached her, she got up and started running but eventually stopped. There was a small cave. We bent over, entered in, and soon heard the sound of fighter jets above the clouds. A sound like thunder had already been rolling through the mountains, but now the ground began to blow up and I saw big bombs fall to the ground and explode. The mountains became a hell on earth. The sound of the explosions was continuously rising from the ground and stones and trees were flying into the air. I was worried about Saro and the fate of his group and asked, "Hevala Rûken, why didn't you tell hevalê Saro to throw away their radio while it was turned on?"

"Heval, I myself learned that from hevalê Saro. Don't you see? The squadron is bombarding two places. Our little radio must be on in the other area."

Hundreds of bombs were falling from the sky, exploding, and destroying everything in those mountains. The boulders were jumping into the air and a part of the mountain was sliding down into the valley. I thought of Saro and missed him. Three days ago, he had described a similar situation to me, but I thought he was laying it on thick and expressed my doubts. I could not believe that the Turkish regime would dispatch fifty-three heavily loaded bombers to fight a small group of guerrillas and I asked him with a suspicious tone, "Don't you think fifty-three bombers is too much? Maybe it was thirty-five or three and a half."

"Heval, I could count to one hundred before I went to school," Saro replied kindly.

"Yeah, I believe you. And I could count a hundred dough balls. But dough cannot fly and the supersonic planes cannot be counted with fingers, especially when they drop bombs on us."

Saro turned to the mulberry tree and took out two loaves of bread. He handed one of them to me, ate a piece of his bread, and gave his response.

"Hevala Jîncin, I did not stay in the war zones for a long time and did not directly see any planes during the bombardment. But why did I tell you about the fifty-three bombers? There was a place where I stayed alone with another comrade, but on the evening of the bombardment we had two more guests. I do not know why my comrade thought fighter jets would bombard us that night. He was an experienced comrade and said several times, 'Tonight we will be bombarded either by Turkish aircrafts or by Iranian artillery.'

There was an open area near our site. On that day, our comrades tested their DShK there. Apparently, the test shots were audible to the Iranian bases. He said we couldn't stay there that night. If the Turks didn't bomb us, the Iranians would certainly fire at us with mortars and cannons.

When our two guests arrived, saw the situation, and heard the arguments of my fellow inhabitant, they thought his words were reasonable. They also insisted that we had to leave our position. I was known for my laziness, but I was ultimately able to persuade, or perhaps force them, to stay there. They slept, but I stayed awake and kept working on my computer. When the aircrafts took off, I was immediately informed by radio that a squadron had flown out to bombard us. Swiftly, I wrote down the take-off time. After six minutes and fifty-two seconds, I got a message from Xinêre that they hadn't flown toward them. A few seconds later, I also heard from Garê that they hadn't shown up there, either. The bombers were coming from Amed's military airport to our position and would arrive within ten minutes and forty seconds. Then I counted the flight time. I deducted the distance from Amed to Garê and Xinêre. About four minutes remained until they reached our point, but the planes had to fly first over Garê and Xinêre to reach our point through Turkish airspace. Maybe they flew to other places. Suddenly, I remembered the words of my comrade, 'Tonight, either the Turks or the Iranians will bombard us.'

Perhaps the two countries had coordinated and the bombers were flying through Iran's airspace. I quickly woke up my comrades and ran to a hole in the rock that was three hundred meters away from us. When we reached there, I looked at my watch. We had one minute left. I had a small camera with me. I turned it on and put it on the ground. The explosions were so numerous and so unbearably loud that it was impossible to count them. Additionally, the bangs overlapped and you couldn't tell them apart. Later we looked at the video recording; there were fifty-three bombers.

Based on my research, these bombers were loaded with either four rockets and a half-ton heavy bomb, or two rockets and a one-ton bomb. They dropped all their bombs on our area. Theoretically, they could have returned to the airport in Amed and recharged, although the time was brief. We ourselves made a lot of jokes about this theory. The comrades asked me if I was sure that there had been fifty-three or whether some of them had returned to recharge. I replied that I honestly did not know. It was dark and I could not read their registration plates.

'Next time you should only worry about reading the plates. The bombs will fall anyway.'

In the middle of the terrible explosions, flying rocks, whirling dust, and rising adrenaline you cannot count how many bombers have flown by and how many bombs they carried. There's a whistle inside your head, your ears are buzzing, and your eyes are burning. If we didn't have the camera, we certainly would not have known how many fighter jets there were. It does not change the number of bombs dropped if it was fifty-three individual bombers, or if some of them went and returned again. Before I watched the recorded video, I thought it was a maximum of fifteen bombers, but we were bombarded by fifty-three charged bombers. The area became flat ground, as if it was plowed and the soil had been sifted. It was as though the season had suddenly changed. There were no leaves on the branches and the mountain had split and slipped down into the valley. Even the geography of the area changed. After we crawled out of the hole, we no longer knew the terrain."

"And you had a GoPro camera with you right at that time?" I asked him rudely.

"I always have one in my backpack."

Saro bit his bread lightly and said nothing. He looked tired of trying to prove to a skeptical woman the truth of those things that were obvious in his viewpoint. The previous two times, he had talked about his life much more, but he had not been so exhausted. On the first night, he told me that he would tell me his life story in three rounds. Like a superstitious person, a terrible idea hit me like lightning. Maybe I would never see him again. I turned to Rûken and asked, "Heval, are you sure the other comrades are safe?"

"They cannot be far from the bombardment site. I hope they have reached a safe location."

The thundering continues as the bombers fly above the clouds, firing their missiles and dropping their bombs. They're invisible, but I could have counted their bombs and missiles if I'd thought of it in the first place. We're far enough away from the blasts for this low cave to protect us from blast waves, but the bangs and the scenes are awful, nevertheless. The entire area is under heavy shelling. Here there is no war between two belligerent parties, but a war of people against trees and stones, between experienced military technology and the virgin environment. The green valley below can no longer be seen. The trees and stones jump into the air and fall to the ground with great force. The mountain parts are cut up by bombs and thrown into the valley. Each outburst of anger is followed by another and the mountain is hurt even more. It's just too many bombers for thirteen lightly-armed guerrillas and I'm terribly concerned for my comrades, who have become so dear to me. Why did I step on Saro's toes?

Why did I act like I understood the rules of war here better than he did? Just because I had attended a course on symmetrical and asymmetrical warfare in Germany for a few months? The global rules of war simply do not apply in Kurdistan. This name cannot be found on any map and no one cares when its natural landscapes are destroyed, when its people are gassed, chased away, and burned. People say the Kurds are to blame for not wanting to give up their damned identity, instead of being promoted to the ranks of the Turks, Arabs, and Persians.

It was never important to me whether I was a German or a Kurd, but now I feel like a Kurd, because I felt like the rug had been pulled out from under me, since this part of my identity hurts me so terribly. It's hard to be a Kurd and only the Kurds can bear it. For more than a hundred years, these mountains, villages, and cities have been bombed and the fascists have not yet understood that the Kurds will never admit defeat. There are millions of stupid Kurds who will never be subdued. More than thirty, forty, or more bombers are now deployed against fourteen lightly-armed Kurds. We might all die today, but there are more than forty million other Kurds outside of these mountains. You can reduce the number of Kurds to thirty, twenty, or ten million, but that doesn't change the number of crazy Kurds who will never accept their oppression by the ruling world order. How large must the number of these bombers be, how many thousands of bombers must the fascists possess, in order for Rûken, Arjîn, Gulbehar, Satyar, and Nadîr to return from this cave to a normal life in a town or city? I turn and watch them. All I can see on their faces is deep concern for their comrades. As soon as the bombers disappear, Rûken comes to the mouth of the cave and listens for outside voices and sounds. There is no drone in the sky. She turns on the radio and calls for Saro.

"Where are you, heval? Rûken is here. Do you hear me?"

"Yes, heval, I hear you."

I scream cheerfully when I hear his voice.

"How is your situation?"

"We have two injured."

"Flesh wound or deep? Who are the injured?"

"Hevalên Akam and Dêrsîm. Shrapnel from a bomb hit Dêrsîm's injured leg and Akam's belly was wounded by several flying stone particles."

"How is hevalê Akam? Can he talk?"

"No, heval. He has bled a lot. Rûnahî got out the stones, stitched his wounds, and injected him with two syringes. He is unconscious."

"You must leave that area immediately. Soon the helicopters and special units will appear. Do you have a stretcher?"

"Yes, heval, Rûnahî has one with her."

"Great. Then you have to leave the area. Can Dêrsîm show you the path?"

"No, heval. We must carry her too."

"Then stay right there. We will distract them from you. You should leave there only when the Turkish forces have moved toward us. I'll turn off the radio now. At the first opportunity, I will contact you again."

"Ok, heval."

Rûken put the radio in her backpack and turned to me.

"Hevala Jînçin! It's only going to get worse for all of us. The six of us must draw the enemy's attention as soon as the choppers reappear. If we don't make a mistake, we will escape the attack. If you hide well under a two-cubic-meter rock, the missiles will not harm you. Your whole body has to be covered and you have to hold your backpack in front of your head so that the flying pieces of stone don't hurt you."

"Ok, heval."

"Then run as fast as possible. This area is very unsafe."

Rûken went out of the cave, ran down diagonally from the right side, and we followed her. Soon the combat helicopters appeared, but we had already reached the appropriate location. Rûken and Nadîr were running around, popping their heads out from behind the stones, and jumping in various directions across the stones like geckos, until three Cobra helicopters descended and found us. Before they launched their first rocket, we had already crawled behind the big rocks. Gulbehar was near me, as usual. I tried to conceal my fear, while I didn't believe these rocks could protect us from the modern Cobra rockets. But, to my amazement, their rockets were totally ineffective. Rockets were hitting the rocks, detonating with a terrible explosion, and throwing stone particles into the air, but the comrades were crawling under the rocks as freely as if they were playing a game of hide and seek.

The helicopter rotors were turning above us like windmills and shooting their rockets as we watched them under the big rocks. After a while, all of their rockets had been fired and they put the area under a torrent of gunfire. Bullets were falling like rain and whistling around us. My whole body was shivering and my heart was pounding. I shrunk down and huddled myself under a big rock, but the comrades were crawling without fear and firing at the helicopters as their heads and torsos became visible. Soon, another five Cobras appeared. That was certainly the purpose of our comrades' hide and seek game.

Over the top of the mountain there was no place to land and the pilots had tried several times to land on a plateau opposite us, but Nadîr and Arjîn were shooting at the landing forces with their BKC, forcing them to rise again. Suddenly, one of the Cobra helicopters was shot down by an RPG-7. I looked for Gulbehar, but she was not in her position. She must have climbed the rock wall and fired at the Cobra. The pilot and units jumped out, and it exploded immediately afterwards. The other helicopters moved away from us and landed at various locations on the other side of the steep valley. Rûken yelled, "Hevalên Arjîn and Satyar! You should stop their advance until I take the comrades to a safe place. In twenty minutes we will have reached there. Arjîn already knows where the spot is, but if you have to break up, Satyar, you have to run about fifteen meters below your current spot and turn to the left side of the mountain. There you will see a hole in the ground. You must not enter the hole under any circumstances. The Turkish army will use poison gas. Sixty meters after the hole, there is a cliff. When you reach that location, call us quietly. One of us will pull out their hand and show you where we are. Hevalên Gulbehar and Jîncin! Creep eight meters downward without being noticed and wait until the last helicopter flies away, then run quickly around the mountain to the cliff and wait for me and hevalê Nadîr."

Before all the Turkish units got out on the plateau opposite us, we crawled to our planned starting point, and waited for the helicopters to fly away. As soon as the last helicopter was gone, Rûken shouted, "Run, now!"

Gulbehar got up and ran to the mountain gorge and I ran after her. The comrades were shooting nonstop to cover us. Soon after, we arrived safely behind the gorge. Because of the stress, I did not see the hole in the ground. I just looked at Gulbehar's feet and ran behind her. Rûken and Nadîr also managed to safely cross the gorge and reach us. There was no hiding place to see. In front of us there was an abyss more than three hundred meters deep. From the left, after a few meters of very steep rocky terrain, there was an even deeper gorge, into which one could not descend and to the right of us was a vertical rock wall. I asked Rûken nervously, "Where is this hiding place?"

"Behind this rock wall. You have to climb six meters to the left, then you'll see a cleft behind the edge of the wall in which we can hide."

Although I had climbed artificial rock walls in Germany, they were a few meters high and below us there was always a thick air mattress. It's a whole different challenge to climb a three-hundred-meter rock wall under the rain and with the fear of being shot. Before I could express my surprise, Rûken climbed from the left side. In less than two minutes, she disappeared behind the rock ledge. Then she poked her head out from the cleft and ordered Gulbehar to climb. There was no visible place on the rock wall to grab onto with your feet or fingers. It was raining hard as a battle went on behind the mountain. There were continuous shots and explosions. Gulbehar started climbing the wet rock wall from the left side. Nobody said anything. I could not look at her and closed my eyes tightly until the danger of her falling had passed. Now it was my turn, but I was terribly afraid even looking at the rock wall. Gulbehar threw a balled-up end of Rûken's waist shawl to Nadîr. He wrapped the shawl over my chest and shoulder blades, then tied it firmly under my left armpit. He tied his own shawl under my right armpit and climbed up a few meters.

Fortunately, Nadîr was a strong man and stood in a suitable spot, so I gave my life to him. Soon I realized that no danger threatened me. They could keep me in the air. The rain knocked on my head and I even dared to look out on either side of me. The real danger no longer came from the rock wall or the heavy rain, but from the forces behind the mountain who were advancing. I reached the rock ledge and put my foot on it. The heavy rain was knocking on Gulbehar's head and the big drops were dripping over her black eyes and eyebrows onto her cheeks. She moved back so I could put my left foot on the slatted surface of the rock cleft. It was a tall but very narrow cleft, less than forty centimeters. I had to turn at the edge of the chasm and go sideways into the crevice. Gulbehar took my waist scarf while I turned. Nadîr climbed alone and got into the cleft. Then Rûken told us to bend down so that she could come forward over our shoulders. Only then did I understand that we could not sit down. Our knees were pressed against the wall when we tried to sit.

We moved back deep into the cleft. I turned my head to the right to watch the process of Rûken climbing over us. Rûken apologized as she moved along. Gulbehar opened her legs and lowered her head. Nadîr pushed me toward Gulbehar and I pushed her to Rûken. She put her left foot on Gulbehar's left shoulder, threw both her hands around Gulbehar's neck, and tried to get on Gulbehar's shoulders. Gulbehar closed her legs, stood, and helped Rûken until she rode on her shoulders. I stuck to Gulbehar as closely as I could. She crossed her left hand behind my back, put her right hand around my chest, and with both of her hands firmly grabbed the shawl above my waist. Then I did the same with Nadîr and opened my legs as much as the distance between us allowed me, in order to enable Rûken to cross over Gulbehar's shoulders onto my shoulders. Gulbehar lowered her head and Rûken glided her buttocks over Gulbehar's neck toward my right shoulder. Nadîr stuck to me until Rûken could sit over my shoulders. I closed my legs and stood up and Rûken rode on my shoulders. Then I bent my head and Rûken glided her buttocks over my neck and got ready to come down from Nadîr's shoulder. I grabbed Nadîr's shawl with all my strength, while Gulbehar held my waist. Rûken stood on Nadîr's shoulders and panic ran through my body: any movement could throw our commander into the valley. Fortunately, Nadîr was strong enough to take her off of his shoulders and put her on the ground on his lefthand side. I was still gasping. Rûken went sideways to the rock cleft, slowly poked her head out and said, "Our comrades have gotten into some unexpected trouble."

"Can you see them?" I asked.

"No, but Arjîn has reached the peak. New soldiers must have also attacked her from the right side."

I strained my ears, trying to discern something among the gunshots. But all I heard was an indefinable jumble of shots. I could read great concern on her face and didn't want to bother her with any more stupid questions. So I asked Rûken, "Heval! What happened to hevalê Satyar?"

"He is shooting near the hole. There must be someone with the Turkish soldiers who knows this area well."

"Even our hiding place?"

"I do not think so, otherwise they would have attacked us with a Cobra. They suspect we would have slipped into the hole. That may be their aim, too."

Over time the shots grew louder and louder behind the mountain. Periodically, there were also terrifying explosions. I had many questions in my head that I found inappropriate to ask in this dramatic situation. Finally, Nadîr expressed exactly what I felt.

"Mortar shells, bazookas, grenade launchers, machine guns, so many things for only two people?"

"Heval, we should help them. We cannot leave them to their fate. Either we escape or die together," Gulbehar said.

"That means suicide for all of us. Our only chance to save ourselves is this hiding place. We will all get killed if this place is exposed."

"But how can they reach us? They're besieged on all sides."

"And how can we help them if we put ourselves in grave danger? We endanger them even more if we go toward the soldiers. Here, the quantity of forces does not matter."

Rûken was silent again and said after a while, "Arjîn has noticed that we've already reached the hiding place."

"How do you know?" I asked.

"She doesn't shoot in volleys anymore. She shoots purposefully."

"Do they have a real chance to save themselves?"

"Hevala Jînçin! Nobody knows yet what the outcome of the battle will be. This morning we got out of the same danger. We can only hope that they last until it gets dark."

"And how can they climb in the darkness through this wall?"

"If it happens, we can pull them up with a shawl. The Turkish forces will believe they jumped into the gorge."

I thought that she herself hadn't believed her own theory. It was only noon. How could they fight with a couple of bandoliers of cartridges against hundreds of experienced soldiers until the evening? I did not want to make the situation even more complicated with my hopelessness. I could quickly distinguish the individual shots of their BKCs from those of the soldiers. Each of their shots illuminated a glimmer of hope in my heart. This situation went on for four hours, until we heard the Turkish soldiers' footsteps. They were coming toward us on the gorge and after a short time they went away again. I listened to their voices until they were gone. Nevertheless, we still remained silent for a long time after we couldn't hear their voices, until Rûken whispered, "Well, one of our problems is already solved."

"What did they say?" I asked her.

"They said, 'they could not have fled from here. The others must have also gone into the hole.'"

"And what do they mean by 'the others?'"

"Presumably, Satyar went down in the hole or pretended to."

"And when can we get out of here?"

"They will not leave this area for at least two days."

"What!! We have to stay in this state for at least two days?"

"Yes heval, they will not leave until they are convinced of our deaths."

My whole body began to scream and I continued furiously.

"How long can we stay here standing without food or a drop of water? It's not raining anymore."

My bladder hurts terribly. I haven't peed for eight hours. I took off my pants and underwear and laid them on my shoulder while looking at Nadîr. He had already turned his head to Rûken. Gulbehar moved back to the end of the rock cleft so I could spread my legs apart. Then came the loudest pissing noise I've ever heard. My urine went down like a rotating vortex in the crater through the crack in the floor. It took a very enjoyable minute before my bladder was emptied. I felt well again and had no concern for my comrades outside. We were in mortal danger as well.

I got dressed again and the other comrades peed too. After everyone relieved their burdens, Rûken asked me to open my shawl and I gave it to her. I opened my shawl and handed it over to her above Nadîr's head. She knotted one end of my shawl with hers and handed it to me in front of Nadîr's chest. I kept it in my hand and she began entwining and twirling both shawls around each other. Then did the same with the shawls of Nadîr and Gulbehar. Then she tied the two sets of enmeshed shawls together and turned them into a very long chain and made a circle around one end of it that could be tightened by pulling. She twisted another end around her waist and handed the rest of the shawl to Nadîr. He did the same and gave it to me and I in turn handed the rest to Gulbehar, who tied it around her waist.

Only then was I convinced that she had thought about a possible rescue operation for the comrades. If they reached the gorge in the dark, we would have been able to pull them up within a few seconds. The image of Arjîn 😊 and Satyar made me very happy, but it was getting dark and they had not turned up yet and we had heard no sign of them. The frustration and thirst became more unbearable. My mouth was dry, my legs were numb and my whole existence ached.

Rûken was constantly asking me to go to sleep, but how could I sleep in this narrow place, standing and thirsty? I fell asleep a few times with horrible thoughts and after a short while I woke up from thirst or pain, or from the loud male voices of the soldiers.

It was getting light out and the chattering of soldiers grew louder. A group of them was on the peak above us. The roar of their laughter reached us. For all of the next night we waited for them to evacuate the area. The next day, there was no saliva left in my mouth. I couldn't wet my lips and had to keep silent. The soldiers above us were laughing loudly and I saw their pee flowing down like thin waterfalls from the heights over a deep valley on Rûken's left side or in the blue river below.

Earlier in the evening, Gulbehar was stammering to Rûken about how it was better to get out of here before we died of thirst. Rûken squeezed her eyes close, slid a finger into her throat to try to get some moisture out of her salivary glands. Finally, she whispered in a muffled voice, "Only bear it until tomorrow. We will all get out of here."

We stayed there and I had constant nightmares during the night, even when I was awake, for short moments. The next morning, when I woke up, I saw a smile on Gulbehar's face. The soldiers were getting ready to leave the area. It took three hours, until the time of the horse. They were gone and during that time we massaged each other's legs. First, Rûken climbed down from the rock wall. After her, Nadîr climbed down with a shawl that he fastened around his waist, with another end of a shawl tightened under my arms. After both of them were positioned in a suitable spot, I had to get down from the wall, but they both stood in a reasonably high place and pulled me up. We pulled Gulbehar up even more easily. I was exhausted and wished to lie down on a huge stone in front of the sun and sleep, but walked slowly behind them. I looked at Rûken, who was climbing the stony mountain. Soon she called us, "Water!"

I jumped in the air and ran to her. On a big stone she had found a puddle of water. She put her index finger in the water and sucked it off. She did not taste any poison and poured a fistful of water in her mouth. She swished it in her mouth and finally swallowed it. Then she told us, "drink like me. You must not drink more than a fistful in the first round."

I did the same and waited for the others to drink a sip of water. After ten minutes I was not thirsty anymore and followed them in looking for our comrades. We went toward the hole in the ground. The end of a burnt waist shawl was tied around a stone at the hole. It was evident that poison gas had been thrown into the hole. Rûken took a handkerchief from her pocket and tied it around her mouth and nose. I also took my handkerchief and wrapped it around my face. Nadîr did the same, but he put his flashlight in his mouth under the handkerchief. He turned the flashlight on and we went into the hole. Gulbehar stayed above near the hole. We went down twenty meters into the hole and for the second time in my life I saw a corpse. I was shocked yet again, not from regret but from a sudden feeling of disenchantment with life. If I had not known what a happy and lovely man he was, and what incredible vitality shone on his ever-laughing face, I would have seen his dense beard and thought him a fanatic jihadist.

Nadîr sat next to him and took him firmly in his arms. Nobody said anything and I was the only one with hot tears flowing down my cheeks. Nadîr gave me his flashlight, put his hands under Satyar's armpits and picked him up. Rûken took his feet and brought him out of the hole. I put the lighter in my mouth, picked up his BKC, and followed them. Outside, I stared at his face and hands. They were swollen, but not because of death. He must not have been wounded and fought until his last bullet, then crawled into the hole. I went back into the hole and found his two hand grenades on the ground next to the place where he had fallen. I hung the grenades on my magazine belt and went outside again.

We looked for Arjîn and found no trace of her. At the spot where Rûken heard Arjîn's last shots, some bloodstains were visible on the stones. We split up to look for her and I was the first one to see her corpse. Her naked body had been dismembered. They had cut off her breasts and laid them beside her head. Her thighs were bloody from rape. I screamed in fright and fainted.

When I could open my eyes, her body had been covered with two scarves. Rûken didn't let Gulbehar or Nadîr see her body. I sat up and looked at Arjîn's face, her light brown curly hair, and her big amber eyes. I leaned down and kissed her cold cheeks and eyes several times. Only then did I remember that her naked body had been shot up. Rûken switched on the radio and called the comrades.

"Wow, where have you been, heval? We almost went crazy worrying about you! Are you alright?" Saro shouted with enthusiasm.

"No heval, two comrades have fallen. How are Akam and Dêrsîm?"

Saro did not answer for a few seconds, then asked in an upset voice, "Which of our heroes have fallen?"

"Arjîn and Satyar."

Hearing their names again put me into another state of shock and I broke down. But I heard, as if in sleep, that Akam and Dêrsîm were fine. I raised my hand and looked at my watch. It was six past twelve. After an hour, someone appeared on the opposite plateau, where three days ago the helicopters landed their special forces. Zinar ran to us. He sat down beside Arjîn's corpse, took her hands, lowered his head, and burst into tears. Rûken pulled the hoe and shovel out of his backpack. I helped Gulbehar and Nadîr bring her corpse down through the huge stones. Soon Zinar was helping us as a fresh force. When he saw Satyar's corpse his face wilted and I saw no trace of a smile on his face until I left Kurdistan.

CHAPTER 15

THAT EVENING, WE prepared our act of revenge. At nightfall, Saro and Rojano went on a reconnaissance mission. We planned to perform a surprise raid on a Turkish base in our vicinity. Gulbehar, Nadîr, and I slept until the next day. When I woke up, I heard Saro talking. I opened my sleeping bag, slightly lifted my head, and looked in the direction of his voice. On my right side, in a corner of the cavern, they sat under the light of a battery lamp. I turned my head to the left. There was someone sitting next to a little fire. On it was something like a pot or our black kettles on a low flame. I wanted to go to Saro and get informed about their mission, but my mental state had deteriorated and my whole body was cramped after the past three terrible days. An unbearable feeling that I was sick of life itself overwhelmed me in waves, though it made me forget the annoying tingling in my legs for a while.

I looked at my wrist. My wristwatch wasn't there. I might have lost it somewhere yesterday. I should have taken better care to protect Dêrsîm's souvenir. I lie on my back and try to sleep, but I can't. My thoughts swirl around our act of revenge. The frightening image of Arjîn stands before my eyes. If I hadn't been so dead tired last night, I wouldn't have closed my eyes. Nobody said anything about Arjîn's mutilated body, but a silence full of rage had engulfed the cavern space. I crawl out of my sleeping bag, put it in its case and go to the comrades. Rojano was leaning on the cavern wall and Saro sat opposite her. They did not notice me before I greeted them.

"Good morning, heval."

"Good afternoon, hevala Jînçin."

"What time is it?"

"It's past twelve o'clock," Rojano replied. Then she continued, "your watch is with hevala Rûnahî."

"Where did I leave it?"

"At the spring."

I look at Saro, "What did you find out during your reconnaissance? Do we have a chance to attack them?"

"After lunch we will discuss it."

"Lunch without bread?"

"Comrades are baking bread."

"Then I have to empty my belly. It is knocking furiously on my ass."

They did not laugh. I left the dark cavern in the direction of the bright toilet, until Rojano called to me.

"Heval! Wait, you cannot find it alone."

She grabs the small radio from Saro and follows me. After passing through a dark, narrow corridor, it becomes light again. There is a battery lamp and a fire for baking is burning. On a blanket, Akam is lying next to the battery lamp. A serum hangs over his head. I sit down next to him. He is unconscious and deep in sleep. A few meters to the right of him, Rûnahî and Zinar are getting ready for baking. Many dough balls are arranged in front of them. I ask Rûnahî, "How is hevalê Akam?"

"The risk of his wounds becoming infected has almost passed, but the possibility of internal inflammation is high. Last night, hevala Rûken talked ten different times with a doctor by radio. Based on the symptoms, his small intestine is not able to actively digest food due to his injuries. If it is not treated, prolonged inactive digestion can endanger his health."

"Do you think he will be treated?"

"I think so. Hevala Rûken took care of this. Tonight a sympathizer should bring us the necessary medication and also blood for infusion. As long as nothing bad happens and they provide the medicine, hevalê Akam will soon be able to eat the medicinal soup."

I wanted to ask for my watch, but the poop pressure returned. I pinch my buttocks and said, "I hope the medication arrives safely."

Like a lightless motorcycle I turned into the room on the left, which led to a large exit. Rojano ran in front of me with a flashlight on. Rûnahî called me, "Heval, your watch is with me."

"Thanks, heval. I have to go where even the prophets went. I have to push a stick of clay out of my backside."

I follow Rojano to the bright exit. In front of the exit there was a huge stone that seemed to have been the cavern door before our arrival.

Yesterday, it could not be distinguished from the rock. That huge stone, like other parts of the rock, was covered in moss and lichens, and even the rim of the stone was not obvious. Rûken climbed up the rock wall and took three crowbars from a hole. We had to use them to push the huge stone into the cavern and open the entrance. If we had been healthy and in good spirits, it would have been easy. But we had two injured comrades, four of us had been stuck in a narrow rock cleft for three days without water or food, and the other five had not eaten anything in the last three days, besides goosefoot and black salsify, out of concern for their comrade's unknown fate. It took more than an hour to open the entrance and go into the deep cavern.

Dêrsîm is keeping watch in front of the stony door. Our big radio is beside her. A rolled-up gray blanket was hanging from the roof of the cavern.

"Good afternoon, hevala Dêrsîm."

"Good afternoon, hevala Jînçin. Are you ok?"

"I am better. How is your leg?"

"It's not serious, just a flesh wound. Hevala Rûnahî removed the stone particles."

Rojano leans forward and walks out of the mouth of the cavern. I follow her. In front of the exit there is flat terrain about one meter wide and then a gorge more than thirty meters deep. To the left, the rock is not crossable, and on the right lies a narrow path only for goats and stubborn people like me. I follow Rojano over the narrow, stony goat path. I cannot understand why we have to close the cave mouth with that big stone at the end of our mission. Can bears really walk along this narrow fifty-meter-long path? Rojano jumps like a deer over the stones, maybe full of hopeful thoughts for our act of revenge. I do the same, but out of fear of another movement in my intestines leading to me shitting my pants.

Soon there was soft, flat ground under our feet. Rojano sits down under a chestnut tree, beside a canister full of water in which half a bottle is floating. With her index finger, she points to another chestnut tree less than ten meters away: the designated women's toilet. I go there, sit down under the tree, and use a stone to dig a hole, into which I can lay my shit and hide it, like a wildcat. My urge to have a bowel movement was abruptly over as soon as I sat down on the hole. My stomachache was getting worse, but I didn't have any poop pressure anymore. After four days in which I didn't go to the toilet, the feces had become hard and dry. I had to press constantly to empty my rectum. I haven't had such severe constipation for years, maybe since childhood. I press with all my strength, but the shit won't come out. It's supposedly a result of the three cans of mortadella that I ate last night before going to sleep.

When we went into the cavern, I looked for something edible before doing anything else. I ran after Rûken with a flashlight. In a big room behind the cavern there were many old, big plastic barrels full of different foodstuffs, but practically only two edible things were available: sugar and mortadella. All the vegetarians opted for sugar. I asked them with wide eyes, which were clearly visible in front of the switched-on battery lamp, "What? Sugar for dinner after three days of forced fasting? It'd be an affront to my belly." I said in amazement.

"Soon we will bake bread and get back to normal."

"No, hevala Rûken, I won't have sugar for dinner. That would be too offensive to my stomach."

I attacked the mortadella and ate three cans of it. I wanted to avoid upsetting my stomach, but I ended up fucking myself over. It tasted too good. My teeth bit into the delicious boiled sausage and my tongue loved it, but my intestines didn't take it well and now I have to push like I were birthing a stillborn. I scream in anger.

"Come out, shit!"

"What did you say? I do not understand German," Rojano asked me.

"I'm talking to my ass. This worthless feces will not come out. I wish I had money on the line like that gambling preacher."

"What?"

"Have you never heard that joke?"

"Which one?"

"A Friday preacher is playing cards. He knows it's haram to gamble, but he bets a lot of money that he can't afford to lose, thinking God is on his side. To win, he needs the dealer to drop a four on the table, but instead he drops a three, which in turn makes the preacher drop a deuce."

Rojano laughed. I laugh too and a piece of shit moves down.

"Heval, tell me a joke so that I can drop this damned feces. Otherwise, I'll have to press and moan here until evening."

"Heval, last night I wanted to tell you that you should not eat too much mortadella on an empty stomach."

"Why didn't you say that?"

"Would you have listened to me?"

"No, I do not think so. So, shall I scream or will you tell me a joke?"

"Okay, it sounds like a good thing to talk about preachers while shitting. One day, a Friday preacher decides to travel by train. After getting to the station, the first train passes beside him like a rocket. Heart pounding, he immediately takes a taxi, returns home, and sacrifices a cow to God. His wife angrily asks him, 'What is this all about?' He replies, 'God's mercy has saved us. A train flew by me, traveling in the same direction that I was. But if it had been traveling sideways, it would have killed us all!'"

Through a perfect combination of laughter and pushing, I dropped my first piece of feces into the hole. The other pieces came out easier. I filled the hole with soil and put a stone on it so that the other comrades would know that I had already mined there. I lift the bottle and wash my ass, get up, tie my trouser string with my clean fingers, and go to Rojano. She looks sad. We cannot easily free ourselves from the burden of yesterday's terrible events. She is silent. I take the half-bottle out of the canister and wash my hands and face with the soap. We go back to the cavern. Dêrsîm sits in front of the stone door. She stretches her half-leg and puts the gun on it.

"Heval, go inside. I'll keep watch," says Rojano.

"Go and have breakfast, hevala Rojano, then you can replace me."

"I've lost my appetite. I ate sugar a few minutes ago."

Dêrsîm picks up her Kalashnikov with her right hand and presses its butt into the ground, then struggles to get up using her right leg. I would like to help her get to the comrades so that she won't put pressure on her wounded leg, but she walks in front of me with the turned-on lighter in her mouth. The first loaves are already baked and their scent gets stronger with every step. I'd like to eat, but no one goes to eat, not even Tewar, who has now been replaced by Saro. I go to the comrades who just slept. Rûken is packing her sleeping bag. Gulbehar sits next to hevalê Ferhad beside the fire, and Nadîr ought to have walked out from the other side of the cavern.

"Good day, hevalno."

"Good day," they greet me back, without another word.

This grim, unpleasant atmosphere lasts until the end of our belated breakfast. Then we drink tea. I drink a very dark, sweet tea and Dêrsîm is now the only one in our group who doesn't smoke. Rûken takes a quick look at all of us and says, "Hevalên Dêrsîm and Tewar, keep watch at your previous posts. Be attentive. If the drone suddenly appears, pull down the blanket and furtively move back from the exit. Only return to your places when I tell you to. Ok, hevalno?"

"Yes, heval."

Both of them went off without complaining. We went to another side of the cavern where Akam slept. He was still unconscious beside the battery lamp. Rûnahî and Zinar were baking the remaining dough balls. Rûken asked Saro, "What do you think heval, is there a chance?

"I will explain the situation to you quite factually. At the base, more than eighty soldiers and NCOs are stationed. We will face four main problems getting into the base. In each of the four corners of the base, there is a tank equipped with thermal cameras. The thick concrete walls are also equipped with motion sensors. Behind the walls, the ground is most likely mined. So, we cannot go over the wall into the base. Apart from these obstacles, there are also two dogs. They will notice us even before we reach the surveillance coverage of the thermal cameras."

"These are not new. Such precautions are taken in almost all major bases. How can we overcome it?"

"As usual, we have to make thermal shields and approach the base in the dark. Then we wait until dawn. Right before sunrise, the thermal cameras are practically nonfunctional. During this time, the air near the ground is cold and heavy and the drones take blurry images. Then we wait until the right moment, when someone approaches the base against the wind and throws in the peppered pieces of meat. That will keep the dogs occupied for half an hour. That comrade will stay there until the guard opens the main door for the first incoming car. He will go in and kill the guard while, simultaneously, our sniper will shoot the driver, his companion, and the other guard on the watchtower. You have done much harder things than the rest. It won't be difficult.

Rûken did not interrupt him until he became silent. Then she asked me, "What do you think, hevala Jînçin?"

"In principle, it is feasible. But I think his plan is risky."

I turned my head to Saro. The battery lamp was behind him and I could not see his face.

"Heval, I see questions in this attack plan. Let me ask you something."

"By all means."

"Do the motion sensors work through infrared or high-frequency measurement?"

"By infrared."

"Do you know how far their coverage is?"

"I don't know. Does it play an important role?"

"Yes, it can play a big role. Can you explain your heat shields?"

"I did not invent it. They have been used by comrades many times. We make it with heat-insulating fabrics. Rescue forces used these fabrics during snow accidents. The rescuers cover the injured people with this fabric, so that their bodies don't get cold on the way to the hospital. This fabric doesn't let any heat escape beyond it. We will make a wooden frame and stick the fabric onto it, then hold it like a screen in front of us. Behind these screens you will stay hidden, both from the tanks and the thermal sensors."

"But we need a windy day to cope with the problems the dogs pose. On such a day it would be difficult and dangerous to walk behind such big, light umbrellas. We should wear the heat-insulating material as clothing."

"But these fabrics are very thin, hevalê Jînçin, and cannot be sewn."

"No, they can. There are a lot of thermal insulation fabrics that you can sew. These fabrics eliminate the first type of heat transfer, namely conduction. For dealing with the heat radiation effects, we can stick your thin fabric or something similar into the inner part of the clothing as lining. In our case, we will not have the problem of heat flow at all. We can just wear insulated clothing under our military gear and walk straight towards the sensors with similar caps and also swimming goggles. This solves the first problem."

"But how can we get these materials?"

"The sympathizers who bring us blood ready for infusion seem most likely to be capable of buying such materials. One can hardly distinguish them from normal fabrics."

"And what about the other problems?" Rûken asked me.

Instead of Rûken, I directed my eyes to Saro and asked him another question.

"You said that three or four soldiers should be eliminated by our snipers. Do we have silencers installed on our DShK?"

"No. You can't put a silencer or a muzzle flash suppressor on our modified guns."

"And how loud are their shots?"

"Very loud. But they will only be used by our snipers when the first group is already inside."

"But there are eighty armed soldiers positioned there too. We have to build a soundproofing tent for the sniper."

"Is that possible?" Rûken asked me with great interest.

"Yes, we can sew a sound-absorbing layer into a tent. But I have to know the sound frequency of our DShK. Can a heval tell us or send us recorded shots of the weapons?"

"I don't think it's possible. We cannot talk by radio for more than thirty consecutive seconds. We can talk on various other radio frequencies for thirty more seconds, but it is not enough to convince them of such ideas. To be honest, the whole thing sounds a bit unrealistic to me," Saro declared.

"But I think it's quite feasible. If I go to the village instead of hevalê Zinar and have internet access, I will be able to do everything. I just need to know what ranged weapons we're using. Then I can find out their sound frequency myself," I said, turning to Rûken.

"As I said, these weapons were modified and rebuilt . . . but I can help you with that. What do you say, hevala Rûken? May she go to the village?" Saro had almost changed his position.

"This is dangerous. As a blonde girl with blue eyes, hevala Jînçin will be flashier in the village than Erdoğan. Leave it. I'll ask our sympathizers if it's even possible."

"Hevala Rûnahî should also come along. We need a trustworthy and skilled tailor there... If you are not against it." I turned to Rûnahî and added.

"Why should I be against it, if it is feasible?"

Late that night a sympathizer brought the drugs we needed. He covered his whole face with a keffiyeh. First, he took out a blood bag and the necessary blood transfusion items from his backpack. Gulbehar turned on another battery light so that Rûnahî could inject the blood into Akam's veins. The sympathizer left his backpack there and went to another room in the cavern with Rûken. I could see the reflection of their lighter lamp but couldn't understand a word of their conversation. After fifteen minutes he left the cavern without exchanging a single word with us. Then Rûken came to us and told me, "Tomorrow evening he will come back and take you to the village. Your hair should be cut into a male style and dyed black. Is that okay with you?"

"Yeah, sure."

"Great. Be ready. We both have to do reconnaissance. You also have to go see that military base. Take enough water and bread with you. Most likely, we will not be able to return until tomorrow evening."

It took more than three hours to reach the base. The sky was moonless. We could see the guard on the watchtower with our night binoculars and the sentry and both dogs in front of the gate. We waited for dawn. The base was big. Apart from the tanks, there were two helicopters and several civilian and military vehicles on the base. I wanted to know from what positions and directions our snipers should fire so that I could calculate the height and size of the windows needed in the soundproof tent. Rûken lay down on her stomach, lifted her head, and brought her Kalashnikov towards the guard on the watchtower and said, "Hevalê Ferhad is supposed to shoot from this spot and altitude." She crawled to the right, pointing her rifle toward the base gate.

"Hevalê Nadîr will best be able to shoot the truck drivers in this position."

She wanted to crawl further to the right. I prevented her.

"Wait heval, let me write it down in my notebook. Do it from the beginning."

Rûken did it again and I wrote down the shot positions and the distance between the comrades. As soon as I put my notebook on the ground she told me, "Now tell me what you want to do."

"Heval, now I know where to put the panes of glass in the tent. We have to place three sets of double-sealed, soundproofed windows in the tent at specified points. In the center of each pane of glass will be a small round hole through which the comrades can shoot."

"And you think your tent can block the sound of three Zagros rifle shots? They pop off incredibly loudly."

"Why not? We cover the inner layer of the tent with an air cushion and fill it with suitable sound-absorbing gas. Also do the same with the two-layer glass panes. This location is two kilometers from the base. They won't hear the shots."

"Do not you think that our sympathizers will endanger themselves if they look for the materials needed for your plan?"

"No heval, the fabrics can be bought at hardware stores. The other things can be found at glass stores or aquarium retailers. Don't worry, I will take all the necessary precautions."

"Thanks, hevala Jîncin. Now we have to eat something. Soon her routine life will begin."

Rûken looked at the watchtower with her binoculars and said, "Go behind that big rock."

I bent down and went behind the rock. From there one could keep an eye on the base without being observed. Rûken came and sat down beside me, opened her backpack, took out a loaf of bread and a bottle, and put it on a small stone in front of her. I did the same, but I put the bread on my notebook and ate it with a big appetite. Rûken kept looking at the base with binoculars. After a while, she gave them to me. Another soldier was on the watchtower and the previous guard had been replaced. I wrote the time of the guards shifting in my notebook.

"We should also find out at what time the next guards at the gate and on the watchtower will be replaced."

Before the drone could be heard, we were already in a safe place, under the rock face in a narrow cave. We stayed there all day, observing the base with sharp binoculars. While I was busy drawing into my notebook the various parts of the base, armory, command office, dining space, dormitories of the soldiers and officers, gas tanks, etc, Rûken was writing down the soldiers' traffic patterns. Before twilight, she had written several pages. We returned to the cavern under the umbrella. Tewar informed us that the sympathizer had already arrived. He was standing beside Saro in our foodstuff depot with his head covered. Rûken asked him, "Have you been waiting for us for a long time?"

"More than an hour."

"You have to wait another hour. Is that ok?"

"No, heval. It would be too risky for our comrade to wait for us in the car any longer."

"But you yourself said that her hair should be cut and dyed."

"Forget that, hevala Rûken. We can host them at Mîrza's home. Do you agree?"

"Have you talked to him?"

"No, but I can call him on the way."

"And what will you do if he doesn't answer the phone?"

"That wouldn't be a problem. We three can open the door. It's cold out; if hevala Jîncin washes her hair, she will catch a cold. What do you say?"

The sympathizer had a hoarse, masculine voice. He must have been over forty. Rûken was silent for a while and then said, "Ok, you know the situation better."

He turned his covered head towards me, "Heval, are you hungry or can you endure two more hours?"

"We can leave right now."

Saro gave me a slip of paper that contained the list of necessary things to buy for our operation. I put it into one of my zippered vest pockets. The sympathizer grabbed his umbrella from the cavern wall. Rûnahî had two more in her hand. I took one of them and followed her toward the cavern's small exit. The sympathizer drew a cell phone out of his pocket and sent a message to someone. Probably the driver who should no longer wait for us. He pulled up the hanging blanket door and crawled through the exit. I heard the whirring drone. He opened his umbrella before leaving the hole. Rûnahî and I did the same.

It was cold and I was glad that I did not have to go outside with wet hair. The sky above us was no longer dark blue. So, we had to be surrounded by the villages and residential areas. Our anonymous, masked comrade was walking quickly ahead and Rûnahî was bounding behind him. I had to walk faster not to lose them. I had an umbrella over my head and listened to the surrounding areas. There were no sounds except the buzzing drone and the pounding footsteps of the comrades. The man was walking so fast that we almost had to run. For two hours we ran after him, but he never turned his head. Suddenly I just couldn't run anymore. I almost even dropped my umbrella. I softly called to Rûnahî.

"Heval, do you have water with you?" The man also heard, came back to me, and said, "Heval, if you can keep running another five minutes, we'll take a break."

He stretched out his long left hand and helped me to get up. He slowed his pace and I followed right after him. The roar of a river could be heard growing louder and louder. For the first time, the sympathizer turned to us and pointed his hand to a place to the left, deep in the darkness. He made a detour and we climbed about twenty meters until we reached a giant stone. With his free hand he took night binoculars out of his jacket pocket and watched the surroundings, then asked Rûnahî if she had water. She carefully put down her backpack with her left hand so that her entire body remained under the umbrella. Then she pulled a bottle of water out and handed it to me. I sat down on the ground and drank a few sips under my umbrella. The man was talking on his cell phone, "I'm fine, thank you, and you?"

" . . . "

"I need your help. Can you lend me thirty thousand lira?"

" . . . "

"In an hour I will knock on the door."

I asked our sympathizer, "So, we have another hour to walk?"

"In less than ten minutes we will reach the place."

That was the best news I could hear. But what did he mean by an hour? What kind of funny secret language was he speaking? Soon it became clear to me. After ten minutes we had reached the place, but we had to crawl along a dark, narrow cave path for over four hundred meters to reach the door. The cave exit was about ten meters high on the rock wall, sufficiently large to pass through and small enough not to be conspicuous. Everyone crawled into the hole and closed their umbrella behind them.

Without that fucking thing over my head, I actually enjoyed crawling through the cave with the lighter in my mouth. The sympathizer crawled slowly and calmly. I followed him without any stress, watching the narrow passage until there was a strong smell of manure and a bright light that appeared at the end of the passage. There was a big and luminous room in front of us.

Our pathfinder got up and went to the light. After a while I could get up, too. Mîrza was waiting for us. He held a battery lamp up in his left hand. Our pathfinder walked up to him. They greeted each other with a nod. Mîrza made the same gesture to me and, as a sign of respect, put his right hand over his chest, without letting his blue shirt become dungy. I bowed my head amicably and put my hand on my heart. He handed me the battery lamp. I took it and followed them. With every step, Mîrza left dungy footsteps on the floor of the room, which was no longer the same cave, but was perhaps a manmade one. At the end of the hallway there was a very thick wooden door. Behind the door was a large stable, where many sheep and goats were sleeping. I walked over the dung with a feeling somewhere between fear and disgust. I suddenly thought of Rûnahî and wanted to know how she was reacting to the dungy ground in the stinky room. I turned the battery lamp over my head so I could watch her well. She strode beside me and the sheep. The two men stayed near the gate and tried to shut the door. Even though I knew shutting that heavy door was difficult work, the idea of helping them disgusted me. The door had no handle and was dungy as everything else. Mîrza wiped the edges of the door with his dirty hand and only then spoke to our guide.

"Can this heval speak Kurdish?"

"Yes, she speaks fluently."

Mîrza turned his eyes to me and said, "Heval, can you hold up the lamp to let me see the crack in the door?"

"Yes, of course."

I lifted the battery lamp and he took a metal wire from a hole in the wall and put it in the crack of the door. Then he sat down and did the same with the crack on the bottom side. Then the two pulled the gate towards them and closed it. The filthy door could hardly be distinguished from other parts of the wall. Nevertheless, he leaned down, grabbed a handful of dung off the ground, and covered the top of the door with it. He bent down a few more times and cloaked the door with dung so perfectly that it was no longer distinguishable from the stable walls. They both went toward the exit of the stable and I followed them for almost twenty meters. The stable was seven meters wide, but they walked very carefully to avoid treading on the farm animals. By now it was nearly dawn. In the yard, the housewife was waiting for us. Her body and clothes were clean. She greeted and hugged me.

"Welcome, heval."

"Thank you very much. We woke you up too early."

"Wow, you speak Kurdish better than the Kurds."

"I'm already one," I said that, and only then did I remember that I should introduce myself as an Englishwoman.

"Are you a Kurd?"

"No, but I love the Kurds."

She hugged me again and said, "My name is Hinar."

"I'm Jiyan."

Rûnahî walks past a huge, calm Kangal dog and points her finger at what must be a cleaning spot. There are two clean slippers in front of the door. I take off my shoes and put on a pair. Behind the door there is a medium-sized room with a sink, and two more doors facing each other. One door is half-open and a shower is visible. I turn on the sink faucet and feel a shock. A sudden aching feeling grips me. For the past seven months, I have always put my hands in the well or in the springs, streams, and rivers that have been flowing for millions of years. Soon, I must leave this floating world.

Rûnahî goes to the bathroom. I put the battery lamp on the sink and wash its handle with soap. Then I also wash my hands, feet, and socks and hang them on a drying rack next to the heater. Rûnahî comes out of the toilet and I go inside. The toilet bowl and whole of the floor are carved from a yellow stone.

The ewer is already full, but I turn on the tap. The water flows from its pipe until I get up and open the toilet door. Hinar was waiting for us in the yard. She led us to a staircase on the right. We climb the stairs and soon find ourselves in a large hall. Several yellow and black floral awning mattresses frame the bare, smooth concrete floor on all sides, except in the window area where a television sits on a television cabinet. Hinar takes out a napery from the cupboard and spreads it on the concrete floor. I ask her, "Heval, can we take a bath first?"

"Yes, heval. But please do not come out of the bathroom before I call you. Our shepherd can emerge at any time to graze the cattle herd. Go quickly to the bathroom. I will bring you clean clothes."

"No need. We already have clean clothes with us."

Rûnahî took her backpack off from her back, opened it, and pulled out two pistols. She checked whether they were secured and then handed me one of them. I put it in my pocket, took out the plastic bag with my

---

* Pomegranates.

clean clothes, left the hall, and went down the stairs to the bathroom. The bathroom was modest, but high enough. The floor, walls and ceiling were lined with cement and about three square meters in size. Hinar switched on the lamp and Rûnahî noticed our washed shoes immediately. Before Hinar closed the door, Rûnahî called her, "Hevala Hinar, please never do that again. We must not leave our personal work to anyone else. This is strictly prohibited."

"I know, heval. Don't worry about it. Take a rest for a few days. We know how difficult life is in the mountains."

She closed the door. The lightbulb shone brightly under the ceiling. There was a floor drain under the door. Several nails had been pounded into the wall. I hung the plastic bag for my clean clothes from a nail. Then I undressed and hung my dirty clothes on some other nails. There was an upturned plastic tub under the shower, in which there was some shampoo and two bars of soap. I picked up the soaps and smelled them. The green one smelled like cucumber and the yellow one . . . I said loudly, "Lemon."

Rûnahî smiled at me. "Cucumber or lemon. Which do you want?" I asked her.

"Lemon."

"You have to think carefully. Lemon or cucumber?"

"Ok, cucumber."

"You may also use mine."

"Thanks for your generosity."

Rûnahî hung her clothing bag on a nail with a smile, put the shampoo beside the tub, and poured warm water into it. She added shampoo to the warm water, put her right hand in, and swirled it around until the shampoo had completely dissolved and turned to foam. A strawberry fragrance engulfed the bathroom. She took off her clothing pieces one by one and put them in the tub for soaking. I was standing by, watching her. She finally said, "Heval, take a bath until I've washed my clothes, then you have to wash your clothes, otherwise Hinar will wash them."

I turned on the faucet, checked the water temperature, pulled the lever up, and went under the shower. I washed myself twice with soap, but Rûnahî was still washing her clothes. She brought each piece of her clothing up to her eyes and one by one looked for any stains or dirt. My nose was filled with the scent of lemons and strawberries. I leaned over and picked up a shampoo that smelled like narcissus and washed my hair.

By then, she had finished washing her clothes. Now it was my turn to wash my clothes, but it raised a new problem. Where should she lay or hang her washed clothes? I was supposed to wash my clothes in the tub, we were not allowed to leave the bathroom, and the walls did not seem to be clean enough for her. I looked at her and she noticed that I had finished my shower and was waiting for her. Finally, I pulled my clean clothes out of the bag, hung them on the nails, handed her the plastic bag and said, "Heval! You can wash this bag and put your clothes in it."

Rûnahî's eyes lit up with joy, as if her dreams had come true. She took my bag, went to the shower half-crouching, and vigorously washed it with the soap. After, she put her washed clothes in it. Only then was she content to hang the bag on a nail and start washing herself. I poured shampoo into the tub and let the warm water flow in it, laying my clothes into the tub all at once and kneading them leisurely with my left foot. At the same time I looked at Rûnahî bathing. She washed herself carefully and went over her whole body with a washcloth. One hand washes the other. No spot was neglected. She pulled her feet out of her bathing footwear a million times, rigorously rubbing any discolorations or spots she found from her feet to her scalp. She cleaned most intensely between her toes and behind her ears. She was still busy with her self-polishing when we heard the front door slam open. I heard the shepherd's voice and then the cattle herd. When it was quiet again, Hinar knocked on the door and called us. I was already dressed and went to the door, but Rûnahî stayed there, presumably to wash the bathroom. I went out of the bathroom and asked Hinar where I could hang my clothes.

"I'll do that, hevala Jiyan. Go upstairs. It's late."

I went into the yard and then upstairs. As soon as I reached the hall, a fourteen-year-old girl ran up to me. She hugged me tightly and kissed my cheeks several times. I hugged her back and kissed her soft, round cheeks. When she finally went back, I could see her big, fox-like eyes.

"Welcome, hevala Jiyan."

"Thank you, darling. What is your name?"

"Şevîn.* Please sit down there."

She gestured with her hand to the furthest part of the hall on the left where the tablecloth was spread on the floor. The thin flatbreads on the

---

* Created from the night.

plastic sheet caught my eye. Next to them lay many bowls full of yogurt, cheese, olives, thick grape juice, and quince marmalade. Opposite me was a samovar on a small, low table positioned against the wall. Atop it stood a white porcelain teapot. A big red rose was imprinted on the teapot, recognizable even from eight meters away.

"Do you drink tea before breakfast?" Şevîn asked.

"I am waiting for hevala Rûnahî, but you can have breakfast."

"I already had breakfast. I have to leave soon. The minibus will leave in twenty minutes. What should I bring you from the city?"

"What?! You're going to town for my sake?"

"No heval, I go to the city every day except Friday."

"Why? Is there no school here in the village?"

"Only an elementary school. For high school, the children have to go into town."

"But the nearest town is forty kilometers away from the village."

"Yes heval, every day we have to travel eighty-six kilometers, round trip."

"Isn't it hard?"

"Very much so, heval. But maybe it's better that way. We can bring in everything the comrades need from the city."

"That's risky, though. The party should not be endangering children."

"No, hevala Jiyan, not every youth does this. The bus driver is my uncle. He has a good relationship with the soldiers. He also brings forbidden things to them."

"What prohibited things?"

"I only know about whiskey, but they also secretly take cigarettes from people. Don't worry, hevala Jiyan. They don't suspect us. What should I bring you? My dad talked about a list."

"Yeah, right. Do you know where my backpack is?"

"It's supposed to be in my parents' room."

Şevîn got up, went to the samovar, and then to the left toward a wooden door that was next to the metal door of the staircase. She knocked on the door softly and Mîrza let her in. Soon after, both of them came out of the room. My backpack was in Mîrza's hand. He smiled at me drowsily. Şevîn sat down cross legged next to me. Mîrza handed me the backpack and sat on his side over the cushion to look at us directly. I opened my backpack, pulled out my wallet, took out the requirements list, and read it to myself. Then I pulled out my notebook and a pen from my pocket and said to Mîrza, "Heval, unfortunately you have to go into town tomorrow, too. Will it make you look suspicious?"

"No heval, that's ok. Sometimes I drive to town several times a day."

I turned to my right and handed the notebook and pen to Şevîn.

"Hevala Şevîn, we need a cheap, used laptop. It does not matter if its CD player and keyboard are broken. Only the USB connection and internet access must be operational."

"I have a laptop. It works well."

"We cannot use it. You have to buy a used laptop from a small shop that isn't monitored by a CCTV system. You just have to check if you can download something from the internet and transfer it to the USB. Tell the shopkeeper that you only want to download movies with the laptop. Then buy an anonymous SIM card with fifteen gigabytes of internet and let the seller activate the SIM card. Then, in another store, buy a new laptop and a memory stick. I'll write for you the required brands. I will disassemble the used things tonight, then you will have to throw them away tomorrow morning. I'll tell you how and where. That's all you have to buy for me. The list from hevalê Saro is with your father. You or other people can buy his requirements. Did you catch all of that?"

"Yes, heval."

I tore off a sheet of paper, wrote the required brands on it, and handed it to Şevîn.

"Hevala Şevîn, can you read my handwriting?"

She read the list while humming and said, "Yes."

"Then add them to your list with your handwriting."

While Şevîn was writing down the list, I pulled out three five-hundred euro notes from my wallet and handed them to Mîrza.

"What's this?" He asked me, eyes wide with wonder.

"The money for buying these things. For my and hevalê Saro's equipment."

"I cannot accept."

"Why not?"

"Does my family really look that poor?"

"I didn't mean it like that. You're endangering your life and this work is incredibly valuable and important. Please do not misunderstand me. I want to pay for this action myself."

"Heval, that's an insult to us. I don't want Hinar and my mother to hear about your suggestion."

"Heval, if you knew why I've made this decision, you would understand me."

"We do not understand such things and Şevîn will also be silent about this."

"Heval please, Şevîn has to go to school soon. I do not want to discuss this anymore."

"Then take your money back. The party gave my friend some very different orders."

"This is not the party's business. It's my personal decision."

"We do not follow personal decisions."

I was turning red with anger and shouted, "Personal decision was the wrong expression. It's my personal wish." Then, like a little child, I broke into tears. Mîrza looked at me with his mouth agape. I remained silent until I was able to control myself again. Then I added, "I am prepared to give my life for this action. I do not want to take a risk. Everything has to run smoothly. No matter what it costs."

Şevîn took the money from me and gave it to her father. He looked me in the eyes and said, "Pardon me heval, I didn't mean to offend you. What will hevala Rûken say about it?"

"She understands the situation."

Mîrza put the money in his shirt pocket, got up, and went back into the room. Şevîn shook my hand with a smile, shuffled on her knees towards the samovar, and picked up an orange school bag. She got up and went to the staircase. She looked at her wristwatch, turned around, and said, "Today my father will pick me up from school earlier. We'll get back before it gets dark. The stuff on hevalê Saro's list will be easy to find. See you in the evening."

"See you."

She goes down the staircase and soon the sound of her steps fades away. I stare at the tablecloth. The loaves of bread are completely round. I lift a loaf of bread. It is as thin as cigarette paper and forty centimeters in diameter. The first time I ever ate this kind of flatbread was in Qeza Şêxan. I liked its taste very much. My mother tried to learn how to bake this kind of bread to make my father happy. Over the two weeks of our accommodations there, she could not learn this seemingly simple job.

We took all the necessary things for baking the bread, such as a rolling pin, wooden board, and even speciality equipment for the dough back to Germany. Not only my mother, but even my aunt and her staff could not bake a single flatbread with it, neither round nor square in shape. Something always went wrong. Sometimes the dough was torn when stretched, sometimes it rolled or stuck to other surfaces. And when a stretched, free-form dough didn't stick while preparing it, it would stick to the heated tandoor oven and burn. My aunt even bought a potholder and a flat pan at the flea market, but to no avail. After three weeks of trying, everyone was disappointed, and the cooking tools were moved into the basement. Only after the death of my father did I find these baking utensils again. They had been stored away well in a thick, blue plastic bag. For me, the baking experiments were just a gimmick, but for the others it was a way of fulfilling my father's wishes.

Now I can understand how much they adored my father. Xemo had a small circle of friends, but in this circle he was very popular and they were always trying to fulfill his slightest wish. The term "desire" now has a tremendous impact on me. The action of avenging Arjîn's terrifying death is currently my only desire. I was never a vindictive person. I didn't try to take revenge for the bad behavior of others; I would just break all ties with the hated person. But wasn't that an even more brutal form of revenge? My aunt didn't do anything to me, but I threw her out of my life forever.

When I saw her cold corpse on the mortuary bed, I realized how important she was to me, but it was only after a month that I understood how she loved me, when my father told me that, three years prior, she had transferred all of her property to me. For two years I avoided seeing her, but she never regretted or tried to correct her mistake. She is said to have made a request of me on her deathbed, that I should not sell the cafe-bakery until all of the employees had retired. It ruined me. I was ashamed to enter the bakery or her house. My father oversaw the cafe-bakery. It wasn't a complicated job. Those four women were like family and were very reliable. They were honest and responsible for their work. They themselves would continue on with their work better than ever.

I visited them a year ago. It gave them more joy than seeing the sun in one's darkest hour. They saw my aunt in me. I did not tell them that I had found the baking utensils and someone who could bake the round, thin flatbread. But I promised them that I would visit them more often after I had come back from Kurdistan. Now I have the opportunity to learn this kind of bread making. Hinar or her mother-in-law would certainly teach me. I can record a video of them preparing the dough and baking it and ask them to send it to me later. I will surprise my aunt's staff even more grandly by baking flatbread that tastes and smells like the kind that my father always wished for.

Why has it all become like a dream? Why did my aunt transfer her shop to me? She was not even fifty and was still perfectly healthy. Perhaps she was afraid that if the bakery were left to my mother, she would have sold it and fired her employees. My mother certainly would have sold it. But I could have done the same.

I never thought about selling the cafe-bakery or her big house, because I couldn't have done anything with the money besides buying the same kind of property. And the property I already had was full of memories. My aunt was my first music teacher. Those romantic melodies from her flute, like many of the things she said to me over the years, are deeply rooted in my being. You have so much money that you can spend. Hinar shouted for the third time, "Daye Xecê!"

* Daye: Grandmother. Xecê: Khadijeh, an Arabic name; the name of prophet Muhammad's first wife.

CHAPTER 16

THE VILLAGE HAS approximately nine hundred inhabitants. A large part of the village can be seen from the women's room where Rûnahî and I slept. The houses are mainly made of stone with flat roofs. The front doors and windows display a wide range of colors. The colorful curtains are mostly floral. Downstream, the green cemetery of the village can be seen and on the other side of the large river there are wide fields of vegetables and cotton. Mîrza's house is high above the other houses in the village. From here I mostly see old men going to the mosque several times a day, immediately after the call to prayer, and performing the ritual washing for prayer in the small pool in the courtyard. In this house, only Daye Xecê prays. However, she does not hurry to pray and only stands for prayer when she has done her tasks, even when the prayer time has already passed. Apparently, she is reluctant to pray in the direction of the government's military base. We cannot see that base from the window of the women's room. It is located on the highest hill in the village and is clearly visible from Daye Xecê's room, which is between ours and the hall. Daye Xecê and Şevîn sleep in that room.

We feel at home here. We are even allowed to enter the couple's room and its door is always open during the day. I can sit in there behind the green and red-flowered curtains and use binoculars to look at the big city far away.

Although my goal is to write a realistic novel, for security reasons I will not reveal the names of the city and village. I even changed the physical characteristics of some people, but I don't want to ignore the name of Daye Xecê or Şevîn's fox-like eyes. So everything remains realistic, but a different kind of realism that one can call Kurdish. I never ever want to draw the attention of the Turkish secret service to this family.

All the villagers call Daye Xecê by this name, even the elders. Her snow-white hair comes out under her dark green headscarf and spreads over her face and shoulders. It reminded me of Daye Amîn, my father's grandma, whom I never saw. My father often went silent when I asked about her. He always told me that she was very generous and lovely, especially with children. Her bags would always be full of sour-sweet candies and her hands were famous for how generously they handed them out. Presumably, this generosity is one of the personal characteristics possessed by those who are crowned as "Daye." Behind the curtains, I see the children run cheering toward Daye Xecê.

Şevîn's fox eyes are also a unique sign for me. They do not reflect deceit, but the sense of responsibility of those young people who have outgrown themselves. Şevîn is like a young woman when she deliberately puts her life in danger and turns into a teenager when she smiles at those dangers with her tongue sticking out. It's as if she were trying to make a balance between her adult social responsibilities and her adolescent life. Before I had thought of it, Rûnahî mentioned the similarities between Şevîn and Arjîn. She must have meant their smiles, otherwise there was no real similarity between them. Şevîn has a medium-sized and stout body, and her hair is black and smooth. Her round face also looks very different from Arjîn's triangle-shaped face.

Şevîn brings us everything we need from the city. This goes against all conceptions of children's rights and has always been my red line. I hold the opinion that children should not be used for our own interests and should never be drawn into the fierce world of adults. When I found out that she had been asked at the checkpoint why she had two laptops with her, I wanted to prevent her from putting herself in even more danger. But she looked at me like a sensible woman and said, "Heval, nobody forced me to do this. I do this of my own free will."

"Why would you do that?"

"I want to take revenge on the Turks."

"Why though? What have they done to you?"

"Heval, why are you asking me? You also fight the Turks yourself."

"No, I'm not fighting the Turks. I'm fighting against fascism."

"But the Turks are fascists."

"Hevala Şevîn, you can't say that. Not all Turks are fascists."

"I don't know. I've only ever seen fascist ones."

"Where?"

"Here in the village, in the city, at school. Everywhere, only the fascists are in charge. They tease our Kurdish accents. They insult all the mothers and even grandmothers who attend school with Kurdish clothing on. They are not ashamed of harassing women with white hair. We are punished if we speak Kurdish with each other."

"Really? I thought those kinds of outrageous rules were over."

"Furthermore, not only mayors and members of parliament, but also many teachers have been getting fired. After the attempted coup, the situation got even worse. I don't want to go to town for school. Why should I have to go to the city every day? In the Turkish regions, nobody travels eighty kilometers to school by minibus. In winter, we shivered from the cold in the minibus all day. The Turks have no budget to build schools in Kurdish regions, but there is always money for bombs and military bases. The Turks even killed my aunt."

I turned my head to Hinar and asked her, "I didn't know your sister was murdered. Who killed her?"

"The doctors," Şevîn answered me and continued, "they kept her waiting until she died, because of her Kurdish clothing. In the twenty-first century, nobody dies from appendicitis. Even one of the doctors said it."

I turned my head toward Hinar to ask her a question, but she was crying. Şevîn was already aware of the danger of her activities, like many other children in Kurdistan. Like Rojano, who has carried heavy loads on her back like a man since childhood. In her youth, perhaps she also stuck her tongue out in response to questions that were inappropriate for her age.

We let Şevîn continue her activities. She cheered up again and filled the whole home with her loud laughter. She even tried to help us sew the sound-absorbing tent and the heat-insulating clothing, but, like me, she did not have suitable skills for that kind of work. Hinar was a master at sewing and cutting. Şevîn had to go to school, as before, and I was assigned another job that I was happy to do. I had to take care of the family son, a cute three-year-old boy who never cried, but was hyperactive instead. As soon as I got the opportunity to explain to Hinar and Rûnahî what they had to do, he would reappear in the women's room and pull me into the yard to play.

He made me run after the chicks umpteen times. I caught one. The chick chirped in my hand, his cackling mother forcefully expressing her desire to get her chick back. Arkan* wanted the same chick, as well. I followed the son, but he couldn't hold the chick and soon it escaped from his tiny hands. It is not easy to catch duck or turkey chicks. Their mothers cluck up a storm until you give back their young. In the beginning, they even attacked me with their beaks and claws. Over time, I managed to convince the poultry of my harmless deeds. But Arkan wasn't fed up yet with playing. For the first couple of days I waited for the necessary goods to arrive and Hinar took care of Arkan. I just played with him on the side and enjoyed it. But on the third day I had to deal with that frolic-bomb alone.

I always had to get the kids and lambs out of the stable so that he could play with them. This job gave me an opportunity to recall an important part of my childhood. Under the pretext of amusing Arkan and keeping him from distracting his mother, I could bleat like lambs and kids, or imitate the donkey's hee-haw with a human accent, which excited Arkan the most.

I felt like I was eight years old and taught Arkan what sounds the animals make in Kurdish. I was deep into my game when Daye Xecê caught me. When I raised my head, I saw Daye Xecê standing there. She was spinning her drop spindle. With her right hand she held up the wool tow and with the two fingers of her other hand she hit the shaft. The drop spindle was spinning without swinging. Daye Xecê looked at me as her left-hand fingertips automatically pulled out the right amount of wool and bound it to the knob and leader string.

"Heval, you are a Kurd," she said in a friendly voice.

"Daye Xecê, I grew up in a village. That's why I learned these terms."

Daye Xecê's eyes were staring at me. She raised the wool tow in her right hand even higher and turned the spindle shaft with three fingers of her left hand. The string was towing when she raised her hand, the spindle was hanging from the ball of string, and she said to me, smiling, "Maybe heval, but you're a Kurd."

She opened the twisted thread from the spindle handle and continued to twist it around the headstock and went to the front gate, opened it,

* Source of fire.

left the yard, and closed the gate behind her. In addition to her routine duties, Daye Xecê kept watch over us, too. Opposite the house, a few meters from their manure storage space, beside a broken wall from where she could watch the two sides of the alley, she sat with other old women. If she suspected that someone wanted to approach their house, she would quickly ring the bell at the gate, so that I would have enough time to return to the women's room. We had prepared for an even worse scenario. All she had to do was press the green button on a simple mobile phone. Then Rûnahî and Hinar would have to take any suspicious stuff downstairs. We would quickly open the secret stable door and stay behind there until one of the family members called us.

Fortunately, nothing worse happened during our stay. They received guests a few times, but I had enough time to leave Arkan alone in the yard and hide in the women's room beside Rûnahî until the guests left. It wasn't suspicious that Arkan called out "dada"[*] behind me for a long time.

The first day of childcare was a lot of fun, but it took a lot of strength out of me. The second day, he exhausted me. When the cattle came back from the pasture, I was unable to milk a sheep or goat like on the first day or to watch the milking, like on the third day. Unlike me, Rûnahî was fine and helped Daye Xecê and Hinar with all of the cleaning activities. Apart from milking the sheep and three cows, the family had to take care of more than a hundred sheep and goats. There was a lot of daily work that had to be done. The stable had to be mucked out constantly, the collected manure put into the wicker baskets and taken out of the house, but not to be thrown away or simply stored. The manure is formed into manure discs by hand and placed in the sun. After this, the dung slices would not stink and would soon be used as dried fuel in the oven and would even be enough to warm you under your bedside table in the baking room in winter.

I am not disgusted by the manure and dung anymore. It is certainly not more disgusting or dirty than the human feces that I have to clean from my ass every day. If I had been allowed to go outside, I would have slung Hinar's plastic veil on my shoulder and carried the dung bin filled with baking ash or the wicker basket filled with stable dung on my

---

[*] Salutation to an older sister.

back. *We humans eat delicious dishes, but our feces smell stinkier than many animals' feces. Some bird droppings even smell good.*

Hinar washed her hands and veils with dish soap at the courtyard faucet right after the manure work, which reassured Rûnahî. She helped the family with the milking, but she cleaned the udders of the cow that she had declared herself responsible for with soap, which surprised no one. After all, hevala Rûnahî was in charge of hygiene in the party, and for the past two years not a single guerrilla under her command had caught a cold. She cut and sewed all the time and cleaned at every opportunity. But she did it diplomatically and thus didn't appear to be addicted to cleaning.

"Sorry, comrades, that we've turned your house upside down," she'd say, grabbing the broom and the cleaning cloths. She sometimes blamed me for the mess that existed, which didn't bother me at all. Even as a child I was a destroyer of order. It always looked like a pigsty around me. I snooped in the wardrobe and ripped apart my dad and aunt's clothing. First my father, then my aunt and her employees, called me "dynamite," "toy bomb," or "water strider" when I got on their nerves. Only now did Arkan make it clear to me how difficult it is to deal with a hyperactive child. My mother must have been happy to put me in the arms of other people after I had disregarded all of her warnings. There were five people in the cafe-bakery, six including my father, but my hyperactivity took several years to calm down with music and then physics.

Little Arkan tired me out in just four days. I could hardly stand on my feet, but I felt good in my heart and went to the women's room laughing. The job seemed to be done. The heat-insulating clothes were sewn and the soundproofing tent was finished. I filled the tent with the air pump. It formed into its intended shape in five minutes. Three small glass panes with round, tight holes for shooting were on the lower part of the tent. The tent's air cushion also seemed safe and airtight. I measured the pressure with an air pressure gauge, closed the valve cap, and waited for an air leak within the following few hours. Then I checked the thermal insulation levels of all the clothes with a thermal sensor. They didn't let any heat out. I would have liked to have slept without dinner, but first I had to be sure that the air cushion was tight. Tomorrow, the bus driver is supposed to bring us the sound-absorbing gas in a fire extinguisher capsule from the city. If everything goes as planned, we can return to our comrades tomorrow evening.

On my knees, I shuffle to the bed blankets, which were wrapped in a sheet, and open it. Everything was like twenty-nine years ago in Qeza Şêxan. The bed sheet was made of wool and possessed a design of black-and-white stripes. The mattress intended for me is covered with a linen fabric and covered with another satin fabric that is printed with colorful songbirds. The checkered quilts are even more colorful, made of seven-thread *cacim*,[*] with each line displaying a different color. Mine is covered with a purple mohair on one side. Even the pillows are covered with painted cotton fabrics. Mine with a partridge and its chickens and Rûnahî's with butterflies. I looked at the bedding for a long time and, as in my childhood, was amazed by so many colors, shapes, and pictures. Şevîn was laughing loudly in the hall and the whole house smelled like I was eight years old in Qeza Şêxan. I make my bed and go into the hall. Daye Xecê and Mîrza are watching a music show on one of the PKK channels. Şevîn sits next to the television cutting Arkan's nails. Everyone wanted to get up when I entered. I ran to Daye Xecê to prevent her. Arkan is faster and grabs my legs. I almost fell over.

"Come back, you water strider!" Şevîn called him and everyone burst out laughing.

"That name really suits him. Heval, where did you get this name from?" Mîrza asked me.

"As a child I was crowned with a dozen such names. My father once said that one girl like me is too few for a city and two girls like me is too much."[†]

"Yes, Kurdish is your father language."

"Yes, Daye Xecê. My father was a Kurd. I didn't want to conceal it from you. But you know the party regulations," I justified my previous contradictory statements.

"You should have said you were a Kurd. Nobody would have believed that."

"That wasn't my decision," I said to Daye Xecê.

---

[*] Cacim, also spelled jajim, is a type of colorful sleeping quilt used in Kurdistan.
[†] A Kurdish proverb.

I lifted Arkan up and hugged him tightly. I would have loved to kiss or even pinch his bright red cheeks, but he was ticklish and moved like a vibrating cell phone on a glass table. I had only two options, either to let him stand on the floor or to lift him onto my shoulders, where he liked to sit for hours. He made his own decision and climbed up me like a flagpole. I helped him. When he got to the top, I twirled around and he giggled with enthusiasm. Suddenly, I saw the fire extinguisher next to the samovar. I immediately put Arkan down on the floor, went to the cylinder, took it away from samovar and said, "Hevalê Mîrza, this gas is flammable. How long has the bottle been there?"

"That heval brought it here recently."

"Then we can leave soon. Maybe tonight."

"We must first discuss your return plan with hevala Rûken," replied Mîrza.

"Heval, mountains don't run away. Stay here for a few days. You were just working over the last few days. Take a rest," suggested Daye Xecê.

"Heval, Daye Xecê will bake bread tomorrow," Şevîn stated enticingly.

"Will you bake flatbread?" I asked enthusiastically.

"Yes heval, but I don't know why you'd want to film an old bag like me."

"Daye Xecê, I want to remember you forever."

"Forever? Well, I've already got one foot in the grave."

"Don't say that, Daye Xecê. You will bake delicious bread for your great-grandchildren."

"Heval, not just bread. No one in the village bakes more delicious walnut bread than Daye Xecê."

If Jarik were here, he would certainly have gone further than Şevîn and said, "In the entire Milky Way." I curled up laughing. Şevîn looked at me with a puzzled expression.

"Daye Xecê, bake walnut bread tomorrow. You have to wear gloves."

"So that I don't bite my fingers while eating?"

"Hevala Jiyan! Why do you know everything? You're not a Kurd after all."

Before I can say anything, Rûnahî enters the hall with a large and round tray full of plates, glasses, and cutlery. Şevîn gets up and walks towards the stairway. I turn toward the TV cabinet and take a dining tablecloth out of the drawer. It is painted like a motley bird. Except for the floor and ceiling, everything in this house is colorful. Four yellow-colored, energy-saving lamps hang out from the white ceiling. I cover the gray floor with the colorful tablecloth. Daye Xecê helps me to spread the napery. Mîrza is already handing out the melamine plates and colored glasses. In the previous days I hadn't noticed their multicoloredness. Seven glasses in seven different colors. The spoons and forks are made of ordinary chrome steel, but their stems are carved in a palm and flower shape.

Although over the last six days there was all this colorfulness at dinner, I hadn't paid any attention to it. On the first day, I immediately took the laptop from Şevîn and went to the women's room. I did some offline research all night, looking for the best possible materials and the places where Mîrza and Şevîn could buy them. On the following evening, the fabrics and materials arrived, and I had to constantly check the work progress in addition to providing childcare. The meals in the house were unusual. For lunch, it was always a simple meal, such as fried eggs, an omelet, or mashed potatoes. Instead, there were real main courses for dinner. These meal customs are said to be due to Mîrza's work schedule.

He goes to his farm every morning after breakfast and does not get back until dark. There, in addition pruning the fruit trees, he takes care of a large vegetable garden at the foothill of a mountain that is not far from the comrades' camp. Mîrza and his siblings have a shared farm on which they use a tractor to plant wheat, barley, and rye. The farm is rainfed and only a few working days a year are necessary for harvesting, but it gives us enough grains for the whole year.

"Or maybe beer," I said laughing.

"No heval, we don't brew beer. But if you want to drink, Mîrza can provide you with red wine." Hinar suggested to me hospitably.

"Do the comrades drink alcohol?"

"No, heval, I've never seen comrades drink alcohol."

In the previous days, we were busy the whole day, but we always had a warm meal and this colorful napery at dinner. I had overlooked these cultural, familial traits. The plethora of colors reminds me of African villages. Şevîn brings another tray with a red plastic sieve full of fresh vegetables and two big jugs. There is smoked do in the glass jug. The other is a clay jug covered with blue glaze. That must be the water. I get up again, pick up the two jugs and place them in the middle of the food blanket. Fresh dill pickles are floating in the do. Şevîn places the vegetable sieve next to the jugs and sits on a mattress beside the napery opposite her father. Arkan runs and throws himself onto her lap. Rûnahî comes in with a large linen cloth and spreads it next to the napery. Soon after, Hinar appears behind Rûnahî with a main course. Bulgur with fried turkey meat.

I forgo washing my hands and stare at the glasses. Şevîn lifts Arkan off her lap and lets him sit next to her. She takes a purple glass for him and an orange one for herself. For Daye Xecê a dark green, Rûnahî a sun-yellow, Mîrza an indigo-blue, Hinar a turquoise, and a wine-red glass remained for me. I don't know if I had chosen the same color in previous days or if it was just left for me. I eat quickly and go back to the women's room.

The tent is firm and appears to be airtight. Nevertheless, I check it again with an air pressure gauge. No loss of air. It brings me peace of mind. Now I can sleep comfortably. I take my toothbrush out of my backpack and walk through Daye Xecê's room into the hall. Hinar stands with a worried expression at the door.

"Is everything ok?"

"Never been better," I say and everyone in the house calms down. I can feel the relief on their faces. I am giddy and go down the stairs like a drunk. Even before dark, my eyelids were heavy, but now my heart is relieved. The chances of success for our act of revenge seem high. I look at my red eyes in the mirror, brush my teeth, and leave the toilet. Rûnahî sees me stumbling in the stairway.

"Heval, go to sleep. You look exhausted."

"Yeah, I couldn't close my eyes last night. Can you do me a favor?"

"Yes, sure."

"You have to measure the air pressure again before you vent the tent. It would be nice if you could find out how many minutes it takes for the air cushion to completely deflate after you've opened the cap. But you can't push the tent. Ok heval?"

"Rest assured."

The cock-a-doodle-doo of their roosters woke me up early in the morning. I felt well rested. I turned to Rûnahî. She was asleep. A sheet of paper laid between us. It said, "The air pressure at twelve o'clock was on three bars, the tent was vented in four minutes and twenty-two seconds." What a good feeling to start the day with. I go into the hall through Daye Xecê and Şevîn's room. No one has seen either in the first or the second room. I pull the light-blue curtains aside and look into the yard. The front gate is closed and it is quiet. The shepherd must have brought the cattle to the mountains. I went back to the women's room and pulled the GoPro camera out of the socket. It was charged, as were the spare batteries. I took the camera and went into the yard, put it on the floor next to the stairway, and entered the toilet. When I came out, Hinar's voice could be heard. She was mucking out the stable with a wide flat shovel. Şevîn was helping her and filling the wicker basket with a smaller shovel.

"Good morning, heval."

"Good morning, hevala Jiyan. You seem fresh again."

"Yes, hevala Hinar, a heavy burden has been lifted from my shoulders. I was able to sleep peacefully last night. How can I help you?"

"You can't help us with a camera here. Go to the kitchen. Daye Xecê will soon start baking the bread."

I went out of the stable and saw a large bloodstain in the near corner of the yard. Mîrza had slaughtered a goat. Its black skin laid in front of the tap and its head next to it. The area around the fur was bloodstained. Mîrza's voice could be heard coming from the kitchen. I looked into the room. He was sitting on the floor, cutting the carcass in two with a dagger on a large round tray. Next to him was another tray and a large black plastic bag. Through the open window I saw Daye Xecê beside the tandoor. I turned on the camera, placed it on the windowsill, pointed it at Daye Xecê, and went into the bread baking room. After a greeting, Daye Xecê explained to the camera how many walnuts to add to the risen sweet dough and how to brush the top with soaked poppy seeds and safflower. It was not difficult. I dragged the dough tub toward myself, took a piece of the dough, and managed to imitate how she prepared her first piece of dough.

"You make dough balls—I'll kindle the tandoor," Daye Xecê said with satisfaction.

I looked into the tandoor. The depth of it was one meter, the same as its diameter. The wall and floor of the tandoor were black. There was a round hole near the bottom on one side of the tandoor that was used to draw enough air from an air duct next to the oven to run it. In Qeza

Şêxan, I was forbidden from putting my hands and feet into the opening, even though it looked like a simple hole.

Daye Xecê opened a sack and took out some dried brushwood and shavings, stuck her arm and torso into the oven, then took some small twigs from a pile of twigs and placed them on the previous fuels opposite the air hole. Then she took a few small twigs from a pile of firewood on her right side and placed them over the dried brushwood opposite the air hole. Now it was time for the dried manure. She leaned three pieces of dried dung around the dried brushwood. Just one match and everything took care of itself. She got up and washed her hands in the sink and came back to the tandoor. The dried manure was burning excellently and a yellow flame rose up out of the deep, black tandoor. Could such a large amount of dough be baked with only three pieces of manure? The dried manure was burning and smelled wonderful.

In the meantime, I spread out a few balls of dough, colored them with safflower, and sprinkled poppy seeds over them. The inner part of the tandoor had turned red. Daye Xecê rolled up her dress sleeve and fastened its long and narrow tails around her arm above the elbow. Then she put the first walnut bread dough on her palm, bent over into the blazing tandoor, and slapped the dough against the wall.

Eleven walnut loaves fit on the tandoor wall. By the time she smacked the last walnut bread onto the upper part of the wall, the first piece of bread had already baked on the lower part and the strange, pleasant scent of baked bread was rising up.

After the first round of baking, I turned the camera off. In less than an hour a tub full of dough had been baked into loaves of walnut bread and filled two wicker baskets. She covered the tandoor opening with its lid and pulled another tub toward her, which contained ordinary dough for flatbread. I watched closely to find out what problem my aunt and her staff had with making the flat, transparent bread.

Daye Xecê took a small piece of dough and formed it into a ball that was three times smaller than our dough balls. While we were filling the surface of the sheet with balls of dough, Şevîn and Hinar appeared. Şevîn had a *meşke** in her hand that Daye Xecê had made from goat skin. Şevîn put the meşke on the floor and went toward a wooden stool on

* Meşke: animal skin tube.

which lay two ropes made of goat's hair. She put the stool next to the meşke, climbed onto it, and tucked the ropes into a metal ring mounted under an overhead pole. She tied all four shoulders of the meşke with the four ends of the two ropes. The meşke was now hanging from the ceiling. Şevîn went to the fridge and I got up to help her. She took out two buckets of yogurt.

"Does it have to be cow yogurt?" I asked Şevîn.

"Not necessarily, but the butter made from cow milk is gold-colored."

"How can I help you?"

"Open the throat of the meşke so I can pour the yogurt in."

I untied the rope around the hairless goat's neck. There was no sign of blood on its cut throat, nor any trace of the dagger that Mîrza was now using to cut another goat carcass into pieces. Through the open window I see the black fur of the newly slaughtered goat and its severed head. From this fresh skin one can make a perfect new butterskin tube that will yield delicious butter and buttermilk. *No, it is not buttermilk. Buttermilk is made from milk, but do from yogurt. Ok, you may be right. Better to call it a yogurt drink.* My mother corrected her mistake. *But that is also wrong. Do is made in a meşke and smoked with fragrant herbs.*

My mother liked to drink do. Me too. I always wondered why people don't drink do instead of Coke. It is healthy and tastes fantastic.

Şevîn empties the second bucket of organic yogurt into the natural container and adds a handful of refined iodized salt. In front of Mîrza are pieces of filet on a wonderful oriental tray. Next to him, Hinar cuts the peeled onions into slices and pure dew flows down from her eyes. Meanwhile, Mîrza puts the waste into the sky-colored hygienic plastic bag, gets up, and throws it away. Then he sits in the hedge's shadow, turns on the tap, washes the fresh ram's skin under the water, and thoroughly cleans the yard's fine tiles.

Şevîn pushes and pulls the suspended and filled skin tube, swinging it like the hammock of civilization. It rustles and drums inside the hose with every thrust. Maybe the meşke used to be a nanny goat and once had a kid's fetus in her womb.

The goat's skin, which bears the abstract name of "meşke" for good reason and shouldn't be called an animal tube, goes on sloshing and flapping like a drum even louder. How easily we can gloss over our crimes with trivializing words. "Meşke," instead of "eviscerated bowels"; "gun" instead of "murder tool"; "cruise missile" instead of "devastating and unmanned long-range box of annihilation." I look at Daye Xecê. She covers the lined-up dough balls with a fabric cover.

"Daye Xecê, you won't bake them?"

"No heval, only after breakfast."

After her words, Hinar takes the tray of chopped meat to the sink and puts them in a large saucepan. She rinses the chopped meat, puts the pot on the sink, pulls aside the curtain under the sink, and takes out a big jar. Before she pours the vinegar onto the meat, I ask her, "Hevala Hinar, what is all this meat for?"

"For the comrades, right?"

"Heval, this meat is too much."

"Let the comrades have enough meat to grill."

"But most of them are vegetarian. Come spring, the comrades start to collect herbs like acanthus and falcaria vulgaris. I won't eat it, either."

"Why?"

"I have no appetite for it anymore. Keep half of it for yourselves. Our comrades cannot grill this much meat."

"Ok heval, I won't pickle half of it. The comrades can roast it or make a broth."

I leave the bread-baking room. Rûnahî stands in front of the poultry coop in the sun and weaves her hair into two Kurdish pigtails.

"Hurry up, heval. They haven't had breakfast yet."

"I'm done."

I wash my hands in the toilet and return to the bread-baking room. Hinar and Rûnahî are smoking the meşke. Şevîn has a container in her hands full of glowing coals on which a fragrant herb burns. Rûnahî holds the wide side of a large metal funnel over the smoking herb. The funnel neck is already attached to the neck of the meşke. Suddenly the room's door bangs open and the water strider comes roaring through.

"Dada."

All three of us turn our heads towards him, but the undefused bomb runs toward Şevîn with his head lowered. This seems to be a game that Şevîn had played with her father in her childhood and that she now plays with Arkan to minimize her brother's sabotage attempts. Şevîn puts her palm in front of her forehead in time and Arkan bumps his head against it like a ram. He wants to keep pushing, but Şevîn grabs him, hugs him, and takes him out of the room.

After smoking, the meşke remained closed and hung up from the ceiling. We had breakfast. Mîrza went to the farm. Daye Xecê heated up the tandoor with three more dung plates and, finally, the activity that I had been waiting for in this house from the first day began. Şevîn was able to deceive Arkan by proposing a "ram-ram" game. He ran out of the bread-baking room and followed his sister to their parents' room.

The yellow flames rose again from the dung in the tandoor. Rûnahî got up and looked around for something and found another pillow of dough on the flour sacks. She brought it, came back to the sheet over the dough balls and sat far away, so as not to appear in the film. She lifted a ball of dough and placed it on the wooden board, pushed the rolling pin over one side of the dough, and stretched it. Then she turned the dough, rolled the rolling pin over the other side, and stretched the dough into a small sphere. Lastly, she put it over her right hand and said to me, "You should move your hands in an imaginary circle and let the dough dance on it."

I looked at Rûnahî's hand movements; it really resembled a dance. The dough stretched in a circular shape. Suddenly she turned her hand and pounded the stretched circular dough onto the pillow. Then she stretched the dough from all sides until it covered the entire pillow surface. Over the course of her work, Rûnahî was describing her hand movements, which were taken from a book. Then she asked Daye Xecê if she could slam the first dough into the tandoor.

"Yes, please heval, you are very capable."

I got up and turned the camera off. With the pillow in her hand, Rûnahî went to the tandoor and sat next to Daye Xecê. Then she leaned her torso down into the tandoor and slammed the pillow against its wall. She took out the pillow and there was no trace of dough left on it. I gasped at her. Could it be as simple as that and we gave it up after three weeks of unsuccessful attempts? Even Hinar was surprised by her skill.

"Heval, you do it better than me. Did you bake flatbread in Baghdad?"

"No, heval, I learned it in Şingal. We are originally from Şingal."

Only then did I come out of my stupor of astonishment and comment on her work.

"No heval, nobody can learn this hand dancing in Şingal or any other village, unless they possess fine motor skills like yours."

Daye Xecê also took a dough ball. I got up and went to the camera. Before I turned to face her, she had slammed the first pillow against the tandoor's wall. She didn't look at the pillow and looked directly at the camera on my hand as if she were asking me to turn it off. Her head and eyes moved upward as the dough was dancing in her hands, then she pounded it almost into a circle shape on the pillow, made a bit of a correction to arrive at the perfect shape, and then slammed it on the tandoor's wall. All in less than eight seconds, without looking at the dough.

I sat next to Hinar, lifted the first dough ball, put it on the wooden board and slowly rolled the rolling pin from different sides over the dough and expanded it. I started hand-dancing but it was much harder than it looked. The dough either tore or became deformed again. Rûnahî constantly instructed me what the problems were, and Daye Xecê squeezed and kneaded my deformed dough, and made new bread dough, as thin as cigarette paper, with a few rolling motions and hand movements.

"If hand dancing is too difficult for you, form the dough with an upper body dance," Rûnahî suggested to me.

I formed the next dough ball with her advice. Laughingly, I danced and worked it out. It wasn't round thin bread, but at least it was flat. After a few tries, I was able to stretch the dough well. Now I had to try the slamming.

"You have to pay attention to the tandoor's wall. The hotter and redder the tandoor, the smoother the slamming. You must remove the pillow from its wall faster," Rûnahî explained to me.

The bread slamming also took several tries. If Rûnahî hadn't brought a second dough pillow, my attempts to learn would have wasted a lot of time and might have even let the tandoor get cold. Then Daye Xecê would have to throw more dung plates into the tandoor and stir the embers with a metal rod to clear the air hole of the ashes.

Rûnahî was like a silent hurricane, while I played with the dough balls without stress. The tandoor was always full and nobody was waiting for me. After an hour, I took my first flatbread out of the tandoor. I screamed with sheer surprise and enthusiasm, held the bread in front of my chest, and stared into the camera like an Olympic champion. A month later, when Şevîn sent me the video recording, Jarik was with me. He laughed at me for hours. In the recording, he always found something new about my actions and reactions to laugh at. Why would I ask Daye Xecê to bake bread with her eyes closed, from making dough balls to slamming dough onto the tandoor wall? Daye Xecê looked at the camera in astonishment and said, "Heval, why did God give me two eyes?"

It is true that Daye Xecê didn't look at the dough or pillow while baking the bread, but why should she close her eyes in broad daylight? Baking bread, turning the spindle, milking, and maybe some other farming activities she did spontaneously and didn't want to turn things that she took for granted into a type of competition.

How would I have reacted if someone had asked me if I could scratch my temples with closed eyes?

Immediately after the baking ended, Rûnahî conducted a cleaning operation, from the same place where we were sitting. She took all the washable things to the sink. Hinar wanted to help her clean. I suddenly found that I had two options. I either had to remain silent and work hard until evening or simply betray her. The second was easier. I turned to Hinar, but told them collectively, "Comrades, no need to interfere. She enjoys cleaning; even a cobra can't stop her."

Rûnahî didn't want to whitewash anything, took my testimony as an impartial statement, smiled at me, and plunged into her work. I went to the water strider and his sister. They were playing with marbles in their parents' room. As soon as I entered the room, he called out "dada" and ran towards me. He called me, Şevîn, and Rûnahî by the same title, but I could often guess who he meant. He called Rûnahî with a tone that seemed like she was his grandmother. He called Şevîn like she was his mother and me like his playmate. However, I did not know whether he was demoting or promoting me with this title. I played with the two of them for a long time until the high water flooded the upper floor and the lifeguard appeared. In her right hand she had a red bucket and in the other a broom and dustpan. Şevîn got up and wanted to help her, but she said, "Keep playing."

We went into the hall, but we had to leave the hall sooner than we thought. She was not allowed to pull the curtains aside and clean the windows, so her work was done unexpectedly faster. After a while, Hinar appeared in the hall. Rûnahî reluctantly looked at the curtains and told Hinar, "Unfortunately, I am not allowed to pull the curtains away. You can bring them down yourself, wash them, and clean the windows in this nice weather."

It sounded like a suggestion, but smelled like an order. Hinar realized Rûnahî's polite orders and gave her an appropriate answer.

"Yes, commander. Thank God you are not allowed to pull the curtains away and bother yourself anymore."

I burst out laughing and simultaneously looked at Rûnahî in her military clothes doing housework. In order not to be driven out of other rooms again, we went straight into the courtyard. The kitchen looked like it had been transported down from heaven. Everything sparkled. The windowpanes, the frames, the whole room shined. All the items were neatly arranged like in a shop window. The walls in the bathroom were gray as before, but they were glowing. The upper floor had changed so much that when Mîrza arrived, he stood frozen in front of the stairway door with eyes and mouth wide open. *Poor Hinar, Mîrza will divorce you.* No, he must not compare Hinar with the party's health commander. His wife is taller and stronger, she is disgusted by nothing, and much more suited for farming tasks.

"Prepare yourselves, at dawn we leave here by car," Mîrza told us.

"That means we won't go through the stable?" I inquired with joy.

"Right."

"Very well then, I'll take a bath."

I went to the women's room and got my clothing. I quickly washed myself and returned to the hall. Şevîn had her laptop on her lap and was waiting for me to install a specific app on it.

"Heval, bring me the new laptop. We cannot use it in the mountains."

Şevîn went into the middle room and soon came back with the new laptop. I downloaded an app and installed it on the laptop. Then I taught her how to use the app.

"When will we get in touch, hevala Jiyan?"

"I am not sure, but it takes a month."

I transferred my recording video to the laptop so that it could later be sent to me via the app. Then I let the camera recharge. We went to the women's room and packed everything. I gave Mîrza the insulating clothing. Rûnahî had put hers and mine in the corner. She had folded other clothes neatly and placed them in a transparent bag. They looked like ordinary pajamas.

Someone knocked on the door during dinner. Mîrza was already at the gate and opened it quickly. I got up and Rûnahî left dinner and followed me to the women's room. The room was dark. I pulled the curtain aside. The driver had driven the car into the yard. Mîrza helped him to put things in the car trunk. He had already eaten dinner and was wearing his thermal-insulating clothes. I also wore the thermal-insulating clothing and my military clothing over it. Rûnahî helped me wrap my waist shawl around my waist. She was already dressed. Maybe her cleaning addiction wasn't annoying because of her speed. I was spinning around as she wrapped the shawl around my waist. I had turned only ten times. She let me know that I had gained weight in the meantime. I smiled at her in the dark.

To prevent Arkan from finding out about my departure, Hinar stayed upstairs with him. She hugged me tightly and kissed me on the cheek several times. I hugged her more tightly and kissed her back. Then I lifted Arkan and pressed him to my chest with all my strength. I didn't tickle him in the dark stairway, but kissed his entire face several times, left him on the floor, and said, "Go to the bedroom. I'll come and play ram-ram with you."

Arkan immediately ran there. I hugged Hinar again, thanked her for everything, and went down the stairway. Daye Xecê stood in front of the car. Şevîn was already inside. "Heval, get out. Please don't come with us," I ordered Şevîn.

"Why, heval?"

"You mustn't put yourself in more danger."

"There is no danger, heval. We've driven into the city many times at night."

"But not with two guerrillas. Get out. There is no way I can let you come."

Şevîn got out. I hugged and kissed her. She let me hug her and even kissed me back, but reluctantly. I said, "Dear Şevîn, I will get in touch with you soon. Check your app from time to time."

She moved her head to my face and kissed me several times. I couldn't see Şevîn's fox eyes, maybe because it was too dark, or maybe because she had closed her eyes while kissing. Meanwhile, Daye Xecê said goodbye to Rûnahî. I left Şevîn and hugged my Daye Amîn.

"Daye Xecê, I will visit you again. You have to tell me about your mother. How she survived the genocide in Dêrsîm and what she told you about the collective suicide of the women on Munzûr Mountain.

"Forget it, heval. By then, ants and snakes will have eaten my body." She sensed the tears on my cheek and comforted me.

"Who knows, I've survived worse things."

"You are right, Daye Xecê, I will visit you soon. Next time as a tourist. Then we can visit your mother's relatives together."

"One can dream, heval. God is great and merciful."

"Yes, Daye Xecê."

I kissed her white hair and got into the car. Rûnahî sat next to me. Mîrza gave us two veils to wear. I didn't know how to deal with it. Rûnahî had to dress me like a bride. First, she covered my hair with it, then my upper body, and finally covered my legs. Mîrza opened the gate and climbed into the attendant's seat. The driver drove off and Şevîn closed the gate behind us.

The alleys were sloping, crooked, and messy, but the yellow streetlamps were shining. We saw no one in the village and soon we were on a flat road covered with asphalt. After ten minutes, the driver switched off all the lights and turned onto a dirt road on the left. It was a full moon. We drove uphill for a quarter of an hour until the car stopped above a valley. In front of the car the masked, fast-running sympathizer appeared with an umbrella over his head. Before any of us got out, I reminded them that caps, gloves, and swimming goggles had to be worn. Mîrza and Rûnahî had already prepared and got out quickly. I untied myself from the veil, put on the cap, gloves, and goggles and got out of the car. The car stood with the engine running until we unloaded its trunk. Then the driver said goodbye without naming anyone and drove downhill.

I followed the car's departure with my eyes. The house lights of a large village could be seen in the distance. The sympathizer and Mîrza took the heaviest loads. Rûnahî and I got loads of less than five kilograms. Our destination was not far, either. In less than twenty minutes, we reached the meeting point where Nadîr and Zinar were waiting for us. They also had two umbrellas over their heads. We greeted each other briefly. The villagers transferred the loads onto their shoulders and made their way back.

"Hevalê Mîrza, thank you and your family. Instead of me, please kiss Şevîn again and apologize for me upsetting her." I told him.

"I'll do the first one. The last one is not necessary. Şevîn will understand."

I squeezed Mîrza's hands, but didn't feel their warmth or roughness. He pressed his upper body to my shoulders without letting our chests touch each other. Rûnahî hugged Mîrza in a very friendly manner. We also said goodbye to the masked sympathizer and climbed the mountain. The cavern was nearby, less than a ten-minute walk from the meeting point.

CHAPTER 17

WE DIDN'T MAKE kebab. We had neither enough time, nor any desire. At night, lighting a fire is forbidden and, moreover, we had no meat to make kebab. Rûnahî had put the meat in the fridge in Mîrza's home. On the bright side, her housecleaning helped re-establish the damaged intimacy, but I hadn't had a chance to explain to Şevîn why I didn't let her accompany us. Then, on the way, I was constantly asking myself if I had the right to dictate to others what is best for them. She was only fourteen, but how would I have reacted if she was eighteen? I probably still wouldn't let her ride: one mustn't put their life in unnecessary danger. But why do I put my life in danger? I don't let anyone order me around, but decide for myself what I wish to do. Why aren't others allowed to do the same? Why did we prevent a young girl's wishes from being fulfilled when we know there are countless other wishes that cannot be fulfilled for her? Why did I break her heart? She was ready to risk her life, but she wasn't allowed to play with her life. I will make the same decision if she tries to do it again, so I guess my belief in freedom reaches its boundary there. Everyone allows themselves to restrict the wishes of others because they think they see something in their hearts that remains invisible to those affected.

The comrades had already eaten dinner before we arrived there. Rûnahî and I were not hungry, so our session started immediately. Dêrsîm and Zinar were keeping watch and other comrades gathered in the kitchen where Akam's bed was still set up. He could speak now and even sit up. In two weeks he should be able to get up without help. The battery lamp was leaning next to him on the cave wall. Rûken commenced her speech by addressing me directly.

"Hevala Jînçin, we are happy that everything went perfectly. We have thought a lot about your plan of attack and are convinced that it is operational. We rely on your skills and abilities. You will stay at the top of the mountain and command the attack. Now tell us how the attack should go."

"Heval, thank you for your trust. My plan is based on an attack pattern that you have thought of and have often practiced. However, with the new precautionary measures we can perform it without risks. The radios have to be equipped with headphones. First, hevalê Zinar will run towards the base against the direction of the wind. We know from which direction the wind will blow on the day after tomorrow. Nevertheless, he has to check it constantly with a wet finger."

"Hevalê Zinar will accompany you to the attack point tonight. Then you can explain it to him," Rûken said.

"Very good. As soon as I see the truck, I will inform him. How long will it take for the truck to reach the base?"

"At least fifteen minutes."

"Then we have enough time. I'll tell him by radio when and where to throw the pieces of meat over the wall into the base. You can also listen to me on the same frequency. After the dogs have eaten the pieces of meat, you should run, following the remaining route, to the rear of the base. I'll tell you when the tower's guard is looking in a different direction. How much time do you need to cover this distance?"

"Don't worry, heval, there will be enough time."

"Who will shoot the gate's guard with the silenced gun?"

"Hevala Gulbehar will."

"Most likely she will be hidden behind the truck in that firing position and I won't be able to see her. She should knock on her headphones three times. I will explain it to her myself. Our snipers in the soundproofing tent must be ready to fire. All four have to shoot exactly at the same time. Then I will have no more work to do until the last stage of the operation. Hevala Rûken, can you tell me how to proceed with the operation after this?"

"Hevala Gulbehar will stay behind the truck with a Kalashnikov, even if the truck continues into the yard. The gate area must remain clear so that the unarmed soldiers can flee through there. The operation should start and end with hand grenades. Hevala Rojano and I will each take more than fifteen hand grenades into the base and throw them into all the rooms. That wouldn't be difficult, would it, hevala Rojano?"

"No heval, by the time it's our turn, the job is done."

"Hevala Dêrsîm and hevalê Nadîr, both of you and hevalê Ferhad should leave the tent after the first shot and shoot every armed soldier exiting the base. Hevalên Saro and Rûnahî should stay outside until the end and keep the situation under control. As soon as the base is occupied, you enter and place the explosives. Hevalê Saro can explain it himself."

Saro looked at me and said, "Heval, it's not difficult to blow up a base completely. In all bases, without exception, there are arsenals. We don't have to carry a lot of explosives. A few small bombs can destroy the base if we place them in the right places. For remote detonators we can use special walkie-talkies. We make their magnetic field ourselves and their signals cannot be influenced by any electromagnetic waves or jammers. As soon as we have left the base, you can use your mobile to activate the bomb detonators over a certain frequency. That will also be the successful completion of our operation. Tomorrow evening, I will tell you the frequency. If something is not clear, ask."

"Thanks heval, everything is clear."

For a few seconds, Rûken looked deep into my eyes with her sharp, black eyes. Then she said, "You can leave now, hevala Jînçin. We'll meet each other there tomorrow evening. Take enough plain and walnut bread with you. For the hevalên there too. On the way, fill your canteens from the spring, but run slowly, hevala Dêrsîm's leg is not healed yet."

Rûnahî remained silent next to me until I packed up. Then she asked me to go to the provisions room in the cave with her. She was walking in the front with the lighter lamp, then put it on a plastic barrel and said, "Heval, I'm glad you've been given command."

"What! The commander? They gave me the simplest task. It's the only task I can do."

"No hevala Jînçin, the comrades have given you the most important task. You deserve it."

"You know, however, the most important and riskiest tasks will be done by the three people who penetrate into the base. I'll stay away from the dangers and do some kind of coordination work."

"Quite the opposite, you will command this operation. We're counting on your qualifications and your cool-headedness. It was a wise decision to return to the comrades without an umbrella."

"Why did we have to keep heavy umbrellas over our heads when we were wearing insulating clothing?"

"You have proven your competence. Hevala Rûken doesn't make a decision like that without a firm sense of conviction. Neither does hevalê Saro."

"You're exaggerating my responsibility. But still, thank you."

"Heval, would you like to kiss the Barat before you set out?"

"Yes I would. Do you have the Barat with you?

Rûnahî put her right hand into her left shirt pocket and took something out. I turned on my lighter lamp and turned its light toward her hands. Rûnahî had a small box in her palms. I understood that I should open the box myself. Maybe it was a ritual, or just her personal belief. I put the lighter in my mouth, lowered my head to point the lamp at the box, and unlocked it. The Barat looked like a little moon. Barat consists of soil, yogurt, sunlight, and human feelings and is round like the little planet we live on. Even an atheist can kiss the Barat. I took the lamp out of my mouth and kissed the humanmade pearl a few times, then went to the cave's narrow exit. Dêrsîm and Zinar were already waiting for me there. We left and reached the new grotto before dawn. It was under the tip of the mountain on the opposite side of the place from which I would lead our act of revenge. The hevalên anticipated a counteroffensive by the Turkish army lasting several days and intended to use this grotto as a fortress to resist. Over the past few days, they've brought everything they needed. Lots of ammunition, two DShK, and enough water and foodstuffs.

Hevalê Ferhad was keeping watch behind the grotto exit. We greeted him and went inside. A few meters below my bodyguard, Gulbehar, slept. Our short greeting had already woken her up. The grotto was very deep and had access to the other sides of the mountain in several directions. Comrades are said to have expanded these corridors with explosives and hoes over the past years.

This grotto was a strategic place and not yet discovered by the Turkish army. After the attack, the comrades would have to defend it against any counteroffensive, no matter how long it took and how difficult it was. That was the recommendation, or better to say the order of the party. I didn't want to distract my thoughts by thinking about such a problematic scenario. That was not a priority for me. I told Gulbehar that I would go to the observation point and needed all the notes they had written down over the past few days. She switched on her lighter lamp and took a small, transparent bag out of her crafted backpack and handed me the booklet within. I put it in my backpack and followed Zinar, who was waiting for me with a turned-on lighter lamp. He was walking in the grotto and merging the darkness and light with his lamp. The grotto corridors were high and after ten minutes we saw the gray daylight again.

The exit was narrow and low. We had to crawl through the hole. The base could not be seen from there. A plateau full of huge rocks lay in between. Zinar climbed up on the rocks with quick steps. I was trying my best to reach him. It took us half an hour to reach a point near the peak. It had been selected by comrades as an observatory. There was a small cave. We went in and unloaded our backpacks. That point was perfect, protected from the drones and just above the base. I took the binoculars out of my magazine belt and looked through them at the base.

They were enhanced binoculars, almost the only NATO military device that could be used against another NATO signatory. It was only in Rojava that I found out that NATO's anti-tank defense missiles don't work against the military armaments of other NATO partners. *No knife cuts its own shaft.*[*] I look through the binoculars at the watchtower guard. His military uniform is no different from other Turkish Armed Forces uniforms. The watchtower is located above the gate. Another soldier is keeping watch behind the gate. Two Belgian shepherd dogs are on leashes next to the gate. Except for these four guards, everyone else is probably asleep. I turn my head to Zinar and ask him, "Heval, do you think we can withstand a major counteroffensive?"

"Yes heval, why not?"

"But they will attack us from all sides with bombers and military helicopters. What can we do against them?"

"That's not a new problem. Eight years ago, they started an enormous operation against us. It was a cold winter and in some places there was over three meters of snow on the ground. But after two weeks they had to retreat."

"Were you there, too?"

"Yes heval, hevala Dêrsîm and I were there."

---

* A Kurdish proverb.

"Tell me how the operation went."

"For three days, it rained bombs like a hailstorm. But we had hundreds of hiding places and loopholes in the mountain. Only one of us fell and her death determined the outcome of the war."

"What do you mean by that?"

"Her name was hevala Dêrsîm and she was the classmate and close friend of our hevala Dêrsîm. At that time our hevala Dêrsîm's name was Nojîn.* After the death of her friend, she fought like a lioness and reversed the outcome of the war. I can even say that the Turkish army's bombardment helped us, too."

"But how?"

"Do you see those huge rocks there?"

"Yes, of course."

"Almost all of them fell down because of the mountain bombardments. After three days of continuous bombardment, the helicopters appeared, but then they were ineffective. We hid behind the rocks and laughed at the pilots. They could neither land on the crest of the mountain, nor on the plateau downstream. With our DShK and RPG-7 we shot down three of their helicopters. The Turkish army launched a massive ground offensive. That made our hevala Dêrsîm go wild. She loaded herself with a bandolier of cartridges, ran towards the Turkish forces with her BKC, shot them, and nobody could stop her. She did not listen to any orders from our commanders and shot several soldiers. The comrades decided to protect her. We gave fire protection and our snipers shot several soldiers, so the Turkish army had to retreat, pull back a thousand meters, and establish a new line of defense.

After their high-casualty retreat, we started a counteroffensive. However, they remained at their front for ten days. Turkish forces were warmly clothed and stayed in warm tents, but it was an unbearable situation for us. One of our comrade's legs froze and had to be amputated. Therefore, we repeatedly carried out surprise attacks on them. At that time, the Turks didn't have this base. Some of our comrades were able to recapture the hill and launch an offensive that night. As a result of our operation, they had to leave the area. From then on, the Turks had no say in this area. Only with the beginning of the so-called peace period

* A new life.

did the Turkish army restore its lost dominance. Under the pretext of establishing weather stations, they set up two bases in this area. Last year, the comrades blew one up."

"What did the comrades do in response to hevala Dêrsîm's actions? How was her deed judged?"

"The comrades understood her mental situation. She took her friend's name and served as a sniper from then on. She is now one of the best in the party. Everyone admires her wholeheartedly."

"Was her left leg healthy at that time?"

"Yes, she had two healthy legs."

Again, I looked at the base with my binoculars. The same guard was still on the watchtower. The dogs seemed hungry and they were running back and forth impatiently as far as their leashes allowed. The gatekeeper was looking at the building from which his replacement was to come. With my binoculars in front of my eyes, I turned my head to Zinar. I could only see his nose.

"Heval, let's have something," I said laughing.

I took a bag out of my backpack, which contained the walnut bread and a plastic jar full of sheep's yogurt. I opened the lid, poured half of it into an aluminum bowl, and put it between us.

"Come on, heval."

He cut a piece of walnut bread, laid it in the yogurt and reluctantly put it in his mouth. I missed his laughing face. I would have liked to ask him how long he had known Satyar, but I didn't want to add insult to injury. We ate unwillingly, as if we were just tanking up. After eating, I asked Zinar if I should keep watch first. "Sleep calmly, heval. I can't sleep right now," he said.

"Then write down what time the guards will be replaced."

"Ok, heval."

I felt hot and didn't want to sleep in insulating clothing. Sitting, I moved to the corner of the hole and started undressing. He turned his back to me. I undressed calmly and his eyes were fixed on the base the whole time. When I woke up after four hours, his eyes were still locked onto the base. I was still sleepy, but I unzipped my sleeping bag and got out yawning. Zinar turned his head to me, "Hevala Jînçin, you can keep sleeping. I prefer to keep watching."

"No heval, you have to sleep, too. If I sleep any more, I won't be able to sleep in the afternoon. We need absolute vigilance at night."

We exchanged our guard turns. He didn't go into the sleeping bag and just lay down on the ground. The base now seemed like a barracks on parade. The soldiers gathered in the courtyard, and someone in a general's uniform moved his hands as if giving a speech. I looked into the notebook. They had performed the same ceremony a week ago, Rûken had noted in the notebook. I hadn't seen her handwriting before, but I knew immediately that she had written the page. From her notes, I could see that she had mainly focused on this operation. Short and practical. The handwriting of Saro and Rojano also revealed their authors.

Saro had written down his observations factually and in detail, with numbers and figures and a view to the future. Who is responsible for the repair and inspection of military equipment? How do the guards react when various officers appear? How many people serve in different departments? Rojano had written her notes briefly and clearly. What time the guards were relieved and, at the end, her statement: "This base is easy to conquer." This sentence gave me great hope. It is nice that she will penetrate the base with Rûken. The Gulbehar pages were more interesting than the others. It was easy to read and understand the locations and situations. Everything is properly archived: the watching times, imports and exports of equipment, and collective tasks are divided into five columns. The times are exactly written, in minutes and seconds. From her report, I was able to find out the guards' replacement cycle. I drew the same columns from the time reports of the other comrades, compared them with each other, and found out exactly what was the detachment cycle of the base, or perhaps the bases in the region. *Oh sweetie, my black-eyed bodyguard, as beautiful as a yellow lemon. Hush heval, be careful, otherwise hevala Gulbehar will kill you. No, she won't kill me. She is my friend and already a vegetarian. How much do you love me? As much as the PKK meetings are long. . . .* Maybe I'm no longer able to laugh at these jokes. Maybe, like Rûken, I will lose my laughing face here forever. I turned to Zinar. He was sleeping. After two hours he asked me what time it was. I turned my head. He was sitting cross-legged.

"Heval, go on sleeping. I'd rather keep watch."

"Thank you, heval. I've slept enough."

"If you're not hungry, go back to sleep. I will wake you up as soon as I want to eat."

He got the point, stretched his legs and slept. I took off my military pants and black panties, and went to the exit half-crouching. I stuck one of my legs out and peed. If Zinar watched, he could have looked at a smooth, white, round butt. When necessary, you can admire yourself. But he had turned his head in the opposite direction. The tin can was buzzing in the sky, but we were out of sight. I got up and pulled my panties and pants slowly back up. After lunch, we talked about our duties for tomorrow's operation. Then I laid on my stomach on the ground and slept until I couldn't anymore. Sometimes I opened my eyes and looked at the cave mouth. There was the silhouette of a man staring at his tomorrow. I got up and told Zinar to sleep.

"Thanks heval, but I can't sleep."

"Heval, you have to sleep. We cannot afford to make a mistake," I said to Zinar imperiously.

"Heval, we should leave soon."

"It's all Greek to me. We have to wait three more hours for the comrades. I prefer to sit outdoors than in a narrow and dark grotto. Or do you prefer looking for a tight hole!"

I go to the cave exit to keep watch and he goes to his cozy corner to sleep. It will get dark soon. I crouch down to my backpack and don my insulating clothing. I feel like I am in pajamas. Then I come back to the cave mouth, sit cross-legged, and put my Kalashnikov on my lap. The first guerrilla in history to keep watch in pajamas. I laugh. Zinar does not respond and seems to be asleep. After an hour I am bored. I wear my pillow cap, gloves, and swimming goggles and leave the cave. A windless, moonlit night. Bad weather for an attack; fantastic for dreams. I feel hot in my military pajamas and would like to take them off and lay down naked. It would be like seventh heaven if one thing led to another. But this party likes to highlight only one part of an argument without finding any solution. Capitalist sexism is not much more intolerable than the PKK's fanatical antisexualism. I run back and forth, spin around, and stare at the sky. It is indigo blue. The drone is buzzing, the stars are twinkling, and I am hot. As a widow once said, "We are not lucky enough to find a dick while sweeping. Neccesity knows no laws."* I go back to the hole. Zinar has already gotten up and looks at me passionlessly. Maybe I can flirt with him in spite of the darkness. The clothes make the man.

"Hevala Jînçin, your clothes are warm."

"Yes, very much."

"For winter it will be very pleasant."

"Then take it off, it's not winter now."

"Heval, it's not a good time to catch a cold. Anyhow, we have to conquer that base."

I felt in his voice neither blame nor advice, but a deep grief. I got cold feet. Maybe I'm depressed or terrified. Not from forthcoming dangers, but from the risk of our operation failing. It is windless and that jeopardizes our plan of attack. I bend over, take my military jacket, put it on while crouching, and pull the zipper up. Then I put on my military trousers and fasten the strap. It's hard in this narrow and low hole to wrap the long shawl around my waist. I pull myself up, take my shawl, and go toward the cave mouth. There I stand on the flat ground and put one end of the shawl in my pants. Zinar takes the other end in his hand. I spin around as he wraps the shawl around my waist. Rûnahî was right: the other comrades turned eleven times. I fasten my magazine belt over it, wear my vest, and wear my backpack on my shoulders. Then I bring my left hand through the leather belt of the Kalashnikov and put it over my shoulder.

We left and moved downstream. Zinar was running slowly and gave me the opportunity to observe the surroundings, so that I could later find my way alone. We were on the path for an hour, but in the grotto we still had to wait an anguishing half-hour for our comrades. Their arrival filled the grotto with life, spirit, and energy. I could see the comrades in the dim light of a lighter lamp. Rojano only had a little backpack on her shoulder, which was unusual for her. With the load on her back, she sat down and put it on the ground. Curious, I went over to her backpack and tried to lift it, but I couldn't. I asked her, snooping, "May I open it?"

"Yes heval, we must open it anyway," Rojano answered me.

I untied its strap. It was full of hand grenades.

"You both have to carry so many grenades with you?" I asked Rûken.

---

* Kurdish proverb

"Yes heval, the machine guns don't do much to bases. Everything has to be done with grenades and snipers."

Tewar had stayed in the cave with Akam and Dêrsîm was keeping watch at the exit behind the grotto. Everyone else had gathered in a deeper part within the grotto. There was not much to explain. The snipers in the soundproofing tent didn't need headphones and all three were given my instructions directly by radio. Zinar would be the first to approach the base with headphones on. Rûken and Gulbehar should also wear their headphones until the shooting had started. I gave Nadîr, Rûken, and Gulbehar three pieces of paper on which were written the frequencies used for communication. After each radio report from my side they would promptly shift to the next frequency, but I had for certain written a name for each frequency so that they could find the right frequency immediately. They took notice of me. Saro gave me the frequency at which I should blow up the base as soon as we were ready to leave there. I switched on my lighter lamp and looked at the note. Saro's handwriting was terrible, but legible.

"Thanks, heval."

Rûken, Rojano, Gulbehar, Rûnahî, Saro, and Zinar took on their back everything they needed, stepped into the pitch-black dark of the grotto, and soon were out of my sight. I wanted to instruct Nadîr how to set up the tent and fill it up with gas, but he told me that Saro had taught him yesterday. After an hour, we stepped into the grotto too, and after half an hour we reached the huge fallen rocks from the mountain next to which the soundproofing tents had to be set up. It was early and a breeze was blowing in our favored direction. I have to climb alone to the observation point and sit there in the dark for three hours. I asked Nadîr to roll me some cigarettes to overcome the heavy burden of the lonely observation time.

I left the comrades and made my way on the rocky path with a weapon on my shoulder that I was not allowed to use, at least until the beginning of the operation. I'm not in any great danger. Apparently for a long time there hasn't been any wildlife on this mountain. I climbed to the top of the mountain to check the wind direction and its speed. I took a sheet of paper from my shirt pocket and held it up to the wind. It was enough to start our operation. I went to my place and unloaded my backpack in the hole. The moon was no longer visible in the sky and there was silence and darkness within the small hole. The drone was no longer buzzing. I was able to take off my thermal insulating clothing, even though it made me pleasantly warm.

At the hour of the buffalo, I took one of the cigarettes out of my pocket and lit it. I hid the red end in my hands, but blew its smoke in the form of rings towards the base. The smoke was indistinguishable from the darkness of the night. In Germany, this ring making was one of my surprise skills as a social smoker. I didn't feel like smoking another cigarette and waited three hours before dawn. The truck arrived earlier than expected. I almost missed it. Through the binoculars I briefly saw a moving object in a blurred view. Maybe it would just be a mirage. I played with the lenses and on the next curve I recognized the truck. I pointed the binoculars at the guards. They weren't looking at the dogs. I gave the first instruction without getting discouraged.

"Zinar, bring the soup to the second table. And then go to Befrîn."

"Got it."

I kept an eye on the gatekeeper. He didn't respond to the thin pieces of meat that were thrown. Then I stared at the dogs. They seemed restless and ran back and forth in the yard. The gatekeeper was replaced half an hour ago and the tower guard only ten minutes ago. Everything was right. The tower guard was looking at me.

"Rûken back home. Then to Dada."

"Ok."

I changed the frequency to Dada and focused my binoculars on the tower guard. He looked in the same direction for a long time. Suddenly he turned.

"Stop." I said.

"Don't worry, we're already home." Rûken replied.

"Then go to Daye."

Again I change the frequency and laugh out of sheer enthusiasm. I had underestimated my comrades. They are all professionals. I look at my watch; we still have five minutes. I see the truck briefly on another curve and wait until the tower guard turns toward the path that the truck is driving up. He lowered his head to the gatekeeper.

"Nadîr, warm the bathroom and go to Arjîn."

"Bathroom is hot."

The gate soon opened and the truck slowly drove inside. Gulbehar tapped her headphones three times. She is said to have been in a good shooting position behind the truck.

"One, two, three," I counted.

I did not hear a single shot, not even from the tent that was only three hundred meters below me, but all four targets fell. The truck drove a few more meters into the yard and then stopped. Rûken and Rojano ran towards the buildings and all hell broke loose. I couldn't count how many grenades exploded. Those who jumped unarmed out of the window into the courtyard were able to escape through the gate, but the armed men were shot by our snipers. Then they were shooting outside the tent and the roar of the Zagros shots echoed across the mountain. Two pilots ran to the helicopters, but they were killed. Hand grenades were continuously being thrown into the rooms and soldiers were running barefoot towards the gate. The armed men either fell or were captured. The base was conquered in less than five minutes. Saro and Rûnahî entered and went to work setting up the destructive climax. The other comrades carried as much usable ammunition as they could. The rest of the ammunition was carried by the prisoners.

They disappeared behind the gate and I saw them again soon after. Five prisoners were running in front and Gulbehar, Rojano, and Rûken were running behind them down the hill in my direction. I watch them through the binoculars. One of the prisoners looked suspicious. He sneakily put his hand into his jacket. I suspected he had a gun in his pocket and tried to take it out. I called them from the last frequency.

"Yes heval, I hear you," Gulbehar replied.

"The prisoner in the green jacket probably has a gun in his pocket."

"Got it, heval."

Gulbehar quickly walked from behind to him and put her gun barrel on the back of his head. He stopped. She searched his pockets and said, "Heval, he only has a cell phone in his pocket."

"Then bring it to me."

"I'll inform hevala Rûken first."

"No heval, let that be my business."

"Ok, heval."

I immediately left my place and ran down the mountain. I stumbled several times and almost fell over out of anxiety and haste. They reached the foothill and climbed up to me. I was running to them. Rûken asked me why I was in such a hurry.

"You'll know soon."

I went to Gulbehar. She was walking a few meters behind them with her gun pointed at the prisoner. He was a thirty-year-old man. He freaked out once he saw me. I took his cell phone from Gulbehar and looked at his photo gallery. It was as if I had been struck by lightning. All my fury went into my left hand and I bashed his head with the butt of my gun. He fell down to the ground and howled like a wolf caught in a trap. I cocked my gun and wanted to shoot him. Rûken reacted in a flash and smacked the barrel of my gun. My shot hit the ground.

"What are you doing, heval?" She screamed.

I couldn't talk. Gulbehar picked up the phone from the ground and handed it to her. I stood there frozen. In the video footage, his foot was on Arjîn's head, holding her two severed breasts in his hands and posing triumphantly for the camera. I was dazed and confused and saw the other comrades as if in a haze. Rojano was biting her lip in anger. Rûken screamed loudly at the man for a few seconds until she calmed down. They wanted to keep walking again. The blood rose to my head again.

"Where are you going, asshole? You have to pay for that," I roared in German.

I pointed my gun at him again. Rûken screamed sharply and stood in front of me.

"Drop your gun."

With trembling hands I pointed my gun at him but Rûken said, "He is our captive and we cannot kill him."

"No he is not a captive. He's a piece of shit. Only a motherfucker can commit such a crime in this world."

"Drop your gun."

I stuck to my decision and wanted to blow his head off, but, suddenly, Saro's voice came from the radio. "We are out. You can do your job. Until we meet again."

At that moment, it was the most pleasant task I could have possibly done. I hung my gun on my shoulder again, pulled the note out of my shirt pocket, looked towards the base and adjusted the walkie-talkie to the written frequency. First a little bang, then a clap of thunder burst over the hill and got louder and louder. Everything blew up in a few seconds. I couldn't see what weapons and locations were exploding, but we later saw above the mountain that the whole base was destroyed. All buildings, the arsenals, all four tanks, both helicopters, and all of the vehicles. The booms were mingling together and their collective echo was more pleasant to my ears than any music. The comrades continued to climb up and soon I had to run after them. I felt a little relieved and called Rûken. She stopped and before I asked her anything, she ordered me to hand over my gun to her. She hung it on her left shoulder and said, "Thanks, heval."

"What do you want to do with the cell phone?"

"I will throw it away. We are not allowed to keep it."

"Then let me send the photos to an anonymous account."

"It's forbidden."

"Why? I'll send it in a safe way."

"But in addition to all routes, there are also detours. Please forget it."

"Heval, I also know the detours."

"I'm sorry, you have to forget it."

"You can't tell me that. I am an expert in this context," I shouted.

"Maybe you're an expert at your university, but you're an amateur in these mountains."

My lips locked in anger. I dragged myself behind them and didn't speak with anyone. As soon as we reached the grotto, all five prisoners were released. Rûken angrily yelled at them in Turkish. I did not react to her and sat on the ground until the prisoners who had run away disappeared. The comrades went towards the grotto and I followed them at a distance. The bombers soon appeared and began continuously bombarding the area. But we were all in the cavern, except Saro. I suddenly remembered his last words. What did he mean by "until we meet again?" Was it a secret message or a normal goodbye? I didn't want to ask anyone a question about it and continued running quietly behind them to the other side of the mountain through the passages. When we reached the large grotto, the bombs were still falling, but not in our direction. Only the backside of the mountain was being bombed. The act of revenge was completed successfully and I saw great satisfaction on my comrades' faces. Routine life was back. Some comrades smoked cigarettes; others nibbled on some walnut bread. The kettle was on the fire and soon after they drank tea. The thundering sky did not spoil the ecstasy of our victory. A heavy burden had fallen from their shoulders. My soul was comforted too, although I had not expected that cell phone souring the successful end of our operation.

I felt humiliated by Rûken. She had exploited my scientific prowess and portrayed me as an amateur right after my mission. I put my head on the backpack without eating or drinking anything. When I woke up it was quiet. There were two large pots on the fire again. Rojano sat next to me and looked me in the eye, "Heval, today you slept like a rabbit, just like me."

"It's very rare for me."

"It's normal. You made the heaviest contribution to this operation." Rûken said.

"Why? Just because I watched you in the distance?"

"No, because you gave us your capabilities and coordinated our operation without any mistakes."

"Heval, you don't have to comfort me. I am not that sensitive."

"I'm glad. Then maybe you can sit up. We are doing our daily meeting now."

I sat up and leaned against the grotto wall. Rûken started talking.

"Hevalno, our operation went smoothly. Nobody made the slightest mistake, except me. I went too far with hevala Jîncin. Therefore, I would like to apologize to her."

Rûken turned her head and looked at me, but I didn't respond to her. She added more.

"I forgot how drastically I used to react to situations like that. I've even shot several prisoners. At the time, I thought it was fair. Morally it may have been correct, but the political and practical results of such actions have been devastating to us. It's exactly what the fascists want. They want to incite nations against each other to the fullest extent possible. They want to deepen our hatred of each other even more incurably. I can even say it would be unfair if we shot that prisoner today. He was definitely not the only Turk who did something like that. His atrocity was accidentally exposed, but there are hundreds of thousands of fascists who can do the same without feeling shame or remorse. They grew up in a culture where even speaking a word of Kurdish was seen as a terrorist attack up until thirty years ago. These soldiers defend the last barricades of fascism. Fascists always sang in their ears that Kurds are terrorists, that we are a danger to humanity, that we are viruses and microbes that must be sweep from the world. Since the AKP came into power, they have another reason to exterminate us completely. We are atheists. It may be normal in Germany to be an atheist, but for soldiers here, atheists are enemies of God and they want to kill us by all means possible. They can throw our comrades into the valleys and mutilate our bodies. The fascists and fanatics have no sympathy for their victims. I have no pity for such villains. Today I would have loved to kill that beast, but that would be wrong. They must have a family and we would have made them our enemies if we killed those soldiers."

"And what did you accomplish by releasing them? You just let them go easily. They will take your deed as a sign of weakness."

"No, heval. They understood that only in the Turkish propaganda films do the brave soldiers disarm the terrorists."

"No matter what the reason, that soldier got away without being held accountable."

"But we also obtained five witnesses. They will tell others we released them in spite of their shameful crimes. They have even seen that a blonde European girl wanted to kill them, but a terrorist released them because she didn't want to add fuel to the fascist inferno. They fought us today and were arrested. Next time they will flee through the window barefoot without a gun. I would rather imagine it like that."

"They fled barefoot to save their lives, but they will rape us again and pose with our cut breasts in their hands if they find an opportunity."

"Heval, do you remember that officer who saw you under the bushes? Why did he ignore your presence? Hevala Jîncin, I called you an amateur today and still stick to my word. I've seen several of the same cases. All of the comrades here have had the same experience. With our new strategy, which is not playing the same game, we will take the wind out of the sails of the fascists. Today's prisoners will not risk their lives for the rulers like they did before."

"You can be right about your release reasons. But why did you throw away the evidence of their crime? I would have been able to send those photos to an anonymous account without any risk. With such evidence, we can achieve a lot that we couldn't achieve with your new, overdue strategy."

Rûken turned to Rojano and asked her, "Heval, you were responsible for archiving the receipt documents for two years. Could we have achieved anything with today's recording?"

"No heval, we have several such recordings in our archive. You can put that in your pipe and smoke it."

"What! You have several such pieces of evidence? Then why haven't you published it?" I asked Rojano in amazement.

"Why should we? The Turks publish those recordings themselves. They've even shared those video recordings on YouTube."

"Hevala Rojano, I don't understand. Of course these soldiers are improvident people, but they are not stupid. Why should they publish evidence that could be used against them?"

"Yes, maybe it could have been used against them, but the politicians work with real means, not assumptions and guesses. By publishing such recordings, they break the heroic image of Kurdish women fighters in the eyes of many people. They say, 'look closely, they are not heroines, but failures. Our soldiers have fun with their hot bodies. They are whores and our soldiers play with them like toys.' Heval, a Kurdish proverb says that a bald man isn't ashamed when his hat has fallen off. Those who organize and, in fact, implement rape and extermination are not ashamed of exposing their crimes. They are even proud of it."

"Darling hevala Rojano, that's only one side of the story, but Turkey is not in another galaxy. Under international law, such acts are called state crimes."

"Maybe, but crime is a normal part of routine life. Heval, do you really think that German politicians aren't aware of what the Turks are doing here in Kurdistan?"

"I'm not talking about the politicians, but the German citizens. We must heighten their sense of solidarity against the organized crimes of the fascists."

"We can't do it, heval. We are too weak, too small, and too isolated."

"Why, heval? The global community is much larger than a regional power like Turkey."

"The world community, yes, but they are not on our side. They see us as terrorists and have sympathy for the fascists. They are playing their cards close to their chest. If the world community were to become aware of their crimes, they would claim that we staged these scenes ourselves to taint the reputations of the honorable Turkish soldiers. They will say that and prove it. Turkey is a state and a NATO partner, and they have systematized their extermination apparatus and institutionalized their crime structure. Therefore, they have the power in their hands. Tens of thousands of propagandists, justifiers, and commentators work on behalf of the Turkish government. We have to keep hiding from the drones, but they sit on their armchairs, with coffee cups on the table and modern computers that are constantly updating. We can't fight with them at the moment. Heval, did you forget how the Turks interrupted the peace process?"

"Yes, I know what you mean, but the PKK also shouldn't dance to MİT tunes."

"You see, hevala Jîncin, you have also been influenced by the Turkish intelligence agency's deception. MİT tried to incite us with all the possibilities. Their mercenaries had performed several assassinations against us. The comrades, however, kept a cool head and weren't deceived by them. But in the end they killed two of their own police officers and put the blame on us. Every heval denied it. But it didn't help and they broke the peace process unilaterally. The AKP harvested the benefits of peacetime and strengthened itself. Honestly, I would have loved to have killed that asshole today, but it was reasonable what hevala Rûken did. We must keep our emotions in check, hoping for the best and expecting the worst. We have to stay away from the dirty games of the fascists and draw a red line through our movement; then we will stand on one side with these soldiers, who mostly come from working class families. We have nothing special, either. They have to understand that we are not the cause of their poverty and misery. We are not mercenaries and we don't believe in paradise. We fight for our ideals and we always have to stick to them. Only in this way will we have a chance."

I was impressed by her eloquent, fluent speech and especially her deep, male, melodious voice and became silent for a few seconds, then I spoke.

"If it were so, as you have described it, then I would be dumb as a bag of rocks. I always blamed the party for its stupid reaction to the Turkish government's provocative activities."

"Heval, you're still speaking in the subjunctive. The problem with intellectuals is that they believe there is something true about everything.

But this is wrong. Some of these media sources tell absolute lies. I'll give you an objective example. Today the Turkish bombers bombed this area for four hours. You slept almost the whole time and the other comrades don't have even a single scratch on their bodies from it. You can listen to TRT English radio in a few hours. There it will be reported with 100 percent certainty that, *"more than ten terrorist ammunition depots have been completely destroyed and over one hundred terrorists killed."* In their reporting it will be announced that *"the terrorists failed in their actions and all were eliminated."* I have formulated it for you exactly as it will be formulated on their radio program in a few hours. I know their language patterns by heart."

"Can you speak English well?"

"Yes, heval."

"Why didn't you tell me when hevalê Saro translated my instructions for you?"

"When?"

"Eight months ago. On the first day when the drone appeared."

"Did you speak to him in English?"

"Yes."

"I did not know."

"I still don't understand one thing. Many soldiers died today. They all have families. How can the army hide their deaths?"

"Heval, the armed forces sign an employment contract with the army that allows them to remain silent about their deaths."

"A written contract? Turkey is a candidate for EU membership."

"Yes, and the European Commission knows that exactly and ignores it."

"And why didn't you tell me about such things before?"

"You were more interested in our past life."

"When do I have to leave here?"

"This evening," Rûken told me in a regretful voice.

"What's the rush?"

"We anticipate a large counteroffensive by the Turkish army. Unfortunately, you have to leave tonight with hevala Rojano and hevalê Zinar before the new comrades come in to provide support."

I calmed down a little and turned to Rojano, "Then we can talk about the remaining issues later."

"No, heval, the time will be too short. Hevala Rojano has to take care of the new group issues."

"Well, hevala Rojano was promoted. I am pleased."

"Last year hevala Rojano was responsible for this group, but she couldn't get along with the administration. Therefore, she was transferred to us at will. Tonight you will travel with hevalê Zinar. He will accompany you to Başûr. From there you will fly to Germany."

Rûken said nothing, nor anyone else. I suddenly became upset. In the next few hours I would have to leave my comrades, maybe forever. Until the evening, my comrades and I recalled many wonderful memories together, but they remained silent about Arjîn and Satyar. Before leaving, Rûnahî let me kiss the Barat again, with the same ritual. Zinar and I were on our way for two weeks. Each guide gave us a new group. We only ran at night with an umbrella over our heads. After fourteen nights we reached a party base in Başûr. Only then could we get into a car. After two hours, we reached Silêmanî. The next day Zinar took a taxi to the airport. On the way he gave me my handbag. All my things were in it. There were two stamps on my passport. Silêmanî, entrance and exit. Officially, I spent the past eleven months in Başûr. There was WiFi at the airport. I switched on my cell phone and sent a message to Jarik on Telegram.

"Hi, bald head."

I immediately got an answer by secret chat, "Hi blondie. You didn't commit *seppuku*?"

"No, I'll stay alive until I bury you."

"Where are you now?"

"In Silêmanî, soon I will fly to Germany."

"How was your adventure trip?"

"Adventurous. I have three booklets with me. I wrote a couple of them. One is from a friend. He wrote about the Şiwan Battalion. Do you know this battalion?"

"Yes. Leave the booklets there. You can ask them to send it to you when you arrive in Germany."

"And if they get lost?"

"At least I will give you PDF files. When do you arrive here?"

"I'll be at the Düsseldorf airport at seven o'clock in the evening. Two hours later, I will be in Frankfurt."

"We'll meet there."

"Ok, until then."

"See you."

Jarik immediately deleted all the messages. I switched my cell phone off and put it in my handbag. Zinar sat opposite me behind the table.

"Hevalê Zinar, I want to drink a beer with you. Do you agree?"

"Ok, heval."

I went to a buffet, bought two beers and came back to the table. With my lighter I opened the beer bottle so violently that the lid made a popping sound, blew up in the air, and slammed against the ceiling. Some travelers turned to look at us, but I opened the second bottle even more violently. The foam spilled over the table. I handed him one of the bottles. Then I looked Zinar in the eyes and banged my bottle against his.

"Noş!"*

"Noş, heval," Zinar replied without any emotion.

"Heval, when I think of you I would like to have your laughing face in front of my eyes."

"I'm trying, heval."

"One more favor."

"Tell me, heval."

"The next time you meet hevala Gulbehar, give her a lemon on my behalf."

"No, heval. I don't want to fall to a comrade's bullet. I've survived several air strikes."

I laughed and Zinar smiled with me. I took a big sip and Zinar took a sip. The beer was cool and didn't taste like much. Soon I was slightly drunk and asked him about his hiding places. Zinar laughed more and more.

"Heval, you can hide something here, too. There are also many gaps and holes in this hall."

"Not necessary. A guerrilla has no business at the airport. We prefer to go on foot."

"Even as far as Germany?"

"Even to the moon."

"But you can't walk there."

---

* "Cheers!"

"Then I'll give it up. I prefer to watch the moon from below."

"Hevala Zinar, why don't you look at me when you talk to me?"

"Heval, you look strange in civilian clothes."

"Even stranger than in my pajamas?"

"That was also a type of military clothing."

"Which one suits me better?"

"You look free in any clothing. You've smoked cigarettes with all of the comrades except me. Now it's just us two, drinking a brew."

"Nice rhyming. Was it deliberate?"

"No heval, it was splendid, but unintended."

"Unfortunately I have to fly soon, otherwise I would find out if you only get quick answers and rare things from your pockets or whether they hold the right rhymes, too."

"Well, if I had a secret, you know I wouldn't speak of it."

"Got it. How long do you need to walk from Kurdistan to Germany?"

"What's the path like, uphill or downhill?"

"Only a few mountains and then a flat sea. Can you run across the water? You've already been recognized as a prophet by us."

"Heval, your recognition is not enough. God should decide. I will only reach the age of a prophet in the next year."

I leaned over with a laugh, moved my chair back, got up, opened my backpack, and handed over my three booklets to Zinar. He also got up and accompanied me to the departure gate. There I turned and hugged him. He put his right hand on my shoulder and I kissed him on the cheek. He remained calm and said in a friendly voice, "Heval, I hope you reach your home safely."

I quickly turn around so that Zinar won't see my eyes. Where is my home? The impassable mountains of Kurdistan or the plains of Frankfurt? I'll be on the plane soon. A window seat was booked for me. A smiling German lady sits down next to me. Her left hand is in a plaster cast. I greet her with a nod and look outside. The aircraft is taking off, climbing up, and I can see the mountains from above. We move away from the ground more and more and my view widens. The city of Silêmanî is behind us and can no longer be seen. From the sky, I can see the mountains, towns, even some villages, but no signs of guerrilla life, neither in Başûr nor later in Bakûr. In an hour we are above Lake Van. In all possible directions, I look for the city of Van, from which our beloved cat came.

No city is seen and I cannot guess the direction of the mountains in which I lived for eight months. But I have our underground bunker and the hawthorn trees before my eyes, the cave where Akam may still be receiving treatment, and the mulberry tree under which I slept with Saro.

I had offended him with my stupid reaction. I found an attack by fifty-three bombers to be a total exaggeration. Saro had always been very kind to me. He had sat cross-legged while I leaned against the tree trunk. He was silent as the drone was buzzing. I got up, went to him, and sat close to him.

"You mustn't be upset with me. The numbers are no more important than our friendship."

"Yes, I think so. I hope not to see a single other bomber before you leave us."

"When will I have to leave here?"

"In a few days."

"Why do you want to reject me? Am I not in your good graces? So hasty. I have enough time until next semester." I looked at him, shocked.

"But soon this place will be like hell. You have to leave us before the Turkish army operations begin."

"I also want to see some battles."

"Come on, heval. There are no nice things in battle. Real wars are different from those you have seen in cinema. In war, ruthlessness dominates. Human emotions are subjugated and hatred stirred up. In war, blood is spilled, people are killed, and nature is destroyed. You mustn't see scenes like that. After participating in a battle, you cannot go back to your previous life."

"But I also found my previous life to be worthless. I don't want to live in a cage of my own passivity when the world goes to ruin."

"I'm here for similar reasons. But you can't stay here in the mountains any longer. If you want to help us, you can do it in other ways."

"Ok, I'll do it in my own way, but before I make my decision, I want to sleep with you."

"What?" Saro asked me loudly, staring at me with wide eyes. "You aren't serious."

"Why not? Maybe you're a monk, but I'm not a nun. I haven't had sex in the last ten months and I want to sleep with someone before I leave these mountains."

"Sex is prohibited here. This is a careful decision by the party considering the pragmatic implications. We don't have a normal life."

"And in your abnormal life, do you absolutely have to suppress your human feelings?"

"Suppression is not the correct term. We postpone it until the right time."

"Until then, it will destroy your natural existence. You cannot live a healthy life without sex and love."

"Here is full of love. A much deeper and more genuine love that you can hardly find anywhere else. The love here is natural. You have no seductive images in front of your eyes. In the cities, people follow manipulated patterns. Your lover should look like a model, smell like a certain perfume, and their voice should have a special tone. Where can you find hevala Rojano's strange voice?"

"Do you love Rojano?"

"Yes, I love her."

"Did you sleep with her?"

"No. Why are you getting it all wrong? How did you reach that conclusion?"

"But you want to sleep with her."

"Heval, you always seem to be puzzled by everything. I love her like many other comrades. I love her as I love you. I'm talking about collective love. This party was built not only on pillars of ideology, but on a collective love that has made us a family, very different from the conventional power-oriented family structures. No matter where I go in the party, I am immediately accepted as a member of a family. We are not bound by common economic or metaphysical interests, but by generally applicable human principles and common ideals."

"You can give your lovers mutual pleasure and happiness. Why can't you sleep with a woman who has the same principles as you?"

"Because of our collective love. When someone makes another person his lover, he also makes them his private property."

"Oh, that's your problem. Then I'll also sleep with other comrades. I promise you. I have not had sex for a long time and I would like to get laid by several men."

Saro laughed. I pulled his head towards me and kissed him on the mouth. Saro was frozen for a few seconds, then pulled his head back and asked, "Didn't you have a boyfriend?"

"Do you mean Jarik?"

"Yes."

"He is not my boyfriend. He is unbearable as a partner."

"Why?"

"He's crazy."

"Do you think Sharam Qawami is crazy?"

"How do you know Jarik is Sharam Qawami?" I asked Saro in amazement.

"Is there another writer in Frankfurt who comes from Sine?"

"I do not know. Did you meet him yourself?"

"You didn't answer my previous question."

"Yes, he doesn't quite have both oars in the water."

"Anyone who thinks they have both oars in the water usually has neither."

"Nonsense. He is really abnormal. Sometimes he has two huge eyes on his ass and sometimes he forgets his cell phone in the fridge."

Saro burst out laughing. It took a long time. Then he said smiling, "You're exaggerating."

"Why exaggerate? I often called him and his cell phone would ring in my fridge or in drawers. At the beginning of our friendship, I thought he wanted to spy on me."

"We were together in Rojava for a few days. Do you tell Sharam when you sleep with someone?"

"Yes, and he listens carefully to save it in his bald head. No sensible woman wants such a man as a partner."

These sentences made me feel hot again. I roughly pressed Saro's body to my own and put my lips on his mouth. I put his right hand on my breast. He squeezed it and I lay on my back on the ground. Saro didn't have any desire for sex, but his penis was already hard and I didn't want to let the opportunity slip through my fingers. I would like to sleep with someone while the drone is buzzing up there. Men have often raped women in history, why can't a woman do the same after ten months of not getting any? I undressed completely with an enjoyable rhythm.

"What are you doing? We are not on the Hawaiian Islands," Saro said laughing.

"The shepherd will not cross the river and until that drone is up there buzzing, our comrades are stuck. The bird has eclipsed us. We're already on an island."

I grabbed his rod, took fate into my own hands, and accepted the charges for his package. Saro squeezed me and I enjoyed his weight. Smoke rose from my head and my spirit swelled with pleasure. After two strong orgasms my craving was stifled.

"You birdie, I screwed you!" I screamed at the drone.

Saro stood there with a wide-open mouth. Then he stammered, "I think you and Sharam are a perfect match."

"That means I'm crazy, too?"

"Sharam showed fewer symptoms of disease."

"I know, but two crazy people are too much for a house, though one is not enough."

I laugh. The flight attendant asks one of the passengers what he wants to drink. I look inside. The man takes a coffee. The flight attendant pushes the trolley closer. The lady next to me asks for a glass of red wine. I ask for the same and fold down the table flap. In addition, like everyone else, I get a sandwich in a bag. The lady opens the bag with one hand and puts it on the tray table.

"You shouldn't have done that," I tell her.

"Why not?"

"Not only is food placed on these tray tables, but people also change their babies' diapers on it. And they don't clean these trays often."

She took the sandwich, leaned over the lap of her neighboring passenger, threw it into the trash bag, and turned back to me. "Please take mine. I'm full," I told her.

She takes it with a smile, "Thank you."

"My pleasure."

"What's your name?"

"Kajîn."

"I am Claudia. Do you work in Kurdistan?"

"No, I was there as a tourist. And you?"

"I went there to see my friends."

I lift the plastic cup from the tray table, turn to the window, take a sip, and think of the mulberry tree under which Saro politically slept with me. He didn't offend me, either in the remaining eight hours of the same day or in the next few days. That was not out of humility, but out of intimacy. I could easily feel it from his eyes and our conversation. So when our operation was done and I didn't see him in the grotto again, I wanted to know what had happened to him. I asked Rûken during her speech at the criticism meeting, but she didn't respond to my question and kept talking. When the meeting ended, we drank tea. Then she asked me, "Wouldn't you like to smoke one of your political cigarettes with me?"

I bent over with laughter and said, "Yes, gladly."

We went out of the cave. There was no drone and we sat under the open sky.

"Hevalê Saro had to go to another group. If the supposed Turkish army operation doesn't last much longer, he will visit us briefly before returning to Rojava," Rûken said.

"Why did he go so unexpectedly?"

"The comrades had problems with the communication devices. He should have gone there earlier. Because of our operation, he had to postpone it until today. But I'll give you his email address."

"Yes, that day you deliberately let me accompany him. You probably know a lot. If you want, I'll tell you about the mulberry tree." I told Rûken, smiling.

"Not necessary."

"I still thank you. You will remain my commander forever."

"Thanks, heval. I have a request for you."

"Yes, please."

"I want you to talk with your mother again."

"Ok, hevala Rûken, but why is that important to you?"

"For personal reasons. I am indebted to my mother. Six years ago, she came to the mountains to visit me with great joy, but in the end she left crying. It was a very tragic time for me. A comrade who I loved had recently fallen and it was during this period that she wanted to persuade me to leave the party. I got angry and told her that she should never visit me again. After two years, my brother called me to say that my mother was terminally ill and wanted to talk to me. I was driving from Şingal to another place. When I arrived, I called her, but she had already died. I cannot forgive myself for my cruelty. Mothers always see their daughters and sons as little children, no matter how old they are. I cannot explain how painful this feeling of guilt is."

"I understand you well. I made the same mistake with my aunt."

"I imagine that she will pick you up from the Frankfurt airport. It is said to be a large airport."

"Yes, a wide flat plain. Hevala Rûken, may I ask who your boyfriend was?"

"He wasn't my boyfriend. I hadn't known how much I loved him until a snake tried to bite him."

"He was bitten by a snake?"

"No, heval. You once asked me how I could get rid of my ophidiophobia."

"Well?"

"I used to fear snakes like the devil fears holy water. I ran away while other comrades caught them. We even had a snake that was fed by the comrades. This harmless snake always came to our location and disappeared after eating. I had only heard that, but I had never dared to stay close when it entered the cave. Seven years ago, something happened that made my ophidiophobia disappear and that revealed my love for that comrade to myself and other comrades. I was reading a book in a grotto. Suddenly, I saw a black snake near that comrade. It was crawling toward his feet. I spontaneously ran, took the snake by its tail and hit it against the wall. Not once, a hundred times. Then I kept stomping on its head with my shoes over and over again, as if it had bitten my comrade. From then on, I was no longer afraid of snakes, but I didn't hurt any others."

"What happened to your friend?"

"He was shot by drone missiles. A traitor had put a GPS sensor in his vest."

"I am so sorry, darling hevala Rûken."

"Thanks, heval."

"That's when you lost your laughing face?"

"No, heval. Already before that."

I take a sheet of paper out of my handbag and briefly write this last story. Claudia stares at me and says, "You can drink my wine, too."

"Thank you very much."

I didn't sleep last night, in order to sleep peacefully on the plane. I drink the glass, lean my head against the window, and quickly fall into a deep sleep. I wake up over Germany. It is not necessary to look at the flight monitor to find out. The neat square fields tell me themselves. It gives me a good feeling. This sudden turning of pages, from stony gray mountains to flat green forests and fields triggers a beautiful feeling in me. I stare at the square fields and fall asleep again until the plane lands at the Düsseldorf Airport. The children rejoice excitedly. I go down with Claudia through the passenger boarding bridge to the passport control section. The check-in no longer takes time and my passport receives an entry stamp. Claudia is not finished yet. I wait for her and accompany her to the baggage claim area. She wants someone to help with her heavy suitcases. We take the escalator down to the hall. My hiking backpack comes first. I lean forward and my handbag nearly falls onto the baggage carousel and gets swept away. I pick both of them up, carry the backpack on my back and my handbag on my shoulder until Claudia sees her big blue suitcase and smiles.

I say, "Can you keep my handbag for a moment?"

"Yes, sure."

I give it to her and lift her suitcase off the conveyor, put it on the ground, and drag it after me.

"Thank you, dear Kajîn. I can carry your bag."

"Not necessary."

In the waiting hall I see Sharam and my mother. A woman is hiding behind them. It is Güzel. She comes up to me and says, "Çonî başî?"*

"Ez pir başim, to çonî?"†

"I'm fantastic."

She hugs me and kisses me again and again. She releases our embrace reluctantly and my mother comes and hugs me. Her hug is even tighter and she kisses me like a little child. On behalf of Rûken, I hug her heartily and kiss my mother with deep feelings. Forcibly, she moves away and Sharam gives me a hug. I kiss him and he takes me in his arms mischievously. Then he turns to my mother and introduces Claudia to her.

---

* How are you? Are you okay?
† I'm fine, what about you?

"Perye le cilî mirova."*

My mother and then Güzel shake hands with her. Claudia turns to me and asks a question, "How long have you been in Kurdistan?"

"Almost one year."

"A year as a tourist, hevala Jînçin?"

I burst into laughter and say, "No, as a terrorist."

* She is an angel in human form.

ABOUT THE AUTHOR

Sharam Qawami is an Iranian-Kurdish writer and literary critic, born in Sanandaj, Iran in 1974. He started his university studies in horticulture at Razi University in 1995. In 1998, he was expelled from the university for political reasons. Qawami has written many short stories, poetry, novels, and literary critiques over the years, resulting in the authorship of several books. Most of the books written in Iran have not been licensed by the Ministry of Culture and Islamic Guidance.

In his works, Sharam Qawami has taken steps in a distinct direction, moving beyond the dominant literary movements and groups of literary critics, and has avoided adapting to government-dependent art, conservative art, and propaganda. The work *My Mother's Most Historical Wound* was his first collection of short stories; he obtained a license to publish it in Iran in 2001. In 2003, the license application for his first work of fiction was rejected in Iran, so he published the book in Iraq. His second novel, *Birba*, is norm-breaking. His discussion of religious, cultural, and political taboos in the novel was deemed too radical, leading to his arrest. After the book was published without permission, he was imprisoned at the Islamic Revolutionary Guard Corps' Sanandaj Intelligence Prison. In 2007, he published a book of literary criticism, *The City of Groups and Bands*, in Iran. The book serves as a critique of one of Bachtyar Ali's populist fiction works. Due to the meticulous reading and analysis required to write the book, as well as the intellectual richness found within, this critique serves as an educational reference for fiction literature and holds a special place among Kurdistan's educated class. In 2008, he published his third banned novel, *Long Overcoat Wearer*, in Sulaymaniyah, Iraq. Iranian security forces prevented the publication of a Persian translation of this novel. In 2010, he published a collection of poems entitled *We Are Just Getting Old Lonely* without permission.

Sharam Qawami settled in Germany after being forced to leave Iran in 2010, where he resides today. In 2017, he published his first novel in German, *Brücke des Tanzes*, followed by a Kurdish translation. Sharam Qawami's latest work of fiction, *Rojava,* was written simultaneously in Kurdish and German. The Ministry of Culture and Islamic Guidance of Iran did not issue publishing permission for the Kurdish and Farsi manuscripts of *Rojava* due to their breach of Iranian laws. The author decided to publish *Rojava* in both Kurdish and Farsi without permission. The book is now available in both languages within Iran, but the Iranian secrect services do not permit its sale and so confiscate *Rojava* from bookshops.

ABOUT COMMON NOTIONS

Common Notions is a publishing house and programming platform that fosters new formulations of living autonomy. We aim to circulate timely reflections, clear critiques, and inspiring strategies that amplify movements for social justice.

Our publications trace a constellation of critical and visionary meditations on the organization of freedom. By any media necessary, we seek to nourish the imagination and generalize common notions about the creation of other worlds beyond state and capital. Inspired by various traditions of autonomism and liberation—in the US and internationally, historical and emerging from contemporary movements—our publications provide resources for a collective reading of struggles past, present, and to come.

Common Notions regularly collaborates with political collectives, militant authors, radical presses, and maverick designers around the world. Our political and aesthetic pursuits are dreamed and realized with Antumbra Designs.

www.commonnotions.org
info@commonnotions.org

BECOME A COMMON NOTIONS
MONTHLY SUSTAINER

These are decisive times ripe with challenges and possibility, heartache, and beautiful inspiration. More than ever, we need timely reflections, clear critiques, and inspiring strategies that can help movements for social justice grow and transform society.

Help us amplify those words, deeds, and dreams that our liberation movements, and our worlds, so urgently need.

Movements are sustained by people like you, whose fugitive words, deeds, and dreams bend against the world of domination and exploitation.

For collective imagination, dedicated practices of love and study, and organized acts of freedom.
By any media necessary.
With your love and support.

Monthly sustainers start at $15.
commonnotions.org/sustain